Double Fault

ALSO BY
KATE SCANNELL

NONFICTION
Death of the Good Doctor—
Lessons from the Heart of the AIDS Epidemic

FICTION
Flood Stage—
A Novel

Immortal Wounds—
A Doctor Nora Kelly Mystery (1)

Lethal Control—
A Doctor Nora Kelly Mystery (2)

ESSAYS AND COLUMNS
www.katescannellmd.com

Double Fault

A Doctor Nora Kelly Mystery

KATE SCANNELL

Double Fault: A Doctor Nora Kelly Mystery. Copyright 2024 by Kate Scannell. All rights reserved. Printed in the United States of America.

First Edition, 2024. Word Haven Media

Cover and interior design by Maureen Forys
Cover photo © iStockPhoto | SimonSkafar

Library of Congress Cataloging-in-Publication Data available upon request

ISBN: 979-8-9908981-0-3 (print)
ISBN: 979-8-9908981-1-0 (epub)

For Diane

And in loving memory of
Zee

*. . . truth will come to light; murder cannot be hid long;
a man's son may, but at the length truth will out.*

SHAKESPEARE, *The Merchant of Venice*, Act 2, Scene 2

It takes two to make an accident.

F. SCOTT FITZGERALD, *The Great Gatsby*

*Do not grieve over someone who changes
all of the sudden. It might be that he has given up
acting and returned to his true self.*

SOCRATES

ACKNOWLEDGMENTS

I AM GRATEFUL TO FRIENDS who regularly encouraged me to continue writing this series.

Once again, I thank my brave and patient first reader, Diane Buczek. I am indebted to Susan Riter, Ruth Palmer, Jean Kaufman, Leslie Lopato, and Terri Rubinstein for their good-hearted and close readings of this book. For her steadfast support, I am grateful to Leslie Larson. And for her keen and insightful editing, I give thanks to Adrienne Armstrong. Any mistakes in this book are entirely my own.

CONTENTS

Part One

Thanksgiving,
November 28

2019

Lake Temescal Beach House

Northeast Oakland, California

UNDER THE STREETLAMP, he appeared older than his seventy-some years. The hollows under his cheekbones accentuated, and his white hair illuminated. His loose-fitting wool coat hinted that he may have shrunk a little. He flipped up its collar and rubbed his palms together.

"Dr. Balaban?" someone called out.

He turned toward the caller and saw his research mentee, Owen Landry, approaching in the far reach of the streetlamp's light. Such a large man, and everything about him big—his Louisiana accent and sonorous voice, his hulking stature, his oversized emotions, and his unearned good fortune.

Dr. William Balaban answered, "Hello, Owen. Thanks for meeting me here."

"No problem," said Owen. "Everything is closed now, anyway. Oh, and happy Thanksgiving."

"Did you have a nice holiday?" Bill asked.

"I did. I went in early to the lab to check on my bone-cell cultures so I could meet my parents for a Thanksgiving brunch."

"Ah, so that's why I didn't see you there this afternoon."

Wondering whether he had disappointed his mentor, Owen said, "I would have notified you I wasn't coming in then, but I didn't think you'd be there today. Last Thanksgiving, I was on hospital call, so I didn't know what to expect. Sorry."

"That's okay," said Bill. "Glad you got to see your folks."

"Yeah, they're my bedrock. Then, after brunch, I got to pin a femoral fracture and reduce a dislocated shoulder in the ER."

"Not the most traditional way to celebrate the holiday."

"Well, how about you?" asked Owen, zipping up his old varsity jacket. "Did you celebrate the day?"

"I'm not terribly fond of Thanksgiving. I spent my day and evening in the lab."

Owen knew that Bill often used the lab to escape his unhappy marriage and home life. But to do so on a major holiday seemed remarkable. He tugged on the visor of his black and gold Saints cap and asked, "Is everything all right? You sound sad, maybe upset."

Bill looked away and said, "Both."

Stuffing his muscular hands into his jacket pockets, Owen sensed that something bad may have happened to prompt this private meeting, at this late hour, behind Lake Temescal's shuttered Beach House. He said, "Well, can I help?"

"I certainly hope so," said Bill.

"Sure thing. What do you need me to do?"

"Can you be available in the ER at eleven tomorrow morning?"

"No problem. I'm supervising that hospital triage drill in the morning that I told you about. But it ends by eleven." Owen hesitated, not wanting to sound intrusive, but asked anyway: "Do you need me to do something for you, Dr. Balaban? Or for your wife, Ellie?"

Bill shook his head. "It's for Dario Parker."

Owen's eyes widened. "The kid getting stem-cell injections?"

"Unfortunately, yes. Dario called me a few hours ago, after falling on the tennis court. He was concerned about some pain and swelling in his arm. So, I told him to drop by the lab, and I'd take a look. And when I examined him, I palpated a tense muscle compartment in his forearm and realized he had a compartment syndrome."

"Wow, I'm sorry to hear that. He must've gone to a different ER, because I would've been notified if he came to ours."

"Actually," said Bill, squaring his bow tie, "I told Dario he had an infection that required IV antibiotics—something that could wait until morning. I gave him orals to tide him over until then, and a few oxy for his pain. But clearly, he needs a forearm fasciotomy. And, *obviously*, it would be best if *you* performed the surgery."

"But you . . . you didn't send him home like that?" said Owen, shifting his feet. "And, why 'obviously' me perform his surgery?"

Bill looked sidelong at him, wondering why this junior doctor was questioning him. Hadn't he supported Owen Landry sufficiently to have earned his unquestioning trust? Having generously nurtured his career—gifting him dedicated lab space, securing research grants, soliciting funds, publishing papers—he expected a show of good faith from his mentee. Instead, here he stood, disrespectful and ungrateful, much like his wife Ellie.

"I'm sorry," Owen said. "I must not be getting something. Because you're not actually sending Dario to the ER tomorrow, without a clue he's going to need his forearm cut open. Right?"

Pure insolence, Bill thought. *Arrogant moral superiority.*

"Dr. Balaban? Help me understand."

Bill rubbed his rheumy blue eyes and said, "Take it easy. I have a plan to make things right by you *and* Dario. Tomorrow, Dario will get the surgery he needs. And you, by performing that surgery, can make certain that no one becomes the wiser about your injection."

Owen flinched and took an involuntary step back. "*My* injection?"

"Look, I'm not assigning blame for his compartment syndrome. But let's be logical. You did give Dario his most recent stem-cell injection. And you administered it in his *forearm*. I assume you aimed for the tendons. But who knows? Maybe you accidentally hit muscle instead? Or did damage by applying excessive pressure on the syringe? Perhaps you mistakenly nicked a blood vessel? Certainly, as the chief Ortho resident, you know about those potential causes of a compartment syndrome."

"You can't be serious," Owen said, his voice cracking. "You think I don't know how to inject tendons? I'm an orthopedist—I can do them in my sleep."

Bill tilted his head and said, "Still, no one is infallible, right?"

"But none of what you suggested happened," Owen insisted. His forceful speech created steamy swirls in the cold night air.

Turning his palms upward, Bill said, "Still, we're left with a surgery that must be performed. And I've already instructed Dario to show up in the ER at eleven, because you'd be there to help him."

Owen looked away, with a sick feeling in his gut.

"It's up to you," Bill said with a tired sigh. "You can choose to control Dario's surgery and explore his arm for any trace of our treatments, or you could choose—"

"'*Our* treatments'?" said Owen, shaking his head. "No, you're the one who's been treating Dario. I only gave him one injection. And I only did that as a favor to you, while you were away in Costa Rica at your stem-cell clinic."

Suddenly, an amorous couple emerged from nearby hedges and skirted by. One carried a blanket, the other a wine bottle. After they moved beyond earshot, Bill said, "You're aware that Dario's father is the major donor to my lab—the same lab that allows *you* to pursue *your* research projects and lucrative ortho-device patents. In simple terms, Donald Parker controls your future. And I believe he'd be quite upset if he were made to think you made a serious error treating his son."

The oxygen in Owen's lungs instantly depleted, and his mind blanked.

"Owen?" said Bill, stroking his gray-stubbled chin. "Should I worry that you're not capable of performing the surgery?"

After forcing out an imprisoned breath, Owen managed, "Where is Dario's father in all of this?"

"His parents know nothing yet. They're spending the long holiday weekend in Napa, and Dario didn't want to bother them about his arm. And he is eighteen—the legal age of consent."

"But . . . but you made Dario think he only had an infection. Not a life-threatening surgical emergency!"

William Balaban looked wearily up to the vast night sky. How had he come to occupy this small earthbound moment teeming with mundane predicaments? Throughout life, he had been a bright star himself, to whom others looked up in awe. How had his light faded so resolutely? When had he fallen from the heavens so ingloriously that people like Owen—people like his wife—just stepped over him now?

"And," Owen continued, "that . . . that *lie* is going to be exposed when Dario has the surgery. The kid is going to have a flayed-open forearm. He's going to freak out, and his father's going to freak out. Dario won't be able to play tennis on his scholarship—"

"Keep your voice down and listen," Bill interrupted. "What will be made obvious tomorrow is that Dario had a compartment syndrome that required an emergency fasciotomy. No one will doubt that. And you'll be considered Dario's savior when you perform that surgery."

Owen narrowed his eyes and asked, "Why are you even finding it necessary to imply that I caused his compartment syndrome? You said Dario fell. So, why not just assume it was caused by a muscle crush injury from the fall?"

Clenching his jaw, Bill struggled to rein in his impatience. There was still so much he had to do before morning. During his own days as a surgical resident, such contentiousness toward a senior physician would have earned a suspension. Finally, he hardened his voice and said, "Attributing it to a fall is precisely what we're going to do. But to support that claim, we must control the narrative so the subject of Dario's stem-cell injections isn't raised."

"I don't know," said Owen, staring down at his worn black sneakers. "Something doesn't feel right about this." He remembered his parents at brunch today—so proud of him, and so grateful he made the time to see them. What, he wondered, would they advise him to do now?

"Oh, that's right," Bill said with a sharp laugh. "I forgot—you're infallible. Your injection had to be perfect, so you have nothing to worry about."

Owen pressed on his temples, as if trying to force out the right decision from his head, all the while his gut told him to decline involvement in Dario's surgery. Still, here he stood with his mentor, who had always supported him. Was the cynical comment about infallibility only intended as another valuable lesson? But why did it also sound threatening? Or, did it?

"Cat got your tongue?" said Bill.

"I don't know what to think. But it feels like you're intentionally not saying something. And that's why I don't understand what you're really asking me to do."

"Owen," Bill said, as if in lament. "I'm just trying to protect you, son. I've always had your back—you can't deny that. Yet, all of a sudden, here you are doubting me. And that hurts."

Staring shamefacedly at his mentor, Owen privately agreed that he'd never been given cause to doubt him. For two years, every Thursday afternoon, he'd worked in Bill's lab. Bill was always present—reading newspapers or medical journals, watching videos on his laptop, making professional and social calls—doing anything to avoid going home, it seemed. And when Owen finished his afternoon's work, Bill routinely ordered food deliveries, and they would discuss science and medicine over dinner. Finally, Owen said, "I'm sorry. I mean no disrespect. But it still feels like you're not being straight with me."

Bill placed a hand on Owen's broad shoulder and looked meaningfully at him.

"What?" said Owen, offset by Bill's grip, uncomfortable with his invasive stare.

"Son," Bill said. "You need to trust me. You're better off not knowing some things. And I would do the surgery myself if I could. But I'm just a retired neurosurgeon."

When Owen returned a confused and doubtful expression, Bill said, "Look, I'll be with you in the ER tomorrow. I plan to be there before eleven, and I'll text you where I am. All you have to do is show up for Dario's surgery. Then you explore his forearm, and lavage the heck out of the incision to remove any lingering cells. And if you see anything unusual, bag it and bring it to me. I'll get rid of it."

Part Two

Friday, November 29

The Palmer Medical Research Center

Near Oakland City Hospital

DR. WILLIAM BALABAN exited the Palmer Medical Research Center and looked up, catching the cool mist of morning fog on his face. From the top of the stairway, he saw container ships hugging the Port of Oakland, and ship-to-shore cranes stretching toward them. Gray-green waves rippled in the bay. He snapped a mental picture of this view as a memory keepsake. Then he deeply scratched his cheek, pulled on his gloves, and descended the stairway.

Midway down the stairs, he glanced back to see the center's security door close with finality. Then he clutched his chest, doubled over, and clumsily reached for the handrail. Passersby gathered at street level below and looked curiously up at him.

Gymnasium, San Sebastian Prison

Marin County, California

Elaine "Ellie" Balaban looked up from her cellphone and stepped downstage. "Why?" she beseeched her audience of two.

Dr. Jack Griffin, her "artistic director" (she always air-quoted his title), grimaced. He glanced at young Luis, seated beside him, and thought, *I was insane to plan this holiday show for the inmates.* But because Luis was so thrilled to serve as his assistant director, he told himself to forge on with "Holiday Cheers!" with as much good cheer as he could manufacture. Still, he could not refrain from whispering to Luis, "Within theater circles, Ellie is someone we would call a 'prima donna.'"

The exotic term delighted Luis, who asked, "What does that mean?"

"It's Italian," Jack answered. "It translates as 'first lady,' but it means 'diva.' You remember what 'diva' means, right?"

Luis nodded while he committed "prima donna" to memory. He found himself thinking about the colorful map of Italy that hung like a jaunty boot on his third-grade classroom wall.

After tousling Luis' curly black hair, Jack stood up in the prison-gymnasium-cum-theater and asked, "What's the problem now, Ellie?"

"This is becoming unbearable," she said, descending the stage and approaching him.

"Indeed, it is," Jack muttered, coaxing Luis to follow him into the aisle to meet her halfway.

When the three stood together, Jack adopted a sympathetic tone and said, "I understand, Ellie. But we both knew from the beginning that this show didn't aspire to be Shakespeare or Sondheim or Miranda. It's a small production on a dime-store budget, intended for incarcerated people who would otherwise spend the holidays behind bars. So, please, perhaps we can lower our expectations a bit?"

"It's not about the production value," she said, her face filled with injury.

Jack smiled stiffly and said, "Pray tell, then. What's the problem?"

"The 'problem,'" she said, holding up her cellphone, "is Bill. As I told you this morning, he's not been well. And now I've been notified that he's having *another* meltdown."

Luis' eyes widened while he envisioned a man literally melting down.

"I'm sorry to hear that," said Jack, offering her a consoling hug. Up close, he noticed the thickness of her stage makeup, and he imagined her needing a crowbar to pry it off. "We understand if you need to leave rehearsal."

Ex–daytime TV star and wannabe serious stage actress Elaine Balaban took Luis' small delicate hand in hers. Then, peering into his dark almond-shaped eyes, she wistfully said: "Young man, surely, you've heard the old theater adage: 'The show must go on!'?"

"Yes!" he answered—it was one of Jack's regular refrains.

"Well," she said, "that adage also applies to living one's life, even when the obstacles seem insurmountable." She pivoted to Jack and said, "As we speak, Bill is being transported from the research center to the ER at Oakland City Hospital. I'm worried. But I suppose, at least, we can take comfort in knowing he'll be cared for by his old colleagues who love him. You mentioned yesterday that Nora would be working in the ER today?"

"Yes," said Jack. "That's why she couldn't accept your invitation to join us here for lunch today. But she was sorry to miss you, and after all these years. Though, it looks like you *will* be seeing her, in a different context now." He explained to Luis, "Ellie's husband is a physician who mentored me and Nora and Fred and Carl during our early careers. He and Ellie were like patron saints to us, when we were young doctors."

"That's sweet of you to say," said Ellie. "But forgive me. I need to get to the ER."

"We'll hope for the best," said Jack.

"Thank you," she said, smiling bravely at Luis. Then she retrieved her cane, put on her dark glasses, and walked toward the gymnasium exit, her thin shoulders held back, her head held high.

In rapt attention, Luis watched her take leave. Her mannered style of walking, in sync with her cane's rhythmic striking on the floor, charmed him. And when she passed through the exit door's security lights, her blonde pageboy shone. "Prima donna!" he whispered.

Ward A, ER Exam Room #7

Oakland City Hospital

Dr. Nora Kelly shared an anxious look with ER Head Nurse Sarah June Ferguson: Ortho was taking too damn long to respond. Already, their patient's cold left hand and puffy fingers had lost sensation. The manometer confirmed the perilously elevated pressure within his forearm muscles, responsible for compressing his radial artery and diminishing blood flow to his hand. By every clinical and objective parameter, eighteen-year-old Dario Parker had a life-and-limb-threatening compartment syndrome. And, taking his history into account, the symptoms had been present longer than the optimal six-hour window of opportunity to surgically intervene. The elevated pressure must be released *now*.

Glancing worriedly at Dario, who lay writhing in pain, Nora wondered, *Why would an intelligent young man with such a blatantly distorted forearm and hand wait so long to come to an ER? How did he even tolerate the pain overnight? And to expect such angry swelling to disappear after a dose of IV antibiotics? He must have consulted the internet for such awful advice.*

Staff nurse Lizbeth Tanner appeared in the doorway, panting, shaking her head, signaling her failure to summon the Ortho chief resident. Fergie pulled her aside and whispered, "You checked the OR?"

"Yes," Lizbeth whispered back. "And the surgeons' lounge. The recovery room and cafeteria, too."

After removing her thick bifocals, Fergie dragged a hand across her shaved head, cupping the nape of her copiously tattooed neck. Then she silently mouthed, "Freakin' unbelievable."

Absorbing the news, Nora shook her head with dismay. She and her team had cemented Dario Parker's diagnosis and prepared him for the fasciotomy he so urgently needed. All Ortho had to do was waltz in and make the incision. But where the hell were they the last fifteen minutes? Not answering their pager, not responding to the hospital's overhead PA? With an awkward smile, she faced her patient and said, "Dario, if we hope to save your left hand, we need to make that incision now: the 'fasciotomy' that I explained earlier."

"What do you mean, 'if'?" he said, his voice muffled behind an oxygen mask. "Yeah, we want to save—" His entire body clenched as pain surged through his forearm.

Nora winced and asked, "How about more fentanyl before we begin?"

"No," he said, his good hand strangling the bedsheet. "I can deal with the pain. Just hurry, please."

"Okay," she said, situating herself at the bedside. "Are you still sure you don't want us to call someone? Your parents? A friend?"

"No one," he said. "Let's do this."

After Nora gave the thumbs-up to her team, Fergie texted the on-call nurse anesthetist, whom she had put on alert, to inform him they were ready to proceed with the fasciotomy. Lizbeth organized the surgical instruments on the overbed table, while Nora prepped Dario's forearm for the incision she would make to relieve the pressure.

Although annoyed by the Ortho team's unavailability, Nora was confident about performing the procedure without them. *In fact*, she thought, *I've performed more fasciotomies than the entire lot of them combined.* She reflected on her early years of broad-scope ER practice—a time predating the ascendancy of surgical and medical specialties that began staking proprietary claims on patients like Dario. *Now OB delivers all the babies. Plastics sutures every facial wound. Ortho casts even minor fractures . . .*

Through a corner of an eye, she saw the nurse anesthetist saunter in, and she reflexively did a double take. His sleepy eyes nearly drooped to closure. His blue scrubs begged for a good scrubbing, and his oily brown hair spilled out from under his cocked surgical cap. *This guy is supposed to administer conscious sedation to my patient? Is he even conscious himself? Is he sedated, maybe?*

"Hey," he offered in greeting, holding out his employee-ID card for Nora's inspection. "I'm Paul Ling, and I'm new here. But, like they say, 'good as new,' right?" He winked at Lizbeth, who pretended not to notice. "Gotta say," he continued, "this ER is wild. But I like it. I already caught a patient breaking into the narc box. And there's a demented old guy in the hallway, talking crazy on his cellphone, on the other side of this door. Look—you can see the codger peeking through the window. A couple of rug rats with squirt guns shot me in the—"

"I'm Dr. Kelly," Nora interrupted, her jaw tightening. "We're ready to proceed. Consent is signed. And FYI—we hung the antibiotics half an hour ago."

After saluting her, Paul adjusted Dario's IV and infusion pump. Fergie initiated the surgical safety checklist with the team, while Lizbeth placed sterile sheets on the surgical field and repositioned the pillow under Dario's neck.

Although Paul was moving at a snail's pace, Nora reassured Dario they would be "good to go in a minute." She glanced idly at the view box, where Dario's arm X-rays hung, and reconfirmed that all his bones were intact, without evidence of fracture. The isolated fleck of calcium in the soft tissues above his elbow was most likely the residual from an old muscle or tendon injury. *Sports*, she thought, *can be so rough on a body. And to think, this young man is suffering a terrible crush injury, all for want of hitting a little ball over a net.*

Finally, after Paul announced "Good to go," Nora told Dario: "You're going to start drifting into deep sedation. And when you wake up, as I explained earlier, you're probably going to be shocked to see your forearm cut open. But that's also going to mark the beginning of your recovery."

"I understand," he said. "And I'm going to do that rehab afterwards. I need my arm and hand for tennis."

"You're a player?" asked Paul, administering the IV midazolam.

"High school varsity," said Dario, followed by a groan and "college, next year."

"Dario has a tennis scholarship to UCSM in the fall," Lizbeth explained, placing a comforting hand on his shoulder.

"Congrats, sport," said Paul. "UC Santa Monica has a great sports program. But right now, you're heading to dreamland. Mind counting backwards from ten for me?"

Nora wished Dario had invited a family member or friend to be present. Someone to support him, to help him understand the gravity of his circumstances, to encourage him along the arduous road of physical rehab ahead, and to accept the grim likelihood of not playing college tennis. Should she have more forcefully emphasized all of this to him? Should she have tried harder to puncture his entrenched optimism?

Within seconds of receiving sedation, Dario unclenched his right hand and released the bedsheet. Then he locked eyes with Nora and said, "Ten."

She returned a smile, hoping to reassure him.

"Keep counting, sport," said Paul.

"Nine," said Dario, blinking dully, maintaining focus on Nora.

"You're doing good," she told him, while privately reviewing the fasciotomy technique she was about to employ. She would use the 18-blade and cut deep to Dario's fascia to release the pressure.

"What number comes next?" asked Paul.

"Uh . . . eight?" he slurred, looking probingly at Nora.

"That's right," she said, wishing on his behalf for a more expeditious sedation. "And, after that?"

But then Dario's head shot off the pillow. He sat upright, and his trembling hands reached for her. Lizbeth tried to restrain him, while Fergie struggled to stabilize his left arm and protect the sterile field.

"Sport, it's okay," said Paul. "The meds are just making you edgy." In a loud aside to Lizbeth, he said, "Some patients resist going under. We just give them more sedative."

Overhearing the aside, Dario vehemently shook his head, his fearful eyes remaining fixed on Nora. His lips moved, as if he were trying to tell her something. But only coarse throaty sounds emerged from his mouth.

Nora coaxed him back to a supine position, holding his unsettling stare. Then, suddenly, he mouthed a silent scream and fell back, listless and unresponsive.

Adopting a professorial tone, Paul said, "Let's all relax. The guy is just agitated by the meds. It's *opposite* of what we expect from them, but it can happen. It's called a 'paradoxical reaction.'"

Nora prized her ability to dismiss insufferable behavior at work—a well-honed talent born of abundant practice working with colleagues. Now drawing on those skills, she imaginatively shoved Paul into her blind spot and set her focus exclusively on Dario. Then she abducted Dario's arm and infiltrated one-percent lidocaine along her planned incision line. Fergie handed her the 18-blade, which *thwapped* into her gloved palm, and, in one swift move, Nora made an S-shaped cut that extended from Dario's wrist and up toward his elbow.

The room fell silent while everyone stood in stunned witness to Dario's freshly flayed forearm. Even Nora released a breath that, unbeknownst to her, had been waiting for release. Then slowly, as she lowered the scalpel, the room reanimated, like an orchestra following a conductor's baton. Lizbeth cleared the bloodied drapes and gauze, and, having never seen the interior of a living person's forearm, she internally reviewed the names of the exposed muscles and tendons. Nora removed her safety goggles to inspect the incision and explore the soft tissues for evidence of necrosis. But then Paul distracted her again by loudly proclaiming, "This your first rodeo, ma'am?"

When Nora shot him a reproachful look, he pointed to Fergie and said, "Just saying, your nurse is turning green."

Nora turned to see Fergie awkwardly backing away from Dario's bedside. She saw her lean against the medicine cabinet and press a hand over her abdomen.

I'll be damned, Nora thought. *In all the years we've worked together, I've never seen her so upset—not viscerally, at least. And we've seen so much worse than this!* Hoping not to sound judgmental, she nodded toward the door and told Fergie, "Go. We got this."

Still, Fergie hesitated. But after Lizbeth offered her an emesis basin—which she grabbed in the nick of time—she blurted out "Sorry" and dashed out of the room, while Nora and Lizbeth looked on with concern.

In the immediate next moment, Paul yelled "Shit!" and Nora irritably turned to him again. This time, he was pointing to Dario's cardiac monitor, on which PVCs gyrated chaotically across the screen.

"What the?" Nora muttered, dropping the scalpel. She called out Dario's name and shook him. And, getting no response, she said, "Call a code!"

Paul pressed the code button and began chest compressions. Lizbeth ripped open the intubation tray and handed the laryngoscope to Nora. After displacing Dario's tongue and epiglottis with the laryngoscope's blade, Nora visualized the vocal cords and passed the endotracheal tube through them. Lizbeth took over the compressions, and Paul attached the tube to the ventilator all the while Dario's cardiac tracing seismically quaked. When the Code Team arrived, several of its members appeared to be shaken to see Dario's flayed arm bounce on the bed in sync with the chest compressions.

A nurse drew labs and a blood gas. Cardiac defibrillations and medications followed. Then, additional defibrillations and more medications. And after thirty-two minutes of attempted resuscitation, Dario was officially declared dead.

Ward B, ER Exam Room #12

Oakland City Hospital

After waiting for the ER nurses to vacate her husband's exam room, Ellie asked Bill, "Did people actually *witness* your meltdown?"

Bill nodded.

"And you're sure about that?"

"I am," he said. "In fact, it was a spectacle. A circus, really. My research colleagues watched me through the windows. Gawkers gathered on the sidewalk. Two ambulances and a fire truck arrived, and EMTs with their bulky gear negotiated their way up the stairs to attend to me." He pulled the threadbare hospital blanket up to his chin and frowned.

"And *you're* frowning?" she said. "Well, I had to leave rehearsal and drive from Marin to be here before eleven. My nerves are shot from the Richmond Bridge traffic. If anyone should be frowning, it ought to be me."

"Well," he said, "we can both frown."

She looked at him as if she were sucking a lemon. "You needn't be so insensitive. I had to leave something I love to be here and help you with a problem I did not create."

"Of course, you're right," he said, staring up at the crumbled-waffle ceiling. "I should be more gracious. I should have welcomed you with chamomile tea and butter biscuits." He grabbed an applesauce cup from the bedside stand and offered it to her. "It's the best I can do now."

"Please," she said, waving her hand dismissively. When he responded by pulling the blanket over his face, she yanked it away and asked, "What's wrong with you?"

He did not want to admit to his fresh humiliation—let alone, to share it with her. Besides, he needed to focus on his plans already in play.

"Seriously, Bill?" she persisted. "All my efforts to help you, and, still, I can't know how to do that when you continue to shut me out."

"It's just that . . ." he said, looking away, mindlessly setting his sights on a plastic water pitcher. "When the ambulance brought me here, not a single doctor or nurse recognized me. And, even after learning my name, no one here had even heard of me."

Ellie tutted. "So, you're surly because your ego was injured?"

He sat up in bed and faced her. "It was *disrespectful*, Ellie. And it felt like a callous erasure of my life. I worked at this hospital for *decades*. I rose through the ranks: chief resident, staff physician, head of neurosurgery, residency program director. I launched its clinical research program and—"

"This is not a job interview," she said.

He persisted undeterred: "I'm an integral part of this hospital's living history. I would hope to be treated accordingly. At a minimum, to be recognized for my efforts to keep this hospital alive."

She looked sidelong at him, figuring she had two choices. She could reveal what was on her mind, but at the risk of further wounding his ego. Or, she could try to assuage him, but at the expense of exhausting her last thimbleful of patience.

"Ellie?" he said. "I've just laid bare my feelings, and all you do is look strangely at me?"

She stifled an eyeroll and said, "Given the mess you've gotten us into, your diminishing professional status should be the least of our concerns. Besides, you left clinical work here eons ago. How can you expect the current hospital staff to recognize you or know your name? I was on television for years, and, even so, some people still don't—"

A wiry young woman with a prominent cleft lip entered the room in green scrubs. After nodding in acknowledgment of Ellie's presence, she asked Bill, "How is your headache now, Mr.— Sorry, I mean, *Doctor* Balaban?"

Ellie estimated the doctor's age—or disappointing lack thereof—and determined she was too young to have seen her early television work in order to recognize her now. Still, for years Ellie had volunteered her precious time on the hospital's auxiliary board, and she had attended numerous social events and fundraisers in support of Oakland City Hospital—*including* this young doctor's residency program. "Excuse me," she said, stepping forward. "I am the doctor's wife, Elaine Balaban. And you are . . . ?"

"I'm Dr. Lena Grabowski," she answered, snapping on a pair of blue nitrile gloves.

"Staff, may I presume?" asked Ellie, though quite certain she was not. But extending such a basic professional courtesy to her and her husband seemed the minimum honorific that the hospital should offer them.

"Not yet," said Lena. "I'm still a third-year medical resident, on my ER rotation. And I'm the doctor who phoned you earlier about your husband."

"Of course," said Ellie, pursing her lips while solidly aligning with Bill's experience of being made to feel invisible and disrespected. Trying to solicit some due recognition, she continued, "Normally, I would have recognized your voice. As an actress, I've undergone considerable vocal training. But with what is happening to my husband . . . Obviously, it's been disorienting."

"I get that," said Lena, removing the stethoscope from around her neck.

"Excuse me," said Bill, pressing his fingers against his forehead. "Sorry to bother everyone, but . . . but my headache . . ." His eyes rolled back, his hands dropped to the bed, and his body stiffened.

"Dr. Balaban?" said Lena, checking the cardiac monitor but seeing nothing abnormal.

Ellie shook his shoulder and cried out, "Don't leave me!"

After calling for a nurse, Lena placed her stethoscope on Bill's chest to listen to his heart and lungs. But he suddenly stirred and emitted a guttural groan. Then his eyes orbited within their sockets and landed on Ellie with an inquisitive stare. "Who are you?" he haltingly asked.

Ellie shakily replied, "I am Ellie—your wife."

He returned a skeptical squint.

Dr. Lena Grabowski put her hands on her hips and said, "Well, *something* just happened. I'm not sure what, but we're going to figure it out." She asked Ellie to step aside, out of Bill's view, so she could command his full attention. Then she fired questions and commands at him to evaluate his capacity to hear, move his limbs, track her finger, open and shut his eyes when instructed. She followed her initial neuro evaluation with a mental status exam, during which he correctly stated his name and identified Oakland as his current location. But when asked for the year, he replied, "2013." In naming the current president, he confidently proclaimed, "My man, Reagan." And when tasked with subtracting nine from one hundred, he answered, "About eighty."

After completing her assessment, Lena said to Ellie: "So, I'm sure you can tell that something is impairing your husband's—" She stopped and faced Bill, remembering to address the patient directly, being all too familiar with how it felt to be overlooked because of some perceived impairment. Resuming the conversation, she told him: "Something is affecting your ability to think and remember. Please be patient and give us some time to diagnose the cause. For now, I'm going to order STAT labs and a head CT."

After the young doctor left, Ellie scolded Bill, "What are you doing? You were supposed to wait until Nora got here!"

"It was taking too long," he said. "Are you sure she's working here today?"

"I made certain of that," said Ellie. "Jack told me so yesterday, and he confirmed it this morning. I've already looked for her once. I'll look again when my presence here isn't required."

Nora's Office

Oakland City Hospital

Nora sat at her desk in the shocking aftermath of her patient's inexplicable death, her heart aching, her nerves knotting. She stared at her hands that, minutes ago, held the life of a young man they were supposed to save. They didn't seem to belong to her.

Minutes earlier, her next-of-kin notification call to Dario's parents had felt eerily stilted. All that the father said in response to news of their son's death was that they would immediately drive back from Napa. Perhaps, by the time they arrived here, after their immediate shock, they would have words and feelings to communicate. *How painful these calls are to make*, she thought, *but how much more painful to be a parent receiving one.* Reflecting on her own daughter's sudden death, she felt oddly grateful that she hadn't learned about it from a stranger's unexpected call. *Because, as horrific as it was to witness Caitlin's death, I knew for certain that she was gone. I didn't have to muddle through denial. I wasted no time in useless bargaining with gods. It was direct to grief for me—pure, unadulterated grief.*

But then, of course, the trauma of witnessing her death, and the onset of my panic attacks . . .

Still, I had my eyes on Caitlin when it happened, and I'm not haunted by worry that she may have suffered. I saw how happy she and Michael were when the rogue wave grabbed them from the beach.

Nora wearily rubbed her temples and looked at the wall clock, deciding she would claim a few more minutes of respite before returning to her shift. She leaned back in her chair, wondering how some of her colleagues never needed to take a break in routine after one of their patients died.

Now her eyes shifted to the colorful dartboard hanging near her bookshelf. Plastic magnetic darts—three red, three green—remained in place after last week's game with Fergie. Focusing on the vacant bull's-eye, she again questioned what she may have missed to explain Dario Parker's death. Yet, no matter how often she reviewed his case, she couldn't even hit the proverbial target.

Still, for a final time, she revisited every step of the surgery preceding his death. *I walked into the exam room and met Dario. He professed to be in "perfect health" until "a dumb fall" on the tennis court the day before. He was in obvious pain, and protecting his left arm. The moment I sat down, he straight-out asked, "Can you just hit me up with the antibiotics?"*

But it was evident at first glance at his swollen forearm and hand that he likely had a compartment syndrome—something that required urgent surgery and hospitalization. Responding to his question, she had stammered back, "The antibiotics?"

Their ensuing conversation proved wrenching. She hated watching his pained but optimistic expression transition to disillusionment and distress, while she gently disabused him of his naïve expectation. But steadily and efficiently, she built the case for her diagnosis. On a paper towel, she also drew a diagram to illustrate how the forearm muscles were normally arranged in separate bundles or "compartments," each containing nerves and blood vessels. Then she demonstrated how a firm membrane called "fascia" wrapped tightly around each compartment, so that if something injured the muscles inside it—"say, like a dumb fall"—they could swell and generate pressure. "So, you can see," she explained, "how too much swelling and pressure inside that compartment could compress its arteries and nerves, and cut off the blood and nerve supply to your hand and forearm."

After Dario professed to understand, she proceeded to confirm her diagnosis by performing a clinical exam. Along the way, she explained her findings. First, she palpated a firm muscle compartment in his forearm, and his pain intensified when she passively stretched it—"telltale signs, I'm sorry to say." She then demonstrated its compartment-specific muscle weakness, and detected a diminished radial pulse at his wrist—"consistent with threats to the nerves and blood supply." And, despite her clinical certitude, she inserted a manometer into the affected compartment to document its elevated pressure. At that juncture, Dario had no further questions, and he signed the surgical consent form.

He had a classic case of compartment syndrome, Nora concluded yet again. *And his surgery was flawless.*

Still, self-doubt crept into her consciousness—a reliable intruder whenever a patient died on her watch. And its capacity to disturb always multiplied when a death, like Dario's, was incomprehensible.

How impossible, too, to shake her memory of Dario's face all the while he was, in retrospect, dying. His anguished expression while he struggled to communicate something to her. His eyes, brimming with fear and urgency. His reaching out for her . . .

And that insufferable Paul Ling. She rued her uncritical acceptance of "paradoxical reaction" as his explanation for Dario's agitation. A chill spiked her spine now as she considered an alternate cause—that Dario may have been *genuinely* agitated but rendered incapable of communicating his experience because of the drugs. *What was disturbing him? What was he trying to tell me?*

Needing distraction, Nora walked to the dartboard and gathered her three green darts. She threw the first from behind the desk and watched it land on one of Fergie's reds. The contact felt comforting, and additionally reminded her to check on her friend.

While repositioning herself to lob the next dart, she speculated further about her imminent meeting with Dario's parents. Knowing firsthand how it felt to lose a child, she could imagine their shock and grief. And, like herself, they had been ambushed by the tragedy and thrown into a future of unfathomable loss. She pictured herself sitting with them in the private conference room, bearing witness to their suffering, offering counsel and comfort, and sharing her own story if that seemed appropriate. She released the second dart—*Phwitt!* It landed on the four, single ring.

Then a knock on the door sounded. She turned to see Owen Landry, chief orthopedic resident, boldly enter her office.

"Dr. Kelly," he said, as if in accusation. His deep sonorous voice made it sound as though he were sentencing her in a courtroom.

"Excuse me?" she said. "You can't just barge into my office."

"That compartment syndrome," he said. "It should've been Ortho's case." His thick fists knotted at his sides.

Nora stared incredulously at the stocky young resident who, less than an hour ago, was nowhere to be found. And here he stood now, unapologetically, stewing in grievance.

He stepped closer and said, "Do you have any idea how rare it is to have the opportunity to perform an emergency fasciotomy?" As his voice tightened, his Southern drawl accentuated. "This is a teaching hospital, and I've got Ortho residents who need the practice."

"So, where the hell were you while we were paging you to the ER so you could avail yourself of that rare 'opportunity'?" *The audacity*, she thought. *The bloated narcissism of this man-boy!*

"I was in the backlot, supervising the disaster-preparedness drill for the hospital," he shot back. "A *mandated* drill for our accreditation. Do you not read the memos? All you had to do was look out a window to see us."

"That's absurd," she said. "I'm not your babysitter. I'm not paid to keep watch over you like that. But *you* were obligated to be available to me and this ER." She cocked her head and added, "Do you not read or answer your pager?"

"I took off my coat to role-play a victim during the drill, and my pager was in the pocket. But it couldn't have been more than a few minutes. Besides, you could've waited."

"We waited until the very last minute for you. We had everything ready, and all you had to do was strut in and pick up a scalpel. But the clock was ticking on that patient's arm."

"Yeah, well," he said, widening his stance. "Now 'the clock' has stopped ticking for the patient."

Nora's palm ached from its vise-like grip on her last dart. Owen Landry, a junior physician, was trying to evade responsibility for his unavailability earlier. He was outrageously blaming her for not searching for him outside the hospital. He was displaying no emotional reaction to the sad fact of a young man's death, beyond anger at losing an "opportunity" to perform surgery. And what was he insinuating now, by his blunt comment and aggressive posturing?

But before she could marshal a fitting response, he pivoted away, only pausing fleetingly at the door to say: "That patient's death is on *you*."

5th Floor Hospital Stairwell

Owen Landry ran up the stairwell, trying to discharge his panic. He knew he had fucked up royally. Not only did he just go ballistic on a senior ER physician—he essentially accused her of killing a patient! He also had failed to secure Dario's surgery and deliver on his promise to Bill. And, if Bill's disturbing innuendos last night at the Beach House possessed any merit, perhaps he had also sabotaged the chance to save himself; because now the body belonged to the county Coroner's Bureau, and who knew what they might find during their investigation for the cause of death?

Panting when he reached the 5th floor landing, Owen plopped himself down on the staircase. His palms sweated and his stomach burned as his body absorbed the coolness of the metallic stairs.

How foolish to have allowed himself to become stuck in his awful predicament. Why had he agreed, if only once, to inject stem cells into Dario as a favor to Bill? Even at the time, he had felt hesitant, knowing almost nothing about those cells, or about any science backing their purported benefit. And at the Beach House last night, why didn't he follow his own moral compass, which was definitely pointing away from involvement in Bill's plan for Dario's surgery? He should have listened to his gut and declined Bill's cryptic and intimidating request.

"But it's fucking too late," he whispered, holding his forehead, shame washing through him. He had capitulated to Bill on both occasions.

What pathetic character weakness that reveals! What profound moral failing!

He imagined his parents' grave disappointment should they ever find out. He could almost hear his father's rebuke over abandoning one's principles to satisfy another man's needs.

On top of everything, he had yet to inform Bill that he missed Dario's surgery, which was bound to elicit his anger—even retribution, perhaps. And he was likely to face some form of disciplinary censure by Dr. Kelly.

Owen punched the stair rail, and it rattled loudly. A fitful paralysis of his mind took hold as the onslaught of his failures and fears intensified.

He stood up slowly and looked down through the stairwell, at the ground-floor entrance to the ER, beyond which Bill would be waiting for him. But how to tell him about missing Dario's surgery, especially when he was already so upset? When Bill had phoned him just before eleven, he was panicking about their plan, which only heightened Owen's own anxiety and kept him from answering his pager. Would Bill become angry enough to withdraw his support or evict him from the lab? And suppose the coroner uncovered evidence of the stem-cell injections—something Owen might have prevented had he performed the surgery?

At a minimum, his companionable relationship with Bill would fray. And if the awkward estrangement made it untenable to coexist in the lab, it would be he, not Bill, who would be forced to leave—ironic though that was, since only he, not Bill, was conducting genuine research. While Owen actively searched for answers in petri dishes to address questions about human health, Bill sleepily rested on his laurels, repackaging his old research data for publications in throwaway journals that paid. Bill used the lab as a man cave to escape from his wife, and to dabble in stem cells for the money.

Grasping the stair rail, fearing his career was in free fall, Owen counseled himself to get a grip. He needed to think rationally, like a scientist. He needed to be practical, like a doctor. So, what were the real-world odds that a notoriously understaffed and underfunded county coroner would conduct a sufficiently detailed and expensive postmortem to detect injected stem cells? And then, to go the mile to prove they were a genetic mismatch with Dario's native cells? *None! No chance for a 'CSI: Oakland' scenario here!*

And besides, despite Bill's undercutting insinuation, he knew he had directed his stem-cell injection into Dario's tendon without causing any peripheral damage. *The coroner won't discover anything to implicate that in Dario's death. And the autopsy will merely confirm predictable evidence of Dario's compartment syndrome, which will be attributed to his self-reported fall.*

He relaxed his hold on the railing. Yes, maybe a few days after the coroner settled matters as such, Bill would forgive him. Hopefully, that might even transpire before next Thursday's lab unit, when Owen expected to find out whether his osteoblast cell cultures were compatible with the experimental bone cements he was testing and hoping to patent. *Yes—logically speaking, that's how things will proceed.*

And yet . . .

It occurred to him that Dario's parents had not yet entered the equation. How to account for the potent new variables they were bound to introduce? How were they going to react to their son's death, and on whom would they try to pin the blame? How could the father not speculate about a possible connection between the stem-cell injections and the compartment syndrome that necessitated the disastrous fasciotomy? And, given the circumstances, how likely was he to continue his philanthropic support of the lab?

Weighted with dread, Owen descended the stairwell, thinking along the way, struggling to remain logical. By the time he reached the ground floor, he had chosen to believe that Donald Parker was not going to point the finger at him or Bill's lab, because doing so would require him to disclose his own complicity. He would have to admit that he had cajoled his son into receiving stem-cell treatments for the purely speculative goal of boosting muscle and tendon strength. He would have to identify himself as the person who paid handsomely for the injections, while stipulating they be kept confidential. Yes, if Donald Parker chose to stir up troubling questions, he would have to answer personally to many of them. *And that is not going to happen.*

Owen squared his shoulders and stood tall. Then he pushed the ER entry door open and headed toward Bill's exam room.

Afternoon

Fergie clutched the wastebasket, willing her stomach to settle down. The vomiting had ceased—or so she hoped—though her gut kept burbling, reminding her who was in control. Hearing footsteps now, she looked up and saw Lizbeth enter the locker room, bearing a water bottle in her hand and a concerned expression on her face.

"Are you all right?" she asked, handing the water to her boss, whose sickly pale skin made her blue tattoos pop starkly across her arms and neck.

"I think so," Fergie answered, with little conviction.

Lizbeth counseled herself to act normal, but she was rattled to see her mentor looking so frail and unlike herself—the unflappable, rock-steady ER veteran, who modeled nursing like a superpower.

After gulping down the water, Fergie sank back into her chair and said, "Thanks."

"No problem," said Lizbeth, taking the wastebasket from her, expecting—but not experiencing—a refusal to be helped. "I'll be back in a sec," she said, heading to the restroom.

Lizbeth emptied the wastebasket into the toilet bowl and saw the vomit disappear after a quick flush. She thought how great it would be to have the power to eliminate all terrible things with such a simple flick of the wrist. Things like wars and pollution, poverty and homelessness. Diseases and injuries and accidents. Sordid politicians and corrupt corporations. And the death of Dario Parker.

Now rinsing the wastebasket at the sink, Lizbeth glanced into the mirror and paused, wondering how many times, throughout her years at Oakland City Hospital, that she had seen herself reflected in it. First, as a high school "candy striper" volunteering in the ER. Later, as a nursing student on clinical rotation. Later still, as a specialty trainee and, finally, a bona fide member of the ER nursing staff.

She studied her reflection, sensing some change in her visage over those years, though unable to identify a blatant physical alteration. Her tawny brown hair was still swept behind her ears, her long thin face remained smooth, and her charcoal gray eyes shone as always. But then, when softening her gaze before turning away, she spotted it: The change she had sensed was internal, something she had "seen" in the visages of her mentors, Fergie and Edna. And now she could see it in herself: the effortless projection of her own confidence and authority.

Ward A, ER Hallway

After texting a colleague to thank him for holding down the fort, Nora exited her office to resume her shift. Before checking the whiteboard to assess the status of her patient load, she peered down at her old rust-colored Keens and grounded herself in their magical powers to keep her safe and strong at work.

But, with her first step down the hallway, she was thrown off balance by a powerful tidal force, drawing her toward the exam room in which Dario had died. She flashed back to her last view of him—the endotracheal tube dangling from his mouth, his flayed and bloated arm, his lifeless body on the bloodied white sheets—everything left in place for the coroner to deconstruct during the forensic investigation. And that "everything" also set solidly in her memory, as if encapsulated in amber.

Willing herself to forge on, she headed to the whiteboard. After squaring the readers on her face, she saw that every exam room under her charge was purportedly occupied—including room 7, from which Dario's name had not yet been erased.

Ward B, ER Hallway

Owen Landry paced the hallway while his last nerve frayed. It was taking forever for the nurses to vacate Bill's room. And the woman at the bedside—presumably, Bill's wife—must be glued to her chair.

All the while he waited to deliver his bad news to Bill, his gut knotted. Paranoia rushed in to fill the widening gaps in his reasoning.

He obsessively checked emails on his phone, and he liberally texted assignments to his residents. Occasionally, he traipsed into the crowded waiting room to retrieve an old magazine.

Then one of the ER interns passed by and walked to the Ward B whiteboard. Watching her change the clinical notation alongside Bill's name, his jaw dropped.

What the hell is Bill up to? And what is his wife doing here? What have I gotten myself into?

Nurses' Locker Room, ER

When Lizbeth returned to the locker room with the cleaned wastebasket, she found Fergie hunched over in a chair and asked, "Still feeling sick?"

Fergie grimaced. "I'm mostly feeling embarrassed. Nothing like this ever happens to me."

"Well," said Lizbeth, "you're only human."

"No, it's freakin' unbelievable. I've seen crazy-times-ten worse here, and nothing ever gut-punched me like this."

Lizbeth's full lips formed a tight red O through which she dramatically exhaled. "Come on," she said. "That *was* pretty upsetting. And the guy was only eighteen."

"Wait," said Fergie, sitting upright. "You're talking as if the guy is dead."

"So . . . you didn't hear the code?"

"*That* young guy?" said Fergie, her brow furrowing. "No! It must have happened during my Olympic puking in the toilet. What happened?"

Lizbeth shrugged. "Everyone is bent about it. Even Dr. Kelly. *Especially* Dr. Kelly. But the second you left, Dario crashed." She snapped her fingers for emphasis. "We coded him for thirty-two minutes but—"

"Excuse me?" someone called out.

Recognizing the voice of their stalwart ER desk clerk, Fergie replied, "Come on in, Leon."

"Sorry to bother you, ladies," he said, stepping into view.

"Why the frown?" asked Lizbeth, eyeing him with concern. "What's up?"

"Well," he said, scratching his cheek. "I suppose you could say 'hackles.' Yes, that's what's up. The parents of the young man who died? They're in the waiting room. And here's a heads-up: They are *very* angry. In all my years of clerking in the ER, I've rarely been so grateful for all the security guards we got here."

Fergie winced and said, "Thanks, Leon," although feeling anything but thankful for the news. Over recent years, she had witnessed—and experienced firsthand—the escalation of violent emotions and physical threats from patients and families. And she was aware of the punishing psychic tolls and physical injuries that her staff were made to suffer. But when she stood up to accompany Leon to the waiting room, she staggered.

Lizbeth held her back and said, "Sit down. I got this." She explained to Leon, "Fergie is sick."

"No," Fergie protested. "I'm good to go. And it's my job as head nurse."

A corner of Leon's mouth turned down. "I'd listen to Lizbeth," he said. "I can guarantee two hundred percent that you vomiting on those people is just going to make a bad situation worse."

"I can meet with them," said Lizbeth, guiding Fergie back to her chair. "Besides, I was in the room when Dario died. And, naturally, his parents will have questions about what took place."

Ward A, ER Hallway

After making certain that her patients were stable, Nora headed toward the nurses' locker room to check on Fergie. But on the way, she ran into Lizbeth and Leon, and, noting their somber expressions, asked, "What's going on?"

"Well," Leon answered, "Lizbeth is about to talk with the parents of that young man who died. The Parkers. Actually, the father's a Parker.

The mother has a different last name—Greene. Still, they got the same anger."

Nora exhaled wearily. And Lizbeth, as if hearing Nora's private doubts, insisted: "I can do this, Dr. Kelly. I volunteered to be their first encounter. Besides, Fergie's still sick."

Leon stepped back to evade Lizbeth's view, and he shook his head vehemently. Nora, knowing how accurately he read the many strangers who approached him daily at the registration desk, smiled politely at Lizbeth and said, "If it's okay, I'd like to accompany you. The parents will want to talk with me anyway."

Ward B, ER Exam Room #12

Finally, everyone had vacated Bill's room. Owen charged in and stood red-faced before his mentor.

"Well," said Bill, "you certainly took your time to get here."

"I had to wait for everyone to leave, so we could talk privately," said Owen, clenching his fists. "But I didn't get the Dario Parker case."

Bill blinked hard and said, "What?"

"The timing was off. Maybe Dario came in earlier? Maybe while I was running the disaster drill? Still, I couldn't get here at eleven, when you told me to—because *you* were freaking out on the phone with me then! So, I didn't take care of business because I *couldn't*."

"No, no, no. That's not what was supposed to happen."

"Well, that *is* what happened. Nora Kelly was in the ER, and she just *grabbed* the case. Hell, it was over by the time I got there."

Slumping against the headboard, Bill moaned.

"She could've waited," Owen said. "She *should* have waited for me and my team. That's standard protocol."

Bill watched his research mentee twist himself into one big muscular knot. *Such a golden boy, so unaccustomed to obstacles. Everything has been handed to him on a silver platter—his lucky draw from the gene pool, loving parents, a smart-enough mind, and the research support he so blithely accepted from me. Even a goddamn dimple in his chin.*

Following an unwieldy pause, Owen said, "So, what do we do now?"

"First, I must be frank," said Bill. "I'm very disappointed in you. I relied on you, and I've made so few demands . . ." He looked away and continued, "But at this point, I'm not sure there's anything different we can do."

"I'm sorry, Dr. Balaban. But I explained what happened. And you still haven't told me what you're—"

"Well," Bill interrupted, staring pensively at the ceiling, "even if Nora saw some anomaly in Dario's tendons or muscles, she'd likely dismiss it as evidence of an athletic injury in our fall-prone patient. And, of course, she'd have no reason to test any lavage fluid for stem cells. Still . . ." He cocked a brow and continued in a cautionary tone, "Still, knowing how exacting she is, I advise you to check her operative note to make sure she didn't see something unusual."

Owen pinned him with a piercing glare. "'See something unusual'? Seriously? How would she have had time to note *anything* after the surgery, when Dario reportedly coded before she even set her scalpel down? And now? Now the coroner has the body, and they're going to look very carefully for a cause of death, and who knows—"

"The coroner? What's the coroner got to do with this?"

Standing rigid now, Owen said, "Did you not hear a Code Blue in this room?"

"I did hear a code! I heard two, in fact. It is an ER, for godsakes. But they don't broadcast patients' names."

"Well, hear this—Dario Parker is dead," Owen said.

Then, for a moment that felt like an eternity, the two men stared at one another.

ER Waiting Room

When Nora, Lizbeth, and Leon entered the packed ER waiting room, a middle-aged couple shot out of their seats and beelined toward them. The man—white, fashionably attired, over six feet tall, with mahogany-colored hair and a matching mustache—said, "Dr. Kelly?" The woman—brown-skinned, trim, a few inches shorter, wearing a short bleached Afro—said, "We are Dario Parker's parents."

"Yes, hello," said Nora, with a pained expression. "I'm so sorry about your son. We're all heartbroken." She pointed to Lizbeth and continued, "This is Lizbeth Tanner, one of our ER nurses who was also with Dario. And I believe you met Leon from the reception desk. Perhaps we can all go into the private conference room to talk."

But Donald Parker—the CEO of Parker International—thrust his hands into the air as if giving witness, and he turned to address all the people in the waiting room. "No!" he loudly proclaimed. "There will be no talking behind closed doors. We demand transparency about whatever happened to our son. We want the public to know that our boy . . . our *healthy* eighteen-year-old boy, who was headed for college next fall . . ." He took a moment to repair his breaking voice. "Our son *walked* into this ER, after taking a simple fall on a tennis court. And"—he snapped his fingers—"he died." After surveying everyone in the hushed room, he asked, "Just how does that happen? Someone, anyone, tell me how that just happens."

"Please," said Lizbeth, stepping between him and his hypervigilant audience. Already, Leon had summoned the security guards.

Donald Parker's wife, Lori Greene, placed a hand on his arm. But he brushed it off, pointed at Nora, and shouted, "This place is crawling with surgical specialists! Actual surgeons. But my son had to die because *this* doctor . . . this *ER doctor* performed a *surgery* on him that she had no business doing!"

Nora's heart walloped against her chest. Though skilled in conducting difficult conversations, she tended to falter when ambushed by someone's rage. And what a cruel and unfounded allegation he was lodging against her. How had he even conjured that up? She struggled to maintain composure, but she couldn't ignore all the people in the waiting room, who were either staring at her or trying to act as if they weren't. Several began filming the dramatic encounter on their cellphones. Finally, she managed to say, "Mr. Parker, I'm genuinely sorry about your son's death. He was—"

"That's right," he exploded. "My son *was.* My son *was* alive this morning when he entered this ER. He *was* a good boy . . . My god, he *was* . . . My god . . ." He threw his head back and moaned. This time, he did not brush off his wife's hand.

Lori Greene, eyeing Nora coolly, said, "Dario's with the coroner now."

Nora couldn't tell whether Lori was conveying a question or a fact. She answered or agreed, "Yes."

"Tell me," Lori said. "Did the simple courtesy of calling me or my husband even occur to you, before you performed the surgery?"

Nora replied, "Dario told us more than once not to notify you. He said you were in Napa for the Thanksgiving weekend, and he didn't want to intrude. And because he was eighteen, we honored his decision."

"Please," Lizbeth entreated the couple, "it would help if we could talk privately."

"That's not going to happen," said Lori, ushering her husband away. "Any future communication will go through our attorney."

ER Nurses' Station

After ingesting a peppermint capsule, Fergie felt better. Still, as a precaution, she reassigned a nurse to cover her primary duties, and volunteered for less taxing chores, like IV insertions and blood draws. When she scored a peaceful moment, she went searching for Nora, and found her working on a computer at the nurses' station. "Hey," she said, "Lizbeth told me what happened in the waiting room with Dario's parents. It sounded rough. How are you doing?"

Nora appeared to grasp for words, then said, "I don't know how I'm doing. I'm massively distracted, for sure. And shaken up. And not just from meeting the parents." She logged off the computer. "There's Dario's death itself—so shocking, on so many levels. And Owen Landry bursting into my office to scold me for stealing his surgery."

"Ugh," said Fergie. "That guy can be such a pain. At least he's a decent Ortho surgeon."

"Wait," said Nora. "What about you? I'd been on my way to check on you when the parents arrived."

"I'm near to normal now," Fergie said. Then she cocked her head toward an empty exam room, and Nora followed her in. After closing the door, she said, "So, I was floored to hear that Dario died. What do you think happened?"

Hunching her shoulders, Nora said, "I wish I knew. I keep going over *everything*. But it looks like we're going to have to rely on the coroner for answers."

How rare to see Nora sound and look so defeated at work. But, having learned from the few prior occasions, Fergie knew to say: "Do not freakin' tell me you're blaming yourself."

Nora's hazel eyes glistened. "But, you know, maybe I missed something. And maybe I was too distracted during the surgery. Too annoyed with Ortho for being AWOL. Too irritated by that pompous nurse anesthetist, Paul Ling."

"I'm pleading with you, as a friend: Do not go down that dark road again."

"Or maybe I was too *focused*. On Dario, I mean. We had been locked in an epic stare all the while he was being sedated. And, early on, he was grimacing and trying to speak, but he couldn't. He looked agitated and desperate the entire time. And then, suddenly, he went under, I did the fasciotomy, and he died. End of story."

Fergie handed her a tissue. Nora dabbed her eyes and continued, "Maybe Dario's parents are right. I should have just waited for Ortho."

"First," countered Fergie, "Ortho wasn't responding a good ten-maybe-fifteen minutes, and we had no idea when and if they might. Second, how could you have waited any longer, when Dario's hand was already ischemic? Look, I know how hard you take a patient's death. But I and everyone else know how skilled you are."

"But you didn't see everything that happened in that room, Fergie. You weren't there the entire time."

Fergie placed her hands on her hips and looked inquiringly at Nora, wondering whether she had intended an accusatory tone. After a beat, she said, "True. But I wish I had been there—for you."

Nora cringed. "Forgive me, please. I realize how that might have sounded. I'm just upset. And besides, I even encouraged you to leave when you did."

"No problem," Fergie said with a dismissive wave of her hand. "We're good. Obviously, Dario's death is affecting both of us. I'm floored by how sick I felt when you made the incision and—"

An insistent knock on the door preceded a woman's voice: "Nora? Dr. Nora Kelly?"

Fergie and Nora looked at one another and shrugged. Then Nora steeled herself, finger-combed her long chestnut-brown hair, and straightened her white coat. She opened the door to find an elderly woman with a cane, whose free hand was poised to knock again. Instinctively, Nora noticed clinical evidence of osteoarthritis in the woman's fingers, and she privately questioned the woman's choice in footwear (*High heels while needing a cane?*). The woman also wore dark glasses (*Why, inside a building?*) and a floral silk scarf (*With beautiful blue roses.*). Her smooth face appeared to be constructed with layers of makeup (*Like a mask.*). Her hair, in a bright blonde pageboy, was surely a wig or had been creatively dyed (*Because that yellow doesn't exist in nature.*).

The woman frowned and said, "You don't recognize me, do you?"

Fergie excused herself and slipped away. Nora stepped into the hallway, struggling to identify her visitor.

"I'm Elaine Balaban," the woman offered. "Bill's wife?"

Nora tapped a palm to her forehead in sudden recognition. "Of course! *Ellie.* Sorry. It's just so out of context to run into you here. And after all these years?"

"Decades, actually," Ellie said. "Except for the funerals, of course."

"Yes, well," said Nora—the least lame reply she could marshal. Then she relievedly recalled, "Oh, Jack tells me you're working together on a holiday show for the prison inmates."

"We are," she replied. "He was kind to reach out to me, although I suspect he was desperate for help. And, I'm sorry—I didn't intend to make you uncomfortable. In fact, I should be apologizing for ambushing you like I did. But Jack told me you'd be here, and when I saw you enter this room with that young man who just left, I thought—"

"Oh, that was Fergie, a woman. Head nurse here. A good friend."

"Ah," said Ellie, arching a brow. "All this 'gender fluidity' confuses me. And perhaps I would have seen *her* better had I not been wearing these." She removed her dark glasses and stared at Nora. Her filmy blue eyes glinted with tears, and a maroon bruise rimmed the right one.

Nora gasped and asked, "What happened?"

"I'm all right," said Ellie, although her tone suggested otherwise. "And I'm not in the ER because of *me.*"

"Well, that black eye is certainly *yours*," said Nora.

"I mean, I'm here because of Bill. He is not . . . *himself.* And he hasn't been himself for nearly two years."

Nora strove to project equanimity. But she was shocked to imagine Bill capable of harming Ellie—anyone, really. Still, she wasn't going to dismiss any woman's intimation of domestic violence. "Are you saying that Bill gave you that shiner?"

"No," said Ellie, with a doleful look. "Not as *himself.* But, as the person he's become? Yes, *that* person hit me."

Jack's Home

Rockridge District, Oakland

After a stopover at Fentons Creamery for an emergency ice cream fix, Jack and Luis arrived home and began their Friday-night ritual. They assembled the chessboard on the coffee table and tossed a frozen pepperoni pizza into the oven.

Jack said, "I can't believe you're still hungry." In addition to devouring a Fentons Special, Luis had consumed a full breakfast at the house before his subsequent lunch of burgers and fries at the prison commissary.

Patting his slender stomach, Luis said, "It's still got room for pizza."

Jack marveled at how tall and strong Luis had grown within the past year of living at the house—since having reliable access to food, really. He said, "I think your stomach is made of elastic."

Luis laughed and, after placing chairs around the chessboard, asked, "Are you going to call the prima donna before we play?"

"Ah, what a great memory you have! Your vocabulary is exploding. I better watch what I say around you."

"But are you?"

"Call Ellie Balaban? Why would I do that?"

"Well," said Luis, scratching an ear. "Because she was worried about her husband?"

Jack's face flushed. "You're right," he said in a confessional tone. For, as maddening as Ellie could be (*and was*), she'd been generous to help produce (*and, at her suggestion, star in*) the prison's holiday show. Last month, when he solicited her help, years had passed since he had initiated any contact with her or her husband. But she was the only actor he knew who was likely to be free—time-wise and salary-wise. So, he picked up his cell, walked to the kitchen, and phoned her.

Ellie answered with a breathy "Hello."

"Ellie?" he said. "You sound winded. Is everything all right?"

"I'm in the ER hallway, rushing back to Bill's room. I had been talking with Nora in the other ward."

"Well, take a moment to catch your breath."

"You needn't be concerned," she said in her theater voice. "In fact, I've arrived. I'm standing outside of Bill's room now."

"Great," said Jack. "So, how is he doing?"

"Not well," she whispered, furtively glancing through the door lite into his room. She saw the backside of someone in a white coat, who was talking to her husband.

"I'm sorry, Ellie. Can you say more?"

"I'm trying to be discreet," she said. "I don't want Bill to overhear. But, truthfully? He looks more confused and agitated than he did just a half-hour ago. Oh, Jack. What is it? A stroke, perhaps? Dementia worsening? They know nothing yet." She huffed and added, "Or, I should say, the *third-year resident* caring for Bill knows nothing yet."

"But it's still early, isn't it?" said Jack. "Do they even have any test results yet?"

"I don't know," she said. "Like I told you, I was out talking with Nora and—" The "someone" she had seen in her husband's room grazed her shoulder on their hurried way out and continued undeterred down the hallway. "How rude!" she exclaimed.

"Sorry?" asked Jack.

"People act so crudely these days," she said. "The lack of professionalism among the staff here is shocking."

Disinterested in sharing her affront, he said, "Well, back to Bill?"

She spoke in a normal volume now. "Well, thankfully, Nora promised to be here in a minute, after making some call. I'm sure we'll get better answers then."

"You must be—what?" said Jack, realizing how astute Luis had been to prompt this contact.

"I'm beside myself," she replied. "Bill doesn't even recognize me sometimes. He thinks it is 2013, and Ronald Reagan is the president."

"That's worrisome."

"Well, yes, it is. And I'm sorry, Jack—but, right now, I can't even think about our holiday show."

"Of course," he said. "But please forget about that. I was only calling to check on how you were doing."

"Oh?" she said, surprised by his expression of personal concern. She wondered if he might be feeling acutely sentimental, reminded of Bill's mentoring in the waning '80s. Bill had taken the "gang of six"—Jack, Nora, Fred, Lydia, Carl, and Cheryl—under his wing during their residency. He had championed them professionally and tended to their growing pains as young doctors. He had lauded their earnestness and intelligence, their fierce comradery and work ethic. With monthly regularity, he and Ellie had hosted elaborate cocktail dinners for them at their home. Still, she thought, before Jack's recent call to solicit her help with the show, no one in the gang had initiated contact with her or Bill since their residency ended in 1990.

"Yes," said Jack. "Luis and I were both worried about you."

"Well," she said, "I appreciate your concern. Though I suppose, depending on what Bill's CT shows, we might be able to resume rehearsals soon."

"No," he said, perhaps too emphatically, but realizing an opportunity to cancel the beleaguered production. "I mean, I think you should focus on Bill right now."

She hesitated. "I'm sure you're right. But we can't let the inmates down."

"They will survive the loss," he said. "And you must rest and take care of *yourself*, as well."

Ellie sighed. "But as you and I know, sometimes 'taking care' of yourself equates with taking care of others. You're a doctor, tending to inmates' physical health, and surely you experience personal gratification from that? Also, as a former thespian yourself, you understand the theater's healing power to mend broken spirits. As an actor, I feel it's my duty—if also a selfish reward—to offer my healing gift to others."

When their conversation ended, Jack took a moment to shake off his discomfort with the call. But Ellie's haughtiness and judgmental attitude had transported him back in time, to his days of socializing with the Balabans in their home. How uncomfortable and invisible he regularly felt at their dinner table. And though they never explicitly judged his sexuality or requested he not bring a date, they remained conspicuously incurious about him, while plumbing the depths of his friends' lives and relationships. They sat like bookends at opposite ends of the table, keeping the conversation "polite" and within their socially acceptable straight norms. Even the banter between them—barbed as it often was—tended toward joking about their married life.

Jack shook off his dispiriting mood, then returned to the living room, where Luis cheerfully awaited him.

Fred's Office

Oakland City Hospital

Dr. Fred Williams sat at his desk in his 10th floor C-suite office, deciding which administrative crises to prioritize for weekend review. Surely, the imminent pharmacists' walkout required more robust contingency planning. He should also acquaint himself with next week's court case against his OB department. Still, the nursing and durable-medical-equipment budgets required urgent sign-off. And Infection Control had yet to address the skyrocketing rates of hospital-acquired *C. difficile* and MRSA infections—a threat to the hospital's forthcoming accreditation.

But now the early evening bell rang in the hospital's chapel tower, signaling the time for his daily ritual. He walked to the window overlooking the courtyard and offering a panoramic view of the East Bay Hills, and took a meditative breath. Then he entered the present moment, insulating himself from all the pressing external demands on him. He professed his gratitude for his wife and two children, and he prayerfully spoke their names aloud: "Vickie. Ella. Charlie. *Amen.*" He also thanked his mother and grandparents for their sacrifices, which made his good life and career possible. He included his friendships with Nora, Jack, and Carl among his blessings.

Though lasting little more than a minute, his ritual possessed hours of staying power. Carving out the moment to reflect on the love of family and friends helped him to feel humanized at work. As chief of staff, he often felt objectified—treated as a means to an end, with the staff always wanting something from him: bigger salaries, departmental promotions, additional hires, enhanced benefits, designated parking spaces, et cetera.

Now renewed of spirit, Fred returned to his desk and packed the files for his weekend review. But as he snapped close his briefcase, his cellphone chimed with an alarming text from Nora: *Call STAT.*

When Nora picked up his call, he said, "Hey, I'm just leaving the office."

"Glad I caught you," she whispered, scanning the hallway to make sure Ellie wasn't nearby. "Because I thought you'd want to know that Bill Balaban is here in the ER."

"Hell, no," Fred muttered, immediately awash in guilt. How many times had he promised—but failed—to visit his old friend and mentor? And now, had he lost that opportunity? "How bad is he?"

"Can't say," Nora said. "I'm just about to go in to see him. But you should know—"

"What room is he in?"

"Twelve, Ward B. But wait. His wife, Ellie—"

"I'm on my way," said Fred, ending the call, darting out of the office.

Ward B, ER Exam Room #12

Sitting at his bedside, Ellie asked her husband if "this Owen Landry person" had come by yet.

"It's taken care of," Bill answered.

"So, then, we've finished with that part of it?" she said.

He nodded.

"Good," she said, fidgeting with her scarf. "But what's taking Nora so long? She promised to be here 'in a minute' after making some call and—"

Fergie entered the exam room and said, "I'm here to draw more labs."

Ellie peered above her dark glasses for a better view, noting Fergie's shaved head, copious blue tattoos, thick bifocals, and compact athletic figure. "So," she said, "I hear you're the head nurse?"

"Yup," Fergie answered, applying a tourniquet around Bill's arm. Recalling their earlier encounter in the hallway, she guessed, "I gather you're the wife?"

"I am," Ellie returned with poorly concealed judgment. But since when did nurses look so unprofessional, and address patients and families so informally? "In fact," she said, "we've been married to each other for more years than you—"

"Excuse me?" said Bill, his eyes widening. "Did you just say we're married?"

"Oh, Bill," said Ellie with a dismissive tut. But when she removed her dark glasses and extended her hand, he declined to receive it.

And that's when Fergie noticed Ellie's black eye. Reflexively seeing the couple through a new lens, she questioned whether she and the staff had been too quick to attribute the scratches on Bill's cheek to his fall on the stairway. Considering the possibility of domestic violence now, she felt queasiness return to her stomach. After filling the blood vials and releasing the tourniquet, she planned to seek out Nora for urgent consultation. But, as if in a telepathic response, Nora appeared in the doorway, though with a tight expression on her face.

"Hello, Bill," said Nora, approaching. "I'm sorry to see you here."

He massaged his stubbled chin and asked, "Are we married, too?"

Ellie dabbed her eyes with her blue floral scarf and turned away. Nora replied, "No, we're not married. I'm Nora Kelly—one of your old students. And I've been working here on staff since 1990, if you can believe that."

"For god's sake," Ellie exclaimed, pivoting back to Bill. "She's *Nora*. You took her and her friends under your wing during their residency. You must remember the 'gang of six'? Nora and Lydia, Fred and Jack, Carl and Cheryl?"

Bill eyed Fergie and said, "That's right, the old gang. Which one are you? Wait, I know. You're Lydia!"

Fergie shook her head.

"My mistake," he said. "You're Cheryl, of course."

"Please, stop," Ellie pleaded. "Lydia and Cheryl are *dead*. My god—they were both *murdered*, Bill. We attended their funerals. You can't remember something like that?" She buried her face in her scarf and wept.

Nora reeled internally, blindsided by Ellie's hardball delivery of the still-painful fact of Lydia's murder. She braced herself and said, "Why don't we just focus on the present, and do what's needed to understand Bill's—"

Fred rushed into the room. But his smile capsized immediately, when he saw the wounds on the Balabans' faces and Nora's worried expression.

Bill wagged a finger at him and said, "Fred Williams! You *finally* came to see me."

Fred looked sheepishly around, aware that Ellie and Nora knew about his repeated cancellations on Bill over recent years. He cleared his throat, guiltily wondering if Bill may have been trying to talk with him about a volatile domestic situation. "Yes, I'm finally here," he said. "And I'm sorry it's taken me so long. I've been so damn busy, and not a good friend to you."

"Well," Ellie managed, sniffling, "you're here now. And so is Nora."

"And," said Lizbeth, now in the doorway, "so are the police and a lawyer. They're here about that patient of yours, Dr. Kelly."

Good Earth Landscapes

Lakeshore District, Oakland

DeeDee Alcindor knocked on the glass door and looked in at Red, who was kneeling on the dusty floor, taping drywall with Gianni. The renovation of their soon-to-launch garden and landscaping store appeared to be on track for its grand opening in January.

Gianni laughed when he saw Red's smile stretch ear-to-ear while he waved to DeeDee. "Go on," Gianni told him. "I can finish up." Red brushed himself off with his mastic-caked hands, only dirtying his clothes more. "Wow," said Gianni, "that girl *literally* messes you up!"

Red thanked Gianni, threw on his black leather jacket, and stepped outside. The wind blew off mists of drywall sand from his orange-red hair, which caused DeeDee to step back and say, "You need to be vacuumed!"

"Agreed," he said, brushing off his jacket. "But I didn't expect you this early. Thought I'd have time for a shower." Peeling caulk remnants off his hands, he added, "Hey, and didn't you have plans for the day?"

"I did," she said. "Sorry. I should have texted you first."

"You're joking," he returned. "I'm happy to see you *any* time." Still, she looked worried; even her cobalt-blue hair and silver nose ring appeared dim. He immediately feared she had come to dump him— something he'd been expecting since the day they met. His pale skin turned improbably whiter, causing his freckles to darken and his red hair to redden. "What's wrong, Dee?" he asked.

Familiar with the telltale signs of his insecurity, she stroked his smooth cheek and said, "It's not about us or you."

He exhaled sharply. "Sorry. There I go again, railroading you with my shit."

"It's okay," she said, reflecting on how far they had come toward understanding each other's psychological quirks. "But it's about something that happened this morning. Do you have time for a walk-and-talk?"

He hugged her and grabbed her hand. Then they drove Red's crew cab truck to Lake Merritt, and walked its shoreline in easy silence. Having learned how to "respect her process," he simply waited for her to speak. Meanwhile, he thought about his new business venture with Gianni and reasoned that, with continued good luck and hard work, they'd be able to open on schedule. After their remarkably stressful, though highly lucrative, last year spent in court as whistleblowers against Greeley Enterprises, they could look optimistically forward to a more relaxed and financially secure future.

Strolling with DeeDee under the lakeside pergola, he marveled at his hard-won good fortune. Just yesterday, at this precise location, he helped to fund the second annual Thanksgiving cookout. One year earlier, at its inaugural event, he'd been a hungry and unhoused recipient of its offerings.

Finally, DeeDee stopped and looked directly at him. She swept her blue bangs off her forehead and said, "So."

Recognizing that signaled her readiness to talk, he asked, "What's up?"

"So," she began, resuming her stride. "You know how I tend to get depressed around the holidays?"

He nodded, recalling their first Christmas and New Year's together last year. Though they had each been estranged from their respective families, she, unlike him, had suffered the estrangement.

"And," she said, "remember me deciding to do something about that? To say 'yes' to opportunities to connect and celebrate with other people?"

"I remember," he said.

She tightened her grasp on his hand. "Well, this morning at coffee I ran into a guy named Joel Plawecki. We used to work together at the research center across the street from the hospital. Anyhow, he invited me to their annual 'all-purpose holiday party' today—Christmas, Chanukah, Kwanzaa, and New Year's all rolled into one. So, I decided to go—me, with my new positive attitude."

"And?" he said, tracking a yellow kayak being pulled onto shore.

Her dark brow tented over her hyacinth-colored eyes. "And that whole thing made me feel ten-times worse."

"Well, that sucks," he said. "But we both know attitude adjustments are fucking hard and—"

"It's not that," she said, pulling him aside. They braved a gang of urban seagulls that were pecking at trash, and headed to a park bench under a rustling oak tree. They sat down and huddled, looking out—to the lone brown gondola navigating the choppy lake, to people strolling in their winter coats, to the necklace of LED lights surrounding the lake that would begin to glow at dusk. Finally, she said, "The whole thing made me sadder because, when I got to the Palmer Research Center, it was swarming with ambulances, and EMTs were working on somebody halfway up the stairs. Then, when they carried that poor guy down on a stretcher, they passed right by me, maybe two feet away. And I recognized the guy. Besides Joel, he was the only person I was hoping to see at the party."

"Sorry, Dee," he said, stroking her hair. "That's upsetting. Who was the guy?"

"His name is William Balaban. *Doctor* William Balaban. I saw him maybe every day I worked there as the receptionist. And I always appreciated him because he was one of the few researchers who greeted me or talked to me like I was a human being. And he smiled at me like he meant it."

He hugged her tighter, and she continued: "But it was so weird. When he passed by on the stretcher, I called out his name, and he turned and looked right at me. And, Red, I'm absolutely positive he recognized me. But then he just kinda flinched and turned away, acting like he didn't know me."

"Whoa," he said. "Hard to imagine him—*anyone*—not recognizing you. You're totally unforgettable." When she didn't respond to his attempted endearment, he persisted: "Truth? How many hot women with blue hair and silver nose rings has he ever met? And it's not been much more than a year since you left that job. Maybe he was having a stroke or something?"

She shrugged. "I stood on the sidewalk and watched the ambulance take him across the street to the ER. And after that, I just didn't feel like going to the party."

"Huh. But that was hours ago, Dee. What have you been doing since?"

"I went to the ER to find out how Dr. Balaban was doing."
"And?"
She frowned and said, "And then things just got much worse."

The Parker-Greene Estate

The Uplands, Berkeley, California

Dario's parents—after prickly communications with the hospital's nurse manager, terse discussions with the police, consultation with their attorney, and completing necessary paperwork—finally exited the ER. When they stepped onto the outdoor portico plastered with "No Smoking" and "No Loitering" signs, they froze. Sparrows flitted overhead, an ambulance siren whirred, two girls passed by with vape pens that shrouded them in lingering smoke.

Everything felt surreal. How could the world appear so normal and carry on so unfazed?

For Donald Parker, the past violently broke away, like a bridge segment collapsing at his heels. He stood unsteadily at the break, afraid to move forward, not trusting the future to hold him.

For Lori Greene, Dario's death could not have happened. Yes, of course, she saw the evidence, and she spoke with the doctors and nurses. But, in essence, it was inconceivable. There had to exist a more credible explanation for Dario's sudden absence. And besides, if Dario were truly dead and taken from her, her own flesh would be bleeding right now.

Finally, Donald said, "We should go home."

Lori faced him, her golden-brown eyes brimming with questions, her mind weighted with dreadful considerations. *How do we stop being Dario's parents? How is it possible we suddenly have no one to call "son"? And "go home" to what, Don? How do we live in a house, where Dario is everywhere and nowhere at once?*

While waiting for her to speak, he wrestled with remorse. Two days earlier, against her wishes, he had supported Dario's request to be excused from Thanksgiving weekend at his COO's Napa estate. Their tennis coach had advised more intensive training for Dario, given his faltering progress ahead of the imminent early-welcoming ceremony for UCSM team recruits. The coach was also wary about Dario's escalating excuse-making to cancel lessons—pains in the arm, fatigue, exertional short-windedness on the court: "things to be expected" during training. But Donald wondered now whether Dario had been shamed into staying behind, and how much his own implicit judgment might have contributed to that. And, he had to concede that, had he agreed with Lori's wish to give their son a holiday break from the demanding routine, Dario would not have been left behind to fall on a damn tennis court, and to die alone.

"Don," she finally said. "It makes no sense, right? We can't be expected to believe that Dario *vanished*. Someone is playing a trick on us. Gaslighting us. Yes, that's it. Because we *saw* him on Wednesday, right? We *heard* him on the phone yesterday. He can't be gone . . ." She threw a hand over her mouth and sobbed.

He held his wife until she could stand unsupported. Then, realizing they were too distracted to drive, he decided to leave their black Tesla in the hospital lot and summon a taxi. During the ride home, they sat in stunned silence. The driver occasionally checked on them in the rear-view mirror.

When they arrived at their mansion, their housekeeper Nadja met them at the door and offered condolences that they simply couldn't absorb. She said something about dinner and . . . ?

Lori headed straight for the staircase leading to their master suite, and her husband followed. He closed the bedroom door behind them. Lori sat on the bed and doubled over, muttering unintelligibly.

Minutes later, they heard a knock on the door, which they chose to ignore. But Nadja's voice followed: "Is there something I can do to help?"

"No, thanks," Donald replied, while coaxing Lori to lie down. He pulled off her shoes and draped the duvet over her. "I'll call you tomorrow, Nadja."

"But your dinner is—"

"We're fine. Tomorrow, okay?" he said.

When convinced that Nadja had left, he lay down beside his wife, waiting for her juddered crying to stop.

Minutes passed, and Lori said, "Dario is gone. Just . . . gone?"

Donald Parker, renowned venture capitalist, knew how to conduct big business with authority and panache. He possessed a notoriously keen eye for startups with lucrative potential, and he knew precisely when and where to place hefty capital investments. His expertise was lauded—in corporate management, accounting, micro- and macro-economics, and everything in between. He commanded respect as an international financier and philanthropist. And he had risen from abject poverty to become a top one-percenter in the country.

But on this occasion of losing their son, he knew nothing, and he felt powerless. He possessed no expertise or talent that could bring Dario back, and he had no one he could call to "just fix it." On a more fundamental level, he felt as though he had forgotten how to think. Because he couldn't fathom how to go on, or conceive a way to deal with his guilt. He could not imagine how he and Lori were going to survive this unfathomable tragedy, this seemingly forever brokenness.

Evening

Grady's Irish Pub

Jack London Square, Oakland

Jack carried the drinks to the table: a merlot for Nora, a Manhattan for Fred, and a can of diet coke for himself that he had wedged under an arm. He was abstaining from alcohol tonight so he could help Luis with homework later. As he had learned the hard way, mastering fact families in multiplication and division was challenging enough while sober. But, as he set down the drinks, a text arrived from his housekeeper Zofia: *Luis in bed with a book, homework done.* "That's funny," he remarked.

"What's funny?" asked Fred. "Tell us. We could all use a good laugh."

"Well," said Jack, "it appears that Luis is considerably more efficient with his math assignments if I'm not there 'helping' him."

Nora smiled wistfully, recalling how she and her husband Michael used to suffer through their daughter's calculus homework, never understanding the point of it, or even believing in it. Still, now, she wished she could reclaim that time, any time, with him and Caitlin.

Fred winced with Jack's comment, reminded of having been an absentee father to Ella and Charlie during their grade school years. Still, privately, he admitted not regretting any missed opportunity to study any kind of math with them.

"So," said Jack, hunching his shoulders. "All that got me was a half-smile and a wince? Tough crowd tonight." When they responded by reaching for their drinks, he said, "Okay, I give. What's going on? And why did you invite me here tonight—beyond having a chance to watch me flop?"

Nora gently squeezed his shoulder and said, "You didn't flop. It's just that we both had a rotten day at the hospital."

"Rotten and then some," said Fred. "We came here straight from work, after the police left the ER."

"The police?" said Jack, eyeing the bar.

"That's right," said Fred. "They went so far as to secure one of Nora's exam rooms as a potential crime scene. There's yellow tape everywhere. Can you believe that? Not a great confidence booster for the patients who saw it. The police even confiscated—"

"Whoa!" said Jack. "I'm going to need something medicinal after all." After waving to the bartender and calling out for a glass of pinot, he continued, "So, pray tell. The police were there because . . . ?"

"Because," said Nora, "a patient died right after I performed his fasciotomy. His death was completely unexpected. Inexplicable, even in hindsight. It feels horrible."

"And, of course," said Fred, "the coroner hasn't had time to determine anything yet. Still, the parents of the deceased already lit a fire to the situation. Their silk-tie attorney, the police, the coroner's office, the media—all involved now."

"How dreadful," said Jack, taking Nora's hand. "It's agonizing enough to lose a patient. But to be under legal and criminal scrutiny, as well?" His brow arched, and he added, "I've been there."

Fred and Nora exchanged a knowing look. Although each of them had apologized to Jack on multiple occasions, the thorny issue of their inadequate support during his wrongful imprisonment still surfaced regularly.

Immediately sensing their discomfort and surmising the cause, Jack said, "Sorry! Honestly, I didn't mean to resurrect old ghosts. I was just attempting to commiserate."

"I still feel bad about it, though," said Fred.

"Me, too," said Nora.

Jack made a pretense of pulling out his hair and said, "You're both such guilt queens. Especially you, Fred."

Fred nodded in agreement and said, "All right now. Should we go back to the young man's death?"

Nora lowered her eyes and said, "The boy's parents—of course they were devastated and angry—but they accused me of incompetence."

Jack scoffed. "That's ridiculous."

She appeared unfazed by his vote of confidence and tightened her grasp on her wineglass. "I had gone out to the waiting room with Lizbeth and Leon to meet them and escort them to the private conference room. But they refused to go. And they had a preconceived idea about what had happened. So, instead, in the middle of that packed room, they broadcasted that I wasn't qualified to perform the fasciotomy."

Fred took over for her. "They claimed a surgeon should have operated on their son. I don't know how they even knew one hadn't at the time."

"He was just eighteen," Nora said. "An aspiring athlete, headed to UCSM next fall on a tennis scholarship. He is . . . *was* the son of Donald Parker and Lori Greene."

Jack's jaw dropped, and he grabbed Fred's Manhattan. "We're talking *the* Donald Parker? The venture capital king?"

"One and the same," said Fred, reclaiming his drink.

"Well, no wonder such drama surrounding the boy's death," said Jack. "But, frankly—no disrespect intended—with all the wealth and power in that family, I'm surprised their son sought care at OCH in the first place. Must have been a trauma case?"

Nora shook her head. "Not *technically*. But it did leave me traumatized."

"Dario walked into the ER, of his own accord," Fred explained. "He came in with a forearm crush injury after taking a fall the day before."

"But the injury had evolved into a compartment syndrome," said Nora. "And by the time I started the fasciotomy, it was well beyond six hours of him having symptoms."

"So," said Jack, upturning his palms, "you *had* to do the surgery."

"Well, me or, allegedly, someone more qualified. But, yes, it had to be done."

Fred intercepted Jack's second reach for his Manhattan and said, "There's something fishy about the whole incident. The boy's death makes no sense to me, either. But that's why I'm confident that any facts emerging from the autopsy will exonerate you, Nora. And besides, I can't think of anyone *more* qualified than you to perform a fasciotomy. You've done more than most 'qualified' surgeons."

Jack thrummed his fingers on the table, longing for his wine. "Still, it feels like there's more to the story, because you're both so grim and—" He tapped a palm to his forehead and said to Nora, "I know! You can't figure out how you might have caused or prevented your patient's death. You're doing what you always do whenever you assume you're in control—or should have been."

"Thank you, Dr. Freud," she said, feigning a smile.

"But it's true, right?" he asked.

She sat back and folded her hands in her lap. "Yes, I feel like I should be able to understand what happened to cause Dario's death. And understanding that, I could have prevented his death."

"So," said Jack, looking sidelong at her, "if you'd been omniscient and all-powerful, your patient would be alive now."

"Your sarcasm, noted," she said. "But I'm also rattled by watching him die. And by his parents' hostility. And by an insufferable Ortho resident who barged into my office and insinuated I had *killed* Dario."

"All right now," said Fred. "You're getting revved up. You'll be needing my inhaler soon."

The bartender arrived with Jack's pinot and, eyeing the empty glasses and everyone's tense expression, suggested, "Another round?"

The three nodded. After the bartender left, Nora said to Jack, "Anyhow, thanks for listening."

"You kidding?" he said. "I'm glad you invited me here tonight. And, I agree—most definitely, a rotten day. And, a painful one, too."

Nora and Fred sighed in unison.

"Whoa," said Jack. "Synchronized sighing? What am I missing now?"

"Unfortunately," said Nora, "you only heard about half of the rotten day, and not the half we had wanted to discuss with you."

"There's more?" he said, incautiously swirling his wine.

"I'm afraid so," Fred replied. "We wanted your input on a separate matter. If Carl were in town, we would've invited him, too. But he left last night for his vacation, right after Carrie's dinner."

"So, then, it must have something to do with our gang-of-six-now-four?"

"Yes," said Nora. "It concerns Bill Balaban and his wife, Ellie."

Jack cocked his head and said, "Interesting. Ellie left rehearsal early today, because she said Bill was being taken to the ER with another 'meltdown.' And later, on the phone, she told me she was in the ER, waiting on you to see him."

"I did see him," she said. "And Fred did, too. Bill was not *compos mentis*. He scored poorly on his cognitive exams—only sixteen on the Mini-Mental, and four on the Clock Drawing Test."

"And," Fred added, "he didn't remember being married to Ellie."

Pretending shock, Jack said, "How is that even possible?"

Nora shot him an eyeroll and said, "According to Ellie, Bill has been in cognitive decline, and hasn't been 'himself' for nearly two years."

"And his labs and CT showed nothing useful today," added Fred. "But the neurologist and social worker will see him tomorrow, and he's scheduled for an MRI at noon."

"That's mind-blowing," said Jack, digesting the news. "No pun intended. But, *Bill*? He was such a brilliant neurosurgeon, and the best clinical neurologist around. How ironic for him to lose his mental faculties." He gulped the remainder of his pinot. "It's like Martha, the oncologist, dying from gastric cancer last spring. Or Brad, from ID, dying with strep pneumonia a month ago."

Feeling increasingly guilt-ridden over his inattentiveness to Bill, Fred said, "I should have visited him when I had the chance. Or, the *chances*, honestly."

Jack set his elbows on the table, looked inquiringly at his friends, and said, "Frankly, I'm surprised you're both so upset over the Balabans. I mean, what's happening to them sounds terrible. But terrible things happen to people all the time, especially at their age. Sadly, Bill and Ellie will have to go through this trial and tribulation. But they'll also be able to afford a lot of practical support—more than most people."

Nora furrowed her brow and questioned him: "You did see Ellie's black eye at rehearsal this morning, right?"

"Come again?" Jack said.

"And in the ER, Bill had deep scratches on his face," Fred added.

"Well, no," said Jack. "I didn't see any black eye. And, of course, I wasn't in the ER to see Bill."

"Ellie told me Bill didn't mean it," Nora said. "At least, not the Bill she used to know."

"Fuck," Jack muttered, running a hand through his thinning blond hair. "So, you're suggesting domestic abuse?"

"Well," said Fred, "it adds up. We've got Ellie's black eye. And there's Bill's scratched face, that we *assumed* happened because of a fall. It's hard to know. We can't rely on Bill for information—he's a completely unreliable historian. And Ellie is unwilling to complain or discuss Bill's violent behavior. But whatever is happening between them seems dangerous."

"Obviously, it's hard to sort things out at this point," said Nora. "But Bill and Ellie live alone and have no family we can consult."

"Hell," said Fred, "they used to say the six of us were as close as they'd ever come to having sons or daughters."

The bartender arrived with the second round and cleared the empties. Before leaving, she said, "Just holler if you need another."

Fred loosened his necktie and said, "I don't know about you guys, but I feel like I let the Balabans down, big time. I rarely saw them after our residency ended, except at hospital fundraisers and such. Even then, I never took them up on their social invitations. I mean, I think I was . . . I think I hesitated because, you know, Vickie was never keen on keeping up the charade of our marriage, except when it was 'absolutely necessary' for my work. But then, a couple years back, when she and I started working on our marriage . . . Well, that's when Bill started inviting me out for drinks, for coffee, in order to . . . what? Now I wonder if he was needing to talk to someone about losing his mind. Or confide in someone about domestic abuse. And yet, every time I accepted his invitation, I ended up canceling."

Jack said, "But you were kinda busy, pal." He looked to Nora as if seeking permission to continue. She caught his drift and added, "I agree with Jack—you were repairing your marriage and fighting to get your family back, Fred."

"Still," he replied, "I could have explained that to Bill, instead of just ditching him."

"If it makes you feel better," said Jack, "I'm as guilty of forsaking Bill and Ellie after residency. Except for calling on her recently to help with our holiday show at the prison, I never initiated contact with either of them. Of course, like you, I saw them at Lydia's and Cheryl's funerals, but only to say 'Hello.'" He let out a huge breath. "But, yeah. They were generous to the six of us. And Bill was a devoted mentor—though a bit on the obsessive side. Remember the cocktail dinners at their house?"

His friends smiled in warm recognition, and Nora said, "I *definitely* remember the high-octane cocktails. But not a whole lot more." She closed her eyes, stealing a private moment to reenvision one raucous dinner at the Balabans, during which she and Lydia drunkenly kissed.

"And all that after-dinner cognac in their parlor?" said Fred. "God, we were all so young and resilient."

"Yeah, memorable times—well, maybe not for Bill right now," Jack said. "And I can't say they were always comfortable for me. Still . . ."

Nora leaned in toward her friends and said, "It was strangely upsetting when Bill didn't remember me today. And then, to hear him ask Fergie if she was Lydia or Cheryl? Ellie also got upset, and she reminded Bill they had both died—though he didn't recall that, either. At least Bill recognized you, Fred."

Fred huffed. "Being the only black person in our residency program likely made me unforgettable." His shiny bald scalp reflected a shaft of ceiling light to form a luminous halo above his head.

"I'm getting nervous," said Jack. "Because I have a question, but I'm afraid to ask it, because I think I already know the answer, and I simply don't want to hear it."

His friends waited for him to continue.

"Okay," he said. "I'm afraid you two think we should somehow intervene in the Balabans' lives."

"Well," said Fred, "don't you think we owe it to them?"

Jack squinted and said, "I'm not sure. I mean, their *alleged* fight could have been a one-off event. We don't know, right? Is it any of our business to butt in, *especially* after not being involved in their lives for *decades*? And if Bill is displaying violent behavior as a behavioral manifestation of his dementia, well, that's a whole other level of intervention they require. Why not call on Adult Protective Services to conduct a formal—and *professional*—evaluation of their domestic situation?"

"APS isn't what we had in mind," said Fred. "Not yet, at least. Besides, Ellie made it clear she would deny any problem if asked."

"We just don't know enough," Nora chimed in. "We need better information about their home situation. And, like Fred said, the problem is that Bill is an unreliable informant, and Ellie is refusing to address, let alone report, any violence between them."

"There's a time crunch, too," said Fred. "Ellie plans to take Bill home from the ER tomorrow, after his neuro consult and noontime MRI. And if we just allow that to happen while suspecting an unsafe home environment for them . . . Well, talk about letting them down again, and at their most vulnerable."

"Whoa," said Jack, holding up a hand. "Something is off. Yeah, going back to your original question, Nora: I did see Ellie at rehearsal today, but she did *not* have a black eye. I'm sure about that now. Because I saw her face up close when we hugged. So, when she got that call about Bill and left to meet him in the ER . . . Well, when could he have possibly hit her?"

Fred blew air through a corner of his mouth and said, "It's possible she and Bill could have fought in the ER. Wouldn't be the first time a couple duked it out in an exam room."

"Or," said Nora, recalling her encounter with Ellie in the ER hallway, "maybe you didn't see her shiner at rehearsal because she was concealing it under that thick makeup she was wearing. Like plaster, really. Maybe some of that makeup rubbed off after your rehearsal? I mean, she *was* tearful when I ran into her. And she was wearing dark glasses in the hallway—probably trying to hide the shiner."

Jack inhaled a deep breath and released it slowly. "I suppose that's all possible."

Silence passed easily among them while each held their private counsel. Finally, Fred nudged Nora with, "A penny for your thoughts. I hear those gears cranking."

Nora tilted her head. "Something just struck me as odd about Bill being transported from the research center this morning."

"Well, that's hospital protocol in a 911 situation," said Fred, "even if the patient is only a hop-skip-and-jump away from the ER entrance."

"No," said Nora, "not that. I mean, how could Bill have been conducting research there without someone noticing his mind slipping or his behavior changing?"

"Actually, it's not difficult to remain under the radar there," said Fred. "A lot of researchers work in secured labs, in near-total isolation. On their *top-secret* projects. And with little direct oversight for long periods of time. I think that suits a certain kind of personality."

"But we're talking about Bill," said Nora. "He was always sociable, always involved in hospital functions and professional events. I can't imagine him not interacting with coworkers there."

Jack said, "Well, remember how Cheryl—god rest her soul—used to hibernate in her research cave? She would disappear for ages, and that would drive us crazy sometimes."

"To your point, Nora," said Fred. "Don't you still serve on the Institutional Review Board? Do you remember Bill completing any research projects lately? Submitting grant proposals? Publishing any papers?"

"Come to think of it," she said, "I don't recall seeing any recent reports or updates from him. I think he's mostly recycling his old data, and re-dressing it for bottom-tier journals. Oh, and he's supervising Owen Landry's research—on paper, at least."

"All right now," said Fred, firmly setting down his Manhattan. "We've put a lot of big questions on the table tonight. But the most pressing one is: What are we going to do about Bill and Ellie tomorrow?"

Part Three

Saturday, November 30

Nora's Home

Montclair District, Oakland

GLANCING AT THE ALARM CLOCK, Nora estimated that, at most, she had obtained three hours of sleep. Too many nighttime gremlins had occupied her mind, murmuring their worries and fears.

Now at six a.m. and unable to sleep, she was resigned to start her day. Lying in bed, and keeping her promise to her ever-vacationing therapist, Dr. Solène Barteau, she began with her Morning Gratitude exercise.

So, what three things make me feel grateful this morning? Well, for one—I'm grateful I don't have to work today (and, in my state, all the better for any patient). Two—I still have Thanksgiving leftovers from Carrie's in the fridge. And, three . . . ?

Unable to conjure a requisite third item, she rolled over in frustration, only to face the palpable vacancy on Alex's side of the bed. *How strange,* she thought, *to experience absence as something tangible.* But she could feel the carved-out hollow in his pillow that uniquely held his shape, and she traced it with a finger. She could smell his citrusy body soap. She could see his coppery hairs on the sheets. And when she reached into his absence, her heart registered ache.

She reminisced about their first Thanksgiving together, two days ago. Because of him, the holiday had been less freighted with loss—of Michael and Caitlin, her parents, and, of course, Lydia. *Ah,* she suddenly realized, *and that's my third gratitude. I'm done!*

But, as often happened, the Morning Gratitude exercise backfired. Because searching for gratitude always required sorting through all the chaff for which she was decidedly ungrateful. And that larger pile of considerations had expanded greatly since yesterday. Dario Parker's sad and upsetting death rested on top of the heap. Then, her disturbing interaction with his parents. The police, treating her like a criminal. Fergie getting sick. Bill and Ellie's worrisome predicament. Alex gone for the month, visiting his ill parents in Tepoztlán. The persistent leak in the laundry room. Bix's long-overdue flea medication. Forgetting her Prius' service appointment . . .

She scrunched her white comforter over her mouth and screamed with abandon into it. Then she flung it aside—"Some comforter you are!"—and headed to the bathroom for morning ablutions. While brushing her teeth in front of the mirror, she noticed new strands of gray in her hair and fine creases radiating out from the corners of her eyes.

Choosing not to look for further proof of passing time reflected in her face, she returned to the bedroom to dress. She donned a pair of black jeans and one of Alex's white-collared shirts, then headed to the kitchen to prep the coffeemaker and deposit frozen waffles in the toaster. When breakfast was ready, she carried it to the table and opened her laptop to check the morning headlines. She automatically bypassed the national news, which had become a repetitive litany of worrying economic news and dyspeptic analyses about next year's presidential race. As if on cue, her tuxedo cat Bix jumped onto the table and held a threatening white paw over her keyboard. "Don't worry!" she told him. "We're not going to read that depressing stuff."

After he withdrew his paw, Nora said, "And as you know, you're not supposed to be on this table. You're lucky Alex isn't here." But throughout her pro forma reprimand, she petted his head and rubbed his nose until he tired of it and leaped off the table.

She returned her attention to her laptop, eager to check the local news. But the first thing she saw knocked all the wind out of her. The lead story on the *Oakland Register* website featured a dramatic photograph of Dario Parker's parents. Standing alongside them was the infamous celebrity attorney, John Norris, poised like a heavyweight boxer in a million-dollar suit. The headline read: "Parents of Deceased Local Athlete Demand Answers from Hospital." The article's byline credited Fergie's husband, Winston Wang.

"Holy shit," she muttered, closing her laptop, unable to read more. Then her mind froze, and she sat motionless at the table, sensing the dark and powerful headwinds barreling toward her.

Fred's Home

Berkeley

When Fred entered the breakfast nook, his wife Vickie looked up from her plate and said, "Morning, Chief." She wore her burgundy nightgown, and her jet-black hair was tied back in a yellow scrunchie. He spiritedly saluted her and joined her at the table. But while she poured his coffee, he noted her tight expression and asked, "Everything okay?"

"Eat first," she said, loading his plate with soft-scrambled eggs, organic apple slices, and whole wheat toast.

He obligingly savored the nutty aroma of his chicory coffee and took a bite of toast. Then he looked at her and said, "Okay, there. So, tell me."

She implored, "Please eat before you lose your appetite."

"Now you're just worrying me," he said. He took a moment to replay their intense conversation last night; had he said something wrong? Clearly, he was still on probation with her, but what did he do this time? He stared anxiously at her and asked, "What?"

Feeling she had no choice, she answered, "Well, I may as well just show you." She handed the *Oakland Register* to him.

Its front-page headline and photograph instantly alarmed him. "Oh, hell," he grumbled.

Vickie watched his expression progressively sour while he read the accompanying article. *Healthy 18-year-old man . . . local high school athlete, headed to UCSM on a tennis scholarship next fall . . . parents grieving his unexpected death after he underwent a surgical procedure at Oakland City Hospital . . . lawyer questioning ER doctor's expertise, asking why a qualified surgeon did not perform the operation . . .*

Fred tossed the paper aside and stared up at the ceiling.

"Obviously," said Vickie, "this is the same case you told me about last night. But you never mentioned it was Nora's case."

His heart ached. He knew how the media coverage was going to distress Nora. And he dreaded yet another onerous lawsuit and publicity nightmare for the hospital. He pushed his breakfast aside and said,

"It's tragic enough when a patient dies. And so hard on the family and friends. On the doctors and nurses and hospital, too. And then you get someone like John Norris—lawyer for the rich and famous—who calls a press conference and starts to kick up dirt while the patient's body is still warm! Before any coroner's investigation, he's pointing fingers and insinuating guilt." He scoffed, and continued, "Looks like he even dragged the parents out to the parking lot to get this photo op yesterday! Look at the shock on their faces. It's cruel."

"Fred, please. You're getting too worked up."

"And Norris—insisting he's 'out to obtain justice' for the family? Really? Justice before any facts? Before an autopsy? Justice that destroys good people's careers in the meantime?"

"Still gotta eat," she said, pushing his plate back toward him. "And, yes, the boy's death is tragic. His parents must be completely devastated."

He just propped an elbow on the table and held a hand to his head. She persisted, "I thought Winston's article was evenhanded, though. You do understand he was *obligated* to report what was said during that press conference."

"But, my god," said Fred, jabbing his finger on the newspaper. "*This* photo and *this* headline alone practically condemn Nora and the hospital. And look at Norris, so poised and sure of himself. He's charging into a tragedy with his guns drawn, before questions can be legitimately addressed, and all he wants to do is shoot! And Nora and the hospital are easy targets." He pushed his plate away again. "It makes me sick, all of it."

Vickie put down her teacup and wondered at the irony of her physician-husband being made so frequently "sick" by a hospital. Problems at Oakland City—legion and unrelenting—were like invasive pathogens, always getting under his skin. She said, "Well, you want my layperson's diagnosis? I think you're suffering a bout of 'hospitalitis.'"

He grimaced and said, "Yeah, well, maybe I concur."

After sprinkling salt and pepper on his eggs, she placed a fork in his hand and said, "You know full well that if *our* healthy son or daughter walked into an ER with arm pain after falling, and died right after an operation performed by a nonsurgeon . . . Well, you would be out-of-your-mind shocked and angry, too. You'd be itching to point a finger."

"But Nora is an ER veteran," he countered. "She's a trauma expert. I'll put money down she's performed more fasciotomies than any surgeon within a hundred-mile radius."

"I understand that. And the fact of her experience and expertise will only aid her defense, right? Now, please—eat this breakfast before it gets cold."

While he picked at his eggs, she said, "By the way, you also didn't mention last night that Lori Greene was the dead boy's mother."

"Meaning what?" he said. "You know I never reveal names of patients or their families."

"True," she said. "You're strict about maintaining confidentiality and privacy. But news like this, involving *that* family? It was bound to go public at high speed." She pointed to the photograph and added, "And I'm supposed to have lunch with *her* on Wednesday."

"Lori Greene?"

She nodded. "Our gallery's been planning an exhibition of her new work in January. It will be her third show with us. The first two sold out before opening reception. She's quite an accomplished artist. She has pieces hanging in major museums."

Fussing with his napkin, he tried to recall whether Vickie had ever mentioned a personal or professional relationship with Lori Greene. If she had, perhaps she had also talked about meeting Lori's husband, Donald Parker? The possibility of a connection between her and Dario's parents tightened the knot in his stomach. Still, he hesitated to ask his wife for clarification; for, had he not been so oblivious to her and the kids over the years, he might be able to answer his own questions. And, reluctant to reactivate tensions over his years-long absence and relationship with Lydia, he merely said, "Huh."

Vickie hunched her shoulders and said, "But who knows whether Lori will still want to show, let alone take lunch, so soon after her son's death? I can't imagine what she's going through, poor woman."

He cleared his throat while also trying to clear his mind. Ethically, what was permissible to tell Vickie about the circumstances surrounding Dario's death? Or, for that matter, about his predicament with the Balabans?

"Anyway," she continued, "I know you must be worried about Nora. The family's charges—or, at least, their lawyer's—are damning. And isn't Nora alone right now?"

"She is," he said. "Alex left early yesterday morning, to visit family in Mexico. One or both of his parents are ill."

"Well, invite her over for dinner tonight. Ella is making chicken Marbella, and Charlie will be out with friends."

After downing his coffee, he said, "I'll ask her later. Right now, I need to go to the hospital."

"No, Fred! It's *Saturday*. You have the day off. We just agreed—you're already sick with hospitalitis! And yesterday, you promised to look at matinee options with me."

"I know. I'm a terrible husband."

"Well, not to *me*! Because it's the *hospital* you're married to. And you keep choosing it over me, even when it makes you sick." She stared defiantly at him. "You've been an absentee member of this family . . ." She held her tongue, not wanting to resurrect their past troubles over Lydia.

She was right—he knew that. He stared back, consumed with regret, wondering if they had been foolishly optimistic to plan their "marriage redo" next month.

"Fred," she said, "you have a choice."

He shook his head. "It doesn't *feel* like I do."

"So, it's all about *your* feelings? What about mine? Or this family's?" Receiving only his silence, she briskly turned away.

Watching her leave, likely returning to the difficult past they had worked so hard to reconcile, he called out her name and said, "Please." She stopped at the doorway, her back to him.

"What I mean is," he said, "I don't feel like I have a choice about going into the hospital—at least, not a good one. Because Bill Balaban is in the ER, and I'm worried about him and Ellie."

She pivoted back to him and said, "Well, I'm sorry to hear that. I know how important he was to you and your old gang. Weren't you supposed to visit him—?"

"Yes, yes, yes," he answered brusquely. Then, "Sorry. It's hard. I've been feeling guilty about always canceling on him. And I'm walking a fine line between the Balabans' privacy rights and wanting you to understand what's really going on."

"Honestly, Fred. Your hospitalitis is so bad, it's spreading to *me*. Because now I feel sick with worry about you and me and—"

"Bill has severe cognitive loss and behavioral problems."

"What?" she said, stepping closer.

"According to Ellie, he's been in decline the last couple years. Then yesterday, something acute happened to him while he was leaving the research center. Maybe a stroke? A seizure? We're not sure yet. He's been in ER observation overnight."

"But I still don't understand why you need to go into the hospital."

"Because, if Ellie has her way, she's going to take Bill home right after his MRI at noon, and before . . ."

"Before what?"

He hesitated. "Before it's possible to arrange for in-home intervention and support."

Vickie cocked her head. "And just what do you think *you* can do about that, *Doctor*? You know that's the social worker's job. Besides, you wouldn't even know how to—"

"It's more than that," he said, feeling the rigid barrier he had steadfastly maintained between her and his work begin to bend. "When I saw the Balabans in the ER yesterday, Ellie had a black eye, and Bill's cheek was covered with scratches."

Carrie's Home

The Oakland Hills

Over morning coffee, Carrie Chandler debated whether to take down her Thanksgiving decorations, because she was still feasting on leftover joy from the dinner here two days ago. It was a whopping success, by all accounts—in dramatic contrast to last year's dinner, when only Carl showed up.

And how heartwarming to have shared the holiday with people who had celebrated it with Lydia in this house. Nora and her partner, Alex. Fred and his family. Jack and Luis, Fergie and Winston, Lizbeth and Aditya. And Carl, of course—the first to arrive, precisely on time. Red and DeeDee brought their guitars and led everyone in a raucous singalong.

Reenvisioning all those people around the table, Carrie said aloud, "Thank you, Lydia, for leaving me your warm home and loving friends."

In this afterglow, she finally felt certain that she had made the right decision to move into her sister's home. Since her own husband's death three years ago, she had been seeking a sense of renewal and purpose. She had begun symbolically by dropping her married name, Chamber. And, after taking up vegetable gardening, she became a self-proclaimed know-it-all on heirloom tomatoes and Romano beans. After a year of Mandarin lessons, she studied Asian cuisine and learned about the new herbs she could cultivate. On weekends, she volunteered at the local community library. But it was not until the present moment that Dr. Carrie Chandler knew her life could be made whole and meaningful again.

Scanning her exuberantly decorated walls, she marveled at the seamlessness with which her personal decorations meshed with those from Lydia's attic. And she happily reflected about the new contributions from this year's gathering that would join the collective trove: Lizbeth's string of LED-light turkeys, and Luis' multicolored renderings of pumpkins in outer space.

How could she possibly take down all these tender and joyful mementos? And yet, today was already the last day in November, and she could hear the December holidays beckon. And how busy they would be, with all the add-on festivities: a bon voyage for Fergie and Winston before they embarked on their honeymoon in China; a celebration of Fred and Vickie's "marriage redo" at Grace Cathedral; and the near launch of Red and Gianni's garden and landscaping business. Yes, December 2019 was going to be massively celebrated (and massively decorated).

With her spirits enlivened by such happy prospects, Carrie retrieved the Thanksgiving storage boxes from the attic. She packed away the cranberry garlands and the glow-in-the-dark pumpkins. She swaddled faux-rosemary sprigs and autumn wreaths in bubble wrap. The pinecone centerpiece and scarecrow diorama were returned to their original, dedicated cartons.

Before her last trek to the attic, she walked through the house, scouting for overlooked tchotchkes. But when she stepped into the living room, she startled, starkly reminded of its baseline state, exactly how Lydia had left it. The mission furniture, the colorful patterned rug, the silk table runners, the extensive collection of local artists' works—everything so vividly reflecting her twin's sensibilities that Carrie felt Lydia present in the room. "Lydia," she whispered, "I'm overwhelmed. All this joy I'm feeling is because of you. I'm so grateful. And I'm so fucking sorry for what I did to you."

Nora's Home

"Open up!" someone yelled, and Nora flinched.

She had sheltered herself in her home and turned off all the lights. She had drawn the living room shades and locked all the doors. *Whoever is at my front door is crazy to think I'd answer.*

She returned her obsessive attention to her laptop screen, scrolling through the poisonous texts that kept popping up. Her landline rang yet again, with another hostile call from a stranger. And despite all the vile threats and demonizing comments that people were posting on social media, she remained helplessly addicted to viewing them.

Knock, knock, knock!

She shuddered and reached for her cell, intending to call her friend Detective Darinda Johnson for advice about the intruder. But she stopped when she heard, "Nora! It's me."

After setting down her laptop on the couch, she tiptoed to the door and peered through the peephole, through which she saw Fergie's emerald eyes enlarged in its lens. While opening the door for Fergie, she furtively surveyed the driveway for strange people or cars.

"Hey," said Fergie, appraising her friend. "I tried calling." She and Winston had seen the online media assaults against her and had begun to worry.

"I'm sorry," said Nora. "But I fell into a rabbit hole."

"Yup, I figured that," Fergie said, taking a seat on the couch near Nora. "Pretty nuclear stuff online today. But it's like a dark fortress in here. Are you all right?"

"No," said Nora, "I'm terrified." She angled her laptop's screen so Fergie could see it. They viewed an unsettling image of Donald Parker pointing at Nora in the crowded ER; its caption read, "Parker CEO Points Blame for His Son's Death." Below that, they read disparaging comments that called for Nora's death (*An eye for an eye! That's a Px in the Bible!*), her imprisonment (*Lock her up!*), and the revocation of her medical license (*Call this number to demand the hospital fire her!*). Someone had even posted her personal phone number and home address, below a skull-and-crossbones picture.

Fergie drew her hand across her neatly shaved head and groaned. "That social media stuff is disgusting. I'm sorry, pal. Things are fucked up enough in the world, without people shitting their minds on everyone else."

"That's exactly what it feels like," said Nora. "Like verbal defecation, all over my life."

"Okay," said Fergie, closing the laptop. "I think you've had enough. I know I have. I'm cutting you off from this shit."

Slumping back against the couch, Nora closed her eyes and said, "My life was completely different twenty-four hours ago. The one I have now after Dario's death is filled with hatred and vitriol. I'm even afraid to leave my house."

Fergie reached into her backpack, pulled out the *Oakland Register*, and tossed it onto the coffee table. "I picked this up on your driveway, coming in. I was going to wait to give it to you, but it seems moot now. Clearly, you've seen the online version."

"Yes, I read Winston's piece a couple of times."

Scrunching her face, Fergie said, "I hope you understand, Win is just doing his job. He had to report what they said at that press conference yesterday."

"I understand."

"And he has no editorial control over the headlines they choose for his articles. Or the photographs they use."

Nora nodded. "I remember all about that. And, frankly, I think his reporting was objective. But, god, I shook when I saw that photograph of Dario's parents and their lawyer. I felt like I was facing my accusers who were about to condemn me, and I couldn't say anything in my defense."

"Yeah, that photograph was charged. And it was taken in such a raw moment for the parents. They had that deer-in-the-headlights look."

Slumping deeper into the couch, Nora said, "Hey, don't worry. I know you and Winston are on my side. I'm just surprised that I have any 'side' to be taken. But I do—lines have been drawn. Big, thick, angry lines."

Peering over her bifocals at Nora, Fergie said, "Enough. You and I are getting out of this dark cave, and leaving the even-darker internet behind. We are moving into the light! We're going to take a walk at Lake Temescal, brave the world together, and you're going to talk about whatever comes to mind."

When Nora didn't respond, Fergie nudged her off the couch, dragged her to the entryway, and draped her jacket over her shoulders. Then she picked up Nora's car keys and wallet and said, "Here. We need to take separate cars, because I've got a dental appointment in a couple of hours. But I'm going to tail you to the lake, so don't even think about trying to shake me."

The Parker-Greene Estate

Donald Parker sat on the sofa with the *Oakland Register*, studying the front-page photograph of himself and his wife. How absolutely still, almost lifeless, they appeared. Not the slightest hint of their roiling grief, their turbulent hearts, or their quaking minds. He wondered how it had been possible for him to look into the camera with such a blank expression, all the while collapsing under the weight of his loss and guilt.

Lori soundlessly appeared in the doorway, her brown eyes swollen, and her normally angular cheekbones rounded by swelling. He startled and said, "Morning, sweetheart. Did you get any sleep?"

When she looked at him as if from a faraway distance, he said, "How about I make us some breakfast? I told Nadja not to come in this weekend. I figured we could use the privacy."

She seated herself in the armchair across from him.

"Please," he implored. "You haven't eaten anything since yesterday morning."

But she had no desire for food. Just imagining the mechanical work required for eating felt taxing. She needed to reserve any remnant of her energy to get through the next moment.

"Well, I put away last night's dinner," he said. "So, if you get hungry later . . ."

She scanned the living room walls, adorned with her paintings—each one so bright and lively, a visual poem expressed in living colors that swirled across the canvas. She knew she had created them, but they no longer seemed to belong to her—or her to them. She looked at her hands—empty, like her heart—and wondered whether she'd ever again feel as alive as those paintings.

Donald hid the newspaper behind a sofa cushion, hoping to spare her the trauma of seeing their photograph. And he had to stifle the urge to come clean and tell her everything, because here she was, already so fragile.

"Don," she finally said. "I need time alone today."

"Okay," he said. "I'll fend off the press, manage any calls. I'll cancel our meeting with John Norris today. Whatever you need."

"Just to be left alone."

"Understood," he said, but not without worry. "Well, I could easily disappear for an hour or two. I need to call a taxi and retrieve our car from the hospital lot. Then I should drive by the office for a quick minute. But I'll check back on you—"

"I don't want to be checked on, Don. I don't want to be disturbed. Not even by you, no matter what."

He pulled down on his mustache and said, "All right. Just promise you'll eat something?"

She stood up slowly. Then she walked to Dario's favorite painting on the wall, took it down, and carried it through the hallway to her studio.

Donald heard his wife's studio door close, and its lock click. Then he picked up his cell to call Bill Balaban.

Lake Temescal

Northeast Oakland

Midway on their walk around Lake Temescal, Nora and Fergie stumbled upon a rotting . . . what? "Ugh," said Fergie, "smells like a fish, way past its expiration date."

Nora said, "It could be a small bird? I think I see a—" She stopped, seeing Fergie step back, a hand held over her stomach.

"Sorry," said Fergie. "I guess I'm just being Ms. Sensitive again."

While using her shoe to shove dirt over the mystery corpse, Nora said, "Well, speaking as Ms. Sensitive, have you had further thoughts about what happened in the ER yesterday? I never saw you that upset."

"That was crazy-times-ten. But, no. I have no idea why Dario's case got to me like that. And, thanks for asking, but we're here to focus on you—not me."

Nora nodded, and they returned to the trail. As they crossed a playground teeming with laughing children, sudden wind gusts whipped up scents of eucalyptus and pine

"You were right," Nora said. "Dragging me out of my dark house and thoughts was a good idea. I was feeling so edgy and scared, and—"

From out of nowhere, a Rottweiler bounded toward them and nearly knocked Fergie over. Its owner approached with a leash in hand and exclaimed, "Oh, he likes you!"

But Fergie would hear none of that. She pointed to a sign that instructed all dog walkers to keep their dogs "on leash," and she snapped: "Well, *I* don't like *him* pouncing on *me*. Maybe he can't read, but you probably can."

The owner scowled and, after looping a finger under her dog's studded collar, walked away. Nora glanced at Fergie with her brow arched. Fergie said, "Sorry. I can't stand people who assume privilege like that. Like they're so special they don't have to obey the rules."

Nora linked arms with her friend and coaxed her back into their walk. Once their strides synchronized, she restarted their conversation:

"So, I keep going over Dario's death, as if the zillionth-plus time will reveal what happened. But it doesn't."

Fergie picked up a discarded beer bottle and tossed it into a nearby bin. "I know how bent out of shape you get when you don't understand a case. Especially a death. But, you know, you always figure it out."

"But in Dario's case, my mind is jammed, and my intuitions are gummed up. So, I'm having trouble thinking diagnostically. And with so many fingers pointing right at me, it's hard to see much else."

After pausing for a small newt to cross their path, Nora continued, "Then . . . god . . . that look on Dario's face haunts me. His terror and agitation. His struggling to tell me *something*." She shuddered. "And his parents—their rageful eyes keep burrowing deeper into my psyche."

"It sucks now, I know," said Fergie. "But I promise, things will get better. Time is going to heal. It always does."

Nora looked away, unconvinced. Fergie persisted, "And you have to trust yourself, because you *should*. The coroner's findings are going to vindicate you, and people will realize you did nothing wrong. His parents will see the light of day, and the media shitstorm will quiet down."

"I hope you're right," said Nora. "All that can't happen soon enough."

"It's too bad Alex is away," said Fergie, looking sideways at her. "I mean, right? Have you talked with him about any of this?"

"No," she answered. "His parents are ill, and he's having to care for them. I'm going to wait until he's settled and has some freed-up mental space. By then, I might also have a clearer picture about what's happening for me."

"Have you spoken with legal?"

"Not since yesterday in the ER, while the police were there."

After descending the stairs near the picnic area, Nora picked up the thread: "Whether or not the coroner 'vindicates' me, the parents are probably going to sue anyway. Meanwhile, the press is going to . . . well, continue to press on me. And the internet is going to continue its bloodlust attacks. So, right now I'm just trying to keep my head above water." She pointed to the lake and added, "Like those ducks."

At the end of the lakeside trail, they stood in the parking lot, where they had left their cars. Fergie asked, "What's that mantra you always say before work?"

"One breath at a time, one day at a time."

"Okay," said Fergie, "let's go." Then they took a deep breath, exhaled together, and said, "One breath at a time, one day at a time."

Nora smiled and said, "Thanks. You're a good friend."

"Back at you," said Fergie. "And now, your friend needs to run off to the dentist. You know, I'd invite you over to the house tonight to distract you, but maybe seeing Win isn't such a good idea right now?"

Nora echoed, "Maybe seeing Winston isn't such a good idea right now."

They hugged and parted ways. Fergie drove off in her bright red Subaru, but Nora lingered in her sage-colored Prius to return the call she had received from Fred during their walk. He testily answered, "Where have you been?"

Jolted by his brusqueness, she said, "On a walk with Fergie at Temescal. But why the snarky tone?"

"Sorry," he said, taking a beat. "It's just . . . It's so damn frustrating. We're in the ER, but Ellie had persuaded the staff to rush Bill's MRI so she could take him home earlier. They left before we got here. Hell, they didn't even wait for the neuro consult or social worker!"

"Damn," Nora muttered. In the grip of her personal turmoil, she had forgotten about the intervention they had planned together.

"Hey," said Fred, "neither of us really expected you to show. Not with everything happening to you."

Jack seized Fred's phone and told Nora, "We mean that, darling."

"Hi, Jack," she said, fending off tears.

Fred retrieved his phone and said, "Nora, me again. We're having dinner at the house tonight, and Ella is cooking. So, come. This is an order from your chief. It'll be a good distraction."

"I'll go if you go," Jack said in the background.

"Did you hear that, Nora?" Fred asked.

Nora knew her friends were rolling out a safety net to break her fall. "Yes," she answered weakly.

"And, sorry," said Fred. "But, full disclosure: Our dinner is going to include a business meeting. We need to come up with a 'Plan B' for the Balabans, short of siccing APS out on them."

Late Morning

Kaufman's Party Store

SAN LEANDRO, CALIFORNIA

Carrie Chandler grabbed a second shopping cart to accommodate all the discounted post-holiday-sale decorations she was purchasing for next year's Thanksgiving. It was hard to imagine how she would fit them in for display, but that was always part of the fun.

Sorting through the bins, she marveled at the human spirit behind the creation of such unique handicrafts. She selected two boxes of wind-up head-bobbing turkeys—likely to be voted *the* hot item in the 2020 gift bags. She found a dozen-pack of necklaces strung with plastic letters that aspired to spell out "Happy Gobbling!"—three were broken and missing a letter or two, but their minor misspellings were excusable at the discounted price.

Finally, she rolled her carts to the last aisle, where she rummaged through the "Slightly Used" items in the bargain bin. It was a ruse, she knew; everything inside it had been "fully" used or abused, and then shamelessly returned for refunds.

But something near the bottom of the bin stared fetchingly up at her, and she fished it out. It was a pair of resin-scarecrow shelf-sitter dolls who were stitched together at the waist. They had flaccid arms and dangling legs, and the label on their inexpertly repackaged box claimed: "They love to sit on a window sill and keep your happy company!" Noting a missing black-button eye on each doll, Carrie muttered, "'Slightly used,' *my* eye," and almost tossed the pair back into the bin. But she hesitated, suddenly enamored of the twins' complementary flaws and—despite the evident trauma—their insistent half-smiles and plucky determination to make others happy. *Yes*, Carrie thought, *like Lydia and me.*

At the checkout counter, the clerk offered Carrie "a free sample of hot apple cider" while he tallied her bill. "You might as well have some," he advised, "because it's going to take me a while. I have to manually enter each marked-down price."

She accepted his offer of a small plastic cup that contained lukewarm fluid, which tasted like hospital-standard apple juice. Still, she raised her cup in appreciation.

He said, "Yeah, and happy holidays to you, too."

But Carrie was raising a glass (of sorts) for a different reason: She was experiencing her second epiphany of the day, and her clarity over that was intoxicating. Yes, she was certain now—she would accept the job at Oakland City Hospital and become its director of hospice and palliative care.

She said to the clerk, "Actually, I was also toasting to my new job."

He placed his hands on his hips and stretched his back. "Well, congratulations. Wish I could be celebrating the same."

Waiting for the bill's final tally, Carrie reached into one of the shopping bags to reposition the shelf-sitting dolls comfortably on top.

Bill and Ellie's Home

Trestle Glen District, Oakland

Ellie walked to the bedroom dresser and reflexively reached toward her neck, expecting to return her blue-roses scarf to the drawer containing a half-dozen identical others. But there was nothing to grab. "Of course," she murmured, recalling that she had discarded her makeup-stained scarf in an ER wastebasket.

"What did you say?" asked Bill.

"Nothing, really," she replied, tugging on a false eyelash. "I had to sacrifice one of my scarves at the hospital. Ruined. All the makeup and mascara. All the *tears* I shed."

"You still have plenty others, don't you?" he said.

"Tears? Yes, and you have certainly tested that."

"I meant *scarves*."

"That's not the point," she said, appending a huff. "You would never succeed in the theater, Bill."

He was tempted to reply, "And you know what that's like." But he knew that would only infuriate her more. Instead, he said, "You're right.

I simply became a neurosurgeon and researcher. I merely saved lives, taught generations of doctors—"

"Oh, stop," she said, wiping off her eyebrows. "I didn't mean it that way. It's just that you don't know how to be, let alone stay, 'in character.'"

He rolled his eyes, though she persisted: "You and I had a plan—a script, if you will—to get you out of the trouble you caused with your stem-cell dalliance. But, no. You had to go off script and—"

"I've asked you a million times not to refer to my stem-cell work as a 'dalliance.' I'm providing innovative treatment and cutting-edge regenerative medicine."

"Yes, well," she said, raising a ghost brow. "Explain that to the courts and media."

"And yet, not once before this mishap did you complain about my stem-cell work. I suppose you didn't mind the income it generated for us?"

She slammed her dresser drawer. "That remark was mean and unnecessary. Besides, I had no idea those cells could cause any problem, until you told me about that young man! You always made them sound safe and routine. You never mentioned they could cause a life-threatening infection! And then, I try to help you out, but . . ." She waved dismissively at him.

He folded his arms across his chest and sighed.

"Don't give me that," she said. "You're the one who panicked and flubbed your lines. *You* went off script and screwed things up. And the audacity—you continued to keep me in the dark about what was happening. You lied to me!"

"You're exaggerating," he said.

"Really?" she said, her eyes narrowing. "Yesterday, in the ER, you told me things had been 'taken care of' while I was out in the hallway, talking with Nora. But then I find out, *a day later*, that wasn't true! You waited until this morning, while we drove home from the hospital, to tell me about your panicky call to this Owen Landry person, and him missing the surgery on that young man!"

He held his palms toward her and said, "Calm down."

But she continued undeterred. "And then, on top of everything, I had to learn about that young man *dying* from the newspaper on our welcome mat, when we arrived home!" She slipped off a black pump and tossed it at him. "I can't—and won't—help you with this mess if you continue to lie and keep secrets from me!"

"All right. Do you honestly want to know what made me panic on that call? It was *you*. You and your so-called script!"

"Oh, so it's *my* fault?" she said with a cutting tut.

"Because you had railroaded me, like you always do. And I had developed misgivings about your 'script' once I had a moment to think it through. So, yes, I freaked out. And I didn't want to tell you about that, because I didn't want to be railroaded by you again. I didn't want you involved anymore."

She walked up to him and said, "Do not blame me for your screwup yesterday. It was *your* spinelessness and *your* call that ruined our plan. *You* are the saboteur! My script—had you and your mentee followed it— would have absolved you of responsibility for your stem-cell 'mishap.' And now, on top of everything, a young man is dead, and we have no idea if the coroner will find something that traces back to you and your 'innovative treatment.'"

Bill plopped down in an armchair, turning his back and a deaf ear to his wife. He tried to console himself by remembering that soon— though, not soon enough—he would be free of her. But until then, he would hold his tongue, as best he could, and stay the course of his plan. And at some future point, Ellie would discover in painful retrospect why he withheld information about changing the script, the true circumstances of Dario's death, and the reason for Owen missing the surgery. Besides, had he kept her apprised of such things, she would have made things worse with her oversized reactions and bulldozer instincts.

Presently, while Ellie continued her litany of complaints, he grappled with new concerns arising from Dario's unexpected death. *That's going to affect things. And now it's just a matter of days before the coroner's report comes out and ruins everything.*

But he was not going to share his evolving concerns about his predicament with his wife. She would only view it through a narrow lens that focused on her self-importance and welfare. His current situation interested her primarily because it introduced risk to her security and comfort. She and Owen were alike in that regard—both blithely entitled to a trouble-free life that depended upon his largesse. They made a good pair.

"Are you even listening to me?" said Ellie, suddenly standing in front of him.

He scratched his gray-stubbled chin and said, "Yes. Just thinking."

"Well, it's about time," she said, walking back to the dresser. "Because you should start thinking about . . ."

But he tuned her out again, and found himself thinking about his encounter with Fred and Nora yesterday. How pathetic that a "visit" from them had required his trip to the ER. Except for brief sightings of them at Lydia's and Cheryl's funerals, he hadn't seen any member of the "gang" in decades. They consistently spurned his attempts to stay connected after their residency ended, always too busy with work and family—with lives that excluded him. But they must know how their abandonment pained him. And, after licking his wounds and swallowing his pride in extending himself to Fred recently—how particularly humiliating it had been to see him yesterday. Over the prior two years, he had canceled each time they had arranged to meet; and the knowing pitiful look on Nora's and Ellie's faces only exacerbated that humiliation.

Seeing Fred and Nora also reminded him how close they used to be—not only as friends, but as like-minded colleagues serving in a noble profession. He taught them, mentored them, and fostered their careers—never anticipating that their successes would ultimately eject him from their lives. But they, like the hospital, had erased him.

How *persona non grata* he'd become in retirement—removed from the hospital and his colleagues, and sent out to pasture in a detached research building. He couldn't even secure a meeting with Fred, to discuss some way—*any* way—he might prove useful to the hospital or residency program.

And how purposeless he felt. When was the last time he conducted any original research? Thank god for distractions like stem cells. And thank god for Donald Parker's deep pockets.

Glancing at Ellie, now removing ruby-red lipstick in the bureau mirror, he wondered how many years of his one precious life he had spent trying to escape her. Their marriage had been ill-conceived from the start, rushed by her parents' impatience for grandchildren. But at the time, neither they nor he was aware that Ellie's private script for her life had excluded roles for children. It did, however, include her marriage to a doctor and a comfortable lifestyle.

"And then," she said, slamming another bureau drawer and pulling him back into his beleaguered awareness. "Then you allow yourself to be intimidated by a *resident*?"

Of course, he thought, *she's already weaponizing the information I shared during our drive home from the ER today. She's trying to belittle me.* But he once again held back and only said, "Owen Landry is not just any 'resident.' He's my research mentee. I provide him with funding and lab space and sage professional guidance."

She wiped away her eyeshadow with a white towelette, transforming it into a miniature watercolor. "Well," she said, tossing it into the wastebasket, "things aren't like the old days. This Owen Landry sounds like a wounded narcissist—self-centered, and concerned only about his career! And disrespectful, too. You shouldn't have excused his not showing up for the boy's surgery. And then you gave him a pass after being angry with you?! Fred, Nora, Jack, and the others—they never would have behaved toward you the way he did."

"Lydia might have," he said. "God rest her soul."

Slathering cold cream on her face, she said, "Well, this is no time for you to be weak and lose your nerve with some whining and unreliable resident. If you're such a great mentor, then mentor him on how to show you respect."

"He's upset and afraid," Bill said. "And I can't say I blame him. Because I involved him. Then I panicked and screwed up the plan that would've allowed the entire mess to disappear."

Pleasantly surprised to hear her husband's self-admonishment, Ellie looked tenderly at him—but, she recognized, in a cued and practiced sort of way, that prompted her to question how she authentically felt about him. It was an actor's dilemma, she thought, to find one's self caught between the art of portraying emotions and the reality of experiencing them. Did she, in fact, love Bill? Did she really know him or, for that matter, care to? Did she even like him? Just how was she supposed to know such things, when their lives were lived so separately, and without positive emotional or sensuous charge between them?

But in theory, she knew how rewarding married life *could* be, having played the fulfilled wife and powerful family matriarch on her soap opera, *The Blue Rose*. That role had empowered her to explore big feelings and express grand emotions. She was enlivened by opportunities to enact outrage and lust and fierceness and joy. She could experience what it would be like to engage in wild, passionate affairs, with both good and evil men. In season four, she birthed a love child with the hunky prince of a small country to whom she later donated a kidney. She survived plane crashes and automobile accidents, and she resurrected—twice!—from a coma. In the final season, she was possessed by the devil—or so an unscrupulous "pastor" had tried to convince her.

"What are you thinking?" Bill asked, largely curious about her unusual silence.

She wondered how she should act toward him, but then decided to shelf that question for another time. Because, like it or not, they were involved in a pressing, high-stakes stem-cell drama now. So, adopting a business-like tone, she replied, "I'm thinking that we can't predict how this situation is going to play out, now that your plan with Dr. Landry failed, and our fate depends upon the coroner's findings. If they find no stem-cell evidence, we're safe. But if they do, and they link that to the boy's infection and death ... Well, obviously, we have a very serious problem. The question is, do we wait for the coroner's report, or do we get ahead of it?"

"And?" he said.

"I don't know, Bill. But at least we can start planning together, now that you've *finally* told me everything. You have, haven't you?"

He nodded, and she continued, "Then we probably have nothing to fear. Since Nora did the surgery, we can assume perfection. She must not have seen anything suspicious, or she would have—"

Bill's phone rang. His face paled.

"Who is it?" she asked.

"Donald Parker," he said.

"Do not answer that," she commanded.

Sunny Day Café

The Uplands

Lori Greene heard the chime from the front door's security sensor. She looked out through her studio window and saw her husband leave in a taxi—finally. Relieved, she slipped out through her studio's exterior door and headed for the Sunny Day Café. In her agitated state, she didn't think to dress properly for this cold, windy day. Still, to shiver was to experience a welcome alternative discomfort, something other than despair.

At the café entrance, she spotted Martin Stanger seated at a private corner table. She had not seen him attired so casually before. But his bulky 49ers jersey did not well serve his long, thin frame. And, even from this distance, she thought his bushy black mustache and eyebrows begged for a trim. When she joined him at the table, he was midway through his black coffee and strawberry scone. A cooling green tea awaited her.

"I remembered," he said, pointing to the tea. "Green for Greene, with a pinch of sugar."

"That's right," she said, trying to warm her hands around the cup. "Sorry I'm late."

Martin shrugged and said, "It's just tragic, Lori. No other word to describe it. I was so sorry to hear about your son."

"Thank you," she replied automatically, wondering how many times she would have to endure the same banal exchange about Dario's death in the upcoming months. "But I didn't invite you here for your sympathy."

He shifted in his chair, scanning the café to reassure himself of their privacy. "Yeah, I figured that," he said, lowering his voice. "I'm guessing you called because . . . Well, when I heard the news about Dario—"

"I need my money back," she said, tightening her grip on her teacup.

With a small apologetic smile, he said, "I'm sorry. That's not possible."

Her brow knotted. "Excuse me?"

"That money has been disbursed, to the coach and test proctor. It's been out of my hands for weeks."

"But I gave you $800,000, Martin. And Dario is dead now. He's no longer going to college."

He shoved his scone aside and somberly shook his head. "This is uncomfortable for me. I don't know how to say it. But, well, you and I never discussed any refund policy. In my book, the money was always nonrefundable."

Words stuck in her throat, but she finally managed to say, "You don't understand."

"I beg to differ. I do understand—that's a *lot* of money." He refrained from adding, *To most people, anyway*. He—a self-made college-admissions counselor, and a high school dropout to boot—often marveled at the oversized distress with which the ultra-rich suffered over their money.

"It's not about the money," she whispered. "I'm afraid someone is going to discover what we did."

"Excuse me?" he said, cocking his head.

"Dario's death is under investigation by the coroner's office. And Don hired John Norris as our attorney to go after the hospital and the ER doctor who, we were told, wasn't qualified to operate on Dario. The media is scrutinizing Dario's story. There's so much forensic and legal and media attention being paid—"

"Hey, hey," he interrupted, "slow down. I can barely keep up." He waited a beat and continued, "Look, I read about all of that in the morning news. So awful to lose a son. And because of an incompetent doctor? Jesus. Of course, you're beside yourself right now."

She forcefully set down her tea. "You're not listening! All the reporters and lawyers, the police, and the coroner? Lots of very smart and very curious people are digging for details about Dario."

He placed a hand on hers and said, "You can't be worried that somebody is going to scrutinize Dario's college application?" When she returned a telling silence, he said, "Nah. Not going to happen. It's in nobody's interest to smear the reputation of a boy who died so tragically in the prime of his life. And his college application isn't public record, Lori. It's irrelevant to—"

"My god," she said, "there is no 'scrutiny' required. It is bold-faced obvious how average, at best, Dario was at school and sports."

"Well, yeah," he said, suppressing an eyeroll. "You and I wouldn't have met and conducted business if he hadn't been . . . you know, 'average.'" He thought, but did not say, *You "bought" this problem upon yourself.* He thought, but did not mention, that, unlike her son, his stepson Jason had excelled at academics and sports but never possessed the means or wherewithal to attend college—the flipside of Dario's privileged circumstances.

"That's not a helpful response," she said, her voice cracking.

After looking away momentarily, he said, "Sorry. But, still, my hands are tied."

"And still, you don't get it," she said, grabbing the table edge. "Because if anyone so much as glimpses at Dario's grades, they won't believe the legitimacy of his ACT scores. They will doubt, for good reason, that he was capable of writing that college-entry essay. And if anyone speaks with his high school coach or teammates . . . with *anyone* who has ever seen Dario *try* to play tennis . . . they'll know he was no athlete." She forcibly shut her eyes, thinking, *How desperate and stupid it was to fake Dario's credentials.*

Martin leaned toward her, his elbows on the table. "Well, remember—you and I agreed to cover all the bases. That was the strategy we shared from the get-go, to snag Dario's early acceptance. And you have to admit, I delivered on my end. The plan succeeded."

She stared quizzically at him. "You do understand, you're in the line of fire, too? And that much money missing from our house account is going to raise suspicion."

He wearily rubbed his eyes and said, "Please don't tell me that you're thinking about exposing our arrangement. Because, if you do, you're going to inflict a lot of pain on yourself and your family and friends— to say nothing about the other students and their parents who've been involved. Now, you need to get a handle on your anxiety."

"'Anxiety'? Your head is in the sand. My husband and I are public figures, and we're charging a hospital and an ER doctor with wrongful death and negligence. We're seeking punitive damages and compensation for emotional suffering and lost years of Dario's life."

"Keep your voice down," he implored.

Her eyes narrowed and she said, "The lawyers and their accountants will be calculating Dario's worth—his many lost years of earning potential, in the life and career he would have had with his college degree. And the defense will try to undermine that. See? They will be *appraising* my son's life, line item by line item, and putting a price tag on him, including the 'investment' we lost in his education. It's a matter of minutes before one of the bean counters concludes the obvious—that Dario not only didn't earn his admission to UCSM, but he wasn't likely to excel in whatever college major he might've pursued. So, how he got accepted in the first place is going to be questioned—"

"Please! People are staring at us."

She lowered her voice and said, "It is going to raise suspicions about a back channel to admission, and that means questions about money. It's a short leap to wonder if bribery was involved. And the $800,000 hole in our house account is going to stick out like a sore thumb." She privately vowed she would not, could not, go to prison. Not now, not ever, and certainly not after losing her only son.

Martin bristled. Was she delivering a veiled threat, trying to intimidate him in hopes of getting her money back? He leaned toward her and said, "You need to remember, as I've said, that Dario's college application materials are *not* public record. And besides, I'm an independent admissions counselor. I work with only one coach, at one university, and he has been loyal as hell for five years. And the only other person in the loop is the test proctor, who happens to be my *stepson*—and, even there, he has a different last name than mine. So, my ship is small, and it's very tight. You and Don are *not* going to prison for—"

"Don knows nothing about this."

"What?"

She fidgeted with her wedding ring. "But I have to tell him."

He scoffed and said, "That makes no sense. And how would getting your money back help you to—?"

"I need to tell Don," she persisted, "before someone else does. Before he reads about it in the news. Before he hears from the police or defense lawyers. Before he finds out about the missing $800,000 from our financial adviser or tax man."

Shaking his head, Martin wondered what his life might have been like if he, like Lori, had been able to withdraw hundreds of thousands of dollars from the family's piggy bank—let alone, without anyone noticing. He questioned whether he should be feeling sympathy toward her now, but it was difficult to empathize with her ultra-rich person's rich predicament. Finally, he rapped his knuckles on the table and said, "You don't need to tell Don, because no one is going to gain legal access to your finances without your permission. And, for the last time, no one can access Dario's college application materials. Period!" He let out a voluminous sigh. "And, if you want my advice, if you still feel compelled to tell your husband . . . Well, tell him you've been secretly putting money aside to surprise him with a nice gift. Money toward another house, maybe? A new yacht? A luxury cruise around the world?" He hoped he hadn't sounded sarcastic.

Lori stared at him, despair and astonishment crossing her face at once. Then she abruptly rose from the table and walked away.

Afternoon

Nora drove to the Safeway—the store's name oddly comforting—to buy wine for Fred's dinner tonight. Plus, a few extra bottles for personal consumption.

Once inside, she hesitated—as always, overwhelmed by the exorbitant number of food options, which seemed comically excessive. Who had the time to choose rationally among them, and then figure how to cohere several into a "meal"? And, of course, the tiresome cleanup afterwards. *Thank god for frozen dinners.*

After loading her cart with a six-pack of wine and a week's supply of frozen dinners, she headed to the checkout. She was feeling less anxious after her lakeside walk with Fergie, and looking forward to Fred's dinner and the additional respite it would offer.

But when loading chicken piccata trays onto the counter, she froze. At eye level, she saw copies of today's *Oakland Register* stuffed into the checkout display.

Donald Parker arrived home after retrieving their Tesla from the hospital lot and stopping at the office to arrange interim leadership of his company. He set his keys and work laptop on the entryway table and then walked to the living room. The silence was disquieting. No music, no son talking on a cellphone, no TV noise in the background. He glanced at his cell—still, after leaving two voicemails, no response from Bill Balaban.

Now he heard the security-door sensor that originated from Lori's studio. But was she entering or leaving the house? What had she been doing during his absence? He walked down the hallway to her studio door and knocked. "Lori?" he called out.

"I asked to be left alone," she answered. "Please, just leave me alone." Muffled, deep-throated sobbing ensued.

His heart sunk. He returned to the living room and stood before the vacated wall space, where Dario's favorite painting had hung. "What have I done to you and your mother?" he whispered.

When Fergie arrived home from the dentist, Winston was, predictably, at the dining table with his laptop. Without looking up, he asked, "How was your walk? Is Nora okay? Is the lake still filled with stinky blue-green algae? How did your dental appointment go?"

She watched him tap away at the keyboard, his eyes fixed on the screen. Did he care whether she answered his list of questions? At what point in time had he stopped noticing her? What had happened to the once-powerful magnetic attraction between them? She removed her black denim jacket and threw it at him.

"Hey," he said, finally looking up. "What's that about?"

Embarrassment flickered across her face, and she said, "I'm sorry. Nothing."

He walked to her and placed a hand over her heart. "I love you, Fergs. Talk to me."

But she didn't know where or how to begin. And she feared that, even if she found a way to launch her tale, it simply wouldn't end. She looked away and said, "I'm still not feeling great. I'm going to lie down."

Finally, Ella Williams was satisfied. The blue ceramic appetizer tray was artfully arranged—centered with assorted crackers and Brie, and rimmed with the parmesan-finished shishito peppers she had roasted. The dining table was properly set for four, and the chicken Marbella—with dried apricots substituting for prunes—was finishing in the oven. She would ask her mother to toss the salad—red sails lettuce, Persian cucumbers, avocado—after everyone was seated. The jasmine rice and steamed broccoli would require minimal last-minute attention.

Fred followed his nose to the kitchen and exclaimed, "Sweetie, it smells fabulous in here."

Ella replied with unflinching confidence, "Well, just wait 'til you taste it."

But when he reached for a shishito pepper, she gently slapped his hand and said, "I told you—*wait* 'til you taste it."

Vickie noted his scowl when she entered the kitchen and asked, "What are you so sore about?"

Ella pointed to the appetizer tray and explained, "Dad tried to ruin my *presentation*."

Vickie tsked and said, "Fred, you should know better."

Fred wished that Charlie was here to reinforce the XY contingency in the room. But, on quick second thought, he realized their son tended to side with the women in the house. He cleared his throat and offered, "Want me to pull up another chair? There's only four at the table."

"No, thanks," said Ella. "I'm not staying for dinner. But everything's on automatic pilot. Mom's going to finish and serve."

"Our daughter finds our company boring," Vickie said in an aside.

"Not true, Mom," said Ella. "It's just fun to cook for you and your friends. But you can save me a piece of chicken." She tossed her white-and-red checkered apron to her mother and kissed her parents goodbye.

While Vickie was tying the apron around her waist, Fred's cell chimed with a text. She saw him half-frown and asked, "*Now* what?"

"Carrie Chandler," he replied. "She's accepted the hospice and palliative care job."

Vickie toyed with the prospect of teasing him about his discomfort in the company of Lydia's identical twin; and, now, he would be seeing a lot more of her at the hospital. But he, catching her mischievous drift, preemptively warned, "Don't even start."

~ ~ ~

"But I finished all my homework last night," said Luis.

"For Monday?" asked Jack. "Not just the math?"

Luis nodded, and their housekeeper Zofia concurred: "He did all the reading and the essay, too."

"Without me?" said Jack, a whiff of injury in his voice.

Luis scratched his ear and said, "Well, only because me and Zofia want to watch an old movie tonight. With popcorn and coka."

Zofia tousled Luis' curly black hair and said, "Yes, Luis' passion for acting and theater is growing—just like him. He wants to watch an old movie with your friend in it." When Jack returned a puzzled look, she explained, "That woman in your prison show?"

"The prima donna," said Luis, beaming.

"Ah, yes," said Jack, "our dear Ellie Balaban. She did lots of TV in her day, mostly soaps and game shows. But you must have had to do some serious sleuthing to find one of her old films!"

"Not really," said Luis. "They're easy to find on the internet. We are going to stream *Broken Rainbows*."

Jack privately gave thanks for being spared the ordeal of watching another of Ellie's melodramatic performances in so short a time. That also reminded him to restock the antacids in his medicine cabinet. "Okay," he said, heading out the door, "you two have a fun movie night. I'll be home late, after dinner."

~ ~ ~

Detectives Darinda Johnson and Tom Burka exclaimed in unison, "What?!" They stared incredulously at the county coroner, who merely shrugged in response.

"But Doctor," Darinda persisted, "you must have *some* idea? I mean, how does something like that even happen?"

Chief county coroner Dr. Annie Klumtree responded with a triad of facial movements. One corner of her generous mouth turned up, then the other side turned down, and her aquiline nose crinkled. "I don't know. But that's my provisional diagnosis for the cause of this young man's death. And I'm sticking with it."

Evening

Fred's Home

"Substituting apricots for prunes was inspired," said Jack, resting a hand on his stomach. "Truthfully, the best chicken Marbella I've ever had. Please relay my compliments to the chef-in-residence."

"Seconds?" asked Vickie.

Nora patted Jack's stomach and said, "I think you mean thirds."

Vickie whispered to Nora, "I was trying to be polite."

"Well," said Fred, "our daughter will be happy to hear that you stuffed yourself, Jack. She's going to grill us about everyone's critique of the dinner." He took the occasion of a relaxed atmosphere at the table and ventured, "So, we had planned to discuss strategy for a Plan B tonight."

Jack whispered an aside to Nora, "Of all times for me to be without my antacids."

"I heard that," said Fred, eyeing him cautiously. "And just so you both know, I phoned the Balabans twice this afternoon, after they escaped from the ER this morning. But no one answered or returned my calls."

"Well, that makes matters even more worrisome," said Nora, her guilt resurrecting over having missed this morning's intervention, and expanding now, too—she hadn't even thought about checking on the couple afterwards.

Vickie stood and started clearing the table. "I'll leave you three to your discussion," she said, heading to the kitchen. "Just carry on. Don't mind me."

After she left, Fred explained to his friends, "Vickie's not, let's say, 'enthusiastic' about me spending so much time on the Balabans' problems."

"Maybe," said Jack, "I could help her in the kitchen and talk with her about that?"

"Hell, no," said Fred. "You're not getting out of this discussion."

"But good try," said Nora, nudging Jack with her elbow.

"Fine," said Jack with dramatic resignation. "So, let's talk about a Plan B. Pray tell, what do you have in mind?"

Fred knew his proposition would generate debate. He also understood how busy his friends already were with the demands of their own lives and work. He scooted his chair closer to the table and said, "I think we need to visit Bill and Ellie in their home."

"Oh, no, please," said Jack, trying not to sound whiny. "Isn't that a bit of an overreach?"

"All right now," said Fred. "Last night, at Grady's, each of you agreed that we *should* intervene."

"I know," said Jack. "And we tried this morning in the ER. But intervening at a hospital feels a *lot* different than barging into their home. I also think they'd find it invasive."

Looking apologetically at Fred, Nora said, "Jack has a point. And . . . I'm wondering if your need to get involved with the Balabans stems from your guilt over canceling on Bill so often?"

Jack sat up straight, surprised by Nora's bluntness. Hoping to support her pushback, he said, "And, sadly, Fred—you showing up for Bill at this point isn't likely to give you the closure you're seeking. Because, from everything I've heard—from what you and Nora and Ellie told me—Bill is seriously demented. It's probably a little too late for genuine reconciliation with him."

Fred's jaw tightened. He knew they were right. But neither they nor the Balabans had been privy to the arduous work and time required of him, over the prior two years, to reconcile with Vickie and the kids. During that period, he had always been happy to accept Bill's invitations—but always, subsequently, needing to cancel because family or work reclaimed priority. On several occasions, he considered explaining his challenges to Bill, but doing so required the time he didn't have to meet with Bill in the first place—replaying a sad and vicious cycle. He finally said, "Thank you both for your curbside psych consultations. But there's another question on the table. Don't you think we have a moral duty to care about the Balabans? They parented us through our medical training and careers. And now *they* need *us*. And they have no one else in their lives."

Placing a hand on Fred's arm, Nora said, "But, the truth is, Ellie made it clear she didn't want any intervention. And *we* don't have the authority to override her wishes."

"But you saw Ellie's shiner!" Fred exclaimed. "And you saw Bill's scratched face. They've each become a bona fide 'danger to self or others.' And that raises the bar for us to—"

"Then we should call Adult Protective Services to run a home welfare check on them," countered Jack. "The APS has the authority to intervene with them."

Fred flicked his hand and said, "You know that APS rarely intervenes in a situation like theirs."

Nora nodded in agreement, and Jack muttered, "Dear god." Fred persisted, "I guarantee APS would not protect them from the bad consequences of Ellie's bad judgment."

After dropping her white napkin onto the table, Nora said, "I surrender. You're right, Fred—we have an ethical obligation to help them." Turning to Jack, she continued, "And I second Fred's proposal. I'm up for going to their house in the morning, so we can assess their safety and welfare. Besides, who knows? Maybe Ellie has been managing as well as can be expected of anyone. But, if not, at least we'd understand their situation, and know how to be helpful. And we'd also know whether calling out APS is warranted."

"So," said Fred, his palms held up, "then we're agreed on this Plan B?"

Nora nodded, while Jack buried his face in his hands and groaned.

Part Four

Sunday, December 1

Bill and Ellie's Home

THE DOORBELL RANG. Ellie blinked several times and glanced at the clock. Then she rolled over in bed and said, "Bill, wake up. Are you expecting anyone at this hour?"

"No," he answered. "Just ignore it."

"Well, it's too early for solicitors," she said.

The doorbell rang again.

"Bill?" she said.

"Fine," he said, throwing on his wool robe and shuffling toward the front door. But when he sleepily looked through the peephole, he was jolted awake by Owen's livid eyes.

"Open up," Owen demanded.

Ellie promptly appeared at her husband's side and asked, "Who is it?"

Placing a finger across his lips, Bill whispered, "Shh."

But Owen continued pounding on the door. "I know you're inside!"

Bill whispered to Ellie, "It's my research mentee, Owen Landry. He's the Ortho chief resident who—"

"For heaven's sake," she said. "I remember what you told me about him. But he's going to wake the entire neighborhood." When she grabbed the doorknob, Bill deflected her hand and said, "I don't want him inside."

Eying him scornfully, she replied, "You are cowering from him again! And you're allowing this bully from the junior leagues to intimidate you. You're his boss, for godsakes! Grow a spine!"

Owen pressed the doorbell.

Ellie persisted, "I'm so disappointed in you, Bill. But I intend to meet this Owen Landry head-on and set him straight." She pushed past her husband, unlocked the door, and greeted their visitor with: "Do you have any idea what time it is?"

Owen answered matter-of-factly, "Seven-forty-four in the morning."

Such a smart-ass, Ellie thought; such a rude and disrespectful smart-ass. She replied, "You must know what I mean." Then, after eyeing him head to toe—from garish baseball cap, to juvenile varsity jacket, to faded jeans and worn black sneakers—she added, "Or, perhaps, you don't have a clue."

"I need to speak with your husband," said Owen. "I take it you're Bill's wife. I saw you with him in the ER."

"I am Mrs. Elaine Balaban," she said. And, though knowing full well who he was, she nonetheless asked, "And you are . . . ?"

Bill stepped between them and said, "Enough. He's Owen Landry, from my lab." He gestured toward the living room, and Owen headed for the couch. Then Bill pulled Ellie aside, into the hallway, and said, "Go back to bed."

"No," she returned. "I'm not taking a chance of you cracking under pressure again."

"I can handle him," Bill said, gritting his teeth.

"You understand I have reason to doubt that," she said.

But he held her back with a steely gaze until she relented. Still, before she turned back to the bedroom, she sternly reminded him, "A *spine*, Bill. Grow one."

After seeing the bedroom door close, he walked to the living room and sat in the armchair, across from Owen. "What the hell are you doing here?" he said.

Owen scanned the room, eyeing the Persian rug, the Limoges plates, the Inuit stonework, the ornately framed oil paintings and photographs. He fingered the coffee-table art books and asked, "For show? Or do you actually read these?"

Deflecting the question, Bill said, "I understand you not wanting to leave a paper trail. But coming to my home unannounced, and making your presence known to my wife and the entire neighborhood—"

"I had an epiphany yesterday," Owen interrupted. "I had to share it with you."

Determined to appear in control, Bill sat back in his chair and smiled artificially. But Ellie's admonition to "grow a spine" echoed irksomely in his head. He stroked his gray-stubbled chin and said, "I'm all ears."

Owen counseled himself to remain calm. Already, he had inflicted his quick anger, triggered by panic, on two senior staff, including Bill. He bluntly stated, "I read your medical record in the ER."

Bill tried not to outwardly cringe. "Why, that's unethical," he said. "And illegal. You had no right to do that—you're not providing me with medical care."

After removing his cap and tossing it onto the couch, Owen said, "You're a fine one to bring up law and ethics."

Bill gripped the armrests of his chair but immediately let go, determined to conceal his irritation. Still, to tolerate his mentee's insolence and claims of moral superiority . . . his sense of entitlement . . . his ingratitude . . . his . . . *his being just like Ellie! And after all I've done to help him and his career! He thanks me by barging into my home, reading my private medical record, judging me, questioning me . . . ?*

"Still, I'm sorry," Owen continued. "I hadn't planned on reading your record. But I was there in the ER so long, waiting for your wife and the nurses to leave, so we could talk privately in your room about . . . you know."

"So, you were bored and decided to pass the time by reading my medical record?"

"Something like that. It was convenient. And I only thought to do it, because I saw your name on the whiteboard and—"

"I see. So, then, you read my record *before* you came into the room. Is that why you were so agitated when you visited me? Even angry, perhaps?"

Owen crossed his arms and said, "I was already shook over what happened with Dario Parker—his death, and me not getting the surgery. So, yeah, reading your record rattled me even more."

"All right. And you have this urgent need to tell me about that now because . . . ?"

"Because there was no time to discuss it in the ER. Before I could bring it up, I heard your wife talking on the phone in the hallway, right outside your room."

Bill studied his fingernails, thinking. *This is no neutral inquiry. He is here to complain, to whine, to threaten, to blackmail. He is here to question me again.* He looked up at his mentee and said, "I wish you had respected my medical privacy."

Owen's smoky dark eyes widened. "Yeah, and I wish *you* had told *me* about—"

"I have my reasons," said Bill.

"Well, I want to know what they are."

"You're disappointing me again. You don't trust me."

Owen stared at the ceiling, as if seeking divine guidance. While he didn't completely distrust his mentor, he also didn't completely trust him. "Dr. Balaban—if I understood what you were doing, it would make it easier for me to trust you."

"It's to your benefit to know as little as possible."

"That's simply not true. Because not knowing what's happening has been tearing me up inside."

And that was the last straw for Bill, the final time he would allow someone like Owen or Ellie to so tenaciously challenge or question him. The proverbial camel's back snapped under the odious weight of their imperious meddling and shared sense of entitlement. "That's enough," he let slip out loud.

"Enough of what?" asked Owen.

Trying to amend his slipup, Bill said, "All that you already know— that's enough. Knowing more would only jeopardize your career."

Owen shook his head. "I've been so worried that I haven't slept for three nights." He put on his Saints cap, stood, and said, "I feel like I fell into some deep swamp. I feel dirty and stuck and unsafe." Then he headed for the door.

"All right," Bill said, throwing his hands up in surrender. "Please, sit down, and I'll explain." He smiled mechanically, trying to conceal his fury over being forced into a tight corner. And while waiting for his mentee's hesitant return to the couch, he desperately strategized over how to appease him.

When Owen was reseated, Bill leaned forward and said, "I guarantee—you're about to learn things you're going to wish you never knew. But then you'll understand how I've been trying to protect you. And maybe that will allow us to trust each other again, so we can come to an agreement about how we should proceed. And I believe you'll be pleased to hear what could be in store for you if you work with me."

Nora's Home

"How is it possible that you're never ready?" Jack complained. "You'd think it would happen once or twice, by accident at least."

"I just need a minute," Nora replied, excavating a waffle from the freezer. "Want one?"

"Definitely not," he said, pretending to gag. "Are you going to toast it first?"

She faked a laugh and dropped the waffle into the toaster.

"Well, look at you!" he said. "Who says you can't cook? Wait, I know. *Everyone*."

"Funny-*not*," she said. "Besides, we have time. Fred just texted—he's running late, too."

"Oh?" he said. "That's unusual. I bet he's just factoring in you being late for our meeting at the Balabans."

She kissed his cheek. "I'm glad you didn't do the same. Because isn't it nice that we get to spend this extra time together?" When he said nothing, she stopped buzzing around the kitchen and said, "Wait a minute. No smarty-pants response? That's not like you."

His lips stretched into an unconvincing smile.

"No way," she said, pointing at him. "What a tell! Fess up. What aren't you saying?"

Jack groaned. "I don't want you dealing with it before our meeting with the Balabans—which is enough tsuris for one morning."

But she just crossed her arms and waited.

"I think it's a mistake," he said. When she remained unmoved, he relented. "All right, fine. Have you seen the news this morning?"

She shook her head. "I decided to avoid it, so I could maintain a tenuous hold on my sanity today. But now? You might as well just hand it over."

With a scowl, he reached into his backpack and gave her the *Oakland Register* that he had collected from her driveway.

Opening the paper, she said, "Yesterday, it was Fergie delivering . . . my . . . paper . . ." Her expression turned grim when she read the headline: "ER Doctor's Competence Questioned in Teen's Death."

Jack had read the story online, so he anxiously waited for her to finish reading the article. When she laid the paper down, he asked, "Are you all right?"

She nodded unpersuasively.

"Still, there's also some goodish news in it, right?" he said. "It mentions that the coroner's preliminary report might be made available as soon as today or tomorrow. So, that must mean the cause of Dario's death was reasonably obvious at autopsy. And since we both know your surgery played no role . . . Well, I think it's reassuring."

"Still, the headline is pretty damning, don't you think? And they practically name me in the article. I'm the only 'veteran female physician' who works in the ER."

He rubbed his forehead. "But Winston's article doesn't *technically* name you. And it consistently uses 'alleged' before any accusation."

She stared at him as though he were an alien. "Please, don't be a Pollyanna right now. This is very serious and upsetting to me. And what did Winston mean, when he wrote about 'heightened' social media threats over Dario's death?"

Jack grumbled, "Fuck."

"So, you must know. I haven't looked at the internet since yesterday. I just couldn't."

"Well, that was a wise decision. And it remains so now. Say, don't you have a waffle to tend to?"

She considered his advice for a nanosecond. "I can't even imagine what could be 'heightened' threat-wise. I thought I saw it all yesterday. But show me. I need to know where the landmines are."

"Tell me why, after all these years of avoiding social media and criticizing it, must you look at it now?"

"I'm waiting, Jack. Impatiently waiting."

"It's a terrible idea. And you've always said it was a colossal waste of time to read crazy shit on the internet."

She fixed him with a defiant stare.

"We're both going to regret this," he said, scooting his chair alongside hers at the kitchen table. Then he tapped on his cellphone screen, and a video appeared—a coarse animation depicting her mortal demise. Nora's face slackened.

"Nora?" he said.

But she couldn't respond. She was using all her energy to contain the shock. Familiar with the terrain of trauma, she felt herself slipping into its dark landscape. Then, in the next video, she saw a GIF of red-faced

Donald Parker, who appeared taller than she had remembered. His stiff finger jabbed toward her like an icepick. She shuddered during the audio replay of his vitriolic accusation: "But my son had to die because *this* doctor . . . this *ER doctor* performed a *surgery* on him that she had no business doing!"

Jack seized his cellphone and said, "See? This is why I didn't want you looking at these crappy—"

"Are there more new videos? I want to see them."

Trying to casually slip his cell into his jeans pocket, he replied, "They're all the same, Nora. The same video, just from different angles of hate and derangement." Privately, he prayed that her PTSD was not being triggered.

"But there are comments, too, with each of those videos," she said. "I want to read them."

"No. Besides, you've always been *super*-critical of those."

"Then, I take it you've read them."

He slapped his palms on the table. "The comments are what you'd expect from highly opinionated people with no knowledge of facts, no concern with truth. They're from media influencers who are generating drama to whip up their viewer counts. From people who hate doctors and hospitals and Western medicine and the patriarchy and the government and even the goddamn vending machines in the hospital cafeteria."

"Do the comments all condemn me?"

"No, not all of them."

"Do they name me?"

"Some do."

"Personal threats?"

Jack sighed in surrender. "That's what Winston was referring to."

Nora rocked ever so slightly in her chair and stared vaguely at the wall. Finally, she said, "Well, thanks for telling me. I know it was hard for you."

He grimaced and said, "God, I hate seeing you like this." Then he walked to the toaster and, as a comfort offering, placed her waffle on a plate and served it to her.

"No thanks," she said. "Not hungry."

"Well, now, that's a worrisome sign," he said. "This is your favorite ultra-processed, nutrition-free brand of frozen waffles."

When she didn't respond, he added, "And only a thousand useless calories per serving. Please—you need to keep up your artificial strength."

But Nora was contemplating a different type of fortification. She knew she needed help to avoid her entrapment in a panic attack, but she didn't want to rely on the alprazolam that her psychiatrist had prescribed. Still, up against escalating physical threats . . . the vicious slander . . . becoming a target for an angry public's unbridled attacks . . . and the looming lawsuit about to drop on her life like a ton of jagged bricks . . . *How did this all happen?* she asked herself. *How did such an ordinary workday, performing a routine procedure on a healthy young man, evolve into this terrifying nightmare?* Her heart began thumping inside her chest while her lungs emptied of air. The nerves in her hands vibrated, and her ears buzzed.

Jack recognized her tell of an imminent panic attack and attempted to keep her focused on their conversation. But she heard nothing of what he said, while her ears rang deafeningly now. He grabbed a paper bag, held it over her mouth, and instructed her to breathe into it. He pinched her arms, trying to distract her. He repeatedly assured her, "You're having a panic attack. It will pass."

Minutes later, her breathing and heart rate normalized, and her light-headedness slowly resolved. He withdrew the paper bag and stroked her back, repeating "okay" until she appeared to reconnect with him. Then he fetched her a glass of water, and a cool washcloth that he pressed against her forehead.

"Thanks," she said, sipping the water. "You're a savior."

He smiled tentatively. For, given the fevered circumstances of her life, he suspected that additional triggers were looming in her immediate future.

She removed the washcloth and looked into his soft blue eyes. "But you've got that telltale look again. You're still holding something back."

"More water?" he said, grabbing her glass.

"No, thanks. You heard what I said."

He grumbled, "I'm going to buy an RFID body suit so you can't read my mind anymore."

"They have such things?"

"No. Probably not. I don't know. But I'll be first in line to buy one, when they hit the shelves."

"Tell me," she pleaded.

He sighed resignedly and said, "All right. I was thinking about your PTSD and panic attacks." He paused to press the washcloth against his own forehead. "And, please don't get me wrong. I understand the huge and crappy things you're up against right now. And I'm aware of the original trauma—I was even with you on the beach when that rogue wave took Michael and Caitlin from you. But . . ."

"But?"

"The thing is, you're so accustomed to being in control at work. You're always capable and fearless and in command, regardless of what medical catastrophe arrives at your doorstep. But, *outside* the ER? I'm not sure you accept what little control you have over life's regular slings and arrows. And, returning to the original trauma, I'll say this for the millionth time: There's no fucking way you could have fended off that mammoth sneaker wave!"

She stared attentively at him, waiting on his next word.

He continued, "Your panic attacks since that horrific day—they also seem to be triggered by threats that ambush you. By bad things you don't anticipate that just sneak up on you, and you discover you have no power over them. Like all this social media crap, or the misguided lawsuit, and even Dario's death."

After a weighty pause, he said, "It might help to recognize that you can't control all the sneaker waves—literally and metaphorically. *And you have to trust that not every wave will annihilate you or someone you love.*"

She closed her eyes and looked inward. *Yes, lots of sneaker waves out there that keep coming at me. Still, what peace can come from acknowledging powerlessness over them?* When she returned her attention to Jack, he asked, "So, what do you think about what I just said?"

She answered him with a long embrace, feeling progressively stronger than she would have imagined possible minutes ago. "I think," she replied, releasing her hold, "I'm going to ask my itinerant psychiatrist for a refund."

Jack smiled and watched her walk to the sink, where she refilled the water glass. He asked, "So, where is your Dr. Barteau vacationing this time?"

Nora said, "Who knows? I learned the hard way not to ask her. Once, when I did, she just quizzed me about my need to know and, still, never answered the question."

"Too bad," he said, "that you can't at least live vicariously through the travels you finance for her."

"True! And her being gone *again*, while so many unsettling things are happening? Dario and me. His parents. The internet assaults, and the lawsuit. The Balabans! Fergie not well. Alex's parents being sick. The hellish presidential campaign with the country gone mad. Seriously, a deadly pandemic wouldn't surprise me right now."

"There's my girl!" he said, grabbing his jacket and backpack. "It's good to hear you sound more like your optimistic-*not* self. And, if you feel okay, it's time we head out to meet up with Fred at the Balabans." But when he glanced at his phone and noted the time, he said, "Oops! We're going to be even later than Fred—"

Another cellphone rang, and Jack said, "Has to be yours. But it sounds kind of muffled."

Nora searched her kitchen, tracking the ring to her freezer, from which she pulled out her cell and sighed.

"A cold call?" said Jack, hoping—but failing—to make her smile. "Look, don't be embarrassed. You were totally distracted."

"It's not that," she said, frowning. "It's a call from hospital legal."

He thought, but did not say, *Ugh! On a Sunday? And so early in the morning?* Instead, trying to remain calm and supportive, he suggested, "Well, let's pick up and hear what they have to say." Still, as a physician, he knew there was no such thing as a welcome call from a hospital's legal department on a weekend. On any day, actually.

Nora tried to ground herself in Jack's metaphor by envisioning the bourgeoning lawsuit as a raging sneaker wave, beyond her control. She pictured herself standing firm, refusing to be swept away by helplessness or doom. Then she answered the call with a cautious "Hello?"

Jack wanted to appear as though he wasn't listening and monitoring her—though, of course, he was. But what he mostly heard was her silence, while the call dragged on. At times, she looked stunned or mesmerized. The hospital lawyer was either a gifted hypnotist or a captivating conversationalist.

Finally, he heard Nora say, "Really?" When he approached her and thrust out his hands to convey *What gives?* she didn't seem to notice.

Then he became mesmerized himself, watching her expression shift several times between confusion and awe. Twice, she said, "A *what?*"

Finally, Nora said, "How sure are they?" A long pause followed, and then: "I have no reason to doubt that. Annie Klumtree is the best forensic pathologist I've ever known."

Concerned about the elapsing time, Jack began a text to Fred to warn him about them being *extra* late to the Balabans. But he stopped when he overheard Nora say, "Yes, I can drive to your office now. Thanks for giving me the heads-up." She ended the call and stood still, while thoughts about Dario flooded her mind.

"What's going on?" asked Jack.

She exhaled through a corner of her mouth. "The hospital just received the coroner's preliminary report."

"And?"

"And, apparently, Dario died from multiple pulmonary emboli."

Jack met her bewildered look with one of his own. "That's . . . well, unexpected. But clearly, your surgery had nothing to do with that."

"Still," she said, her brow knitting.

"Still, yes, it's odd," he said. "Such a young athletic man throwing clots to his lungs? I assume the coroner also found a DVT as the source? Probably a clot in his leg?"

She shook her head. "Not according to what legal read to me over the phone."

"Huh," he said. "So, then, maybe Dario had a blood-clotting disorder? A familial coagulopathy of some sort?"

She shook her head again. "And even if he did, that wouldn't have mattered."

"Because?" he asked.

"Because the clots they found in Dario's lungs—they were not your run-of-the-mill blood clots."

The Parker-Greene Estate

He knew his wife had slept overnight inside her studio, and, by his assessment of their kitchen, had still not eaten. So, Donald knocked on her studio door and said, "Lori, please let me in. Talk to me."

This time, he heard the lock turn. Then the door slowly opened. But when he looked inside, he took an involuntary step back. Paint tubes and brushes were strewn about everywhere. Canvases on wooden easels were slashed. Puddles had formed from overturned brush-soak jars, creating colorful archipelagoes across the floor. Watery rainbows stretched out from toppled glasses on the worktable, and shattered remnants of several shimmered in the ambient light. Near the far window, soggy sketchbooks formed a warped hillock.

His heart pounded so forcefully that he felt it in his neck and skull, and he feared he might be having a heart attack. He wondered if this moment would constitute his last chance to confess his recklessness to his wife. But she was already undone by grief.

Lori stared concernedly at her husband, anxious to confess about the bribery before its inevitable public disclosure devastated him any further. But already he appeared so broken.

"Lori," he managed, one hand on his chest. "I don't know what to do."

She wanted to say something, anything, to ease his suffering. Perhaps it would help to admit that he'd been right all along to caution her against pushing Dario so hard, especially toward college. And had she not recently forced Dario into daily tennis lessons, he wouldn't have fallen on the court and required the surgery that somehow left him dead. *My god, is Don even thinking that himself? Is he blaming me for Dario's death?*

He steadied himself against the wall and repeated, "I don't know what to do."

She had never seen her powerful, self-possessed husband appear so helpless and uncertain. It confused and upset her, and it was intolerable to witness. She was forced to look away. More than ever, she needed to see him as the man he had been before.

"What are you thinking?" he asked.

Still unable to face him, she walked haltingly to her workbench and picked up Dario's favorite painting. Such a simple composition, she thought. Basic geometric shapes—a rectangle, a circle, a square, a triangle—that she had painted with solid complementary colors, straight from the tubes. A casual afterthought creation, using leftover paint, after finishing the still life that now hung in the city's Fine Arts Museum. Finally, she said, "Dario had such simple tastes. He never wanted to be extraordinary. Still, I kept trying to make him into someone else."

Donald went to her and held her. But she pulled away and said, "There's something I need to do."

He scanned her chaotic studio, dreading its cleanup and repair, and said, "It's too much for us to do alone. How about I make us something to eat, then call Nadja for help with the cleanup?"

"No," she said.

"To food? To cleanup?"

"Both."

"Lori," he implored. But her eyes would not meet his; they were fixed on something that he could not see.

"You can go now," she said.

"I don't want to," he replied. "And I'm afraid to leave you alone."

"But that's precisely what I need from you," she said.

He tugged on his mustache, deliberating. Finally, he said, "All right. I have something to take care of, too. But I'll be back within the hour." He dug his fingernails into his palms, trying to feel something other than responsibility for her suffering. Walking out of her studio, he muttered, "It's all my fault."

Hearing his parting words, Lori jolted. Was he irrationally assuming the blame that was rightly hers to bear? She watched him walk down the hallway, her guilt intensifying. After inadvertently engineering their son's death, was she now haplessly destroying her husband's life, too?

"Promise you won't tell Vickie about this?" said Fred, eyeing the butter-basted sunny-side ups that looked cheerfully up at him from his plate. "Or Ella? *Especially* not Ella."

"Promise," said Jack, forking his hash browns to release steam.

Fred blotted the grease on his bacon with a napkin in a pro forma way. "This is one rare occasion that I'm grateful for Nora's tardiness. It was a great idea to wait for her here."

"Agreed," said Jack, peppering his soft scramble. "Although, the reason for her tardiness is unfortunate."

Pointing to the ketchup bottle, Fred said, "A meeting with hospital legal is never fortunate. I expect she'll give us the details later."

Jack passed the ketchup. "Although as soon as she gets here, we'll need to dash off to the Balabans to launch our Plan B. Boy, what a tough and busy day for her."

"Agreed," said Fred. "Say, maybe we should have her text us before she comes, so we can order ahead for her?"

"No. She already ate breakfast."

"I can't believe that's what she calls it. Waffle or fruit pocket?"

"Waffle. But she toasted it first."

Fred grinned and slathered grape jelly on his toast. "Maybe she's on to something with that diet of hers, though. I mean, I'm only allowed to eat healthy at home. But I swear, that's what's going to make me seriously ill one day. Because, food like this here? My body *craves* it, so it must contain essential nutrients I'm not getting elsewhere."

"Hmpf," said Jack. "I think you're just proving the rumor about us doctors knowing nothing about nutrition."

After popping a home fry into his mouth, Fred said, "That's no rumor."

DeeDee arrived with hot sauce and another bowl of foil-wrapped butter pads. Jack and Fred said in unison, "Thanks!"

"You're welcome," she said, lingering conspicuously.

"Everything okay?" asked Jack.

"I hope so," she said. "I wonder if I can ask you something?"

"Of course," Fred said. "What's up?"

"Well," she said, "I've been wondering about a guy who was in your ER on Friday. Is there some way I could find out how he's doing?"

Fred put down his yolky fork. "I'm sorry, DeeDee. I hear your concern. But unfortunately, we can't talk about the young man in the news who died—"

"Oh, no," said DeeDee. "Not him. My *old* friend—well, maybe not a *friend*. But a guy I used to see at work every day. Someone I bonded with." She recalled his unsettling blank stare from the stretcher. "At least, that's how it had felt to me."

"Still," said Jack, handing a paper napkin to Fred. "Doctors can share basic information about a patient's status. I no longer work at the hospital, so . . ."

"That's right," said Fred, withdrawing his pen. "Tell me your friend's name, and I'll make a general inquiry."

"Thanks," she said, pressing her hands together. "His name is Dr. William Balaban."

Highway CA-13, Southbound

Berkeley/Oakland

About a year had passed since the annual fundraiser for the Palmer Medical Research Center, where Donald Parker last saw Bill Balaban. But over that year, he had certainly authorized hefty checks to fund the center, many earmarked for Bill's lab.

Though, given his vast fortune, it was a small price to pay for what he had received in return from Bill. Besides, who knew? His generous financial support *might* spur Bill's lab into making a major medical discovery someday. Or, perhaps, it would foster the development of a lucrative healthcare innovation, like a new blockbuster drug or trendy medical device.

Still, such speculation remained just that. Because Donald Parker readily admitted knowing nothing about whatever research he was funding.

However, now that his son had died, he was intensely curious. His mind was on fire with burning questions for Bill about his work.

Driving to Bill's home now, Donald flashed back on seeing Lori minutes ago—her face swollen, her hair unkempt—falling apart inside her once-sacred workspace, now a livid canvas for her suffering.

Somebody honked, snapping him to attention, and he glanced in the rearview to see a driver giving him the finger. Then, realizing the traffic light had turned green, he drove on with the enraged driver at his bumper.

"Focus," he counseled himself.

Yes, focus on what you're going to ask Bill. Like . . . Why are you not taking my calls? You told me those injections were safe—but were they? What the hell happened to Dario?

Hospital Legal Department

Hank Thom met Nora at the Legal Department's secured main entry and escorted her to his office. Once inside, she took a seat across from his desk, and said, "I'm anxious to see the coroner's report. I wasn't able to absorb everything you read over the phone. And I appreciate you sharing it with me now—hot off the press, and on a weekend, too."

He not-so-furtively scratched his elbow and said, "Sorry, Dr. Kelly. Psoriasis. The ointment's not working."

"Ah," she said without discernible interest.

He withdrew a file from his desk drawer and said, "Yeah, this report was faxed over minutes before I called you. I'm glad I was here to receive it. I'm not usually in the office on Sundays, but I'd fallen behind on my cases because of the holiday." He handed the file to her and continued, "Anyway, I don't understand all the medical jargon in this. But I think I got the gist of it. And I figured you'd want to see for yourself. Right?"

"Yes, thanks," she said, opening the file.

"The one thing I'm certain about though?" he said. "We have a *very* interesting case, Dr. Kelly. I've worked in medicolegal for decades, and, just saying—this case is unique."

Nora put on her readers and began reading the preliminary report. At multiple junctures, she backtracked to confirm what she had just read. On occasion, she thought or said aloud, "What?" She paused twice to look up at the ceiling and gather her fledgling thoughts.

The longer she read on, the more she could hear Annie Klumtree's voice dictating the text. She heard sentences filter through Annie's inimitable accent—part Boston, part Kentucky. She heard her exclaim after making remarkable disclosures about her findings—though, of course, no exclamation marks appeared in the document. And when Nora arrived at the report's summary conclusions, she imagined the animated expression on her old friend's face while she laid them out:

Cause of death: Multiple bilateral nonthrombotic pulmonary emboli.

Preliminary pathology: The emboli are composed of multiple cell types, including bone, hair, and muscle. Genetic and genomic tests pending.

Source of pulmonary emboli: A tumor in the left arm, proximal to a fresh surgical incision in the forearm. The residual tumor is composed of cells that phenotypically match the cells composing the lung emboli. Findings are consistent with a teratoma. Genetic and genomic tests pending.

When Nora finished reading, she leaned back against her chair and said, "Wow." She placed her readers on the desk and stared at Hank.

"You look gobsmacked," he said.

She rubbed her eyes. "If I didn't know Annie Klumtree, I'd wonder if the coroner who wrote this report was a crazed science-fiction writer. But I do know her, and she is solid, the best. I just . . . never saw something like this. And, I wish I never had—poor Dario. God, I'd love to be able to discuss his case with her."

"Well," he said, "that wouldn't be a good idea, given the active lawsuit against you. But the good news is—at least, to this layman's eyes—this report seems to exonerate you in the matter of Dario Parker's death. Because these findings of cause—they couldn't have anything to do with your surgery, right? Even your incision in Dario's forearm—as this report bears out—is located distal to the primary tumor in his upper arm."

When she nodded in a distracted sort of way, he said, "I thought you'd be relieved by the report."

"Sorry. I'm just kind of shocked. It's hard to know what to make of it all."

"I get that. Most doctors are traumatized by lawsuits or the threat of them. And here you've been involved in such a high-profile one. And, well, I've been monitoring the papers and social media . . ."

She shivered, reminded of the posts she saw this morning on Jack's cell.

Smiling sympathetically, he said, "Anyhow, I hope this prelim report alleviates some of your worry. And the sooner the final report is written and released to the public, the sooner the media vitriol will stop. And it will stop, Dr. Kelly."

She knew he was right—and that she *should* feel relieved. Still, Dario died from a most unusual condition. And he died while staring at her with desperation in his face, questions in his eyes, and an urgent message he couldn't vocalize.

"Dr. Kelly?" asked Hank. "You sure you're all right?"

"I'm fine," she said, hooking her readers on her shirt's neckline.

He folded his hands on the desk and said, "Good. You got to stay strong. And, as we both know, regardless of any final report, the parents won't necessarily drop their lawsuit against you or the hospital."

"I know that," she said. "By the way, has their lawyer seen this prelim yet?"

"John Norris?" he said. "I doubt it. The ink's still drying, and it's Sunday during a holiday weekend. The police probably saw their copy, though."

"Thanks," she said, rising from her chair. "You've been very helpful."

Standing and extending his hand, he said, "If you ever want to talk more about any of this, call me, any time. Right?"

"Will do," she said. But, as kind and thoughtful as he had been, he was neither of the two people she needed to speak with. And of them, Annie Klumtree was off-limits. The other person, Dario, was dead. Nora shook his hand and, noting his desk clock, said, "Speaking of time—it looks like your clock is an hour ahead. At least, I hope that's true. Otherwise, I'm *unforgivably* late for a meeting right now."

"It's a cheap time-management strategy," he explained, escorting her to the door. "It helps me keep up with the work I'm behind on. And there's always some of that." He watched her walk down the hallway and called out, "Hope you're going to do something relaxing for the rest of the day?"

She waved in acknowledgment of his good wishes and continued toward the exit. But "something relaxing" today? No chance. Anything but that. Though already spent, she was now on her way to Betty's to pick up Jack and Fred, so they could drive together to the Balabans.

Fred's Home

"Where's Dad?" Ella asked. "At the hospital?"

"That's usually the correct answer," Vickie replied, thumbing through the Sunday paper. "But this time, he's out visiting an old colleague and his wife. People you don't know."

"Shoot," said Ella, plopping down on the couch and leaning against her mother's arm.

"Well, maybe I can help you with whatever?" said Vickie. She turned expectantly to her daughter—such a beautiful young woman, with confident clear eyes and perfect box braids. Tall and dark like her father, but, thank god, with the athletic physique from her family's side.

"You can't," said Ella. "You hate mushrooms."

Vickie put down the paper and regarded her daughter with a puzzled expression. "What in the world?"

Ella laughed. "I was just looking forward to using the chanterelles in a breakfast dish this morning. I already soaked them overnight."

"You got that right," said Vickie. "I can't help you there. I hate the texture of *fungi*. Why on earth do people eat *fungi*? Even the word—"

"Stop, Mom! People eat fungi all over the world. And chanterelles? So delicious, especially when you sauté them with butter and onions. And then you cook that inside a fluffy omelet with grated Gruyère, finishing with a sprig of parsley. Yum!"

"Ugh. I don't care what you add to them, or try to hide them under. I won't be fooled. A fungus omelet will always disgust me."

A cellphone rang, and Ella said, "That one's yours, Mom."

Picking up her phone, Vickie persisted, "You could put whipped cream and chocolate sprinkles on them, and still—" But then she flinched when noting that Lori Greene was calling. Feeling suddenly awkward, she wondered how to speak with a mother who just lost her son. And to someone who was suing the hospital that her husband ran. Why was Lori making this *personal* call? And if to cancel next month's gallery show—an understandable decision—why not just text or email about that? Or did Lori need to take things out on her and the gallery because of her association with Fred, perhaps personalizing her anger in this call?

Ella recognized the caller's name, as well as her mother's hesitancy. She tenderly suggested, "You should answer."

Vickie nodded slowly and then answered, "Lori, hello. I'm so sorry about Dario. I can't imagine what you and your husband are going through. I was planning to wait a few days, respecting your privacy, before checking in with you."

"I appreciate that," said Lori. "Yes, my life is pretty raw right now."

An uncomfortable silence ensued, during which Vickie tried to interpret Lori's tone. Finally, she said, "If there's anything I can do . . . ?"

"There is," said Lori. "That's why I'm calling. I'd like to do a second show. Even next week, if possible. I'm familiar with your gallery's annual community show."

Vickie's jaw dropped. She had just completed the extensive preparations for the gallery's holiday exhibit next week. The annual show in support of local artists was already filled to the max. She had also hung the traditional decorations and prepared the welcome table for the open house, where she would set out the butter cookies, herbal teas, and apple cider she had ordered. How could she possibly wedge in works by Lori Greene and give them due respect, and, at the same time, neither compromise the displays by local artists, nor convert the gallery into a cramped, artless mess?

"I know it's a huge ask," Lori continued. "But, please—I'm desperate."

Overhearing Lori's request, Ella shot her mother a sympathetic look and silently mouthed, "Yes."

"I understand," Vickie told Lori, knowing full well the saving powers of distraction that immersive creative work could provide a grieving artist. Still, she couldn't possibly renege on commitments to any of the local artists now.

As if reading Vickie's mind, Lori said, "I don't mean to interfere with your community show. But if there's *any* way to include me? I'm not expecting the entire gallery."

Vickie rubbed her forehead. "I'm mostly concerned that everything would appear so crowded. Your paintings wouldn't have the ideal wall space or optimal lighting they deserve."

"That's fine with me," said Lori.

"So," said Vickie, "just trying to get clarity: Would you showing with us next week mean that you intend to cancel your show in January?"

"No," Lori said. "I'll have enough pieces for both."

Swept away by Lori's insistent need to work through such a grievous time, Vickie graciously replied, "Wonderful. Yes, of course." After hearing Lori's sigh of relief, she asked, "Shall we discuss the gallery's holiday exhibit over our lunch on Wednesday?"

"Oh," said Lori, "I'm sorry. I completely forgot. But I need to cancel lunch. Especially now that I have so much work to do."

Guest Suite, Carl's Home

Piedmont, California

Winston Wang considered it odd: Why wouldn't the staff at St. Mercedes High comment on one of their star pupils? Be eager to brag about him, even? But every time he contacted someone for background information on Dario, he was stonewalled or ignored. Clearly, he needed to drive to the school and bang on some doors.

He grabbed his Warriors jacket, but went first to check on Fergie. When he found her in bed staring languidly at the ceiling, he asked, "Still not feeling so great?"

"I feel the same as before," she said. "Must've caught something in the ER the other day. It's like working inside a petri dish there."

He sat beside her on the bed and placed his palm on her forehead. "Still, no fever," he said.

"My man of science," she said.

"Well," he said, leering at her, "if it's accuracy you want, I could take an internal temperature."

"Ugh. Go away, Win."

"That's precisely what I intend to do. But I won't be more than an hour, if that's okay with you."

"Oh?" she said. "Where are you going?"

He hesitated to say, knowing that his coverage of Dario's story had been upsetting her and her friend Nora. But he was up against a hard deadline to submit a follow-up piece tonight. And tomorrow was already jam-packed with events that he would be expected to cover: most notably, the second press conference with the parents and their lawyer; and, possibly, the public release of the coroner's preliminary findings.

"You're hesitating," she said, placing a hand on her abdomen. "So, it must involve Dario's case."

He winced. "I'm trying to put together a human-interest story about him."

"But you hate writing those—'puff pieces,' as you call them."

"Yeah, but we're between real-news events. Nothing is happening until tomorrow. And we want to keep the story's momentum going."

"Well, a lot of people—including me—find 'human interest' stories *interesting*. And just as newsworthy as your 'real news.' Sometimes, more so."

"I'm not gonna argue with you. Besides, I gotta admit, I'm getting a little interested myself. It's like the kid was . . . *who*, actually? All we know about him comes from remarks by his parents or their lawyer. But if Dario is or *was* so extraordinary, why do they refuse to talk with me about him? And why do the teaching and coaching staffs at his high school ignore all my calls and emails? You'd think any of them would welcome the opportunity to pay tribute to Dario and his legacy."

Fergie gasped and said, "No, Win! Please don't tell me you're off to hound Dario's grieving parents? Tell me you're not going to their home!"

"Calm down! I'm not. I'm going to his high school."

"On a Sunday?"

"It's a long shot. But there's a football game there today, and I'm hoping to find faculty who knew him."

"Well, good luck with that," she said. "I'm going to take a nap."

"And good luck with *that*," he said, rising from the bed. "But it should be easier with Carl gone on vacation now. It's certainly been quieter."

"Still," she said, "I can't wait to find a place of our own. He's been generous, letting us stay in his guest suite. But there's so little privacy when he's around."

"Copy that," he said. "And I think we can begin looking for a place. Our finances are in decent shape now."

"We'd be giving up the free rent here," she said.

"And the in-house obstetrician," he added. "You know, in case we ever needed one."

"Time for you to go," she said, rolling onto her side.

Hospital Employee Parking Lot

For a Sunday, the employee parking lot was unusually packed. Nora wandered around it, pressing her key fob, listening for a beep to locate her Prius within this interminable metal sea. Finally, she heard it—or so she thought. But then she spotted Carrie and realized the beep was emanating from her white Mini Cooper.

"Drat," Nora complained, anxious about having to interact with Carrie and risking additional delay in meeting up with Fred and Jack. So, she hid behind a cement pillar and waited for her friend to drive away.

Instead, she heard, "Dr. Kelly!"—and in a voice belonging to someone else. Still, that alerted Carrie to her presence, and, seconds later, she and Lizbeth were approaching.

Nora stepped out from behind the pillar with feigned enthusiasm. "Lizbeth," she said, "you must be getting off shift!" Then, to Carrie, she said, "And you're here because . . . ?"

Lizbeth answered, "Yes, I'm heading home now. But I saw you and wondered if you could tell me how Fergie's doing. She didn't come into work today, and I didn't want to bother her at home."

Nora's face flushed. She had been so preoccupied with Dario's case and the Balabans' predicament—and now hugely distracted by the coroner's report—that she had forgotten to check in with Fergie. "I feel terrible," she replied. "I meant to call her this morning, but my life jumped the tracks."

"Wait," said Carrie. "Is Fergie sick?"

But when Nora pivoted to her, she froze to see the identical twin of her deceased best friend staring back with hauntingly familiar intensity and concern.

Lizbeth, having known Lydia from her training years at the hospital, intuited the reason behind Nora's freeze-up and offered to Carrie: "Fergie may have caught some GI bug at work the other day. And, well, things in the ER have also been stressful."

Nora smiled appreciatively at Lizbeth while happening to notice the floral scarf around her neck. "How gorgeous," she remarked. "Such beautiful blue roses. I saw one exactly like it recently."

"Probably in the ER," said Lizbeth. "Mrs. Balaban left it in the wastebasket." She flipped the scarf over to reveal its red, purple, and beige stains. "I fished it out, and she told me to keep it because she had plenty of others at home."

"Well, if I were you, I'd do a heme test on that scarf," said Carrie. "Because it looks like evidence from a crime scene."

Lizbeth laughed and said, "Will do." Then she waved goodbye and walked away.

Carrie squinted at Nora and said, "So, you're still seeing me as Lydia's ghost?"

"No. Yes. I mean, yes, sometimes, but only with certain facial expressions. I'm sorry, Carrie."

"Don't be," Carrie said, waving a hand. "I understand. Besides, you're going to have loads of time to work on that. Because—in answer to your earlier question—*I'm* here to move a few things into my new office."

Nora's face lit up. "So, you're taking the job?"

"I am," said Carrie, smiling back. "You're looking at the hospital's new director of hospice and palliative care. I start employee orientation tomorrow."

St. Mercedes High School

Upper Rockridge District, Oakland

Within minutes of leaving Fergie's side, Winston arrived at St. Mercedes High. He drove their red Subaru along the tree-lined entry, bordered by stone retaining walls through which vibrant green ivy poked. He opened the car window and listened to his tires crunch along the pebble-strewn path, and he breathed in the sweet scent of eucalyptus that wafted from surrounding tree lines. It was all so pleasant, so pretty, so neat and clean—so unlike the entryway to his old alma mater. He couldn't help but wonder how his so-called education might have differed had he been able to feel safe and welcome at school. What would it have been like to look forward to classes, instead of always having to look behind his back?

Finally, he came to an ornate metal gate that looked like a museum sculpture. A security guard wearing a matching blue suit and necktie greeted him: "Sir?"

"I'm here for the game," Winston said. "Hope I'm not too late."

After scrutinizing Winston's face and inputting the Subaru's license plate into his tablet, the guard returned, "Sorry, sir. But our system doesn't recognize you."

"Oh, right," said Winston, thinking quickly to produce his press credential. "I'm with the *Oakland Register.*"

The guard examined the press pass and requested Winston's driver's license to confirm his identity. After entering that information into the records, he returned the cards to Winston and said, "Good to go now." Then he winked and added, "But no matter what, just be sure to report that our team won."

"Good one," said Winston, giving a salute.

The automated gate opened and Winston drove through, following signage to the football stadium. When he pulled into its parking lot, he imagined his little Subaru lamenting: "Everyone here but me is a luxury car."

He entered the stadium and headed for the bleachers, hoping to obtain an overview of the stands. And though he didn't spot a designated faculty section, he noticed an entrance to an adjacent building that had been marked for public restroom access. Hoping it might also provide access to staff offices or a faculty lounge, he chose to investigate.

But when he arrived at the entrance, he was forced to step aside for two young men who were barreling out. Each held a tennis racket and wore white designer sportswear. Although surmising they were too young to be faculty, he happily expected them to be students on the tennis team, who must have known Dario. He called out after them, "Excuse me? Are you students here?"

They pivoted to him, each returning an inquisitorial gaze. The player wearing Lacoste asked, "What's it to you?"

Winston could hear Fergie reprimanding him for "hounding" students at Dario's school—if even by this pure happenstance. But he would offer them anonymity, and protect them from making injudicious statements that they—or their parents—might later regret. He flashed his press card and said, "I'm an investigative reporter with the *Oakland Register*. I'd like to ask a few questions about Dario Parker, assuming you were teammates?"

The students glanced at each other in silent consultation, and struggled to suppress their laughter.

"What's so funny?" said Winston, disturbed by their insensitive response.

"Nothing," said the player in Uniqlo attire. "But you're right. You are 'assuming.'"

Winston's brow knotted. "Meaning what? That Dario wasn't a real mate? That you guys didn't get along?"

"Well," said Lacoste, "you're right again, and on both counts."

Uniqlo tapped his friend's shoulder and said, "Look at the confused reporter. Should we help him out?"

After nodding their mutual agreement, Lacoste locked eyes with Winston and said, "We didn't 'get along' because there was no 'along' to get on with Dario. And, we weren't 'real mates'—I'm speaking literally here."

Uniqlo added, "But that's all we have to say to you about Dario." Then they turned and walked away, each holding up a hand to deflect Winston's repeated plea for further conversation.

Watching the duo depart, Winston said aloud, "What the hell were they talking about?" Or, he thought, *not* talking about? Regardless, his chance encounter with them provided no good copy for his human-interest story on Dario. So, he returned to his original plan and entered the school building.

But as soon as he stepped inside, he froze. He saw an expansive gleaming lobby beyond the designated restroom area. Glass-and-brass display cabinets covered the walls, showcasing the school's sports programs.

He beelined to the gilded lobby and began searching the shelves. A considerable amount of display space had been dedicated to the school's football and baseball programs. The next sectionals featured basketball trophies and swim-team tributes, and the adjacent one contained soccer, archery, and track awards. Finally, he arrived at the tennis sectional, where, surely, he would find tributes to Dario that would interest the *Register*'s readers. He carefully searched its shelves. Then he carefully searched them again. But all he could find was Dario's name listed on the current team's roster.

Bill and Ellie's Home

"Arrived!" the GPS unit gleefully announced.

Donald Parker pulled his black Tesla to the curb and turned off the ignition. He looked through the windshield at Bill Balaban's house: elegant, in a mid-century modernist way, and surrounded by a manicured lawn, populated with Meyer lemon trees and English lavender. He tried one more time to phone Bill, but again received no answer.

He tugged on his mustache, reviewing the questions he intended to ask Bill, and preparing himself for answers he may regret. Their meeting was bound to be tense, given Bill's avoidant behavior. Still, he had to know if he and Bill may have done anything to contribute to Dario's death. Lori also needed that truth, and to hear it from him.

But as he was about to exit his car, he saw Bill's front door open. A stocky man in casual dress, including a pulled-down baseball cap and sneakers, hurried out. Then the door closed, and the man entered a green Honda Civic and drove away.

"What the hell?" Donald muttered, certain now that someone was home at the Balabans. He flung open his car door and strode up to the house. He knocked on Bill's front door and and waited. Then he rang the bell and waited some more.

"Open up!" he shouted, pounding the door.

Finally, in resignation, he stood motionless on the porch, wondering what to do. But in the quietude of that moment, he heard music emanating from the Balabans' house. He pressed his ear against the door—the classical music station was playing inside..

~ ~ ~

Ellie cranked up the volume on the classical station that was playing in the living room. Then she returned to the bedroom, closed the door behind her, and stared coldly at Bill. She was determined that their argument would remain in the bedroom, beyond the earshot of their intrusive neighbors with their armies of private security guards.

"But I told Owen nothing new," Bill insisted. "He'd already read my medical record in the ER."

She was not appeased. "Yet *another* important detail you forgot to share with me!"

"But I didn't know about that until he told me just minutes ago," he said.

She tossed a hairbrush at him, barely missing his head. "Then you should have consulted with me at the time. The moment he informed you, you should have brought me into the conversation! I was here, in the bedroom, a stone's throw away."

He sat at the edge of their bed, fantasizing about throwing that stone at her.

"Your subordinate wields undue influence over you!" she continued. "That bullying, narcissistic Owen Landry is even blackmailing you now. He's gone rogue on us, and he continues to upset our plans." She approached her husband with her hands held out in choke-hold form, muttering, "I could strangle you!"

He closed his eyes and internally chanted, *Grow a spine!*

"I'm talking to you, Bill!"

When he opened his eyes, he didn't like what he saw. He fleetingly considered sharing his observation with her: that she was projecting her own shadow self onto Owen Landry. Instead, he said, "No, you're *shouting* at me."

She raised her voice even louder and said, "No—*this* is me shouting!"

He knew the drill from this point on, being overly familiar with the worn script that always followed. She would begin by chastising him for his weakness in times of crises. She would bemoan the decades of life she sacrificed to orchestrate their social and personal affairs, all the while he pursued his career and academic passions. After that, she would criticize him for declining the more lucrative jobs that he'd been offered over the years—especially in New York, where, surely, she would have enjoyed abundant prospects for stage work. Finally, she would conclude this First Act of her epic grievance with: "You *owe* me, Bill."

At this juncture, he would be expected to agree, and to acknowledge her grave disappointments while convincingly demonstrating empathy. Here, though, he always held back—thinking, but never saying, how she had benefited handsomely from his labor, regaling herself in wealth and prestige; thinking, but never saying, that he had provided her with a comfortable lifestyle that should have enabled her to pursue any dream.

But looking into Ellie's fiery eyes now, and being a practical man, he merely delivered his usual line: "Yes, I owe you."

She cocked her head and regarded him suspiciously. Though he purportedly agreed, his tone *sounded* contrarian. Still, she proceeded to the Second Act of the routine, insisting that she could have, should have, would have become a renowned stage actor had she not been saddled with the arduous business of their married life. But, being the good wife, she had selflessly stepped aside to allow his career to take center stage. Finally, as expected, she ended this act with: "How was I ever going to shine in the shadow of your career?"

Each time she voiced this refrain, he would answer, "You couldn't." But his reason for saying that differed from hers: Because she had no innate capacity to shine—not under the brightest klieg lights, not under a thousand radiant suns. He had seen all her B-list movies, and endured all her C-list musicals. He had miraculously survived overlong hours of her acting on local stages. He had watched reruns of her daytime soap opera and game show appearances on far too many occasions. And, at best, a small handful of her performances were passable. But never did she shine. Not once.

"Well?" she persisted, with a snap of her fingers.

"Oh, I agree," he said, a corner of his mouth rising. "You never had a chance to shine."

She looked askance at him. His response provided faint satisfaction. Needing to exercise her capacity to affect him, she restoked their earlier argument: "We were talking about you and Owen Landry, and what you should have done—"

"I think we're better off just obtaining his buy-in. He asked for little in exchange for his silence."

"Oh? Handing your lab over to him is 'little'? Ensuring that he becomes its director is nothing?"

"In the scheme of things, it's a small price to pay."

"You don't get the point," she said. "The problem is that he so easily extorted that from you. And why? Because he knows you're weak. He sees he has the upper hand, so, yet again, he needn't follow our plan. He didn't show up for the surgery. Then he barged into our home and threatened to upend our plans by exposing them. You should have included me in the negotiations, Bill!"

He held his tongue and headed for the door.

"To think," she said, "of all the time I've wasted trying to solve problems that you continue to reinvent behind my back." She picked up a shoe and flung it at him, hitting his back.

With that, Bill turned to her and yelled "Stop!" so loudly that it startled them both. And he, furious and emboldened, stepped up to her with a raised fist.

~ ~ ~

Nora, Fred, and Jack rounded the corner in her Prius, heading to the Balabans' house. During their short drive from Betty's, Jack had gathered food wrappers and parking-meter receipts from the car mats and placed them inside the clamshell container he found under the passenger seat.

Fred, stretched out in the back, took a prophylactic dose of his inhaler to prepare for their Plan B intervention.

But when they drove onto the Balabans' street, Nora startled and inadvertently tapped the brakes. Jack lunged forward, grabbed the dashboard, and exclaimed, "What?" Then she pulled to the curb a few houses away and pointed to a man who was pounding furiously on the Balabans' door.

Fred looked through his window and said, "Oh, hell. Yeah, that's him."

Jack looked curiously at his friends and asked, "Will someone clue me in?"

"Shh!" said Fred as the man turned from the doorway and descended the front steps. "Don't draw his attention."

After the man got into a black Tesla and drove away, Nora explained, "That was Donald Parker—Dario's father."

Jack winced. "Sorry, Nora. He's probably the last person you needed to see right now."

Fred tapped her seatback and asked, "But what the hell is he doing *here?*"

"I don't know," she replied. "But I don't like it."

"Agreed," said Fred. "It's fishy as all hell that he's visiting Bill. Or, trying to, at least."

"But you've seen them together before, right?" asked Jack.

She shrugged and said, "I don't think so."

"Yeah, remember?" he persisted. "In the ER, on Friday. While Bill was there, didn't you also have that brutal 'conversation' with Dario's father in the waiting room?"

"Well, yes. But I didn't see the two of them together."

"Still," said Fred, "I agree—it's curious. I mean, what are the odds of them intersecting twice, in such a short and difficult time? And why do you think Donald Parker is furious *this* time?"

Nora looked away, trying to fend off repeated traumatization by the sting of Donald Parker's fury. Her memory of being blamed for Dario's death—immortalized now on the internet—kept pushing on her awareness, close to her panic button.

Hoping to alleviate some tension, Fred engaged Nora in the rearview and told her, "This is the second time in my entire *life* that I'm grateful for your legendary tardiness. Because imagine how much worse it could've been if we *had* been on time and were already inside with the Balabans when Donald Parker barged in."

"Not really," she said, emerging from her inwardness. "Because we just saw the Balabans refuse to let Donald Parker in. So, if we had been inside, he wouldn't have been able to 'barge in' on us."

"Ooo-kay," said Jack, thrumming his fingers on the dashboard.

"Also," she said, "*we* may not have been inside for him to barge in on, if the Balabans had also refused to let us in earlier."

Jack hunched his shoulders and said, "Sure. And another possible scenario? Maybe the Balabans simply aren't home to answer the door for *anyone*."

Nora shook her head and pointed to their white Audi in the driveway. "That's unlikely, given that their car is here." She tapped a finger on the steering wheel and continued, "So, are they exclusively avoiding Donald Parker? Maybe over something related to his very evident rage? Or . . . ?" She hurriedly unsnapped her seat belt, and, with a worried expression on her face, said, "Or are the Balabans *incapable* of answering the door? Is our domestic abuse intervention too late?"

"Oh, damn," said Jack, undoing his seat belt and following Nora out of the car with Fred. Then they stood on the Balabans' porch, taking turns knocking on the door and ringing the bell.

"Definitely fishy," said Fred.

"Hold up, everyone," said Jack, placing an ear to the door. "The radio's on. They're playing KDFC even louder than I do at home. Maybe they don't hear us knocking?"

Nora massaged her forehead and said, "Let's see what happens when we phone them simultaneously. Fred, you call Bill? And Jack, you have Ellie's number?" They nodded and called both numbers, but each call went straight to voicemail.

"What do we do now?" asked Fred.

"Well," said Nora, scanning the porch and front yard. "Maybe there's a hidden key out here?"

They proceeded to search the premises. Nora picked up decorative landscaping rocks and shook them for metallic clacking. Jack swept his fingers along the door's casing, only to collect a splinter. When Fred looked under the flower pots, all he found were sow bugs and earwigs.

"What next, Nancy Drew?" said Fred, wiping his hands on his coat. "Seems like I always get dirty when I'm on some mission with you."

"I've told you before," said Nora. "It's Inspector Jane Tennison, please."

He returned an eyeroll, which she ignored.

"Okay," said Jack. "What now, Inspector?"

"Well," she said, recalling the home's layout from eons ago. "There's a door off the back deck, remember?" She gestured for them to follow, then descended the porch steps and walked along the side of the house toward the back. Along the way, they heard operatic music intensify, and Jack said to Fred: "Sounds like Renée Fleming. Mozart, I believe. Yes, *Don Giovanni*—the live recording." When Fred merely shook his head, Jack added, "You really should expand your music horizons beyond Carrie Underwood and Patsy Cline."

But their banter ended abruptly when they saw Nora a few feet ahead, standing rigid by a window, with a fearful look on her face. And when they joined her there and looked inside, they saw Bill's trembling fist poised to hit Ellie.

Ellie startled when she noticed the gawking trio through the window, but she tried not to flinch. Three more intruders she had to deal with today? Urgently summoning her wits, she told Bill, "Do *not* look behind you. I mean it."

Wrestling with his constitutional impulse to defy her, he almost turned to look. But her powerful threatening glare disabled his urge. And when he began to withdraw his fist from the toxic space between them, she whispered, "Hit me."

Though ashamed to admit it, that was precisely what he fantasized doing. But before he could decide a response, Ellie clasped her hands around his fist and yanked it toward her face, acting as though she were struggling to hold it at bay. Then, suddenly, she released his fist and jerked her head to one side. Bill watched her cover her face with a hand and dash out of the bedroom.

Loud pounding on the window made Bill turn toward it now. He saw Nora, Fred, and Jack outside, staring incredulously at him. How long had they been there? What had they seen? He ran out of the room in search of Ellie and an explanation. But he didn't have to go far; she was standing before the mirror in their bathroom, hastily applying makeup. She glowered at him and said, "I swear to god, if you so much as say one *word* to them!"

Against insistent knocking on the back door, Bill said, "They saw us, Ellie! What are you doing? What the hell's going on?"

She turned from the mirror to him—and though her face was plasticized under makeup, it vibrated with rage. "So, *now* you want to hear *my* plan? You expect *me* to figure a way out of this snowballing disaster we're in?"

"Ellie, those three aren't going to leave us alone. This is no time to—"

"You created this mess, Bill. And you consistently lied to me and kept secrets about it. You unilaterally changed *our* plan more than once. You bent over for Owen Landry." She tilted her head and said, "So, I believe we have a new understanding—I'm taking control of the ship now?"

He held her steely gaze and, finally, nodded.

"Good," she said. "So, I'm telling you, in no uncertain terms, the only thing you need to do is to keep your mouth shut." When she aggressively stepped up to him, he falteringly stepped back. She pressed her finger into his chest with each admonishing word: "Not. One. Word. Bill."

In a daze, he walked to the living room and turned off the radio, abandoning Renée Fleming in an improbable high note. Now all he heard was the commotion at the back door, and Ellie trying to reassure everyone that she was fine. He heard Nora repeat, "But I saw you two." He heard Fred insistently ask, "Where's Bill?" He heard the floorboards sound when Jack headed to the bedroom, despite Ellie's protestation. And, within the minute, his three old students surrounded him. Ellie remained in the hallway behind them, pressing a stiff finger to her lips to caution him.

"Hey," said Jack, placing a steadying hand on Bill's shoulder. "Why don't we all sit down and talk?"

Bill complacently lowered himself onto the couch, all the while his mind imploded. This intrusion was piling on new uncertainties, on the heels of being thrown by Ellie, ambushed by Owen, and surprised by Dario's death.

Fred said, "We're here to help you and Ellie. And this time, we won't abandon you."

While taking a seat, Nora glanced back at Ellie, wondering whether she was going to be amenable to any intervention—even after their inadvertent witness of Bill's violence. And how heartbreaking to see her face so heavily—and carelessly—layered with makeup. *How desperate she is to conceal the abuse.*

Jack invited Ellie to come sit with everyone, but she only shook her head. Assuming that she feared being near Bill, he leaned back against the couch and into a new conviction: That his participation in this intervention was the right thing to do, after all—in support of the Balabans and his two close friends.

After clearing his throat, Fred began, "All right now, Bill. How are you feeling?"

Bill returned a blank expression, though he was bristling against Ellie's emasculating control. Still, his mind was chasing that same question: *How am I feeling?* Everything was changing so fast and unpredictably, it was difficult to get a grasp. But then, when he glanced back at Ellie, he knew exactly how he felt: A dark internal spring of venomous energy broke open and began surging through him.

Fred continued, "I'm going to personally see to it that we get you the best neurologist. I'm calling an old colleague at UCSF, first thing in the morning."

"And," said Nora, "we'll get you and Ellie the help you need in order to feel safe and comfortable."

Now Ellie entered from the hallway and sat in the armchair across from Bill. She took his hand and addressed the room: "We are so grateful for your support. Truly grateful. But please understand—Bill and I have been dealing with his . . . his *condition* for a long while. As I informed you in the ER, he's been seeing a private neurologist, so we know the score." She tented her brow while staring intently at her husband and continued, "We have accepted the fact of his worsening dementia, and we no longer fight against that reality. Isn't that right, darling?"

Absent a response from him, she smiled wearily at the group and said, "So, you see. We're simply trying to live our best lives, one day at a time—for whatever time remains for us."

Up close to her, Jack again noted her exuberant makeup and its successful concealment of the black eye that he still couldn't see. Having witnessed Bill hitting her minutes ago, he wondered if it was also covering additional injuries. *How dreadful*, he thought, *that she's stuck in this awful predicament*. With a sad smile, he said, "But the elephant in the room—we need to name it. The relationship between you and Bill has become dangerous, placing each of you at risk—"

"Please, stop!" said Ellie with startling ferocity. Then she looked searchingly up to the ceiling, and her eyes rimmed.

"I'm sorry," said Jack. "I didn't mean to upset you."

She dismissively waved a hand and said, "Bill and I . . . We're fine, thank you all. But we have a clear understanding between us—that neither of us will be leaving this house. No matter what." She turned her tear-stained face to Bill and whispered, "Until death do us part, right, my love?"

Nora's heart sank precipitously, heavy with repeated witness of the consequences from domestic violence, that she'd seen too often in the ER. All the shattered bones and teeth, the mangled faces, the ruptured eardrums and spleens, the rapes, and the forever-broken human spirits. And, she thought, unlike Bill and Ellie, so many of the victims didn't possess the resources to escape. She looked pointedly at Ellie and said, "We can see how much you love each other. Still, we can't just leave you here like this."

Ellie shook her head vigorously. "Bill and I planned for this eventuality. We expected the hardship. And we fully accept it now."

"But we know what we just saw through your bedroom window," said Fred. "And we can't un-see that, or the potential for someone getting seriously hurt."

"We saw how frightened you looked," added Jack. "We saw Bill's fist in your face."

Ellie tenderly stroked Bill's cheek and said, "We made promises to each other, didn't we?"

Bill scanned the room, registering all the somber expressions. Then he laughed nervously and said, "Who are you all?"

The Parker-Greene Estate

Donald Parker paused before entering his home, taking a moment to shed enough rage so as not to further disturb his wife. He had already inflicted too much harm.

He hung his coat on the entryway hall tree and walked to the living room. How achingly empty it was, without Dario on the sofa playing video games, without Lori reading in the window seat.

Heading to the dining area, he prayed to find Lori there and out of her studio, or evidence that she had eaten something. Instead, what he saw made him gasp—the dining room walls had been stripped of her paintings. Only brass picture hooks and the occasional mounting screw showed. And the hardwood floors were smeared with footprints, rendered in red, blue, yellow, and green paint.

He imagined the worst. Fearing that she had resorted to self-destructive impulses, he hurried through the hallway and into her studio. But she acted as though she didn't notice him. He waited in the doorway, watching her rip sheets of brown wrapping paper from a voluminous roll. The paintings she had removed from the dining area were stacked on her workbench, ostensibly waiting to be wrapped. Her feet were caked with the acrylics and oils she had trekked across the hallway and dining room floors.

"I could use your help," she finally said.

"But . . . but what are you doing?" he asked.

"Preparing for an exhibition," she answered.

"But your show isn't until January. And these pictures are from our dining room."

"I've added another show. Next week."

He squeezed his temples. "But the pieces from our *home*? You're intending to exhibit our personal collection? *Sell* them even?"

"Yes. And you could help by bringing me the landscape over the fireplace."

"Why, Lori?"

"It's too heavy for me to take down."

He stared at her, dumbfounded. He could lend his help as she requested, but what exactly was he helping her to do? To take leave of her senses in hopes of numbing herself to her grief? To immerse herself in art as a means of coping? Or was she just dismantling their home, so intolerable now, and removing visual memory of her life spent here with Dario?

The questions overawed him and rendered him incapable of thinking. All he knew with the next moment's arrival was that he was walking to the living room to take down the moody landscape painting that had hung above their fireplace since their wedding. With each step he took at his wife's bidding, his mind progressively emptied while his black Ferragamos collected additional paint.

Jack's Home

Jack cleared Nora's plate from his dining table after they finished Zofia's leftover lasagna. He told her, "See? Another reminder that you're not allergic to real food."

"Funny-*not*," Nora said, holding out her glass for another pour of merlot. "But it was delicious. Please thank Zofia in the morning."

"I will," he said, lifting his pinot to the light to analyze its legs. "Frankly, I wasn't confident there'd be leftovers, when I invited you to stop by. Luis can consume ten times his weight in food."

"What would you have served instead?"

"I had a backup plan. Pizza from Delmonico's—no peppers or onions for you."

"Well, this was much better. Though it wouldn't have mattered. Everything goes well with wine. It's just nice to have some quiet downtime with you."

"Yeah," he said. "You've had a day and a half today! And that visit with the Balabans lasted so long, the three of us didn't get a chance to talk about the coroner's report or your discussion with legal. Too bad Fred had to rush home afterwards."

"It's the Sunday family supper tradition," she said. "He and Vickie and the kids are pretty religious about it."

"Well, Fred will just have to catch up later. And I've got to tip my hat to him. He was right to strong-arm us about the Balabans. I didn't quite agree with him until we were at their house today, front row and center to their predicament."

"And," she said, "we even got them to agree with Plan B. Fred is hooking Bill up with a neurologist at UCSF tomorrow, and Ellie's going to consult with the geriatric case manager that Lola from social services had recommended."

After clinking their glasses together, Jack said, "And that hospice consultation you suggested? A Hail Mary pass, for sure—but inspired, if you ask me."

"We'll see," said Nora. "I'm nervous about asking Carrie for it. And I think the Balabans only agreed to our suggestions because they wanted us out of their house."

"Still," he said, relaxing back into his chair, "inspired, my friend. So, tell me what happened at legal today. And how are you thinking about the teratoma that Annie Klumtree found at autopsy? Could she be wrong? I mean, it's so hard to believe. You should've seen your face this morning, while hearing about it over the phone!"

Nora made a motion with her hands to suggest her head was exploding. "First off, since Annie was the medical examiner, I completely trust the preliminary report: There *was* a teratoma in Dario's arm, and it *was* the source of his fatal pulmonary emboli. The confirmatory stains and genetic analyses are pending, of course. But the cell phenotypes are identical in the teratoma and the emboli."

He repeated her head-exploding gesture. "It's just such a rare tumor in adults, let alone one to embolize to the lungs. And to originate in an arm?" He took her hand in his and said, "I know how upsetting this whole saga has been for you. But you must see now that Annie's prelim proves your innocence in Dario's death. Not that you and I needed that confirmation. But the report will go far in silencing the media witch trials."

When she merely stared into her wineglass, he asked, "So, why the frown?"

She exhaled sharply and said, "Because I don't think I'm seeing the whole picture of Dario's death. It's like I'm watching a movie about it, but suddenly catapulted to the end, where I learn he has a teratoma. It's unsatisfying—like someone edited out critical scenes that would've made his story complete. Something is missing."

"I don't know," he said. "I think you have an end-of-story autopsy report on a very unlucky kid who had a teratoma."

She shook her head. "But, like you said—a *teratoma*, in an *arm?* In a healthy *male* teenager, with no remarkable personal or family medical history? How and why—?"

"What's a teratoma?" asked Luis.

Nora and Jack looked toward the kitchen, where Luis stood in the doorway, wearing his blue-striped pajamas.

"How long have you been standing there?" said Jack. "And why aren't you in bed?"

"I smelled lasagna," said Luis. "It made me hungry. So, I wanted to get something to eat." He walked up to Nora and hugged her.

"Hey," said Jack, "how about I make you a sandwich, and you can take it back to bed. Nora and I need to talk."

Luis nodded, and Jack headed to the kitchen. Then Luis sat next to Nora and asked again, "What's a teratoma?"

"Yikes," said Nora. "Why don't we talk about something more pleasant?"

"Is a teratoma not pleasant? But you were both talking about it."

"Well, it's a medical thing. And not something a person wants."

"Huh," he said. "Like a heart attack? Or cancer? Me and Zofia watched a movie last night, and the prima donna had *both* of them. And she got a bad infection, too. But at the end, she died in a car accident."

Nora knew Luis was all too familiar with real-life death. Still, his blunt plot summary unnerved her a little. "It sounds like a sad movie to watch, Luis."

"It was. Zofia cried. But I told her not to be sad, because it was only a movie. And I said I knew the prima donna was alive in real life. That helped her, I think."

"I bet it did," said Nora, smiling. "That was very sweet of you."

"I still want to know what a teratoma is."

"Double yikes," said Nora, failing to dodge his question. Then, deciding he might be ready to understand the basics of it, she asked, "Well, do you know what cells are?"

"Yes. They're the building blocks of tissue. Like you got liver cells in your liver. And muscle cells in your muscles."

"That's right. So, sometimes a cell misbehaves, and it multiplies and grows way too fast. When that happens, the cells build up and form a mass, and we call that mass a 'tumor.' If it's a tumor that can hurt someone or spread in their body, we say it's a *malignant* tumor, and we call that cancer. But if the tumor doesn't do those bad things, and it's basically minding its own business, we say it's a *benign* tumor."

Luis' forehead creased. "The prima donna in the movie had brain cancer. So, that's because a cell in her brain misbehaved, and it grew into a tumor . . . and that tumor was a cancer because it hurt her?"

Nora nodded, pleased that he had grasped the basic premise. Still, she wondered about the movie plot. *Did its writers attribute the fatal car crash to the prima donna's brain tumor—a neurological complication, perhaps a seizure? And what kind of infection did she have? Did it cause a brain abscess that was misdiagnosed as a brain tumor and—?*

"Dr. Nora?" said Luis.

"Sorry," she said. "I was just thinking."

He scratched his ear; the concept of a brain tumor forming from misbehaving brain cells, or a liver cancer forming from misbehaving liver cells, seemed straightforward. But, a "teratoma"? He asked, "So, you're saying a teratoma is a tumor?" After she nodded, he asked, "But what kind of cells does a teratoma come from?"

"Ah," said Nora. "That's a good question. Because a teratoma isn't like a regular tumor that's made up of only one type of naughty cell. A teratoma is made from *several* different types—usually a mix of cells that can create muscle, bone, and skin tissue."

Luis' jaw dropped.

"Oh, no!" she said, worried that she had frightened him. "Maybe we should've talked about something more pleasant after all."

"No, please!" he said. "This is interesting. But how can that happen?"

"Well," she hesitated, wondering why Jack was taking so long to make a sandwich. "The original misbehaving cell in that case is what we call a 'germ cell.'"

"Like an infection?"

"No. Not 'germ' like infection. 'Germ' also means 'seed' or 'sprout.' And it comes from the Latin word *germen*." She watched him eagerly absorb the new vocabulary words. "So," she continued, "a germ cell is a type of human cell that . . . well, it can sprout reproductive cells—"

"Like egg cells and sperm cells?"

Now Nora's jaw dropped. "Have you graduated from college while I wasn't looking?"

He laughed and said, "We learned about the cycle of life between a mom and a dad and a baby. The egg and the sperm come together and make an embryo that grows into a baby."

"Ah," she said, glancing toward the kitchen, listening for Jack.

"You know about that, right?" he asked.

"Yes . . . I do, Luis. Thanks."

"So," he said, "the whole embryo starts out as *one* cell that doubles and doubles, again and again, and grows big. Those first cells are like seeds, too, right? Because they have to sprout everything that makes up an entire baby in the end."

"That's right," she said. "And because those cells have the potential to create multiple different ones, we call them 'multi-potent' cells. Scientists are trying to use them to treat sick people who need healthy tissues that those cells can sprout."

"I don't get it," he said. "How do you get those cells out of an embryo to treat somebody?"

Stalling for time, Nora yawned theatrically and said, "Do you think Jack needs help with that sandwich?"

Luis shook his head. "He makes them a lot."

"Well, this must be a very elaborate sandwich."

"But you still didn't tell me about your patient. Or how scientists get germ cells."

Nora tapped her fingers on the table, unable to disengage from his intensely curious stare. "Okay," she finally said. "So, those tiny germ cells are very special cells, right? They have so much work to do to create *all* the different cells, for *all* the different tissues and *all* the body organs in a baby. So, imagine if one of *them* misbehaved and grew out of control. That could form a tumor made up of different tissues."

Luis' mouth formed an O. "The tumor is full of different cells! *That's* a teratoma?"

She nodded. "And that's why, in adults, at least, teratomas usually develop in—" She stopped herself from adding, *in a woman's ovary or a man's testicle, where germ cells reside.* Even considering his precocious nature, she felt uncomfortable conducting that part of the discussion with him.

"In an arm?" he asked. "Because I heard you say that about your patient."

"Well, no," she said, grabbing her empty wineglass. "An arm is an unusual location for one, because germ cells don't normally exist there in the first place. And adult teratomas are rare in general." She recalled having diagnosed only two during her entire career—both in women, originating in their ovaries, and each teratoma containing hair, muscle, and bone tissue.

"Then," said Luis, "where do teratomas usually come from?"

Nora smiled tightly and said, "You know who's an expert on tumors? An *oncologist.* And, what luck! I'm going to call on one now." She patted Luis' head and shouted out, "Jack?"

Part Five

Monday, December 2

Nora's Home

NORA IMAGINED DONNING a trench coat and dark glasses before heading outdoors to retrieve her morning paper from the driveway. Media attention had turned gruesome, and her bandwidth for accommodating additional notoriety had narrowed to a wisp. Today, in an act of self-preservation, she decided to avoid the internet entirely.

After setting up the coffee and dropping a frozen pancake into the toaster, she boldly ventured out to the neighborhood public square, praying she would not be seen. But she stopped at the doorway—the *Oakland Register* was waiting on her welcome mat, and two pink camellias were tucked behind its red rubber band. The surprising act of kindness made her smile, even knowing that the Pink Perfection *Camellia japonicas* had originated in her garden.

She returned to the kitchen and placed the flowers in a water glass. Privately, she thanked Reggie—the paper's carrier, now in his fifties, who had been delivering the *Register* for decades—for his supportive gesture.

When she sat down with her breakfast, Bix jumped onto the table and settled near her plate. After sniffing the pancake with evident disapproval, he swatted her with a soft paw and fled. "Fine," she called out after him, "more for me." Then she took a deep breath and opened the paper.

As she expected, the front page featured an article written by Winston about Dario. Its headline and subhead respectively read, "CEO's Dead Son Remembered" and "Inquiry into Hospital Death Ongoing." That was enough to turn her stomach, but not a full 360 degrees.

She proceeded to read the article with anticipatory dread. But, she happily discovered, her dread proved unwarranted. Winston's piece was devoid of controversy and heat, even bordering on bland. The occasional sentence that hinted at a buildup for emotional impact remained merely a hint. There were no moving comments from Dario's parents or friends, no critical statements from the lawyer. The article begged for newsworthiness, offering little more than superficial recitations of Dario's college acceptance and tennis scholarship. Nothing substantive was mentioned about police or forensic investigations—merely that they were "ongoing."

Nora put the paper down and thought, *What relief, not to be pummeled in public again. Still, Winston's piece is so uninteresting, it doesn't even approximate status as a human-interest story. Why did they bother to publish this article, especially on the front page? Where was Winston's usual incisiveness and insight?*

"Argh," she complained to no one in particular, resisting the urge to contact him. But she knew she had to maintain her distance to avoid the appearance—or actuality—of compromising his journalistic integrity over the case. She could almost hear the Parker-Greene's lawyer charging her with attempts to manipulate and bias the press.

And yet . . . she really *should* check on Fergie.

So, after downing her coffee, she called her friend. Fergie answered with, "What's up, Doc?"

"Never gets old," Nora said. "I might, but it doesn't."

"You definitely sound better than the other day," said Fergie.

"Probably because I am," said Nora. "Although the day is early. But what about you? Are you at home or work now?"

"Work."

"Then you must be feeling better, too?"

"Better enough to be here. But we've got so many nurses off, on holiday or sick leave. And knowing I'll be gone soon for weeks, I want to pitch in now while I can."

"Yes," said Nora, "your long-overdue honeymoon is around the corner. But you can't wear yourself out before something like that!"

Fergie laughed and said, "God, the thought of taking a 'honeymoon' while visiting Win's family? Isn't that an oxymoron? Or, negative capability?"

"Whatever—it's likely to involve some challenging moments. But afterwards, you and he are traveling the Wuhan countryside alone, right?"

"That's the plan," said Fergie. "And, speaking of partners—I know I asked the other day at the lake, but have you spoken with Alex yet?"

"No," Nora answered, wondering why she hadn't, despite her markedly stressful circumstances.

Fergie waited a few beats, registering her friend's hesitation. Finally, Nora said, "I don't know why I haven't contacted him. And, before you ask, yes, he's tried to call me. But please, don't ask me anything more about that right now."

"Message received," said Fergie.

"Thanks," said Nora, rearranging the camellias on her windowsill. "I just need one calm and conflict-free day at home to rejuvenate a little."

"Have at it, then."

"I intend to. And, by the way, I may sound better because some good things have happened—besides learning that *you're* better, of course."

"Okay, what else? Share the good news."

"Well, I saw the coroner's preliminary report yesterday, and it's in my favor. Also, the paper today . . . Well, Winston's article wasn't so painful to read."

"Sounds good all around," said Fergie, as the overhead PA blasted a Code Pink to the ICU. She inserted a finger into her ear to dull the volume and continued, "I agree—Win's article was a puff piece. But he couldn't get anyone to provide background on Dario. The parents and lawyer won't talk with him. He even drove to Dario's high school yesterday, but no one would speak with him on—or even off—the record."

Law Office of John D. Norris

The Oakland Estuary

John D. Norris put his feet up on his desk and looked out through his office window at the Oakland Estuary. How still its waters appeared. And yet, he knew how deceptive that had to be, with so much lurking beneath the surface. Certainly, ongoing chemical runoff from the nearby metal refinery. Castaway guns and liquor bottles, too. Without doubt, discarded trash and plastics. And it was merely a matter of time before they dragged out the next body.

He glanced at the fax from the Coroner's Bureau, that he found waiting on his desk this morning. The findings within the preliminary report were spelled out so neatly and matter-of-factly, despite their disruptive impact on his evolving case. Even with his considerable legal talent and narrative skills, he could no longer imagine how to fault the hospital and Dr. Kelly for Dario's death—not when the cause of death was attributed to a preexisting tumor that had metastasized.

Still, the coincidence of Dario's death with the surgery seemed suspicious. And might the coroner be wrong? And would a surgical specialist have done things differently to save the boy?

He had to drastically rethink his strategy now. Yes, he would commission a private autopsy. He would hire independent medical and forensic consultants. And, of course, he would discuss the report and his new approach with Donald and Lori first.

He phoned his office assistant Chris O'Dell and told her to cancel his press conference today.

"You?" she replied, feigning horror. "Canceling a press conference? Who am I speaking with?"

"Hilarious," he said.

"Well," she said, "I expected you were going to do that. I did read the fax when it came through."

"Yep. The report turns everything upside down, doesn't it?"

"Still, I trust you'll figure how to use it *wisely*."

"Where are you? I missed seeing your smiling face at your desk this morning."

"Well," she said, "after I read the fax, I went out to get you bagels and coffee. Thought that might cheer you up, or, at least, refuel your brain to rethink the case. I should be back in about five. In the meantime, though, that reporter from the *Oakland Register* called again."

"No way. Next?"

"Next, you asked me to get hold of Donald Parker. I've been trying all morning, every which way, but he doesn't respond."

"I *need* to talk with him, Chris. Especially now, after this coroner's report. It's more than urgent. It's an *emergency*."

"Right. But I think he could easily have me up on harassment charges already."

"Keep trying. I'll defend you."

"Yeah?" she said.

"Friends and family discount," he said.

Carrie's Office

Oakland City Hospital

Carrie Chandler arranged her desk and straightened the bookshelves in her new hospice and palliative care office. Then she sat down to compile a shopping list for items she needed to brighten the room. The prevailing dark-brown on light-brown on drab-brown color scheme needed some corrective oomph, even for—no, *especially* for—the already-suffering patients and families who would be meeting with her here. Perhaps a peach-colored throw rug? Certainly, a brighter floor lamp. A simple vase or two for the flowers she would always display. And, without question—new sofa pillows to replace the lumpy calcified ones.

Satisfied with her décor choices, she put down her pen and glanced at the window, where her sill-sitting twin dolls now resided. Yes, everything was coming together quite nicely.

Then a knock on the door sounded, taking her by surprise. Who—other than Fred, Nora, and the HR department—even knew she was in the office yet? When she opened the door and saw Nora, she happily exclaimed, "You must be the hospital's welcome wagon!"

"Well, I suppose I am," said Nora, grinning sheepishly, regretting that she hadn't even thought to bring a token welcoming gift. "But I forgot my balloons."

"Come in anyway, and take a seat on the sofa," Carrie said. "But a black-box warning about the killer pillows: You could crack your spine against them."

Nora sat and, after scanning the office, said, "It's . . . nice. In a somber sort of way. A major homage to brown sort of way."

"Agreed," said Carrie. "But I'm planning to spice it up with a few accoutrements. Heck, you just being here already brightens up the joint."

"I hope you'll continue to think that," said Nora.

"Meaning what?"

"Meaning . . . I'm here to ask a favor. Besides, I have a meeting upstairs with legal in an hour. Anyway, I tried emailing and calling you, but nothing was getting through."

"No surprise there," said Carrie, pointing to her desktop computer. "The IT People from IT Land haven't connected me to the rest of the world yet. I realize they have to travel from another planet to get here. But, still."

Nora nodded, wondering how many years of her own life she had lost waiting on hospital-IT fixes.

"So, what's the favor you've been trying to ask?" said Carrie.

"I'm requesting a consultation," Nora answered. "And, given the obstacles with regular channels of communication, I'm hoping we can do business the old-fashioned way—in person, on paper."

"Radical idea," said Carrie, feigning awe. "What's up?"

"I . . . or, I should say, Fred, Jack, and I . . . We're making a referral to you for a hospice evaluation."

Carrie tilted her head. "And you're sounding incredibly hesitant because . . . ?"

"Well, because it's sensitive. It involves a colleague—an old mentor for our old gang."

"Ah, for the legendary gang of six," said Carrie, leaning forward. "So, should I assume that my sister would've been concerned about this person, too?"

Nora nodded.

"Then just tell me how I can help," said Carrie. She tapped a finger to her chest and added, "This new chief of hospice and palliative care is at your service."

"Well," Nora haltingly began. "The situation is also complicated, because our old mentor—Bill Balaban—is demented. We're trying to arrange some medical and nursing care for him and his wife, but there's an immediate crisis at their home. Unfortunately, some of the behavioral manifestations of Bill's dementia include domestic violence toward his wife, Ellie. And, perhaps—it's hard to know—Ellie toward Bill."

Carrie narrowed her eyes and shot her friend a skeptical look.

"Oh, god," said Nora. "Your sister used to give me *that* look, too— just before she'd blow a gasket."

After taking a measured breath to avoid doing exactly that, Carrie said, "Look, I just started this HPC job today. Actually, an *hour* ago. And my first week is supposed to be spent exclusively in hospital orientation.

I haven't even assembled a hospice team yet, let alone met with my assigned social worker."

"We're all aware this is a huge ask," said Nora.

"It's not just that," said Carrie. "Domestic-violence intervention is not a standard HPC service."

"I know, I know. But . . ."

"But what?"

After briefly burying her face in her hands, Nora replied, "Like I said, it's sensitive and complicated. But the only real intervention the Balabans would entertain yesterday was a referral to hospice, based on Bill's dementia diagnosis. We think that's because they're so comfortable with traditional medical interventions. But Bill and Ellie—well, just Ellie, actually—fought us tooth-and-nail on most every other recommendation we made. And, frankly, I wouldn't be surprised if Ellie never contacted the nurse case manager that Lola from social services recommended. I think she agreed to 'consider it' only to appease us and shoo us away."

"You know," said Carrie, "people in my specialty do not possess magic wands."

Nora yanked the sofa pillow out from behind her back and tossed it aside. "I know. But we were relieved when Ellie agreed to entertain hospice, because we knew—if Bill were accepted—they would receive home visits by social workers and nurses. They'd also get vetted referrals for in-home support, elder caregiving, and dementia programs. All of that would provide initial monitoring for their personal safety. It's just a first step, but it buys us some time."

Carrie slapped a hand on the desk. "Who is the primary care doctor for your old mentor? It can't be you, because you don't have outpatients. Fred is Mr. Admin, and Jack works at the prison now. Shouldn't his primary doctor be making this Hail Mary referral to hospice?"

"That would be ideal," said Nora. "But we're in a time crunch, and Bill hasn't seen a primary care doc in forever. Ellie told us about his private neurologist who's been monitoring the dementia for a couple of years. But he's in solo practice and, well, clearly, Bill could benefit from a more comprehensive approach to his medical care. That's also why we want to bring him into our integrated system."

"I don't know," said Carrie, leaning back in her chair.

"Please?" said Nora. "Ellie gave us the neurologist's contact numbers. And she signed the consent form in the ER to request Bill's records; we faxed it over to his office immediately. But it was a Friday, so it's likely to be days, maybe a week, before Fred receives them."

"Fred? Why him? He's no neurologist."

"It's temporary until we can hook Bill into our system with the care he needs. Besides, Fred is the only one among us that Bill recognizes. Also, he's the only one with a clinic here. Well, a half-day legacy clinic on Thursdays, when he sees his old patients. Besides, truthfully, I doubt that any neurologist could help Bill at this point."

Carrie rubbed her eyes. "You're aware that hospice entry requirements also stipulate that the patient has a prognosis of six months or less. So, are you or Fred willing to make that prognostication for your Dr. Balaban?"

Nora shrugged. "We all know how hard it is to accurately predict how long someone will live, especially with a dementia diagnosis. But I think we could honestly say we wouldn't be surprised if Bill died within that timeframe. His disease is advanced by all accounts—our own clinical assessments in the ER . . . what we observed at his home a couple days later . . . and Ellie's understanding of Bill's poor prognosis from their neurologist." She handed Carrie an old carbon-paper consultation form on which she'd handwritten the request for hospice evaluation.

After reading the stated "Reason for Consultation," Carrie shook her head disagreeably. "Your handwriting isn't the only problem here, Nora. The information you've provided is too little for me to go on. And, like I told you, my first week here is supposed to be orientation only."

"But," said Nora, her hands forming a prayer sign. "Maybe while we're waiting on the private neurologist's records, you could get a head start by reviewing Bill's ER record here? We ran tons of blood tests on him, and we did both a CT and MRI."

Carrie pinched her nose and said, "This smells like an ask for special privilege for your old mentor. I mean, HPC resources for a domestic intervention? And concierge medical services from Fred?"

Nora's prayer hands opened in supplication now. "Please, at least take a look?" Then she checked the time and hurried toward the door, pausing briefly to say, "Oh, and welcome to Oakland City Hospital?"

Residents' Lounge

Oakland City Hospital

"What are you doing here?" Owen asked. He put down his cell and looked up from his chair in the residents' lounge.

Ellie Balaban stepped through the doorway and scanned the lounge—so instantly familiar and unchanged over the years. During the pre-cellphone era, she had come here often, looking for Bill in the after-hours. Invariably, she'd find him here, plying the interns and residents with clinical wisdom and pizza. Sometimes, she had to drag him home. She closed her eyes momentarily now, shuttering these memories, and then she locked the door behind her. Eyeing Owen as if he were a lab specimen she was about to dissect, she walked up to him and said, "I know what you're doing."

He folded his arms across his chest, and said, "I have no idea what you're talking about."

She tilted her head. "I *know* what you and Bill discussed at our house yesterday."

"And?" he said.

"*And*," she said, "you need to take responsibility for ruining our perfectly good plan."

"'Perfectly good'?" he said with a scoff. "Well, maybe for the two of you."

"No," she said, seating herself in an old lounge chair that officially merited antique-status now. "You would have benefited, too, had you followed our simple instructions. If you had shown up for Dario Parker's surgery, as you had promised my husband, you could have nipped our collective concerns in the bud. That would have allowed you to escape under the radar from the entire mess and continue your budding career." She hooked her cane on the armrest and continued, "Now, Bill and I did our part. We were there in the ER, as we promised, waiting on you after the surgery."

"But it was your husband who messed that up," he said. "Calling me in a sudden panic about your 'perfectly good plan' and wasting everyone's time. That's what left things wide open for Dr. Kelly to jump on that surgery."

She thrust out a hand to signal "stop" and said, "Not only did you sabotage our plan. You barged into our *home* yesterday! You intimidated Bill and blackmailed him. How could we ever trust you now?"

Owen stood and shoved his hands into the pockets of his white coat, deliberating over how to fence with her. Finally, he said, "Well, if Bill told you about our conversation at your house, then you know I read his medical record in the ER. And since you're raising concerns about 'trust'? Well, imagine my surprise to learn that our Bill had dementia the entire time I've been doing research in his lab."

She flicked her hand and said, "What difference does that make?"

"You can't possibly believe I'm that thick. I mean, why would anyone lie about having dementia?"

"And are you going to answer your own question?"

He widened his stance. "Well, in Bill's case, to escape responsibility for something."

"Such nonsense," she said. "Such drama."

Widening his stance further, he said, "I disagree. Because Bill has been acting different ever since Dario Parker got a compartment syndrome. So, I think that his faking dementia has something to do with that and his stem-cell work."

"Oh?" she said with mock admiration. "And did you share those suspicions with Bill at the house?" Already, she was preparing to strangle her husband for not informing her about this potent allegation. But to her surprise, Owen answered, "No."

The adrenaline surge in her body abruptly ceased with his reply. She weakly managed to ask, "And why not?"

"Because I hadn't figured that piece out at the time. And when I confronted him about the dementia, he told me things were complicated and risky, and the less I knew the better. I didn't believe him at first. But then he convinced me."

"And how did he do that?"

"By pointing out all that he was losing by claiming dementia. His career, his lab, his stem-cell work. So, I realized the situation had to be pretty serious, and I backed down after he promised to protect me and keep me out of whatever. I just had to keep quiet about the dementia."

She forcefully tapped her cane on the floor. "And I'm to believe you simply agreed to that? No, Owen. You were *angry* when you barged into our home. Angry and insolent. I was there."

He pointed at her and said, "Because I don't appreciate being manipulated and lied to. I was asked to do something questionable, without adequate explanation, and then deceived by the dementia—"

"Stop," she said, pursing her lips. "So, we agree—you were angry. And all my husband had to do, to placate you, was promise to protect you from 'whatever'?" She shook her head. "Tell me the truth. What did he promise you in return for your silence?"

He looked away momentarily, then said, "He told me he would protect me and . . . that I could expect to run the lab."

Though relieved that he told her the truth, she pretended surprise. "Well, what a generous gift! You know, Bill worked extremely hard to establish that lab and secure its funding. And I had to sacrifice my stage career for his success." She arched a brow. "But I suppose if my husband is demented, he would have to relinquish his lab to someone. And yet . . ."

Owen tapped his shoe on the floor. "'And yet' what?"

"Well, despite all that you profited from your bargain with him, you still seem upset. And that confuses me. Shouldn't you be happy? I mean, after leaving our house with Bill's lab in your back pocket, and with his promise to protect you and take full responsibility for your stem-cell side gig—"

"Then it's true!" he exclaimed. "He *is* trying to avoid responsibility for something involving stem cells."

Ellie held her tongue, wondering why Owen should be so surprised by that possibility. Hadn't Bill shared his concern about an infectious complication afflicting Dario? Why did Owen think he was asked to do the surgery in the first place? Clearly, she and Owen and Bill were on different pages.

But then Owen put a hand to his brow and said, "Wait. What the hell did you just say? I don't have a 'stem-cell side gig.' I gave that Parker kid only one injection, and only as a favor to your husband while he was in Costa Rica giving them to other people."

"So, you're what, then, Owen? A child? Demented, too, perhaps? Not responsible for your own decisions and actions?"

He stared dumbfounded at her.

She said, "And I might say, you're also sounding paranoid."

"Paranoid?" he shouted. "No. I'm being logical now. Last night, I couldn't sleep again, because I kept thinking about the timeframe for his so-called dementia. It was way too coincidental. Two years—the *same* two years I've been working in his lab? And now . . ." He punched his hand into his palm. "Now I see—you're both trying to pin his stem-cell bullshit on me."

Regarding him with a pitying look, she said, "I feel sorry for you. And concerned. Because it looks like you're about to give yourself a heart attack." She watched him pace furiously and took the opportunity to unhinge him further by charging, "You ingrate! Bill *was* protecting you. He even destroyed *all* the evidence about your stem-cell involvement."

"I told you, I was not involved!"

"How churlish you sound. I happen to know that Bill compensated you handsomely for the injection you gave, because I saw the personal check you cashed. Three thousand dollars?" She flung an end of her blue scarf over her shoulder. "Then you go and blackmail him—*in our home!*—and steal *his* lab in the process. And you whine and complain, when all you're asked to do is keep quiet about his dementia—a tactic that also serves to protect you." She pointed her cane at him. "You don't appreciate that a very accomplished and distinguished man took you under his wing. Bill gave you ample space in *his* lab, to do whatever the hell research you do. He supported your career in all ways. Tell me, Owen Landry— have you ever had to labor over grant writing or fundraising to earn any of that? Have you ever had to ingratiate yourself to philanthropists like Donald Parker to finance your research? Have you ever had to—?"

"You think I should be *grateful* to your husband?" said Owen, his hands fisting. "He's put me and my career at huge risk. And the Parker kid who died—I feel tainted by that. I worry that the stem-cell injec- tions had something to do with his death, and I think Bill worries about that, too. And I think he knows a helluva lot more about that than he's willing to say."

"Dear god," she said, raising her chin. "It's contemptible to insinuate that Bill willfully harmed, let alone killed, this Dario Parker. Reassure me you're not *that* paranoid and hysterical."

"I didn't say he willed it," Owen seethed. "I actually saw how surprised he looked when I told him Dario had died. But the fact is, your husband was way too wound up *before* the surgery. He knew something wasn't right."

She let out an exasperated sigh. "This is becoming tedious. And unproductive. I propose we not deal in further speculation. Let's return to our original understanding and decide where to go from there. Now, all you needed to do was remove potential evidence of the injections during the surgery, irrigate the incision to wash out any lingering cells, and bring any evidence to Bill. That's what Bill told me you agreed to. And, frankly, that didn't sound like a big ask."

"What?" he returned with a tight laugh. "I disagree. Because a day before the surgery, Bill knew Dario had a compartment syndrome, and he said the injections might've played a role. No, actually, he insinuated that *my* injection caused it. So, he was already pointing a finger—at *me*. And I think he was afraid his reputation would suffer if evidence of the injections was uncovered at surgery. So, see, the stakes were high, Mrs. Balaban. And why else would your husband call me and freak out minutes before the surgery? Why his elaborate planning involving me and you, all to protect himself? And, pretending to have dementia?!"

Ellie struggled to control her anger toward Bill, questioning privately, *Why, in god's name, am I just now learning about these troubling details?*

Owen continued, "No, it was a big fucking arm-twisting ask of me to do that surgery."

"You're sounding paranoid again. And, still, refusing to take responsibility—for not showing up for the surgery, for giving that young man the injection, for blackmailing my husband. You sound selfish and so very scared—like a child. So, just tell me, little Owen Landry: What do you intend to do now?"

He stiffened and looked away.

"I see," she said. "You have no idea. That's too bad. But you're on your own now, because neither of us trusts you, and we will no longer be making plans with your welfare and protection in mind." She grabbed her purse and stood. "It will be interesting to see what you decide to do if the coroner finds something to implicate you in Dario's death. After all, Bill said the boy's death was so quick, Nora had no time to even irrigate the wound. So, who knows what might show up at autopsy?"

"This can't be happening," he muttered.

She smiled ever so slightly and said, "Bill was an esteemed clinician and accomplished researcher for decades. He was a good man of impeccable character. That is, until you entered the picture two years ago and began bullying my poor dementing husband into a rogue stem-cell hustle. Then . . ." She tutted and shook her head. "Then you went so far as to cajole him into handing his lab over to you. Such appalling elder abuse!"

Owen shot back, "That's not what happened! And he's not even demented!"

"Well, people often see things differently, don't they?"

"This isn't a matter of opinion."

She sighed and said, "Bill and I are losing so much, trying to solve a problem that you only continue to make worse for us. He has to sacrifice his career and all the income and prestige that entails, in order to put this stem-cell fiasco to rest. And I remind you, he wiped the lab clean of all evidence on *your* behalf, too! He put on a very public display of a breakdown, *embarrassing* himself in front of his colleagues—just so, mind you, he would arrive in the ER *on time* to keep *his* part of the bargain with you. But you? You sacrifice nothing, you're made to feel safe, you get his lab, and you have the audacity to stand in front of me whining now. And you still refuse to acknowledge that we both had your back."

When he took a step back, she took one forward and said, "Here's a question for you: How do you think you'll come off in the final story, and who will get to write that?"

"You're both sick," he said.

"Obviously, you have no answers to the many big questions that are, let's say, 'urgent' in establishing the official narrative." She buttoned her coat. "You're choosing to passively sit back while that story gets written without your input. But I guarantee this: If you don't get on board with us—and keep your promises to us from now on—the final version of that story will include a very sad ending for you."

Owen's head spun. He stared up at the ceiling, trying to steady his whirling thoughts and analyze his predicament. *Okay . . . If all the lab evidence of stem-cell work is destroyed, as she says . . . If the coroner finds incriminating evidence, but Bill accepts the blame . . . If he's absolved of responsibility by claiming dementia, so Ellie doesn't worry about catastrophic claims against their estate . . . And if Bill promotes me to head the lab, when all I need to do is remain silent and "get on board" with them . . .* He took a deep breath, locked eyes with Ellie, and asked, "On board with what?"

Ellie Balaban knew that she owned Owen Landry now, and she took a private moment to savor her victory. Then she tapped her cane on the floor and said, "You are to remain completely silent about any communication between us—past and future. You're to follow our instructions without question or hesitation. And never—never!—are you to barge into our home again. Are we clear?"

He nodded.

"Are you on board?"

He nodded again.

The Parker-Greene Estate

Only after Donald Parker read the warning text from his lawyer—*If U don't open the door now, I'm calling police for a welfare check on U*—did he answer the knock on his front door. John Norris stood on the porch, frowning.

"I'm sorry," said Donald.

"'Sorry'?" said John, tilting his head. "Look, I understand times are rough, but you shouldn't ignore me right now. I'm on your side. And I'm the guy who's going to make things better for you and Lori—or, as better as things can be made during a tragedy like this." Stepping inside, he took stock of Donald's appearance and fell silent. His client's expensive clothes and shoes were covered with paint; a tiny rainbow arched across one cheek, and his brown eyes were puffy and dull. Then, noting the florid disarray in the entryway and hall, he said, "My god. I only threatened that welfare check to force you to answer the door. But, jeez, maybe . . . ?"

Donald looked down and tugged on his mustache, leaving a yellow thumbprint at one end.

"May I?" said John, walking into the living room, not waiting for permission. He gasped, seeing the walls bare of their usual artwork. An aluminum stepladder studded with painted shoeprints leaned against the fireplace. The white area rug was now many-hued. He whistled softly and asked, "What the hell's going on? You're not answering my calls, or texts, or emails. And your place looks scary, Don. *You* look scary. And here we've got a very complicated case before us that requires your full attention and—"

"No," said Donald. "I can't do that."

John withdrew a manila folder from his briefcase, held it out, and said, "Sorry, but we *have* to talk about this coroner's preliminary report. It was faxed to me this morning."

"I don't want to. I just can't."

"You need to, Don. It's making some strange claims, way out of the ballpark. And that just makes me more suspicious of that Dr. Nora Kelly and her Podunk hospital. Would a better hospital—hell, an actual surgeon!—have found Dario's problem and addressed it in time? How the hell did they miss it? The point is, we need to commission an independent autopsy and hire our own forensic experts. I need your approval to—"

"What?" said Donald, as if emerging from a bad dream. "What do you mean, 'out of the ballpark'?"

John placed his hands on his hips and counseled himself against responding sarcastically with something like, "You wouldn't have to ask, if you'd been taking my calls." But, clearly, the Parker-Greene household had been challenged enough. "Look," he said, "the county coroner claims that Dario died from clots that were thrown to his lungs. So, first— that's *not* an expected complication from a compartment syndrome, or the type of surgery this Dr. Kelly purportedly performed. So, did she fuck up the surgery? Did she perform the wrong one? Was everyone wearing blinders during the operation, and not looking at the big deadly picture in front of their noses?"

Getting no discernible reaction from Donald, John continued: "Secondly, the clots in Dario's lungs—they were *not* typical blood clots. The coroner found a tumor in Dario's arm . . ."

But Donald could not absorb John's information and speculations. He heard nothing more while his lawyer droned on about his suspicions and legal advice. What meaningful difference could any words make if they didn't have the power to resurrect his son or restore his wife's sanity? He surveilled his living room and entryway—their hardwood floors now a huge paint palette—and he couldn't picture his life ever looking normal again. So, why take on a burdensome lawsuit that would merely sap his flagging life forces? And to hell with Bill Balaban and stem cells.

"Don?" said John. "You listening?"

"No," Donald answered.

John tossed the case folder onto the coffee table and said, "You've got to work with me here. You have to pay attention. This is *your* case—"

"I mean, no—I don't want to pursue the case."

"All right. I get it. You can't think straight right now. You don't want to dwell on your son's death through the lens of a contentious lawsuit. But—"

"No 'but,'" said Donald. "Drop the case."

The two men locked eyes. John willed his piercing stare to penetrate his client's obstinacy. But Donald only looked calmly back and said, "No private autopsy. No forensic experts. No case."

Nodding in the direction of the hallway, John asked, "Where's Lori? Does she agree with you?"

"She's in no frame of mind to speak with you."

"Yeah?" said John, eyeing him sympathetically, head to toe. "Well, clearly, *you're* not." Then he sidestepped Donald and walked down the central hallway, calling out "Lori?" and following the paint smudges on the floorboards leading to her studio. But when he opened its door, he peered inside and froze.

ER Exam Room

After leaving Carrie's office, Nora stopped by the ER to invite Fergie to lunch before she headed to her appointment with the hospital's legal team. She needed to look forward to something positive after her dreary deposition counseling. But Lizbeth immediately pulled her aside and into a vacant exam room.

"What's up?" asked Nora. "You look upset."

"A couple of things," Lizbeth said, closing the door. "But first—that Ortho chief resident—Dr. Owen Landry?"

Expecting dyspeptic news, Nora grimaced. "What about him?"

"Well, Fergie told me about the trouble he gave you over Dario Parker's surgery. So, I got concerned when she told me he came by here a few minutes ago, looking for you. She said she considered calling security, because he was so fired up."

"What the hell did he want?" asked Nora, a blend of fear and irritation in her voice.

Lizbeth shrugged. "He wouldn't tell Fergie when she asked. But she calmed him down and told him to keep a distance from you."

Nora groaned, regretting this ER stopover, preferring to have remained uninformed about his menacing pursuit before her deposition tutorial. Already, he occupied excessive real estate in her head. "Well," she said, "I should probably thank Fergie for being my bodyguard. Do you know where she is?"

"Sorry. She's tied up in a delivery right now."

"Okay," said Nora. "I'll stop by later, after a meeting upstairs." But when she pivoted away, Lizbeth said, "Wait!"

Registering the urgency in Lizbeth's voice, and suddenly recalling there having been a "couple" of things she had wanted to discuss, Nora said, "I'm sorry. There was something else, right?"

Lizbeth nodded. "You know I just had a miscarriage?"

Nora took her hand and said, "Yes. Fergie told me. And she suggested I say nothing, unless you brought it up. I was so sorry to hear. Such sadness and unspeakable loss for you and Aditya—"

"No," said Lizbeth. "I mean, thank you for the sympathy. But it's Fergie I want to talk about."

4th Floor Hallway

Nora bounded up the stairwell, already ten minutes late for her meeting with legal. She checked her back pocket to confirm it contained her iPhone, not trusting—or wanting to believe—it was faithfully capturing *all* her daily steps.

When she arrived at the 4th floor, she pushed open the door and nearly bowled Fred over. He stepped back in time and complained, "What the hell?"

"Sorry," she said, rushing down the hallway. "I'm late."

"Tell me something new," he replied.

"Funny-*not*," she returned. Then her voice trailed off: "And funny-*not* that I'm heading to a meeting to prepare for a deposition . . ."

"Hold on," he called out after her. "I'm going in with you."

She halted abruptly, causing him to bump into her. He grumbled, "You can't just stop all of a sudden when someone's behind you!"

"But *why* are you coming to my meeting, Fred? Don't you have enough to do on the 10th floor?"

He looked sidelong at her, unsure whether she had intended to sound judgmental about his "admin" work. "Look, I just heard the news about the Dario Parker case."

"What news?"

"Oh? So . . . you really don't know?"

She stared blankly at him, realizing how "you really don't know" so aptly described her lately. She really didn't know a lot. Like, why Dario Parker died during surgery. Why his parents and lawyer blamed her. Why Owen Landry was stalking her. Why the Balabans were behaving so unreasonably. Why Fergie—

"Nora," he said, snapping his fingers. "Listen up. For some reason, John Norris suspended the parents' case against you and the hospital."

She upturned her palms. "'Suspended'? What does that even mean? Is John Norris planning to hold it like a knife to my neck forever? No. I want this catastrophe over, ASAP. I *need* it to end."

"All right now," he said, gently gripping her shoulders. "Let's take a deep breath." After she grudgingly complied, he said, "Okay. Now, I have no idea why Norris is changing course on the case. But I gotta say, it sounds fishy to me."

"How fishy? Like a five-fish level?"

"I'd rate it six fish, at least. Because it makes no sense. For some damn reason, Norris is taking a 180-degree turn, despite the powerful tailwinds he's cruising on right now. He's got the public's sympathy, strong media interest, and favorable press. And everyone is mad at healthcare institutions right now. Hell, everyone is just mad."

"You know what I think?" she said. "I think Norris read the coroner's preliminary report. And he had to see it as a huge wrecking ball against his case. Have you read it yet?"

"No. But when Hank Thom called minutes ago to inform me about the suspension, he said he thought the report was pivotal, too. So, I wanted to join you for the meeting and get all the deets."

"Still," she said, "Norris isn't *dropping* the case."

"My guess is he's rethinking strategy with his clients. But we'll probably get some clarity on that from Hank."

"Huh," she said, tilting her head. "So, you're curious about the turnaround. That's why you want to attend my meeting?"

He smiled and answered, "And because I also want to support one of my dearest friends."

Bill's Home Office

"William Balaban, MD"—the name writ large on numerous plaques and trophies adorning his home office, extolling his clinical expertise, his research endeavors, his civic leadership. Stored in the closet were others that he'd rotate out for display, depending upon his particular mood.

But, among them all, what he most cherished were his clinical teaching awards. They reliably provided him with a sense of pride and purposefulness. Seated in his weathered armchair, he glanced nostalgically at the human skull that resided on his desk, a memento from his years spent teaching neuroanatomy. How rewarding that had been, showing medical students how to identify the pterion and external acoustic meatus, how to locate the glabella and bregma. He recalled wearing a safety pin on his white coat's lapel, and instructively using it to probe the skull's bony grooves through which blood vessels passed to the brain.

And the human brain—how deeply he respected it. What an insular self-reigning world of neurons and dendrites, of ventricles and villi and aqueducts. Such an elegant mystery, endowed with mastery over thought and emotion and movement and creativity. How he admired its constant conversation with the soul, and its refusal to be subjugated to science.

Reflecting now on the generations of medical students and residents who blossomed under his tutelage, he smiled. As always, he likened that paternal experience to parenting—within the profession, of course. And yet, as rewarding as that role had been, it never satisfied his deep desire to adopt or father children of his own—something that Ellie had steadfastly denied him.

Bill scanned his study, seeking solace in the ample evidence of his intellectually fertile past. The wooden plaques and brass plates that lauded his neurosurgical expertise, bestowed upon him by prestigious surgical societies. The framed certificates and newspaper clippings recognizing his civic and political leadership on traumatic brain injury, stroke prevention, and chronic traumatic encephalopathy. The gilded trophies honoring his research, that sought cures for Alzheimer's and Lewy body dementias.

Finally, his eyes alighted on his favorite photograph. He stood, walked to the built-in shelves, and held it in his hands. In the picture, he is surrounded by Fred, Nora, Lydia, Jack, Carl, and Cheryl—the unforgettable "gang of six"—and they are celebrating his acceptance of the "Clinical Teacher of the Year" award for 1988. Even now, the joy was palpable. He pressed the photograph to his chest, wondering whether he had gone too far with his elaborate ruse. Feigning dementia was proving easy—besides, who more capable than he to convincingly pull it off? But it wasn't that easy to act the stranger to people he had loved. His heart now protested what his brain had been telling him to do: to renounce all memories of his "career children" and the profession that had given him life.

He'd seen how his ruse upset Jack, and even worried about it reactivating the trauma of his parents' abandonment. And Nora—how wounded she appeared in the ER, when he denied knowing her; and later, too, while she tried to appeal to him as a friend, hoping to convince him and Ellie to accept help. He even saw how his pretense hurt DeeDee, the sweet young receptionist at the research institute. "Yes," he whispered to himself, "but what can I do about any of that?" Besides, those injuries were wholly accidental. He had not intended for any of those people to stand in harm's way of his plans.

At least he'd been able to spare Fred from such unintentional cold-heartedness by selectively remembering him. Ellie had come up with that strategy to minimize suspicion, after pointing out how often and recently he had tried to contact Fred. And now, despite his constitutional contrariness toward her, he had to admit she was right. Besides, Fred's alliance and advocacy were proving useful in other ways.

Still . . .

Still, it was he being forced to bear the overwhelming burden of "their" strategy. He, alone, made to sacrifice a *genuine* career and revered legacy.

Bill sighed and turned over the gang's photograph, face down on the shelf.

Then he switched off the lights, and headed for the door.

But he stopped abruptly at the doorway, paralyzed by bone-crushing regret that suddenly pinned him down.

He deeply regretted his unhappy and overlong marriage to Ellie.

He regretted his subservience to her, and despised how she always prioritized her own needs.

He regretted conspiring so readily with her to evade responsibility for his stem-cell work—surely, so that *she* would not be too burdened by the fallout.

He regretted having to sacrifice his career children and his professional identity.

He regretted Ellie's refusal to grant him children and grandchildren and great-grandchildren.

He regretted his foolish endurance of her imperiousness, her self-absorption, her narcissism, her so-called acting talent, her tinny voice, her flabby ear lobes.

He. Thoroughly. Regretted. Her.

Jack's Home

Jack's shift at the prison infirmary had been capital-D demanding, capital-E exhausting, capital-F frustrating. He attended to four fentanyl overdoses, and to three cellmates who'd been injured in brawls. He stabilized an inmate who'd been stabbed in the abdomen with a shiv, and then arranged for his transfer to the trauma hospital. He started IV antibiotics for a lobar pneumonia, and assisted the on-call dentist with a tooth abscess. He adjusted doses of antipsychotic medications for several inmates in urgent need of adjustment.

On his drive home across the Richmond Bridge, he somberly reflected on the withering scope of his medical practice since he began his job at the prison. At first, the work was rewarding, allowing him to provide good care to people who seldom received it. Later, though, he realized he was spending most of his time caring for inmates who, to varying degrees, suffered primarily from social ills for which he had no cures. How often Nora had lamented the same about her work in the ER. Still, he increasingly felt less like a physician, and more like a referee for inmates caught in cycles of chaos and violence.

So, what a relief and joy when he walked into his living room and found Luis, Red, and DeeDee playing Uno. They greeted him warmly, and Luis ran up to give him a high five. The signature tomato-and-garlicky aroma of Zofia's baking stuffed bell peppers wafted in from the kitchen. "What a great surprise to see you all here," he said.

DeeDee replied, "Red thought it would cheer me up to come and see Luis," at whom she glanced with affection. "And he was right."

Luis returned her smile and said to Jack, "DeeDee told me how she dyes her hair blue!"

Jack's eyes widened, and he said with trepidation, "I hope you're not getting ideas?"

"I'm getting lots of them," said Luis. "But good ones. And don't worry. I'm not dyeing my hair."

Red laughed and said, "I think the little man caught the theater bug from you, Doc. He's been talking about hair dyes and wigs all afternoon."

"Stage makeup, too!" said Luis. "I even watched some YouTube videos, and I think I figured out how the prima donna does hers."

"Well," said DeeDee, "makeup and hair are essential skills in the theater. They give out Tony Awards to people who do them well. Right, Dr. Griffin?"

"Indeed," answered Jack, realizing how impossible it would have been to predict this conversation.

"So," said Luis, "can I help with hair and makeup for the prison show?"

Jack set down his backpack and said, "Sorry, buddy. I don't think that show is going to happen. The 'prima donna' and her husband are dealing with serious personal issues at home."

"But," said Luis, his brow knitting, "she told me the show must always go on. Just like you say, too."

After a strained silence, DeeDee leaned toward Luis and whispered something into his ear. Whatever she said caused a smile to stretch from that ear to the other.

"Huh," said Jack, bemused. "Want to share your secret with me and Red?"

In unison, Luis and DeeDee shook their heads and tightened their lips.

"Did you see that?" said Red. "They're in cahoots again, just like they were during Uno."

Luis and DeeDee feigned injury. They insisted they hadn't ganged up on him, and that his losses were legitimate. Still, Red pretended doubt and said, "Whatever." Then he threw on his black leather jacket and motioned to DeeDee that it was time to leave. "But," he added, attempting to sound like Arnold Schwarzenegger, "I'll be back."

Jack invited them to stay for dinner, but Red and DeeDee had plans to meet Gianni at a bar. After everyone said their goodbyes at the doorway, Luis grabbed DeeDee's hand and led her out, announcing he would "usher" her to Red's white truck. Jack took the opportunity to pull Red aside and ask what had been troubling DeeDee.

Red thrust his thumbs through the belt loops of his jeans. "She's been having a tough time the last few days, ever since that guy died in Dr. Nora's ER. Anything about that in the news upsets her. Last night, she even had nightmares."

Jack looked curiously at him. "You're talking about Dario Parker?"

"Right," said Red, "that's his name."

"Oh. Was DeeDee friends with him?"

"Nah, nothing like that."

"Okay, then. Like what?" said Jack, crossing his arms.

"Well, like, on Friday, Dee was going to a holiday party at the research center across from the hospital, where she used to work. She wanted to see a couple of people, especially an old doctor who used to be nice to her. Anyhow, she never made it to the party because, when she got to the building, that doctor was outside on the stairway and having some kind of—what?—a bad spell? Anyhow, when the ambulance guys carried him down, right past her, she called out his name. She said he looked right at her, but he acted like he didn't know her. But she's positive he recognized her. Anyhow, she felt hurt, but she also worried about the guy. So, after she took a long walk, she decided to go to the ER, hoping to get information about how he was doing."

"Whoa," said Jack. "So, we're talking about William Balaban?"

In a congratulatory gesture, Red tapped his fist on Jack's arm. "Right again, Doc."

Jack scratched his head. "DeeDee asked me and Fred about Bill at the diner yesterday. And we told her he was safe at home with his wife, Ellie."

"Funny," said Red. "Luis was talking a lot about the 'prima donna' you're working with. And he called her 'Ellie.'"

"Yes, she's Bill's wife," Jack explained. "And definitely, a prima donna. But frankly, I'm surprised DeeDee remains so upset over Bill."

"Nah," said Red. "She's not upset because of *that* guy."

Jack tapped a foot impatiently. "How many guys are in this story?"

Luis suddenly reappeared in the doorway and, pointing toward Red's truck, said, "Excuse me, sir, but the lady in the front seat is asking for her driver."

"Little man," said Red, laughing, "you're one talented usher! Okay, yeah, please inform the beautiful lady that her handsome driver will be there in a sec."

Luis nodded and dutifully headed back to deliver the message, while Red waved enthusiastically to DeeDee.

"Red?" said Jack. "You still with me? Bottom line: What guy is upsetting DeeDee?"

Red shrugged. "She doesn't know his name. But he's a doctor, too. With a Southern accent. And she said he was big. We just call him 'Doc Riffraff.'"

"So?" said Jack, his palms turning upward. "What happened?"

"Well, a lot. When Dee got to the ER, it was crowded. And there was a couple who had just lost their son, trying to get someone's attention. Then suddenly, Doc Riffraff barged into the waiting room and made a beeline to that couple. She said he was loud and angry, and he told the couple that Dr. Nora should've left their son's surgery to an actual surgeon. Like, he might still be alive if she had. Then Doc Riffraff left and didn't even care to check on how the parents were reacting. But Dee said their minds were blown, and they fell apart in the waiting room. Then they demanded that someone come out to talk with them, and the father even threatened the guy working at the reception desk. Finally, Dr. Nora walked into the waiting room, and Dee said it was like watching a slaughter. The father tore her apart in front of everyone, and some people even took videos of it. Didn't Dr. Nora tell you about that?"

"She did," he answered. "But nothing about your Doc Riffraff."

"Well, it got worse. Dee had to take a seat to calm down. When she felt better, she went to the guy at the reception desk and told him she felt sorry for what he had to put up with. She told him she understood, having been a receptionist herself. The guy—Leon was his name—said he'd seen worse over his years of working there, but it helped to understand the different ways people handled grief. I thought that was smart advice."

"I hope that made DeeDee feel better?"

"I'm not done explaining. 'Cuz then Dee asked Leon if he could tell her how Dr. Balaban was doing. And for some reason, he thought that was funny; he said something about someone *finally* knowing who Dr. Balaban was. Then he said he was sorry, too, because, without her being kin, he couldn't give out that information. But then he winked at her, and pointed to an exam-room door that she could see through his security window. He told her, 'But he just might be in that room, number 12—and whoever's inside is stable, sweetheart.' Now *that* made Dee feel better."

Jack was about to say something, but Red stopped him with: "Still not done. Because then, when Dee looked toward that room, she saw Doc Riffraff standing in the hallway outside of it, still all riled up. And he kept peeking into Balaban's room or pacing nearby, like a stalker. That upset her even more, but there was nothing she could do."

"So," said Jack, "that explains her concern about Bill at the diner yesterday. But, like I told you, Fred and I let her know he was home safe. We also mentioned we were on our way to see him after breakfast. So, maybe it would help if you told her that, during our visit, he seemed . . . let's say, 'not bothered' by anything."

"Thanks, Doc," said Red, stepping onto the porch. "I'll tell her. Then maybe Doc Riffraff won't stalk her dreams tonight."

The Palmer Medical Research Center

After downing a second pint at Grady's, Owen Landry signaled the bartender for the check because, finally, clarity had arrived. At least, that's how it felt.

Minutes later, in semi-darkness, he ascended the stairs to the Palmer Medical Research Center and punched in the main door's security codes. He kept his cap visor low and his jacket collar high to shield his face from security cameras. Then he ran up the stairwell to Dr. William Balaban's lab.

He exhaled dramatically upon discovering that his SecurID still worked to open the door; Bill had not changed the code, as he had feared. Still, he hesitated, stung by Ellie's charges that he was paranoid and fearful and ungrateful. Was she right about that? He considered turning back to prove her wrong—to himself, as well as to her.

And yet, here he was, already at the lab, and why not *confirm* what Ellie told him about it being cleared of all things stem cell? That would not equate with being fearful and paranoid. In fact, confirming others' claims was what professional scientists routinely did.

So, he entered the lab and switched on his cell's flashlight. He walked to Bill's desk and searched its drawers, relieved to see nothing relating to stem cells. Next, he rifled through the file cabinets and found no communications with the commercial stem-cell provider AccuCellz, and no correspondence with Bill's Costa Rican clinic or colleagues. The attached workbench was free of client schedules and injection logs. Even the unsightly lime-green binder that Bill suggested he reference for the stem-cell injection protocol had been removed from Bill's bookshelf.

To be thorough, he searched the wastebasket. Then the recycling bin. He checked the cell-storage and incubation units to verify that no stem-cell cultures or telling nutritional additives remained. Finally, he returned to Bill's desk and opened his laptop, using the passwords Bill kept on a yellow sticky note. What a relief to see no files or emails appear after he entered "AccuCellz," "stem cell," "Dario Parker," and "Costa Rica" one-by-one in the search bar.

Owen closed the laptop, feeling his muscles unclench. He could rest now, assured that Bill had, indeed, destroyed all digital and paper trails to his stem-cell business—as Ellie had promised.

Still, how physically and emotionally spent he felt—and foolish, as well. He had worked himself up over nothing, the Balabans appeared to have his back, and Ellie was probably right to call him paranoid and ungrateful. Maybe . . . no, *probably* . . . he should "get on board" with them. He could—and should—step back now and allow them to steer the ship with his welfare in mind.

And, tonight, finally, he would sleep. He imagined collapsing on his king bed and sleeping like an actual king. He would awaken rested tomorrow, ready for work rounds at six, and alert for the knee surgeries that followed.

Putting on his Saints cap, he noted the lateness of the hour and winced. Without the emotional bandwidth to keep his parents in mind, he had forgotten to contact them on their anniversary today. He vowed to call them after his surgeries tomorrow. As always, he would also thank them for their sacrifices, which had enabled his schooling and medical career. He would not mention his current predicament—no need to worry them, especially now on the cusp of its resolution.

While heading for the door, he realized he would be returning here on Thursday for his weekly research unit—and, as usual, Bill would be present. But the current tension between them was unbearable. Then, in a flash of genius, he reasoned that he could avoid Thursday's encounter by performing his research tasks tonight. And, without Bill's usual interference—his constant chatter and repetitive yarns about medicine's "good old days" over a protracted take-out dinner—he could efficiently evaluate his osteoblast cell cultures within the next hour.

Smiling in a self-congratulatory way, he walked to his own desk in the far corner of the lab to retrieve his work logs. Yes, then on Thursday morning he would text Bill to inform him about his change in schedule, and he'd include a blithe comment like "See you next week."

But when he opened the top drawer in his desk, Owen shuddered. He saw the lime-green binder from AccuCellz, Inc.

Part Six

Tuesday, December 3

Guest Suite, Carl's Home

"BUT IT'S ONLY six-freakin' a.m.," Fergie complained. "Don't go."

Winston reluctantly yielded, plopping his head back onto the pillow. "But I've been awake all night," he said. "I might as well just work on my story. As they say, 'It won't write itself.' Which is too bad, because it looks like I'm not writing it either."

She rested her head on his shoulder and said, "It's not like you to be so pessimistic. What's going on?"

With his finger, he traced the tattooed half-heart on her arm that completed the one on his, and said, "I love you, Fergs. And I'm happy we're finally taking a honeymoon later this month."

Fergie rolled away, onto her back. "You're trying to dodge my question. You always say lovey-dovey stuff when you don't want to talk."

"You're right," he said, pulling her back, waiting for her body to relax onto his. Then, "Okay," he said, "ready."

"Go," she said. "The meter's on."

"Well, you won't be surprised. It's about the Dario Parker story. It's going nowhere. And I've been hesitant to talk with you about that, because you work at the hospital, you're friends with Nora, and—"

"Win, stop. You know those aren't legitimate reasons for not talking to me. We're married. And I'm a nurse who understands confidentiality. If you say any more freakin' nonsense like that, I'm turning the meter off."

His free hand dropped onto the mattress. "So, either my story is going nowhere because there is nowhere for it to go. Or, I'm just not tracking the story in the right direction."

"Maybe both?" she said.

"Can't be 'both.' I mean, if it has nowhere to go, then there's also no right direction to track."

She propped herself up on her elbows and said, "I'm jacking up my rates."

"Go ahead. I'll pay."

"Okay. What I meant was, maybe it's nearsighted to focus your story only on medical concerns, like mistakes or malpractice. That's a legit focus, but if you decide it's the only one, obviously, your story goes nowhere else." She looked into his soft, tobacco-brown eyes. "But maybe if you *also* looked beyond that one focus, you'd see what else surrounds your story and take a different right direction."

Winston kissed her forehead and closed his eyes. She remained still, willing him to relax. Finally, minutes later, she felt his muscles slacken against her, his respirations slow. He appeared to have drifted to sleep, and now she could imagine the same for herself.

But Winston was just thinking deeply. His thoughts kept orbiting around his visit to Dario's high school, but landing nowhere . . . until, suddenly, they aligned in a singular path that delivered him to the obvious. His eyes opened wide. He asked himself, *How could I have missed it?* Still, was he remembering the two dates accurately? The only way to know was by checking the photographs he had taken—but they were on his phone, which was charging in the living room.

He had to know *now*. So, moving ever so gently, he tried to extricate himself from bed without waking Fergie. First his arm slowly unwrapping its embrace, then his shoulder's gradual tilt to ease her head onto the pillow. She groaned once, and he froze. Finally, after waiting out a minute of her stillness, he tiptoed out of the bedroom.

His heart galloped while he switched on his cell and scrolled through the photographs he'd taken at St. Mercedes High. The school's verdant entry-way . . . Its ivy-laced stone walls . . . The ornate security gate . . . The state-of-the-art sports stadium . . . A bird's-eye view of the football field, taken from the bleachers . . . The adjacent school building that he entered . . . And, yes! Holy shit! There they were: his photographs of the tennis-team rosters.

He pumped a fist into the air and quietly exclaimed, "Score!" Then he walked to his laptop in the dining room and opened his browser to the UCSM website.

El Gourmet Burger Diner

Downtown Oakland

"I'll be damned," Fred said in greeting, taking the chair next to Nora for their regular Tuesday breakfast at the El Gourmet Burger diner.

"Don't worry too much about that," she replied. "I'll keep you company in the afterlife, too."

Amelia, their usual waitress, swung by to pour his coffee and top off Nora's. "Thanks," they said in unison before she headed back to the kitchen.

"Sorry I'm late," said Fred. "But Carrie phoned while I was trying to park the car. And she gave me *three* earfuls! She's frustrated over not having her computer or phone connected yet. And she's not happy about the consultation request we sent her way."

"I'm not surprised," said Nora. "When I handed her the referral yesterday, on one of the old 'Request for Consultation' forms, she gave me the cold eye, like Lydia used to. The only good thing about the experience, was me getting a chance to smell carbon paper again, for the first time in years. Don't you miss that?"

"Hell, no," he answered. "The carbon dust was bad for my asthma. And I'd get my hands smudged with all that toxic blue ink."

"You're killing my buzz, Fred."

He smiled and said, "Okay, back to Carrie? I think she's got a right to be upset. Shouldn't be taking this long for IT to hook her into the system. And our Balaban referral was a stretch." He mindlessly stirred his coffee, clinking his spoon so loudly against the cup that Nora grabbed his forearm.

"Sorry," he said, putting down the spoon. "I'm distracted, I suppose. Just something odd Carrie told me about Bill's neurologist."

Nora watched him take a dose of inhaler. After his end-exhalation, she asked, "What about the neurologist?"

"Well," he said. "Carrie mentioned you had suggested she begin our 'so-called referral' by reviewing Bill's ER records. But, because she had no access to our system, she needed someone's IT credentials to log in and see them. So, she went to the ER looking for someone to help, and, thank god, Lizbeth was there. Anyhow, Lizbeth printed out Bill's record for her, including the fax we had sent to his neurologist for the outside records."

Amelia arrived, set down their breakfast plates, and then wordlessly slipped away. "Thanks," they called out after her.

Nora whispered to Fred, "Should we say something to Amelia about her droopy eyelids? She must have some trouble seeing."

Fred said, "It's called 'ptosis,' Doctor. And it seems they should have addressed that when she had her cataracts done recently."

"Yeah," said Nora, buttering her cornbread. "I'll find some way to bring it up with her."

"Great," he said, rubbing his hands together. Then he grabbed the ketchup, slathered it on his scrambled eggs with cheddar, and picked up his fork. But she again held his arm.

"What now?" he asked.

"The neurologist?" she said.

"Oh, right," he said, sneaking a forkful of home fries. "He may not exist."

"Huh," she said with a grimace. "Well, that's too bad. And I agree—it sounds odd. You'd think Ellie would have mentioned that, when we sent the request for Bill's records. Unless . . . I don't know . . . Maybe the neurologist just recently died? And maybe Ellie's not aware of that yet?"

Fred chuckled and said, "I don't know about *that*. What Carrie *implied* was that the neurologist never set foot on the planet."

Nora blinked hard. "But Ellie gave us his name, address, all his contact numbers. She signed a requisition for Bill's neurology records, and we faxed that request to *somebody*."

"True," he said, layering grape jelly on his sourdough toast. "But, as a favor to us, Carrie tried to get hold of those records to help confirm Bill's diagnosis and legitimize our hospice referral." He poured more ketchup onto his scramble. "Anyhow, she decided to phone the neurologist—because, as she harshly reminded me, she had not yet been provided with 'twenty-first century means of medical communication.' But it turned out that the number Ellie gave us went straight to an unidentified machine that wasn't accepting calls."

Nora poked her scrambled eggs with her fork, moving them around the plate, thinking. Fred eyed her fries and said, "If you're not going to eat those?"

"Just give me a minute," she said. "I'm trying to digest what you told me. And, as you would say, 'It sounds fishy.'"

He sank back in his chair and nodded. "Well, it gets even fishier. Because then Carrie said she had googled the neurologist, and *nothing* popped up. Zilch. And when she mapped the address Ellie provided, Google associated it with a mailbox-rental facility."

The Parker-Greene Estate

As a career housekeeper for ultra-wealthy families, Nadja Boichek had "seen a lot" that she might not otherwise have seen. The extraordinarily expensive clothes, the lavish parties, the priceless artwork, the ocean-sized pools, the fancy luxury and sports cars.

She'd also "seen a lot" that she wished she could unsee—certain behaviors and proclivities she had unwittingly witnessed while going about her business unnoticed, tidying rooms, washing dishes, preparing meals.

Still, before she returned to duties at the Parker-Greene mansion today, she had never seen such ruinous calamity. Last night on the phone, Donald Parker had warned her that the place was "a mess." He also apologized "in advance" for the "upheaval" and asked her to call whomever she needed to "get the house back to normal, as soon as possible."

At first, she had considered her employer's caution odd. After all, she'd spent her long professional life cleaning up other people's messes. When the call had ended, she even said to her husband, "Do you think Mr. Parker doesn't understand what a housekeeper does? What does he think I've been doing at *his* house all these years?"

But now, in the grim midst of the Olympic mess inside the Parker-Greene mansion, Nadja understood his prudent caution.

The first thing she did was open all the windows and switch on the ceiling fans to rid the house of paint and solvent fumes. Within an hour of arrival, she had contacted an executive cleaning service that promised to come before noon. She also scheduled professional painters and flooring experts to begin repairs later in the week.

Before heading up to the couple's private suite, she hesitated at the bottom of the stairway, reminding herself that she—a *professional* housekeeper—had, indeed, already seen a lot. Then she ascended the stairs, and began her methodical assessment of the couple's bedroom, plotting her initial tasks. First, she removed the paint-streaked blankets and bedsheets and pillowcases, and piled them onto the floor. On top of that, she added the stained robes and towels. The mounting collection resembled an art installation in progress.

She decided to deal with the once-upon-a-time gray carpet when the flooring company visited. Then she checked the nightstands—of course, there was paint on the lamps and coasters. Again, the landline rang—again, John D. Norris was calling, pleading with the couple to "reconsider."

Nadja sat down exhausted on the stripped mattress, avoiding a spot of orange paint, and from this view of the havoc, tried to envision what had happened here. Grief, most assuredly, had visited this house in a violent disposition.

And yet, given the colossal internal disruption here, how peculiar it was to have seen the couple this morning appear so outwardly composed—eerily silent, even. She had watched them casually carry out stacks of Lori's paintings to their car; then, wordlessly, they put on their coats, he grabbed the keys and cellphones, and they drove away.

Yes, she had certainly seen a lot throughout her career, but now she had seen something more.

While staring idly at purple and orange handprints on the bedpost, she reflected on Mr. Parker's request to help get the house "back to normal." But, in her professional opinion, she doubted that a return to normal would ever be possible.

Carrie's Office

On this second day of her job at Oakland City Hospital, Carrie Chandler walked the hallway toward her office, encouraging herself to remain optimistic. Surely, after her heated recital of warranted complaints to Fred, the office should be ready for her to connect electronically to the system, and to connect professionally as a colleague with other medical staff. You couldn't separate the two these days.

But her optimism shattered upon her arrival. Still no nameplate on the door. No office-phone activation. No computer hookup. Even the overhead fluorescent lights stuttered.

Taking stock, she lamented out loud, "I'm supposed to be an expert in pain management. But what can I do here to minimize my own?"

Determined to "do something" about that, she decided to off-load Nora's onerous referral that sat like an albatross on her desk. Besides, hadn't she donated enough of her time to address its ridiculous expectations? So, she grabbed her copy of the request, held her head high, and beelined to the ER.

She found Nora in the Ward A hallway, studying a pneumonia-riddled chest X-ray on the light box. After tapping her shoulder, she plonked the request onto her clipboard and said, "I can't do this."

"Yikes," said Nora, taken aback by Carrie's forcefulness.

"I've got no old neuro records," Carrie continued. "No staff. No computer. No work phone. And, on top of it all, I still have zero reason to think this is a legitimate hospice referral."

"I understand," said Nora with a wince. "Fred told me at breakfast that you—"

"And," Carrie forged on, "I'm not even supposed to begin clinical duties before next Monday. This is my so-called 'orientation week.' And frankly, so far, everything here has been disorienting."

"I'm so sorry," Nora said. "I understand these first couple days haven't been welcoming. And our request for consultation only made things worse." She made a note to self: to bring balloons to Carrie's office later today. "We were just so desperate to help the Balabans, and hoping you might get a head start on a temporary fix for their problems. But that was an unfair burden to put on you. Forgive me?"

Carrie threw back her head and grunted.

"And you're right," Nora continued, pointing to the consultation request. "This isn't your problem. Besides, you've never even met the Balabans."

After murmuring something inaudible, Carrie snatched the request and hurried away.

Nora crossed her fingers and called out, "Does this mean you're reconsidering?"

"I'll think on it some more," Carrie trailed off, heading back to her office.

But noting how defeated Carrie appeared to be over the consultation request, Nora grappled with fresh doubts about Plan B's potential for success—especially given the ongoing technological obstacles Carrie faced. *It's just not going to work like this*, she told herself. Then she texted her misgivings to Jack and Fred, ending with, *What now?*

After sending off her text, she heard Fergie call her to the nurses' station to hear the update on incoming trauma. There was a cyclist-vs.-motor-vehicle accident, a stabbing, two falls at nursing homes, and a construction-site head injury. In concluding the update, Fergie said, "And the X-rays are back, room 5: comminuted fracture. I already paged Ortho."

Nora grimaced. "Wonderful. I get to see Owen Landry."

"Sorry!" said Fergie. "I thought you knew. He wasn't with his team earlier, when the MVA came in. They said he was out sick today. I wouldn't have been so casual telling you about—"

"It's okay," said Nora, her dread receding. "I'm sorry he's sick. But the news spares me from having to swallow a bottle of Tums."

Returning to check on her pneumonia patient, Nora felt her cellphone buzzing in her pocket. Already, Fred and Jack were responding to her text:

Jack: *There is nothing more we can do. I still vote 4 APS*
Fred: *No. We go 2 Plan C.*
Nora: *What Plan C?*
Fred: *The next plan we come up with. Drinks 2night at Grady's?*
Jack: *No can do. Promised 2 help Luis w stage makeup. U R welcome 2 join us*
Fred: ☹
Nora: *Sorry 2. I M having dinner with Annie Klumtree*
Fred: ☹☹

Bill and Ellie's Home

"We needn't worry about Owen Landry any longer," said Ellie, applying ruby-red lipstick in front of the bedroom mirror. "I put him in his place yesterday."

"Is that right?" said Bill. "And you're just telling me about that now?"

"Yes," she said. "And maybe now you can appreciate how it feels when someone withholds important information from you."

"You're being petty," he said. "And what did you even do? Exactly how did you 'put him in his place'?"

She twirled gracefully around to face him, smiling triumphantly. "I went to the hospital, and talked with him, face to face. You should have seen me, Bill! I was *good*. I convinced him to lay low and keep quiet about everything. I told him that you and I would be deciding whatever happens next, and he was never to question us again. And I made him agree, in no uncertain terms, that he had to 'get on board' with that."

"Oh? And he just said, 'Yes, ma'am'?"

She pointed toward Bill's chest and said, "I played straight to the heart of *his* massive insecurities. And I made him believe we had his back—*if* he behaved. I convinced him that you had destroyed all the stem-cell evidence in the lab, so that no one—including him—could be implicated." Now touching up her blue mascara, she added, "But, understandably, he's running scared and paranoid now. We don't want him discovering otherwise. You did remember to change the lab's security keycode like I asked?"

"Darling," he said, coming up from behind and winking at her in the mirror. "How do you expect me to remember something like that, when my dementia is so severe?" Then he slackened his jaw and pretended to wander aimlessly around the bedroom.

She pursed her lips and said, "You're proving my point—you don't know how to act, and you've never respected my craft. That is such an unconvincing and, might I add, offensive portrayal of a demented person. Thank god it was me, not you, who dealt with Owen Landry."

He exhaled melodramatically. "Well, you certainly sound confident about your success with him."

"Bill, I *know* I convinced him! I'm telling you, I was good. Little Owen was scared to death by the time we finished our conversation."

"Whatever," he said.

She slammed her bureau drawer shut. "There you go again! Trying to belittle my skills and expertise."

"Ellie, I didn't mean to. Honestly."

"Is that true?" she asked, her eyes narrowing.

"Yes," he said, upturning her frown with his fingers.

Afternoon

Apartment Building Rooftop

17TH STREET, LAKESIDE DISTRICT, OAKLAND

Staring at the sidewalk twenty-some stories below, Owen Landry imagined himself dead. He would endure a few more seconds of his life during the free fall, but then it would be over.

Relaxing his grip on the rooftop guardrail, he privately apologized to his parents and asked for their forgiveness. And yet, he knew his mother's anguished expression would settle permanently. He knew his father's eyes would forever reflect sorrow and disappointment.

Still, Owen reasoned, it was exponentially better to have to imagine his parents like that for the brief duration of a free fall, than to have to see them like that for the remainder of his natural days and theirs.

While envisioning where his body would land, he realized he'd forgotten again to call them for their anniversary. How selfish he was, how ungrateful—yes, like Ellie Balaban had claimed.

Scooting farther down the roof, he grabbed onto a vent and glanced up through overhanging utility cables to the milky gray sky. The heavens appeared to be trapped behind bars. Or, perhaps he was viewing them through his own imprisonment. Likely, both were true—that's how it felt. No escape, no redemption either way.

The Balabans owned him. They had him in their crosshairs, and Ellie was eager to pull the trigger. They were even *actively* out to get him, planting evidence against him in the lab. And, as his gut told him: They knew something about Dario's death that connected to the stem-cell injections—something they were trying to pin on him. And in the upcoming days, when that was publicly exposed, his parents would be devastated.

They had sacrificed everything for the career he was about to end. He, the first in the family to attend college or even complete high school. He, the first in the family to work with his hands outside of the oilfields or assembly lines. And now he, the first in the family to kill himself.

But what foolish and self-destructive choices he had made, now delivering him to this dire moment. He had compromised his integrity when he agreed to manipulate Dario's surgery. He had ignored his moral compass when he injected Dario with stem cells, about which he knew nothing. In an ethically tainted bargain, he had pledged his silence over Bill's dementia, in exchange for promises of protection and the run of a lab—neither of which was ever likely genuine. Perhaps most formidably, he had turned Ellie Balaban into a vengeful adversary.

Suddenly, his sweaty palm lost hold on the vent, and he lurched down the roof. But reflexively, he lodged a foot into the gutter and stabilized himself at the edge. "Fuck!" he shouted, his heart pounding, furious that he unwittingly broke his fall. *It could've been over by now! Just let go!*

But then a young boy's head popped out of a window, a few stories below. The boy looked up at him, and his mouth hung open in a kind of awe.

Go away, Owen prayed. *Stop staring at me!*

The boy craned his neck to get a better view, and his expression turned quizzical.

Owen imagined its message: *What are you doing up there?* He stared back at the boy, sweat trickling down his back, and he privately replied: *This is none of your business.*

Still, the boy didn't budge; his expression didn't change.

Are you waiting to see if I jump? I swear, you don't want to see what that looks like. It will haunt you for the rest of your life. Is that what you want?

The boy continued watching in silence.

Stupid kid! Okay, if that's what you choose—

But in the moment that followed his foot's partial liftoff from the gutter, Owen froze. He stared at his foot, and then slowly wedged it back into the gutter. Now looking down at the boy, he saw that the choice to jump was his alone. He, not the boy, was uniquely responsible for what the boy would see.

His gut told him not to jump.

His moral compass directed him to spare the boy a forever trauma.

Finally, privately, he answered to the boy's questioning presence: *It's my choice, my responsibility.*

I need to take responsibility for my actions and the life my parents gave me.

Still holding the boy's steady gaze, Owen took a deep breath and chose life. Then he nodded to the boy, pushed off from the gutter, and hoisted himself back up the roof.

Sunny Day Café

They had dropped off nearly two dozen paintings for the gallery's holiday art show. Vickie Williams' warm reception and kindness had touched Lori Greene, who, for the first time in days, felt hungry. After snapping on her seat belt, she told her husband, "I could do with some lunch."

Donald Parker's relief was immediate. He quietly choked up behind the wheel of their Tesla, and said only, "Me, too."

"There's that little café by the house," she said. "They have my tea."

"Perfect," he said, taking her hand.

She stared out through the passenger-side window while they drove in silence to the Sunny Day Café. How out of her mind she had been since Dario's death. How wildly irrational. And destructive, too.

She was afraid to glance over at her husband now, because he had seen her like that—in the way she was just beginning to see herself in retrospect, emerging from the disorienting depths of her despair. She couldn't bear to see the remembered witness of her madness in his eyes, for all that it would confirm about her.

And what did I just do, removing all my paintings from the house? Destroying my studio? Scaring Don to death? She dug her fingernails into her thighs, hoping to externalize some of the pain that kept dragging her inward, back to annihilating grief.

Finally, they arrived at the café. They purchased turkey club sandwiches, salads, and tea, and carried them to a private back table. After waiting for Lori to finish her lunch, Donald said, "We're going to get through this."

When she nodded in response, a tear dropped into her teacup.

"Still, it's going to take time," he said, pulling his chair close to hers. "Lots of time. But it's important we go through it together."

She rested her head against his arm, struggling with her guilt—over going behind his back with the bribe, over pushing Dario to be someone he didn't aspire to be, over losing her mind after his death. But, staring at her teacup, she was reminded of her recent meeting here with Martin Stanger. Though her heart thudded powerfully, it did not drown out the secrets it was longing to tell. Abruptly, with urgency, she faced her husband and said, "I have to tell you something."

"Sure," he said. "But why do you look so afraid?"

She jaggedly breathed in. "Because a substantial amount of money is missing from our accounts and—"

"Oh god!" he said, pulling back. "You knew? I swear, I was going to tell you. But it's been feeling like the worst of times to do that. I mean, you were suffering so much."

She looked at him with a puzzled expression, teetering on crossness. "What are you talking about?"

"The money . . . All the money that I . . ."

"You're scaring me, Don. I don't understand what you're—"

"I did a stupid, stupid thing, Lori. And now he's dead. Our son is dead, and it's my fault."

She cupped a hand over her mouth, stifling a gasp, while her mind reeled around her fear that her husband was, indeed, spiraling downward with guilt that legitimately belonged to her. Worse, she had greased his descent into hell by insulating herself inside her secret, creating impassable emotional distance between them.

"Lori?" he said. "Please, say something."

She shakily replied, "What I was going to say about the money is 'I'm sorry.'"

"Sorry?" he said, his forehead creasing.

"All the paintings we brought to the gallery this morning, for the new show ahead of January's?"

He nodded and waited anxiously.

"Well," she said, biting her lip. "I was desperate and out of my mind. But I did that to raise money, so I could cover up what I withdrew from our account. I knew that withdrawal was going to become obvious at tax time, or when you met with our financial advisers."

"But," he said, "you know I don't care about any of that. I *want* you to feel free to use our money for whatever—"

"Please, stop! I understand that. That's why I didn't think about having to hide it or explain it in the first place. But then, Dario died, and people started looking into . . ."

"Sweetheart, there's no need to worry. What's mine is yours."

She shook her head slowly. "You wouldn't have wanted me to use that money the way I did. And I didn't want you to know about that, because I didn't want to risk you getting involved. But all I wanted was . . . my baby . . . our Dario . . . to get into a decent college."

He shrugged. "I still don't understand why you're upset. Dario's education sounds like a good investment, and I have no problem whatsoever with you 'secretly' using our money to support that." He placed a hand on her cheek. "So, now that your secret is out, I hope you feel relieved?"

"I don't," she said. "And that secret won't be mine or ours to keep much longer. Not with all the lawyers and reporters and investigators looking into our son's life. No. It's inevitable that someone is about to discover that I bribed the school to get Dario admitted."

Donald inhaled sharply. Her shocking confession sent chills down his spine. He hoped he hadn't heard her correctly, but he knew that he had; he could tell it was true, because she was sobbing now. "A 'bribe'?" is all he could manage to say.

She buried her face in her hands.

"Jesus," he murmured. Though a master in creative accounting and inventive corporate financing, he had always steered clear of categorical bribes.

"What I did . . ." she stammered. "I understand it's a felony. And that's why I couldn't involve you. But I know, when people find out, they'll point fingers at both of us. And they're going to . . ." She gulped hard. "They are going to see how absolutely *average* our Dario was."

He looked blankly at her, still grappling with a confession of his own.

She continued, "His tastes, his aspirations, his intelligence . . . everything but his looks . . . they were all so average at best. And still . . ." She wiped her eyes on her coat sleeve. "Still, I kept pushing him to be somebody else—like a scholar, an athlete, someone with ambition and talent and creativity. At a minimum, someone with a college degree. So, against his wishes, I forced that on him. I made him take those damn tennis lessons as a cover for the sports scholarship I bought. And if I hadn't done that, he wouldn't have fallen on a tennis court and required a surgery that ended in his death."

"Shh," Donald whispered, waiting for them both to calm down. Finally, he said, "Dario was fortunate to have you cheerlead for him. I certainly didn't do my share of that. But, Lori—his fall on the tennis court did not kill him. I'm sure of that."

"How can you be?" she asked, her voice infused with doubt.

He momentarily hung his head and then said, "When you first mentioned money missing from our account, I assumed you were going to question *me* about that. I even worried that you were about to suspect me of having an affair."

"That never crossed my mind," she said. "But what money are you talking about?"

Here it goes, he thought. The second seismic quake in their relationship over the span of an afternoon tea. He sat braced, expecting aftershocks, wondering whether he and Lori would be left standing. "Do you remember my 'business trip' to Costa Rica?" he asked.

She nodded. "A couple years ago. You took Dario along. But why bring that up now?"

"Because, the truth is . . . we traveled there for a stem-cell injection. Dario's first one."

"Stem cells?" she said, her eyes narrowing. "For *our* son? But why?"

"Because I thought . . . No, clearly, I wasn't thinking. But I kept hearing about those injections from other people. I heard all this hype about the amazing things stem cells *might* do. My CFO and his wife were receiving them, trying to slow their aging. A colleague on the Arts Council was getting them for aches and pains. Donors in my philanthropy circles were doling out millions to support the market. So, when I heard about athletes and bodybuilders getting stem-cell injections to improve their tendon and muscle strength, well, I thought they might help Dario."

"Even I . . . ," Lori began, grabbing onto the table. "Even I know that is completely unproven."

"Please understand. I wanted the same thing you wanted for Dario. I was hoping the shots might increase his chances of succeeding at *some* sport. We both knew he wasn't getting into a good college on his grades. So, I paid for the injections. I also hired a personal trainer and a sports consultant—Dario rarely saw either of them. I bought gym memberships that went unused. Then, that elite sports camp last summer? Dario barely lasted a week."

"But, you . . . ," she said, pointing at him. "You decided to *experiment* on our son? And you based your decision on the word of mouth from your nonmedical friends? My god, you *paid* doctors to experiment on Dario! Were they even real doctors, Don?"

He stammered, "Yes, a real doctor gave the injections. He started them in Costa Rica, and we continued them here in the States. I funded his research lab—it was a *quid pro quo* arrangement. And, god, I would give anything to turn back time and undo my stupid decision. I would give my own life to bring Dario's back. It's my fault that he . . ."

"That he *died*?" she said. "You keep saying that, but you don't explain why." Then she paused, suddenly intuiting a connection between the stem-cell injections and his insistent guilt. "My god," she continued, "you know something about Dario's death that relates to those damn injections."

He nodded somberly.

"This isn't twenty questions, Don! Don't make me ask."

He held up a palm and said, "Okay. Yesterday, John Norris stopped by the house. He had just received the preliminary autopsy report. But you were in no shape to discuss it with him, and neither was I."

"What did it say?"

"I'm not exactly sure. My mind was kind of shattered."

"Well, try to remember!"

"All right," he said, painstakingly searching his memory. "I got the impression from John that Dario's death had nothing to do with the surgery. He said they found unusual clots in Dario's lungs. And a tumor in his arm ..." He paused, rubbed his forehead, and continued: "When you and I were in Napa, and the ER called to tell us Dario died after a surgery on his arm, I immediately wondered if the stem-cell injections played a role. I didn't know how that could be true—it was more of a guilty reflex to consider it. Still, I needed to understand if that was possible, because I had to know if my foolishness was responsible."

For the first time in days, Lori looked unflinchingly at him. How had she not noticed his unshaven chin, his untrimmed mustache, the maroon circles under his mournful brown eyes?

"So," he persisted, "I tried getting hold of the doctor who provided Dario's injections. But he—William Balaban—wouldn't answer my texts or calls. I even drove to his house on Sunday, but he wouldn't come to the door, and I *knew* he was inside. But that was enough to confirm my suspicions about those injections." He took a quick sip of tea to moisten his parched mouth. "Before that, I'd been holding on to a dumb hope that Dario's death wasn't related to what I put him through. I actually prayed that Dr. Kelly made a mistake or was genuinely incompetent. I wanted to believe what the other doctor told us about her in the waiting room that day."

"Oh, Don," Lori murmured, realizing how much her husband—like her—had been suffering in isolation. They were doubly at fault for trying to change their perfectly good son, and grappling now with the tragic consequences. "But the coroner's report," she managed. "It must contain more definitive information about Dario's death. And you—*we*—can't rely on some doctor not answering his door to determine whether the injections played a role."

"Well, John did leave a copy of the report on our coffee table yesterday. I don't know if that was intentional. He left our house a bit shaken. But I haven't looked at it. I just couldn't."

"Maybe," she said, "we could look at it together. And we could ask our doctor to help interpret it. I'm sure she'd do that for us. She's already reached out about Dario. And we know we can trust her to keep things confidential. We can call her this afternoon, and put some of our questions to rest."

The café manager popped into their private nook and asked whether he could clear their table. "We close at three," he apologized. After they nodded their assent, he hurriedly gathered their plates, teacups, and cutlery and returned to the kitchen.

Donald tugged on his mustache, contemplating how he and Lori would—could?—move on from this raw broken place. Then Lori stood up unsteadily and, buttoning her coat, asked, "What did John think we should do? And what did he say about the stem-cell injections?"

He stood up, faced her, and said, "John was floored by the report and thought we should take a fresh look. He wanted us to obtain an independent autopsy and hire our own forensic experts. But he knows nothing about Dario's injections."

"Well, you need to tell him about them," she said. "And did he make those arrangements for us?"

Donald shook his head. "I told him to drop the case."

"You did what?!" she said, nearly a yell. "You claim to want us to get through this godawful time *together*. But there you go, making a huge unilateral decision like that?"

"You're right," he said, placing his arms around her. "You're completely right. And I swear to god, that won't ever happen again."

Guest Suite, Carl's Home

"So, my office manager tells me you're a reporter with the *Oakland Register*?"

"I am," Winston answered. "Thanks for taking my call."

Steven McArdle, garrulous head tennis coach at UCSM, replied: "You kidding? I love talking about the team. They're a great group of guys. I'll even go on record to predict UCSM winning division title next year." He repeatedly bounced a tennis ball against the office floor and onto a wall, catching its return. *Pwok, pwok, catch . . . Pwok, pwok, catch . . .*

"Well, you sound confident," said Winston. "And proud of your team. You must have some talented players."

"They're all exceptional. Every morning over these last five years, I've woken up feeling grateful for serving as their head coach."

"Fantastic," said Winston. "Maybe we can talk about some of them?"

"Go for it," said Steven. *Pwok, pwok, catch . . .*

"All right. So, I'm looking at a roster of your players, and, hey, sorry. I see you recently lost one of your prospects for next fall—Dario Parker. He was a kid from my hometown."

"Yeah," he replied. "It's a big loss for us. And for his family, of course."

"He must've been quite talented to get a scholarship to join your team."

"Like I said, all my guys are exceptional." *Pwok, pwok, catch . . .*

"Well, this local kid—his death made front-page news here, so I'm especially curious about him."

"How so?"

Winston heard the tennis ball *pwok* louder and faster. "It's probably nothing," he answered. "But I was trying to get some background information on Dario for a human-interest story. And it seemed strange that, when I visited the sports hall at his high school, I couldn't find any tennis trophies or awards for him."

Steven scoffed and said, "Is that what breaks for news in Oakland? How would I know anything about that? Maybe the family has them. Maybe they took possession as keepsakes after the boy died. Maybe the school moved them out for a memorial or—"

"Yeah, you're right. Lots of possibilities."

"So, are you interested in anyone else on the team?"

Winston stared confidently at the photographs he had taken of the two most recent tennis-team rosters for St. Mercedes High. Then he said, "Just a final question about Dario. He was listed on the varsity tennis roster only for his final year in high school—the current one— but not for any year before that."

"Your point?" said Steven.

"Well, I'm confused because Dario's senior school year started just three months ago—and, a month later, there you are, recruiting him during the early-decision admissions cycle. So, can you tell me on what basis you selected him for the team at that time? Without any documented experience? With no recognized tennis accomplishments? How did you determine he was 'exceptional' then?"

The tennis ball silenced.

"Okay," said Winston after an edgy pause. "Let's talk about some of your other players. Because I looked at the UCSM rosters during your five years as head coach. And I found four additional guys who, like Dario, had no internet footprint of excelling at tennis before you recruited them. Can we talk about them?"

The call went dead.

Winston pumped his fists into the air and shouted, "Got you!"

Gymnasium, San Sebastian Prison

Jack spent his lunch break in the prison gymnasium, packing away the stage decorations and audience handouts that were no longer required for the canceled holiday show. He could almost hear the sing-along music sheets striking dispiriting notes from their perch atop the packed tinsel and holly boughs.

Still, Scrooge though he may be for canceling the production, he had to admit relief. The show had become cringeworthy after he yielded its creative control to Ellie. Its most recent iteration featured lute-play-ing reindeer and tap-dancing woodland fairies, and he could see no good coming from that. The inmates were bound to throw shade at the actors—perhaps, even, injurious physical objects. His sole genuine regret was depriving Luis of an opportunity to lend a hand to the production. How wonderful to have seen him so excited yesterday, while discussing theater with DeeDee and—

"Fuck!" he muttered, suddenly reminded of his conversation about her with Red. He grabbed his cellphone and texted Nora: *Need 2 talk*

Nora: *Busy w a CVA*

Jack: *The ortho rez U told me about. Southern accent?*

Nora: *Y*

Jack: *Big guy?*

Nora: *HUGE pain in ass*

Jack: *Calling U now*

When Nora picked up his call, she said, "Seriously, Jack, I can't talk. My stroke patient is—"

"So, just listen," he said. "Last night, Red told me that DeeDee was in the ER waiting room on Friday. And she overheard that Ortho resident tell Dario's parents that *you* were basically responsible for their son's death. Something about you not being qualified."

"What?!"

"Yeah. I thought you should know."

"What a creep!"

"DeeDee would definitely agree with you. He *totally* creeped her out."

"Get the backboard!"

"What?"

"Not you," she said. "I'm talking to my team. Is DeeDee okay? Why did she go to the ER?"

"She's fine. She went there trying to get information about Bill. They used to work together. Apparently, your favorite Ortho res—"

"Owen Landry."

"Yeah, okay. Later, DeeDee saw Owen Landry lurking around Bill's room and—"

"We need the alteplase, *STAT.*"

"Not me again?"

"Not you again. But I gotta hang up."

Sibley Volcanic Regional Preserve

Oakland

The trail sign promised only 500 more feet before reaching the old volcano in the Sibley Volcanic Regional Preserve. But Martin Stanger didn't trust it. Surely, he had already walked twice the total distance of the alleged 0.9-mile hike from the parking lot off Skyline Boulevard— at least, that's what his sore knees and feet attested. And by the time he finally arrived at the volcano, his entire body complained. His lungs demanded more oxygen, his heart commanded a rest, his lower back seized up in protest.

Martin sat on a toppled redwood and waited for his body's grievances to quiet. Idly staring at the old volcano, he thought: what an exacting and audacious request by his stepson Jason to meet up here! And cryptic, too—sent by a text he was asked to delete after reading it.

Meanwhile, anise swallowtails flew overhead, and a pocket gopher peered out at him from a ground tunnel. Something rustled in the surrounding coyote brushes. "Huh," he said, realizing that an eternity had passed since he *intentionally* spent time in nature. And, as always before, his immersion in it felt flat. Nature was so dully repetitive—water, trees, hills, vegetation, sky . . . water, trees, hills, vegetation, sky . . . Even with an ancient volcano thrown into the mix, nature was highly overrated.

Finally, he spotted Jason on the trail and he called out, "Hey, there!"

"Martin," Jason flatly replied, evading his stepfather's attempted hug.

Martin eyed him concernedly and asked, "Why are you looking so ragged?" Hoping to make him smile, he flexed his arms, stood tall, and said, "Look at your old man, after hiking ten miles to get here!"

Jason stuffed his hands into his jean pockets and looked anxiously around. "It's not even a mile from the parking lot," he said.

"Okay," said Martin, gesturing for his stepson to sit beside him on the log. "Obviously, something's bothering you."

After electing to sit several feet away, Jason stared searchingly up, through a canopy of redwoods.

"Well," Martin said, "are you going to tell me what was so urgent and cloak-and-dagger that we had to meet *here*? 'Cuz I'm allergic to nature. Whatever happened to good old-fashioned meetings at bars or coffee shops?"

"Steven McArdle called me," Jason said.

Martin felt the wind knocked out of his chest. He managed, "Steve? Why would he call you?"

Jason stomped on a twig and cracked it.

"Hey," said Martin, scooting closer. "What did he say?"

Jason stood up and shouted, "He asked if a reporter contacted me!"

Dread seized Martin's brain and rendered him speechless.

"What the hell?" Jason seethed. "I thought you were keeping my name out of the whole thing!"

"I was," said Martin. "I *did* keep your name out."

A young couple wearing matching paisley sweatshirts emerged from the trail. They waved to Martin and Jason, who halfheartedly responded in kind. After they finished taking selfies in front of the volcano and left, Jason told Martin: "I wish my mom never married you! We were fine before you barged into our lives. And now I'm in this fucking mess because of you."

Martin turned snappishly away, as though punched in the face. Did the boy mean what he said? "I'm sorry you feel that way," he replied. "But marrying your mother and getting to know you was the best thing that ever happened to me."

"Well, you ruined everything. And if she was alive right now, this would kill her!"

Staring at the ground, Martin tried to steel himself against Jason's cutting words. But they had already pierced his heart. What to do now? Clearly, the boy was frightened and lashing out. But he was also spewing distortions, making it difficult to hope for any rational dialogue now. Would it help to openly reminisce about the backyard barbecue ten years ago, when Jason and his mother eagerly welcomed him into their lives and home? Or about the five happy years that followed before her unexpected death? "Jason," he began, "you're not seeing things in perspective. Please listen to me—"

"Listen to you?" Jason scoffed. "That's how my life got fucked up!"

"All right, that's enough," Martin testily returned. "You can take all your best swings at me at some other time. But right now, I'm the only guy who knows how to help you. And if you want my help, you need to get hold of your emotions. Now, just think for a sec—what else did Steve say?"

Jason forcefully shut his eyes while trying to remember accurately. "He said a reporter from the *Oakland Register* called and asked about Dario Parker."

Martin reflexively kicked a stone into some sagebrush, and a flock of sparrows shot into the sky.

"And," Jason continued, "he said the reporter knew about *everything*. He even—"

"No, no, no," Martin said, shaking his head. "Steve's wrong. Our ship is iron-clad tight."

"Fuck that! The reporter even asked how Dario was recruited to the tennis team, with no athletic background. Then he asked about four *other* guys without credentials who also made the team. You fuckin' believe those are random questions for a reporter to ask Steven McArdle?"

Meeting Jason's furious stare with a look born of painful resignation, Martin Stanger felt his knees soften and his stomach churn. This was the moment that was never supposed to happen, the one with the power to destroy their lives. He haltingly offered, "Look, I don't want you to worry. I'll figure out what's happening with Steve and take care of it. You'll be fine. I promise."

"No," said Jason, "this is a total clusterfuck." He pointed a stiff finger at his stepfather and said, "And the problem isn't just the coach. A goddamn reporter is involved. You think you're gonna control him, too?" He pressed his hands to his temples. "Your tight fucking ship has been torpedoed!"

Martin tried to place a hand on Jason's shoulder, but he backed away. "Look, son," he said, "I'm pissed that Steve called you. He was never supposed to make any direct contact, not even with *me*. Communications always went through the foundation's phone or email—"

"Then why did he call me?"

"I don't know, son. I can only guess—"

"My name is Jason Sullivan, and I'm not your son! Stop calling me that!"

Martin stood rigid, though shaking internally from the brutal impact of Jason's remark. But he had to summon his resilience and act the parent—as he had promised Jason's mother he would. After taking a grounding breath, he said, "Okay, Jason. I won't call you that again. I will feel that it's true, but I won't call you that."

Jason eyed him warily.

"As I was going to say," Martin continued, "Steve wasn't supposed to contact you, *ever*. My guess is he totally freaked out when the reporter called."

"How did he even get my number?"

Martin blew air out through a corner of his mouth. "The only way I can imagine, is from one of his recruits—someone you proctored during the entrance exams. Maybe one of them looked at your phone while you were working on their test?"

"But why not call you instead?"

"Again, I can only guess. But . . . probably to intimidate you as a way of getting to me. Because it feels like an indirect threat—a kind of black-mailing. That if I say anything to anyone about his involvement in our operation, he'll go after you, and he knows I would never let that happen."

"Torpedoed," Jason said, almost a whisper.

"Listen," Martin said, "there's a reason that reporter's story hasn't broken, and why it won't. He has zero factual evidence about our oper-ation, because it doesn't exist." He tapped a finger to his head. "All the archives are stored in here."

When Jason merely looked back, clenching his jaw, Martin said, "On top of that, I guarantee Steve's not going to talk—he's got way too much to lose. The same goes for all the parents. None of them is going to spill the beans about buying tennis scholarships and college admissions for their no-talent sons."

"So, you've heard nothing from the coach yourself?"

Martin shook his head. "He's probably keeping distance from me and the foundation for now. You know, in case—" He stopped himself from raising further worries about the reporter's potential pursuits. "I gotta say, Steve getting to me through you was a helluva good way to send me a message, though. Still, him using you like that pisses me off."

"Well, how do you think I feel about it? And now he's made a trace-able call to *me!*"

"Hang on, Jason. You haven't told me what you said to Steve. How did you answer him?"

"I said nothing. Not a word. I was . . . in shock. I just held my phone and listened. Then I hung up."

"Okay, that's good," said Martin, stroking his chin. "So, here's what we're going to do. I'm going to call Steve right now—"

"You can't. There's no cell reception out here."

"I see," said Martin, nodding knowingly. "And that's why you wanted to meet here. You figured I'd call him after you told me, right? But then he'd know, for sure, you gave me his message. He'd know he fingered you correctly."

"This is that moment," said Jason, his face drained of all color. "It's that moment you promised would never happen."

"C'mon, let's just think together on this a minute. Now, Steve has never seen you. He didn't even hear your voice, and you didn't confirm your identity on his call. So, if I don't let on that you told me about his call, he can't be sure of you. That means I can still keep you out of everything because I can—I *will*—take full responsibility if anything ever comes from the reporter's questioning. Meanwhile, we should destroy your cell, and buy you a new one."

Jason stared incredulously back. "My cell?"

"It's for the best. New cell, new number, no more calls from Steve."

Running a shaky hand through his close-cropped hair, Jason said, "I need to get away from this shit. I need to get away from *you*."

"No, please," said Martin, his hand held out.

Jason backed away slowly, shaking his head. Then he abruptly turned to the trail and hurried away.

Martin watched his stepson vanish behind plumes of kicked-up trail dirt. Then he tilted his neck back and yelled "Fuck!" to the sky, shivering when a bulky gray cloud lumbered overhead and cast him in shadow. After zipping up his jacket, he returned to the trail, consumed with worry over Jason. When he passed goats grazing on the hillsides, he heard them bleat "baa, baa" like a Greek chorus, judging him harshly.

Along the way, he checked for cell reception. When it returned, he rested on a boulder overlooking the canyon and tried to phone Jason. But, met only with the option to leave a voicemail, he chose to say nothing.

Carrie's Office

Carrie sat at her desk, mentally preparing for the afternoon orientation session for new hospital employees. But how she dreaded the inevitable role plays. How she despised talking "personally and deeply" about her professional desires and goals with a roomful of strangers who, like her, were being held hostage by HR. But then her cellphone rang—her *personal* cellphone—and she bristled, recognizing the internal exchange; someone was calling her from within the hospital. "Who is this?" she answered.

"Oh, hello, Dr. Chandler. It's SoShanna from HR. Sorry, but I didn't know how else to contact you. Your office number doesn't appear to be working."

"Yeah," said Carrie, "I'm aware of the problem."

"Well," said SoShanna, "I'm sorry to inform you that we need to cancel this afternoon's orientation."

Feigning disappointment, she replied, "But, so last minute?"

"Unfortunately, HR was just made aware of a pharmacists' walkout."

"Well, that does sound important. Though I was just telling someone this morning about feeling a little disoriented here."

"I'm sorry," said SoShanna. "But we can make up for lost time. In fact, I can meet with you privately, later this afternoon."

"I was just kidding," said Carrie.

SoShanna coughed nervously and said, "HR doesn't dismiss remarks like that."

After reassuring SoShanna that she would be fine, Carrie ended the call, leaned back in her chair, and said, "Sheesh!" But now she had four freed-up hours ahead! Her eyes shifted between Nora's irksome consultation request on the desk, and her sweet sill-sitting twin dolls at the window. Imagining the dolls' sage counsel, she said, "Sure, why not? I may as well be *physically* disconnected from this place, as well."

She grabbed her shopping list for the office upgrades. Then she thumbed through her printouts of William Balaban's ER record and withdrew her copy of the faxed request to his neurologist's office. She vowed to accomplish *something* today! She would A: in person, obtain the information she needed from the elusive neurologist; and then B: purchase a throw rug, a floor lamp, and nonlethal sofa pillows at Bed and Bath.

Postal Supreme

Laurel District, Oakland

When Carrie arrived at the neurologist's purported address, she found herself parked in front of "Postal Supreme"—precisely what the Google Maps gods had divined. The single-story commercial building was squat and cheerless, and its street-facing windows were barred. A crooked sign on the door read "Open." She said to no one in particular, "This is a mistake."

Still, she got out of her Mini Cooper and looked for a building directory. After finding only price lists for various postal services in the front windows, she entered Postal Supreme.

"Ah," she said, scanning the interior. No wonder the name: It *was* supremely postal inside. Postboxes lined the walls, only varying by size and the number affixed to them. A glassed-in cabinet contained packing and mailing materials for sale. Two large copy machines occupied a corner near the service desk, where a young woman sat reading a book. Stacked boxes, ostensibly waiting for transport and delivery, surrounded her.

Carrie rechecked her paperwork. The neurologist's address on the fax included "Num 202" after the street name. Previously, she had assumed that indicated the suite number for his office. But clearly, that was wrong. On a hunch, she searched for postbox 202 and, pointing to it, called out to the desk clerk: "Can you tell me who owns this box?"

The clerk barely looked up from her book and said, "No."

Carrie approached the desk. She made a wide sweep with her arms to emphasize the store's emptiness, and said, "Because it's so busy in here?"

After returning a dead-eyed look, the clerk answered, "Because that's illegal, *ma'am*."

"Do not 'ma'am' me," Carrie said.

"Well, you a cop? You got a warrant?"

"No. I'm a doctor. I'm just trying to help someone in trouble."

"And you think that 'someone' might be inside that tiny box? Yeah, then, I'd agree—they're in trouble."

"You're enjoying this, aren't you?"

But their conversation was interrupted, when a woman briskly entered the store and said "Hello." The clerk waved at her and smiled. And when Carrie glanced back at the woman, she did a double take. For, despite the woman's large sunglasses, Carrie recognized her as the long-suffering soap-opera matriarch from *The Blue Rose*. She considered introducing herself as an old fan, but the actress appeared rushed and, besides, Carrie couldn't remember her real name.

Carrie, returning her attention to the clerk, said, "Look, I was given this address and this box number because—"

"It doesn't matter," said the clerk, grinning.

"This is serious," said Carrie. "Someone's health is at stake."

But the clerk merely tilted her head toward the woman. And when Carrie looked back accordingly, she startled: The actress was hurriedly closing box 202, and then she speedily exited the building.

Piedmont Park

"Five 'exceptional' guys, for sure," Winston said, staring out the dining room window, replaying his phone conversation with Steven McArdle. "But not because of any tennis skills."

After the call, Winston knew he was onto something big. But now he needed to figure out what made those five guys *genuinely* exceptional—allowing them to bypass traditional standards for tennis scholarships. McArdle must have had a reason to select them. But what distinguished them? And what did they have in common? Minutes earlier, he had cross-referenced the names of Dario and the four other recruits, but no pre-UCSM internet connections appeared.

He yawned and stretched, and decided his mind needed a reset. A rejuvenating walk around Lake Merritt, where he did his best thinking, was out of the question, because Fergie had taken the Subaru to work. He would have to settle locally, with Piedmont Park—which he had not yet explored.

He walked the three blocks from the house to the park, braving sidewalk throngs of students who had just been released *en masse* from the neighborhood high school. But the park itself was uncrowded, and its sprawling paths were paved and clean. The sun hung lazily behind ill-defined clouds, performing light tricks on the creek's surface. Locals walked their dogs or pushed children in high-tech strollers, and everyone stayed off the grass, obeying the politely worded signs. The grounds were immaculate, unlike Lake Merritt's. He questioned whether he could think freely and out-of-the-box in such a neat and disciplined space.

But after taking a seat on a green wooden bench, he closed his eyes to the manicured surroundings and waited on what happened next. He took a few meditative breaths, feeling his mind relax and making space for the unknown.

Names began to drift into his awareness. Dario Parker, first . . . Then the other four recruits . . . Steven McArdle . . . Dario's parents . . . But they just continued drifting, making no connections.

So, shifting to his analytical mind, he grappled with his pressing questions. *Why do Dario's parents and their lawyer still refuse to speak with me? Why were the two tennis players at his high school so unforthcoming? Maybe I should track down the other four recruits? McArdle's silence spoke volumes today—but precisely what? Why would he knowingly recruit unqualified players? Did he figure the team could easily absorb a handful of them? But why even do that?*

A flock of chickadees swooped by, drawing his attention outward. He opened his eyes and noticed that the sun had lowered in the sky, and more families and dogs had gathered in the park. He leaned back against the bench, and took a moment to appreciate the peaceful communal scene. But then, out of nowhere, an orange waffle ball bounced toward him, and he deftly reached out and caught it. With a smile on his face, he walked toward the young girl who was approaching in its pursuit. But when he neared her with the ball, she turned away; she ran back to her mother and cowered behind her. The girl's father sprang up from a picnic table and stood protectively in front of his family. He held out his hand to accept the ball from Winston, and, with a cautious expression, said, "Thanks."

Handing over the ball, Winston felt a flare of shame. The parents were treating him like a criminal or creepy trespasser. And though acutely dispirited by their behavior, he replied, "You're welcome," and walked away.

Heading toward home, he remained distracted by the off-putting drama surrounding his innocent return of a lost ball to a girl in an idyllic park. Why did her parents find it necessary to behave so antagonistically toward him? Why such suspicion, and why such overprotection of their daughter, and—?

Struck by his insight, he stopped so abruptly on the footpath that he almost lost balance. "Of course," he whispered, "it's all about the parents!" And, indeed, when he turned back to look at the family, the father was still eyeing him suspiciously.

Winston sprinted home to his laptop. He opened a new page in his reporter's notebook and wrote down the names of Dario's parents. Then he googled the four other recruits and added their parents' names. After he had written down all ten, he began to methodically cross-reference the names on the internet. He began with Donald Parker as a "must include" qualifier in the search bar, omitting his wife's name for its predictable associations. Then he added the names of the eight other parents. But, to his dismay, no links materialized with Dario's father.

"Damn!" he said as Fergie entered through the front door.

She put down her backpack and, having just finished her ER shift, was more than ready to chill. "Well, that's a nice welcome," she said.

"Hi, Fergs," he said. "Sorry. For a hot minute, I thought I was on to something."

She glanced toward the kitchen and said, "Clearly, that 'something' wasn't our dinner."

"Damn!" he said again, and then "Sorry, *again*. I forgot about dinner." He looked sheepishly at her and added, "But if it makes you feel better, you were right to suggest I track in a new direction for the Dario Parker story."

"Fine. But, given the choice, I would've preferred pasta and a salad. And what was so absorbing that you forgot—?"

"I spoke with UCSM's head tennis coach this afternoon. He practically confirmed that he knew Dario had no athletic skills, when he recruited him."

Fergie's eyes widened.

"Yeah," he said, "and get this. I also discovered four other recruits, in the same curious circumstance. And when I asked the coach about them, he went silent and hung up on me. Clearly, he's hiding something."

"It does sound suspicious," she said. "Good work."

"And it gets more interesting," he said. "Because later, I met an obnoxious guy in the park, who treated me like dirt when I tried to return a loose ball to his daughter. And that's what helped me to discover the new track."

"You're going to have to explain that one," she said, kicking off her sneakers.

"Well, the girl's parents were shielding her from me, like I was dangerous. It really put me off. But then, afterwards, while I was trying to understand it, I realized the parents were just being overprotective of their kid. *Overly* overprotective. Still, that's when it hit me—that maybe the story of the five recruits is actually about their *parents*—parents who think they're protecting their kids, when they're actually shielding them against their own anxieties."

"Like, anxieties over their kid not getting into college."

He nodded. "It has to be a huge relief for a parent, when a college actively recruits their kid. Besides, we know the parents *had* to be involved in the UCSM application process, because their kids were under eighteen when they applied for early-decision—"

"Stop! Fine. You don't have to make dinner. I'll throw something together."

He smiled and said, "Thanks. I'll be just a few more minutes. I need to cross-reference all the parents. One down, nine to go."

She stretched her back and said, "You say a 'few' minutes, but we both know that means maybe an hour, right?" She walked languidly toward the kitchen as her voice trailed off: "It's gonna be leftovers, though."

He returned to his internet search. This time, he removed Donald Parker as a "must include" qualifier and replaced it with Lori Greene, keeping the eight other parents in the search bar. And, after pressing the search icon and seeing the result, he shouted, "No fucking way!"

Fergie swiftly returned to the dining room and said, "Well, I'm tired, Win! It was crazy-times-eight in the ER today. And *you* were supposed to cook for us."

"Not dinner, Fergs! Please, just come here and look."

She went to him and peered over his shoulder. He pointed to his laptop screen and asked, "What do you see in this photograph?"

After adjusting her bifocals, Fergie examined the image. "It's a photograph of two women at a fundraiser for the Oakland Fine Arts Museum. I recognize Dario's mom from the news. But who's that she's with?"

Winston drumrolled his fingers on the table and declared, "*That* is Sonya Wisekof. *And* she is the mother of one of the other tennis recruits!"

Fergie looked admiringly at him and said, "Congratulations! You found a solid connection."

He stood up and took a bow.

She clapped and said, "All right, fine. Get on with your work. Keep connecting the dots." And while returning to the kitchen, she added, "But it's *still* gonna be leftovers tonight."

Evening

Suzie's Trattoria

GLENVIEW DISTRICT, OAKLAND

Annie Klumtree was no stranger to Suzie's expansive wine list. In fact, she considered herself a scholar of its text. Without needing to consult it, she straightaway requested a specific 2018 pinot noir for herself, and a merlot for Nora, who wanted something "full-bodied."

After the server left, Annie said, "I hope you were referring to a wine?"

Nora groaned. "Same old!"

"It's damn good to see you, Nora."

"Likewise," Nora said. "I'm just a tad mortified that it took a young man's dead body to bring us together again."

Annie nodded. "It's been—what?—four, five years?"

"That's about right," Nora said. "And I know it's late to say this, but thank you for the flowers and letters you sent, when my daughter and husband passed. And, of course, for Lydia, too." She half-frowned and added, "I believe my losses have sustained Hallmark's business for several years."

Smiling sympathetically, Annie replied, "I received your thank-you cards. And I trusted you'd call one day to catch up, when the time was right for you. And, well, here we are now."

The server returned with the wine and a basket of warm ciabatta, and she promised to return for their food order.

"What's good here?" Nora asked, checking the menu.

"Food?" said Annie, as though it were a foreign word. "Everything here is good. I usually just ask for 'the special.' But first . . ." She raised her glass to Nora, who returned the gesture and toasted, "To old friends."

Nora tasted her merlot and nodded approvingly. "Excellent decision," she said.

"And speaking of excellent decisions? For selfish reasons, I was happy to hear about the lawyer deciding to drop the case against you. Because, honestly, I was *dying* to talk with you about it. You're the best diagnostician I've ever known, and the case is a doozie."

"A 'doozie'?" said Nora. "I haven't heard that word in decades."

Annie crinkled her aquiline nose and said, "But accurate, right?"

"It is," Nora said, appreciating her old friend's expressive facial movements. "And I was dying to talk with you. You're the best forensic pathologist I've ever known."

They toasted each other again and declared, "Mutual admiration."

"But," said Nora, drizzling olive oil on her ciabatta, "the case wasn't exactly dropped. It was 'suspended' by the plaintiff's lawyer. I don't know what that ultimately means. But hospital legal said they no longer had a problem with me contacting you. For now, at least."

Annie scoffed. "'Suspended' my ass! That lawyer read my prelim report and *knew* he had no case against you."

Nora held back tears and shakily lifted her wineglass.

"Oh, no," scowled Annie. "Don't tell me you're feeling *relieved*? You *must* have known all along you weren't responsible for that young man's death. Where's that great diagnostician I was just talking to?"

Struggling to compose herself, Nora replied, "Well, lots of people believed I was responsible. Many still do. And I can't say I entirely blame them. Dario did die on my table. I was even holding the scalpel when . . ." She idly swirled her wineglass and continued, "And for maybe ten, fifteen seconds, I was looking away when my right-hand nurse got sick and left the room. But that's precisely when Dario died."

Crossing her arms, Annie said, "I'm still waiting for that crack diagnostician to return to the table. Because she would understand the difference between 'feeling guilty' and 'being guilty.'"

"It's been hard, Annie. Before your prelim, I was obsessed with making sense of his death. And I kept trying to think of a surgical mistake I might've made, or a complication I caused. Maybe something I missed while I was looking away."

"Keep going. I'll wait until you tire yourself out."

"Then, that immediate lawsuit and all the press coverage—essentially blaming me. I was pilloried on social media. I kept seeing a viral GIF of Dario's father ripping me apart in the waiting room. And so much of the posted commentary was vile—frightening, even. And the dreadful saga keeps giving. Just today, I learned that our chief Ortho resident insinuated to Dario's parents that I was responsible for their son's death."

"I'm sorry," said Annie, reaching for her friend's hand. "It sounds absolutely brutal. And so unjustified. But we both know that anyone who believes your surgery caused the death is wrong. And they haven't read my prelim report."

Nora nodded halfheartedly. "It will be a great relief when that's made public."

"That's the ticket!" said Annie, raising her glass. "And it should be made public any day now. After that, it'll be a few more days for the final report, when we get the confirmatory genetic and immunological tests—"

But Nora just looked away.

"Okay," said Annie, arching a brow. "What the hell just happened?"

"It just now occurred to me how . . . how I could have contributed to Dario's death. I'm wondering if my surgery physically disturbed his tumor. Maybe dislodged fragments from it that embolized to his lungs as the final blow?"

Annie gave her the dead-eye, but Nora persisted, "And, maybe I should've suspected the tumor's presence before I did the surgery? Because I saw a fleck of calcium on Dario's X-ray that I dismissed as likely residue from an old soft tissue injury. In retrospect, I realize it represented bone tissue inside his teratoma—"

"Enough!" said Annie. She signaled the server to bring a second round. "Obviously, I'm going to have to *reel* my old pal back to the table."

She circled her hands around each other in a reeling motion. "Come back, Nora. Come back to your senses. That young man died from complications of a very rare tumor in his *arm* that, logically speaking, no one would have ever suspected *beforehand*—pun intended."

Nora groaned again.

"And it was a *teratoma*, for godsakes," said Annie. "Who gets one of those in an *arm*? You're great, but you're not omniscient. You can't honestly believe you should've been able to *divine* its presence from a speck of calcium on an X-ray?"

"All right," Nora said, holding up her hands in surrender.

"No, I'm not finished. You need to understand that the teratoma had been present and metastasizing for a long while *before* your surgery. Before you ever picked up the scalpel! Because the pathology exam shows most tumor emboli in his lungs were *chronic*—not acute. So, they had to have been there for weeks to months before you even met him."

"But Dario didn't die *then*. Again, the *timing*—he died on my table."

Annie looked sidelong at her. "He was on your table because of a compartment syndrome, and you did the appropriate surgery for that. You just happened to be there when the last straw—the last *embolus*—proved fatal."

"Just seems like too much of a coincidence," Nora said.

"I'm not so sure," Annie said. "Who knows? The kid falls a day before, and maybe enough of the teratoma dislodges—and that partially relieves the chronic obstruction of the blood flow to his forearm? Or, his teratoma just happens to shed another embolus, like it had been doing for a long while? Either way, the sudden relief of the obstruction is the ticket to his reperfusion injury and compartment syndrome. Unfortunately, you had to hop on the train at that time. But a totally separate track leading to the boy's death had already been laid down months before."

Nora gazed at her friend, comforted by her patience and understanding. And how much more reassuring to hear Annie's voice in real time, her emphases and certitude imparting more meaningful dimension to the words she had laid out in her report.

The server arrived with round two. And while Annie ordered appetizers for the table, Nora returned to thinking about Dario's teratoma.

Like Annie says, who gets one of those in an arm? And how did germ cells get into Dario's arm in the first place?

"Yo," said Annie, snapping her fingers. "Remember me?"

But Nora didn't hear her or the background kitchen clatter now. She didn't smell the ciabatta or garlic. She didn't visually register the bread basket at which she appeared to be staring. Instead, she had entered an inner sanctuary, where her senses had receded—a mental clearing, cultivated over years of deeply contemplating the body's elegant mysteries. Her clinical intuition coursed briskly through it now, sifting through troves of scientific facts and diagnostic acumen. It flowed freely and assuredly, carrying her thoughts toward an increasingly visible shore. *A teratoma in a young man's arm, where multi-potent germ cells don't normally reside . . .* She recalled Luis' dogged questioning about the cellular origin of Dario's teratoma. *Yes, how did cells like that even get there? . . . Cells "like that" . . . Cells like . . . like stem cells . . . like multi-potent stem cells that could give rise to a teratoma.*

Annie tapped her friend's shoulder and said, "Nora? Should I worry about you? You look like you're having a spell."

Nora blinked hard twice, and then snapped to attention. She smiled at Annie and said, "Stem cells. Stem cells were injected into Dario's arm."

Bill and Ellie's Home

Ellie phoned Bill to inform him she would be late coming home. After retrieving the fax from Postal Supreme, she still needed to get cash from the ATM and fill their Audi's tank—"at least, to get us through the next couple of days." And now she was stuck at Safeway, "with only one register open. So, if you need something, this is the time to say so."

"Nothing from Safeway," Bill answered, realizing an opportunity to secure additional time for Fred's imminent visit.

"Honestly, Bill, could you be any more obtuse?"

"Do you mean 'oblique'?"

"I don't have time for your contrariness."

"All right. Take it easy. I just remembered needing a couple of things from CVS."

She huffed. "*Another* store?"

"Sorry, Ellie. But I'm out of my eye medications. And while you're there, could you pick up a pack of those disposable blue razors I like?"

Minutes after the call ended, he heard Fred ring the front bell. He opened the door and blinked at him.

"You all right?" asked Fred, doubt pervading his tone.

Bill tapped his forehead and said, "Of course: Fred, right?"

Fred's heart twinged. "Yeah, it's me. And I'm early." After a brief pause, he asked, "Mind if I come in?"

"Please," said Bill, stepping aside and ushering him in.

"Where's Ellie?" Fred asked, scanning the living room.

"She's . . . Huh, I don't know."

Regarding his old mentor with a pained expression, Fred said, "You're not alone here in the house, are you?"

Bill fidgeted with his bow tie and said, "I might be."

Fred rued the sad fact that neither Nora nor Jack had been able to accompany him here tonight. More than ever, he needed their help in developing an emergency strategy for the Balabans. "Bill," he said, "have you eaten anything today? Should I call for a delivery?"

"I think I ate," said Bill. "Not sure. Still, why don't we just go to the parlor for some cognac, like we used to in the old days?"

"Ah," said Fred, smiling politely. "So, *that* you can remember."

Bill nodded. "You know what they say—the oldest memories are the last to go."

Fred followed him down the hallway, fondly recalling time spent in Bill's parlor. The camaraderie they had enjoyed, and the wide-ranging discussions over cognac—about complex neuro cases, groundbreaking articles in the *New England Journal*, the felt experience of becoming a doctor, and . . .

But Fred froze when he stepped into the parlor. Nothing looked familiar; nothing reflected the past or resonated with old memories. The bulky armchairs were toppled over, like defeated Sumo wrestlers. First-edition literary collections were scattered across the Persian carpet. The few remaining pictures on the wall hung askew. And sprinkled like confetti over everything were torn photographs of Ellie and her newspaper mentions. Her cherished daytime soap-opera Emmy lay cracked atop ceramic logs in the fireplace. And before Fred could marshal a response, Bill nervously laughed and said, "Now, where did I put that cognac?"

Glenview District

After leaving Suzie's Trattoria and a warm embrace with Annie, Nora walked toward her Prius, three blocks away. Park Boulevard still bustled with dog walkers and restaurant patrons strolling under the ambient streetlighting.

Although her heart felt lighter, her belly did not—not after the corn and saffron arancini, the pan-roasted Spanish octopus, the gamberetto and baked rigatoni. She regretted not saving leftovers, but vowed to do so the next time—two weeks from now, when she and Annie had scheduled to meet there again.

Turning the corner at Glenfield, Nora happily reflected on their dinner conversation. How wonderful it had felt to discuss a complicated medical case with someone who appreciated nuance and complexity, who eagerly invited diagnostic challenges and—

Footsteps sounded from behind her.

She clutched her shoulder bag and scanned the dark side street. Though seeing no one, she accelerated her stride. But when she rounded the corner to Woodruff, the footsteps grew louder. She could see her Prius ahead, under a streetlamp, and estimated needing a minute to reach it. Her heart rate picked up with the pace of her running. And when she glanced back now, she saw Owen Landry barreling toward her.

"Stop!" he called out.

She defensively positioned her house key through her fist, while flashing back to Owen barging into her office, and to news of him stalking her in the ER yesterday. She clicked her remote and then yanked open the car door, but Owen was now at her back.

When she tried to scream, he covered her mouth with his hand and said, "I just want to talk."

With every muscle in her body tensed, Nora waited for his next telling move. And when he finally loosened his grip, she bit his hand as hard as she could. He moaned and stepped back.

A passing dog walker called out, "Are you all right, ma'am?" His bulldog growled and pulled on its leash.

Nora leaned against her car, de-adrenalizing, keeping Owen in sight.

"Please, help me," he whispered.

"What?" she exclaimed, trying to catch her breath. She stared incredulously at him, thinking: *He looks so small and broken. Not like the monster he's been. His hands are bloodied; his clothes are covered with dirt. And he's asking me for help?*

The dog walker called out, "Ma'am?"

Jack's Home

Jack tried to dissuade Carrie from returning his Tupperware from Thanksgiving dinner, and "certainly not at this hour on a school night." But she had begged him, claiming she'd been on a wild-goose chase, and something about killer sofa pillows. She *had to* accomplish *something* before the end of this miserable, accomplishment-averse day. "So, if I return your Tupperware, I can at least say I'm done with post-Thanksgiving sorting."

Besides, the prospect of her impromptu visit excited Luis. And when she arrived at the door, he grabbed her hand and dragged her to the guestroom, where he and Jack had been experimenting with stage makeup. He flashed his winning grin and asked, "Can I practice on you? I want to win a Tony someday."

Pointing at Jack, Carrie said, "Why not ask him to model for you?"

Jack laughed and said, "I did my time! I scrubbed clean just a few minutes ago. Didn't want to give you a heart attack."

"Please, Dr. Chandler?" Luis pleaded.

"He continues to explore potential careers," Jack explained. "This week, it's work in the theater."

Bowled over by Luis' enthusiasm, Carrie removed her coat and relented. "Okay. But only if someone brings me a tequila." Jack saluted her, mouthed "Thanks," and left for the kitchen.

After analyzing Carrie's face from several angles, Luis asked, "Shall we begin?"

Carrie's brow raised. "Oh, 'shall we' now? My, what a highfalutin place you got here. And all these wigs and makeup—I take it they're from Jack's old theater days?"

"Yes," Luis said, pulling her long white hair back in a pink scrunchie. "But what does 'highfalutin' mean?"

"Well, I'm using it now to mean extra fancy."

"Like a place a prima donna would go to?"

She nodded and said, "Your vocabulary is growing faster than the weeds in my garden. I didn't think anything could outpace that!"

"Thank you," he said, draping a striped bath towel around her neck. "We'll begin with foundation."

"Pretty slick already," she said as he slathered it on her. "Are we going full Hollywood?"

"No, Dr. Chandler. We're doing *theater* makeup. That's more like going full New York."

She laughed and said, "You're right," feeling the day's frustration begin to wane. "But mind turning the mirror so I don't have to see myself? I'm not at my best."

"Okay," said Luis, turning it aside. "And then you'll be really surprised at the end."

When Jack returned with the tequila, he winked at Carrie and said, "Hello, Gorgeous!"

"Yeah, right," she said, grabbing her drink. "And, speaking of the theater, I spotted an old actress on the street today. Well, not literally on the street. In a mailbox-rental facility."

"Say more," said Jack, raising his shot glass to her.

"Well, I recognized her from an old TV program, but I couldn't remember her real name. And the snotty store clerk wouldn't help me out. Anyhow, I thought I'd google the show later tonight." She took a sip of tequila, but Luis politely admonished her to remain still.

"Yes, stay still," Jack warned her. "Or you'll end up like I did, with mascara on your eyeball."

"Okay," said Luis, "now we're going to highlight your cheeks."

"Why not?" said Carrie. "I'd never turn down any highlight."

"Can't have enough of those," Jack agreed.

But when Luis' makeup brush touched Carrie's face, he paused and stepped back. His eyes lit up and he said, "I have an idea."

"Pray tell," said Jack, delighting in Luis' delight.

Luis grabbed a blonde wig, placed it on Carrie's head, and said, "Let's make you up like the actress *we* know!" Then he whispered something to Jack.

"Ah," said Jack, smiling. "That's a brilliant idea. Go ahead, we'll wait."

After Luis dashed out of the room, Carrie picked up her tequila and said, "Finally!" Then she gulped it down and said, "Ah!" But when she turned to Jack to request a second shot, he flinched.

"Oh?" she said. "Do I look that bad? Should I ask Luis to go lighter on the—?"

"No," said Jack, with a stiff grimace. "It's just that . . . you look exactly like Lydia."

Carrie cringed and said, "Of course. Just like my Clairol-blonde twin."

Their discomfort was palpable to Luis upon his quick return with a blue pillowcase. Taken aback by their odd demeanor, he asked, "What's wrong?"

Jack coughed nervously and said, "Dr. Chandler had an identical twin, Lydia, who is no longer with us. And her twin used to dye her hair blonde."

"So," Carrie chimed in, "we were just reminiscing about her is all."

Luis nodded knowingly. "I know people who died, too. I'm sorry about your sister."

"Thank you," said Carrie, taking his hand. "And I'm very sorry about the people you lost."

Luis glanced at Jack, who returned a tender look and said, "Well, before you go on, what do you think of Dr. Chandler's brow line?"

"Hm," said Luis, assessing his handiwork. Then he grabbed a brow pencil and declared, "It needs to be thicker in the middle to look like the prima donna's."

Hoping to keep their conversation off the subject of death, Jack returned to Carrie's prior comment and said, "I rent a private postbox, too. Still, these days, even that doesn't guarantee much privacy, does it?"

"I wouldn't know," said Carrie. "I don't have one. I was only there to track down the neurologist for your old mentor. Nora asked me to do a 'consult'—as *you* well know."

Jack said, "Yeah, sorry about that—I heard our strategy didn't go over well with you. But you went full Columbo? You actually tried to track down Bill's neurologist?"

"Yeah, because I was on my last nerve. I mean, *nothing* was going right today. My office still wasn't hooked up to the current century. Even HR canceled my afternoon orientation. So, I figured if I could move the needle on the so-called 'consult'—"

"You really don't need to keep air-quoting that word," said Jack. "We all understand that our ask was a stretch."

"Yes, please," said Luis. "I need you not to move. I don't want to poke your beautiful green eyes!"

Holding her head stiffly, Carrie said, "Anyway, I had tried phoning the neurologist, but the number I'd been given was dead wrong. So, feeling the pressure from you all, I drove to the guy's address. Or, I should say, I drove to the address on the request for your friend's old records. But that just led me to Postal Supreme. And the 'Num 202' in the address was no medical suite." She tsked and said, "I should've trusted the google gods. Total waste of my time."

"Hang on," said Jack, rubbing his forehead. "That actress you saw there today? What did she look like?"

"Wait," said Luis, "we're almost done." Then he draped the blue pillowcase around Carrie's neck and handed her a pair of sunglasses. When she slipped them on, he stepped aside, angled the mirror back to her, and asked, "What do we think?"

"Well," said Carrie, after taking a beat. "The actress . . . she looked a lot like this."

Guest Suite, Carl's Home

Finally, Winston put down his pen and stared at the chart he had created in his reporter's notebook. After cross-referencing the parents of the five questionable tennis recruits, he had formed a chain of connections among them. Arrows shot across the page, linking at least one parent of each recruit with at least one parent of another. Parent A, Sonya Wisekof, connected to Parent B, Dario's mother, through their fundraising efforts for the Oakland Fine Arts Museum. Parent A also linked to Parent C through board membership on the state's humanities council. C connected to D as co-participants on the regional theater's advisory committee. And both C and D connected to E, a real estate mogul and major donor to the regional theater.

Winston pushed away from the table, then headed to the kitchen for a celebratory beer. Seeing his leftover frittata and veggies on the counter, he was reminded of the lateness of the hour, and he vowed to be more attentive to Fergie. After devouring his food, he opened a beer and returned to the dining room to feast on his chain of parental connections.

Still, he wondered, how did this chain assemble? Certainly, not by happenstance. Someone—or some ones—had to be threading the beads.

He picked up his pen and tapped it on the table, studying his chart. Then he wrote Steven McArdle's name on it, appended with a big fat question mark.

Glenview District

After reassuring the dog walker she didn't need assistance, Nora and Owen stood alone under the dim streetlamp. They stared uncertainly at one another, until she finally said, "You've been nothing but horrible to me. Why should I trust you, let alone 'help' you?"

Owen leaned against the streetlamp, pressing his bitten hand against his chest. "I don't know," he said dejectedly.

"You even told Dario's parents I was responsible for his death!"

"Not exactly. But I shouldn't have said what I said. I'm sorry."

She scoffed. "That's all you have to say to me? *No.* Tell me why you did that."

He haltingly answered, "I was in a panic."

"So, you thought, what? Why not throw Dr. Kelly into one, too? She could use some abuse? I've been attacked and threatened because of what you said!"

He merely shook his head, failing to imagine an adequate apology.

She stayed near her car and kept its door open. "Then explain what you were panicking about."

"You don't want to know," he said.

Boy, does this guy not know me, she thought. "'Don't want to know'? You're talking to the wrong person." She closed her car door and studied him. She had worked alongside him in the ER, throughout his Ortho residency years, but never once did he exhibit anything close to panic. Impatience, sure. Irritation and nervousness, yes. But then to unhinge one day, to panic, to erupt in fury and hostility?

"Forget it," he said, turning away. "Again, I'm sorry."

"Not so fast," she said. "You owe me an explanation." When he hesitated, she continued, "The troubles between us began on the day of Dario's surgery. So, what happened that day for you?"

He stood still, his back to her.

She persisted, thinking out loud about that pivotal day. "You *seriously* wanted that surgery. And when you missed it, you barged into my office like a bull . . . a *bully*, actually. And in a tantrum. All you seemed to care about was doing the surgery—not Dario or his death, certainly not me. At first, I attributed your child-like behavior to your wounded male ego. But then . . ."

He turned to face her.

"But then," she continued, "your *fury* toward me? And *stalking* me— in the ER yesterday, and from the restaurant tonight? You, essentially telling grieving parents that I killed their son?" She released a sharp tsk and said, "God, there's so much more going on than your wounded ego. You need to start talking."

Owen didn't know how to explain, or where to begin. He'd come looking for her—or "stalking" her, he now understood—for one selfish reason. And after all he had done to her, as she so painfully laid out, what right did he have to request her help?

Seeing him waver, Nora fixed him with a clear-eyed stare and said, "For some reason, doing Dario's surgery was an outright *necessity* for you. It wasn't an 'opportunity' for your residents, and it wasn't only your bloated ego that—"

"Please, stop," he said. "I meant it—you don't want to know." Then, recalling Bill's similar but deceitful caution, he added, "For your benefit, not mine, I've told you enough."

Shaking her head, she continued provocatively: "And you've been tracking me down because you need something from me. What could that be?"

"Look, I didn't mean to 'stalk' you or scare you. I only wanted to ask..." He hung his head, then took a deep breath and continued: "I needed to know what you saw during the surgery, and if the coroner found anything."

Nora's eyes narrowed while she considered his request. *That's what he's been needing from me? So, then, he has reason to suspect there was something in Dario's body, and he's been afraid of it being found.*

"Why are you looking at me like that?" he asked. "Please, just tell me what you and the coroner saw."

"Well, I can tell you what I'm seeing right now. You're desperate to know if Dario's body contained evidence of something you did."

When he just looked away, she stepped toward him and said, "And *that* is why you needed to perform his surgery—to see for yourself, and to prevent me from discovering it. The logical conclusion is, you were going to destroy that evidence—because it would implicate you in some wrongdoing."

His stony silence confirmed her suspicion, and she knew she was nearing the truth. *I could jump straight to asking him about stem-cell injections, and telling him about Dario's teratoma. But that would mean skipping over the important in-between questions—ones I may never again have the opportunity to ask.*

"I made mistakes," he finally said. "Big mistakes."

She folded her arms across her chest. "Well, suppose I did find 'something' during the surgery? That wouldn't have implicated *me*—not as a bystander who merely unearthed it in a roomful of other healthcare workers as witnesses. And yet, you essentially blamed me for Dario's death—in my office, and to his parents."

"But I didn't really know if there *was* something to be found. So, when I lost my chance to find out firsthand, I panicked. And I was pissed at you for taking the surgery and leaving me in the lurch. So, then, when I heard the parents shouting in the waiting room, it was a convenient outlet, and I just—"

"Hold on," she said, her mind racing in a new direction. "You believed it was *possible* there was nothing to be found?"

He nodded, then looked pleadingly at her. "So, can you tell me now?"

Nora tried to corral her galloping thoughts. *He seems to be telling the truth. But to be so afraid, and genuinely not know if that's warranted?* She asked, "What did you do to Dario that made you so fearful?"

"I can't," he said, shaking his head. "Things will only get worse. I'm being set up."

"Well, now you know what that feels like," she shot back.

Owen flinched and said, "I deserved that. But what I did to you, it wasn't right, but it was in a moment of panic. I didn't mean to hurt you or anyone else."

"'Anyone else'?" she said, tilting her head. "Who is the 'anyone else' you also didn't intend to hurt? Was it Dario?"

He looked directly at her now, seeing not only her, but also everything surrounding her—the waxing crescent moon, the streetlamp's glow on her face, her sage-colored Prius, the blue house with the red door across the street. This, he knew, constellated the mental photograph he would forever carry, capturing the moment in which everything changed. Then he stammered, "I'm afraid I might've helped to kill Dario."

She knew it was best to remain silent if she hoped for him to volunteer further sensitive information—a communication strategy she employed with tight-lipped patients that usually worked. Still, the silence was excruciating.

"But I'm not sure," he finally said. "And I've got no one I trust to help me figure that out." Then, summoning his resolve on the roof this afternoon, he added, "But I intend to take responsibility for my actions. So, if I played a role in Dario's death, I need to know."

And there you have it, she thought. Now she understood his panic. And making the obvious link to her deduction over dinner tonight, she took a deep breath and said, "You needed Dario's surgery in order to know—*and* obscure—whether you harmed him with stem-cell injections."

Stunned by her charge, he stood rigid and stared blankly back. A white Corvette zoomed by, its radio blaring, and gusty winds rustled the trees. When he could speak, he said, "For you to put that together . . . then there *was* evidence of the cells . . . you must've seen evidence of the cells."

Still strategically withholding disclosure about the teratoma, she said, "I saw nothing during surgery. But you just confirmed my suspicion, Owen. Now I know Dario received stem-cell injections, and you gave them to him."

"Oh, god," he said, his hands held out in supplication. "You have to believe me. I gave him only *one* injection. It was supposed to strengthen his tendons and muscles."

"And you believed that?"

"No. I mean, I didn't know. But Dario's father believed that. He thought the cells could help Dario with performance sports and getting into college."

"Did Dario understand there was no evidence for stem cells doing that?"

Owen shrugged. "I think he took them to make his father happy."

"Well, did that even work?"

"I don't know. Look, Dario was receiving injections before I ever met him. Like I told you, I gave him only one. He didn't ask me questions, and he knew not to talk about the injections."

"Not talk to who?"

"Anybody. Dario told me his father said it would look bad if other people found out, like they were cheating to get ahead in the world."

Nora waited a moment for the sadness to pass through her. What a painful Greek tragedy, unfolding in such an ultramodern context. *This was the secret Dario was struggling to tell me before he died. He suspected or wondered about those injections causing the problem in his arm.*

"Dr. Kelly?" Owen said. "If you saw nothing, how did you know about the injections? Did Dario tell you? Or was something found at autopsy?"

"All in due time," she answered. "First, I want to know what you meant, when you said you were being 'set up.'"

"I've already told you more than I should," he said.

"I'll be the judge of that," she said. "I want to know who is holding a knife to your throat. Because that special someone must have something to do with you and the injections. It has to be someone who—"

Suddenly, a new puzzle piece took shape in her mind, informed by Jack's description of DeeDee's upsetting ER experience. She could almost hear the new piece click into place, expanding the bigger picture. She looked pointedly at Owen and asked, "On the day of Dario's surgery, why were you lurking outside Bill Balaban's room in the ER?"

"What?"

"Someone saw you lurking outside his room, and angry as hell."

"It was nothing," he said, determined to keep her out of the Balabans' toxic web as best he could. "I just needed to talk with him about . . . my research."

Nora watched him with a wary expression, thinking: *He's lying, because he's scared shitless. And it can't be a coincidence that Bill just happened to be in the ER with a "meltdown" at the same time that Owen was supposed to be performing Dario's surgery. It also can't be "nothing" that Owen was waiting to convey to him in an angry, lurking state afterwards. Whatever he had to discuss with Bill was related to the surgery.*

"What now?" he asked, needing to break the uncomfortable silence that followed.

She tersely responded, "I hate being lied to."

Staring at his bitten hand, Owen conceded defeat. He knew he couldn't keep her out of it because she was already inside—seeing him and Bill in the big ugly picture, seeing a connection between them and Dario's stem-cell injections. And, he realized, she was hell-bent on seeing everything.

As if reading his mind, she said, "I'll help you lay things out. *Not* coincidentally, you and Bill and Dario were in the ER at the same time. And after Dario's surgery, you panicked and *had* to talk with Bill. Do you see what I'm suggesting?" She shivered internally from her chilling insight about Bill, but proceeded: "I'm suggesting that Bill shared your interest in Dario's surgery—to seek and destroy any evidence of the stem-cell injections."

Owen said with cosmic resignation, "Yes."

Nora let out a sigh of relief. *Still, this truth really sucks. Nothing feels good about uncovering it. And how demented Bill must be to behave so unethically. But, if the two of them were working together—?*

He said, "You've got to understand. I know what I did was wrong. And now—"

She held up a hand and asked, "If you and Bill were working together, why did you have to lurk around his room after the surgery? Why not just go right in and talk with him?"

"'Working together'?" Owen shook his head. "It never felt like that. It was more like me trying to survive by getting 'on board' with him. And I was trying to tell him that his plan failed—that I didn't get Dario's surgery. But his wife or some nurse was always in his room, so I had to wait a long time. And the longer I waited, the more I panicked. I was afraid of disappointing him and losing his support, and I was scared to death about the coroner getting hold of Dario's body."

Nora struggled to refrain from commenting about his seemingly crass remark. *For now, at least. Because if I say how cold and self-centered that sounded, I'll interrupt the momentum of him talking. And, for the same reason, I can't show my anger. But I am angry. And unlike Dario, he has no fucking idea how it feels to be scared to death.* Finally, she asked, "And your anger?"

Hearing judgment in her question, he haltingly answered. "I was angry at Bill. Because it was his fault I missed the surgery, and, still, I knew I'd be blamed. I knew my career was at risk. So, I lashed out at him, at you, at anyone I ran into that day—even Dario's parents. Again, Dr. Kelly, I apologize—"

"Stop," she said. "Why was it Bill's fault?"

"Because he phoned me, minutes before the surgery, with *his* paranoid freakout—which only aggravated my own, and kept me from answering my pager. But I would've made it to the ER by eleven, and answered your page in time, if Bill hadn't kept me on the call. I would've been there before you could grab the surgery."

"Are you fucking kidding me? 'Grab the surgery'? Dario didn't have the luxury of waiting on you or the god you think you are!"

"I keep making things worse," he said, his hands pressed to his head. "Please, it's just a stupid casual way I talk with some of my surgical colleagues. I didn't mean—"

"Was there even a disaster-preparedness drill earlier that morning?"

"There was. Bill called while I was ending it. Or, trying to."

"Look, I've been holding back. There are things I *really* want to say to you." She took a measured breath and continued, "And I'm losing my patience. Maybe the person holding a knife to your throat . . ." She stopped herself from ending with "has good cause." Instead, she suggested, "Let's just talk about the person who's threatening you, and why."

Owen's brow furrowed. He said, "But we have been."

"What?" she said.

"That person is Bill," he replied.

Nora started to say something, but surprise and confusion throttled her speech.

He continued, "And he went so far as to plant evidence against me."

"No," she said, shaking her head, "that's not possible."

"Well, I can show you that doctored evidence. It's in my apartment. I took it home from the lab yesterday."

Guest Suite, Carl's Home

"You're still sitting here?" asked Fergie, walking into their unlit dining room. Winston's face glowed eerily, illuminated blue-gray by the light from his laptop screen.

Winston checked the time and said, "Sorry, Fergs. I'll come to bed in a minute."

She placed her hands on her hips and said, "You're the worst time estimator in the world. Thank god you don't schedule trains."

Nearly touching his thumb with his forefinger, he said, "I'm *this close* to figuring it out."

She sighed resignedly, sat on his lap, and glanced at the chart he'd drawn in his notebook. "Well, looks like you made connections between the parents."

He nodded. "At least one parent of each recruit connects to another one or two."

Pointing to the big question mark alongside Steven McArdle's name, she asked, "What's that about?"

He kissed her cheek and said, "Well, I can connect the parents as individuals, but not as a group. The only thing they seem to share is having an untalented son, who was recruited to the UCSM tennis team, presumably by the head coach—Steven McArdle."

"What about connections between the parents and the coach?"

"Nothing prior to their kids' recruitment. So, how does this whole shebang work?"

Fergie yawned and said, "Well, the coach has to be involved. I mean, he had to approve the recruits. And, when you asked about them, he hung up the phone on you."

"Yeah. But the task is to figure how he's involved and prove it. But it definitely looks like some shady recruiting over his five-year tenure."

"You'll figure it out," she said, standing up and massaging his shoulders. "But I'm going back to bed. I'm bushed, and this stuff you're working on stirs up my sadness over Dario."

"Okay, night, Fergs," he said.

But she stopped in the doorway and asked, "You said five recruits, right?"

"Yeah."

"And that the coach has a five-year tenure at UCSM?"

He nodded.

"So, that works out to one recruit per year of his tenure. By any chance, was it *literally* one recruit at a time, one year at a time?"

After checking his notebook, he answered, "As a matter of fact, yes."

"Then it's some fixed type of deal," she said. "Limited to one a year. Like an annual scholarship, maybe? Like the scholarship Dario had?"

Winston's jaw dropped. "Babe!" he said, looking so admiringly at her that she blushed. "You're the world's greatest muse. I'll bet you're right— an annual tennis scholarship. That could be the common denominator among the recruits, and the link between their parents and the coach."

"Well, if that turns out to be true, it's crazy-times-ten those kids got scholarships. I mean, besides not having any tennis talent, they all seem to come from wealthy families. They probably couldn't get in on their grades alone, and the scholarship gave them the leg up." But when she saw that he'd already returned his rapt attention to his laptop, she complained, "Hey—how about rewarding your muse by coming to bed with her?"

With a small apologetic smile, he said, "Please? I want to check out your scholarship angle. It'll just take a minute."

She crossed her arms and tilted her head.

"Okay, you're right," he said. "How about ten minutes max, then I'll see you in bed. Promise."

She sauntered over to him and set her cellphone's timer for ten minutes. Then she handed her cell to him and whispered something in his ear that caused his eyes to widen. He watched in awe as she walked provocatively back toward their bedroom.

Owen's Apartment

17th Street, Oakland

Using the personal safety protocol she and Fred had established during their residency, Nora texted him with Owen Landry's address and a photo of his license plate.

Fred texted back: *Got it. Text me when U leave.*

After responding with a thumbs-up emoji, she told Owen, "We can go now." Then she got into her Prius and followed his green Honda Civic to his apartment on 17th Street. Once inside, she waited on his couch while he cleaned and bandaged his hand. Meanwhile, her cell chimed with a concerning text from Fred: *At Bills house now. Waiting 4 Ellie 2 come home!*

Nora muttered, "What the?" and texted back: *Bill is alone?*

Fred: *Yes. And it's a crisis here. Parlor—destroyed. R things OK at Landry's?*

Nora: *Yes. But sorry about Bill—sounds scary*
Fred: *Agreed.*
Nora: *What R U going 2 do*
Fred: *Don't know. We need a Plan C.*
Nora: ☹
Fred: ☹ ☹ ☹
Nora: *I can stop by later?*
Fred: ☺ *Will invite Jack.*
Nora: ☺

Finally, Owen appeared in the living room and set a cardboard box down on the coffee table. He had changed into clean clothes, and his hand was wrapped in gauze. "This is the evidence I told you about," he said. "Everything I could find in the lab that Bill was planting on me, and things I just emptied out from my desk."

Nora opened the box and withdrew a lime-green binder. "Glossy," she said, thumbing through it. "An AccuCellz stem-cell manual that looks like a coffee-table art book." She pointed to its title page. "And here's your name, written in ink."

"But I didn't write that," he said. "It barely even looks like my handwriting."

She put the binder aside to focus on a manila folder that contained communications with AccuCellz, Inc. "You've gotta be kidding," she said. "You can order stem cells online? Like pizzas or shoes?"

He nodded. "It's not illegal to do research with them. Bill usually has some in the lab. And he sometimes sells them to colleagues."

"'Research'? Is that what you're calling what you did to Dario? I'll bet he didn't know you were *experimenting* on him. You know, *legitimate* clinical research requires transparency about what you're doing, and protecting your human subjects. You're obligated to collect safety and efficacy data."

"I know," he said ruefully. "I conduct 'legitimate' research—it's bench research, not clinical, but still . . ." He plopped down on the couch beside her. "I wasn't experimenting on Dario. I had a single encounter with him, one that I couldn't regret more. And Bill wasn't doing research, either. He was using stem cells to practice 'regenerative medicine'—like a lot of doctors do."

Her brow arched. "Well, kudos to the ad agency that came up with *that* marketing concept."

"You may not like it. But there are hundreds of stem-cell manufacturers and regenerative medicine clinics in the U.S. So, to me, what Bill was doing didn't seem so outlandish. And in my specialty, patients always ask about them to strengthen their cartilage and bones. They see ads for those clinics on the internet. They see celebrities endorsing them."

"But what they don't see is truth in that advertising," she said. "Those unregulated, for-profit clinics are making outrageous claims, and giving legitimate stem-cell research a black eye. They advertise stem-cell products as 'potential cures' for just about *anything*. But there's no proof of their benefit beyond a handful of disorders—a few cancers, a few blood and immune-system disorders. People are throwing money at those clinics, not even knowing whether the so-called 'treatments' are safe."

He rested his head against the couch. "Bill told me how lucrative his stem-cell work was. He tried to recruit me more than once. He said I'd get rich a lot sooner than waiting on some ortho-device patent to come out of my research."

She shook her head in bewilderment. "That's not the Bill I used to know—granted, a long time ago. He taught us evidence-based medicine—actual science. He taught us how to interpret studies, critique research, debunk hyped pharma advertising. And now, what? He's gone to the dark side of medicine. I don't understand."

"Well, I've only known him for the two years I've been working Thursday afternoons in his lab. But that entire time, he was involved with stem cells. He even flies to Costa Rica every other month to work a few days in some clinic there. Stem-cell tourism pays off big—tens of thousands of dollars per treatment. In fact, that's where he gave Dario his first injection. And that's where he was, when he asked me to give Dario a follow-up one here."

Surveying the living room, Nora noted its sparse furnishings and naked walls. A few items rested on the TV stand and bookshelves: New Orleans Saints paraphernalia, a small carved statue of a warrior, and a framed photograph of Owen, presumably with his parents. She asked, "Why didn't you accept Bill's lucrative proposition?"

Leaning forward, staring at his parents' photograph, he answered, "To be honest, I thought about it a quick minute. Patients paying me thousands of dollars for a shot. Me, attending fancy conferences in fancy places. Me, paying off my med-school loans and helping my parents out." He shook his head. "But I knew those direct-to-consumer regen clinics were mostly hype. And the FDA still hasn't approved stem-cell treatments for anything in orthopedics." He faced her and said, "I understand you having doubts about me. But I take pride in conducting legitimate research, and I respect the science of medicine."

Yes, Nora thought, *he's right about me doubting him. How can he sound so sanguine and honorable one moment, but so hotheaded and unhinged in the next?* Intending to poke the bear as a test, she said, "Still, you did give Dario an injection."

He nodded soberly. "I made a mistake in a moment of weakness. All because I was afraid of losing my research unit if I disappointed Bill. He also made sure I knew the lab received big bucks from Donald Parker's philanthropy, and that 'we' were returning a small favor by continuing his son's injections in the U.S."

When she tsked, he tilted his head and said, "You can't tell me you've never compromised yourself as a doctor."

She wanted to deflect his question. But of course, she'd been compromised as a doctor. At times, she'd even been complicit with the compromise, trading the devil behind one door for the devil behind another, and just hoping she'd chosen the less hellish option.

He persisted, "With all your years—and I mean no offense by that—don't tell me you haven't had to 'doctor' an insurance claim to get a patient the care they needed. Or manipulate rules to get a sick patient transferred to a tertiary hospital. Or—"

"But there's a huge difference between trying to get patients medical care with proven health benefits, and providing them with bogus stem-cell 'care' with zero known benefit. And then, doing that merely to fund *your* research projects!"

He looked shamefacedly at her, but she continued: "And 'regenerative medicine'? The *only* 'regeneration' happening in Dario's body was in his—" She stopped herself from saying "teratoma" and inadvertently revealing the information she was still tactically withholding. Instead, she took a breath and suggested, "Let's get back to the box?" Then she withdrew another document and said, "This is a stem-cell order form with your signature next to Bill's."

"But," he said, examining it, "I never co-signed this. I've never even ordered stem cells."

She subsequently produced several paid invoices with his name typed in as the authorizing payor. He shook his head each time. Finally, he said, "This is a waste of time. These documents have been altered to implicate me. I was never involved in any money transaction involving stem cells."

"Then what's this?" she asked.

He groaned, instantly recognizing the canceled check she held out. "Shit. I forgot about that. That's the check Bill wrote to compensate me for the injection I gave Dario."

She whistled softly and said, "Three thousand dollars for giving one shot? If I was paid even a fraction of that for every shot I gave . . ."

"Bill said it was the standard administration fee. But each treatment—"

"Okay. Let's stop calling these injections 'treatments.' They don't 'treat' anything."

"Fair. But I was going to say, each session costs about ten thousand total."

Nora slumped back against the couch. *How surreal. Doctors and patients transacting over sham products for sale. And Bill, peddling snake oil? Bill, acting so cruelly—and criminally—toward Owen, and so violently toward Ellie? His dementia must be profound.* Then she shuddered, suddenly reminded that Fred was alone with Bill right now. *Is Fred safe? What did he mean, when he texted about a 'crisis' there?*

"Dr. Kelly?" said Owen.

"I'm sorry," she said. "But I should leave soon." Then, hastily sorting through the remainder of the box, she added, "And I think you're right—it's a waste of time at this point. We got the gist of what Bill was up to and . . ."

"What's wrong now?" he asked, watching her adjust her readers to scrutinize a document.

"This," she said, handing it over to him. "It's an ultrasound image, with a machine-stamped date on it. But no name." She watched his face turn ashen as he examined it. Then he haltingly said, "I have a portable ultrasound in the lab. I use it for tendon research."

"I don't understand," she said. "If you took this ultrasound, what's the point of Bill planting it on you?"

"But I didn't take it. I would've remembered this."

She leaned in and traced the image with a finger. "These look like tendons, right? Muscle, here. Some calcium spicules and—" She gasped and unguardedly exclaimed, "This is an ultrasound of Dario's teratoma!"

Owen startled with her disclosure. "So, Dario had a teratoma in his arm?"

Though instantly regretting her injudicious reveal, she nodded. Still, witnessing his genuine surprise about the news was edifying.

"And that's why you saw nothing at surgery," he said, speaking slowly. "The tumor was higher up, in his arm. So, then, the coroner must have found it."

She nodded again.

He stood up and paced. "I'm trying not to freak out. I'm not going back to the roof."

"'The roof'?" she said. "What does that mean?"

He waved his bandaged hand dismissively and said, "Stem-cell injections causing a teratoma—sure, okay. But, Dario's compartment syndrome? That can't be a coincidence. The tumor must be related somehow."

Of course, he was right: two unusual medical events occurring simultaneously were most likely related. She said, "The coroner had a theory about that over dinner. Just look at the ultrasound again—the whole thing, not just the tumor."

He stopped pacing to examine the ultrasound. "His teratoma is partially compressing an artery to his forearm. That could cause chronic muscle ischemia. But not his swelling and elevated compartment pressures."

"Unless," she said, "that compression was suddenly relieved when a piece of teratoma broke off or metastasized. That would explain the sudden reperfusion of blood to his ischemic muscles. His compartment syndrome, in other words."

Sitting down beside her again, he stared intently at her, his knee bouncing.

Recognizing his desperation to make sense of things—something she fully understood—she dropped her hands in her lap and said, "All right. In fairness, it's time for me to tell you everything. The autopsy? It showed that Dario's teratoma had been metastasizing to his lungs, and that is what killed him."

After a long pause, Owen said, "What a fucking tragedy. And to think, I was involved."

Nora was not only surprised to be feeling any sympathy toward Owen Landry. She also felt inconvenienced by that—it imposed an untimely emotional demand on her, when she still needed to check on Fred, as well as drive to his house later for their brainstorming with Jack. "I have to leave," she said. "I've got a date . . . tonight . . ." Then she looked oddly at him and said, "The *date*."

"What date?" he asked.

She picked up the canceled check and said, "Look."

"You don't have to rub it in. It's three thousand dollars I wish I'd never seen."

"No. Look at the date on the check: October 29, 2019."

"So?"

"So, when did you give Dario his injection?"

After consulting his phone calendar, he answered, "October 31—a Thursday, when I was in the lab, and Bill was in Costa Rica. He wrote that check out a couple days earlier and left it on my desk."

She inhaled deeply and then slowly exhaled. "Dario had his teratoma *before* you injected him."

He stuttered, "What? How do you know?"

"The postmortem pathology showed that most of his pulmonary tumor emboli were chronic. So, they had to have been shedding from his teratoma for weeks to months before the surgery. In other words, before your injection on October 31st."

He stared at her, waiting for her remarks to convincingly enter the realm of possibility for himself. "I want to believe that," he said.

"It's true," she said.

His knee stopped bouncing. Reaching back in memory, he said: "Dario's first injection was in Costa Rica, about two years ago. Bill gave it in Dario's upper arm, where he later gave others, too. But I'm two-hundred-percent positive I gave mine in Dario's forearm tendons—even though Bill tried to convince me otherwise and have me believe I caused the compartment syndrome."

"So," she said, "it's more than likely that one of Bill's injections caused the teratoma."

"Maybe that should make me feel better, but . . ."

"Yeah. There's not a whole lot to feel good about here." Wondering how many other people Bill had injected, she asked, "Do you know what kinds of stem cells Bill used? Were they embryonic? Mesenchymal? Something ordered from Amazon?"

Starting to repack the box, Owen answered, "I only know that the ones I injected came from AccuCellz. I don't know what else Bill might've used. But, obviously, since a teratoma developed, he had to have injected Dario with multi-potent stem cells. I'm skeptical about oversight regulation of the industry in Costa Rica."

She scoffed. "You believe all the for-profit stem-cell clinics in the U.S. are tightly regulated? You think most of their products are FDA-approved?"

"No, I know they're not."

They sat in prickly silence a minute. Then Nora glanced again at the ultrasound and said, "If it's just you and Bill in the lab, and you didn't take this ultrasound, then Bill must've taken it."

"Probably," Owen replied. "I mean, we know he saw Dario in the lab, the afternoon before the surgery."

Her stomach churned, reacting to another sickening insight about her old mentor. She pointed to the date stamp on the ultrasound and said, "Look."

Owen read the date out loud: "'November 28, 2019.' What am I missing this time?"

"Damn," she said, shaking her head.

"I'm sorry," he said. "But, clearly, you're a lot quicker than me."

"It's not that," she said. "It's about Bill. If he took this ultrasound, then he knew about Dario's teratoma a day *before* the surgery."

Owen sprang off the couch and kicked the storage box across the room. "You're right! The bastard knew about it when he strong-armed me into taking the surgery. 'Explore' Dario's arm, my ass!"

She glanced at the scattered documents on the floor, thinking: *What a perfect metaphor for my mind.* Then she said, "And when he took the ultrasound, maybe worried about a complication from his stem-cell injections—he would've had to notice Dario's obvious compartment syndrome."

"Yeah, he did. He told me about that, when we met Thanksgiving night. He even blamed me for it—or tried to. But that's why he asked me to meet Dario in the ER the next morning."

Nora's eyes fixed on him; her expression said, "WTF?" When words finally came to her, she said, "The two of you knew the day before that Dario had a life-threatening condition, and yet you just sent him home?"

"It wasn't like that! Dario had left Bill's lab hours earlier, before I was ever told about it. And it was already late at night, Thanksgiving. Bill said he told Dario his problem could wait until morning, and to come to the ER at eleven o'clock, when I'd be there to take care of his 'infection.' I didn't know how serious it was, or if Bill even made a correct diagnosis. He's a retired neurosurgeon, years out of clinical practice. And, I hope you believe, I had no idea about the ultrasound or the tumor."

This is so wrong, she thought, *so egregiously wrong. But how can I hold someone with advanced dementia accountable for such appalling judgment and outrageously unethical behavior? How can I judge Bill as the seemingly different person he's become? And still . . . still . . . How does such a cognitively impaired person manage to execute such a complex strategy to save himself, in the short span of hours?*

Finally, Owen said, "You've been awfully quiet."

Nora stood up and retrieved her coat. "I'm struggling to understand how Bill was capable of plotting all he plotted—let alone, within less than a day's time after discovering Dario's tumor on the ultrasound. I mean, wow—he meets Dario in his lab, examines him, performs an ultrasound, and sets him up for an ER visit with you the next morning— under a ruse that you caused the compartment syndrome, and a lie to Dario about having an infection. Meanwhile, he selectively destroys evidence of his own involvement in his stem-cell hustle, simultaneously tampering with evidence to implicate you in causing Dario's *tumor*. He concocts an elaborate plan—if even with some last-minute trepidation—to get admitted to the ER so you can help him destroy evidence during Dario's surgery. My god! How does a person with serious dementia do all that?"

For the first time in days, Owen laughed. It was a fleeting, bitter laugh, but a genuine laugh all the same.

"What's so funny?" she said. "I see no humor—"

"Well," he said, a strange grin on his face. "Bill Balaban, with dementia?"

Her forehead furrowed, and, with a hint of admonishment, she said, "He sometimes doesn't even recognize his wife, Owen. He's behaving like a totally different person—*and*, a totally different doctor. He's been erratic and sometimes violent. You work with him—you see him every Thursday. You must have noticed his decline."

"No, I did not," he said, nodding knowingly. "And there's a damn good reason for that."

Fred's Home

Fred grabbed three crystal snifters from the dining room hutch and set them on the table with the brandy. He said to Nora and Jack, "I'm glad we could meet up tonight, and on such short notice. What a day!"

Nora received her pour and said, "I second that."

Filling Jack's glass, Fred said, "It was very disturbing at the Balabans tonight, and I'm dying for your sage counsel."

Jack raised his glass and said, "But mind if I go first? I'm dying to tell you guys about my most curious evening."

"Have at it," said Fred, and Nora nodded, both happy to sit back with their brandy.

"Well," said Jack, with a mischievous grin. "It began with Tupperware, and it ended with a bombshell—a blonde one, to be precise."

"Oh?" said Nora. "What's his name?"

"I wish," he said with an exaggerated frown. Then he launched into his tale about Carrie returning his Tupperware after a frustrating day herself, and getting roped into serving as a makeup model for Luis. "And," he added, watching them expectantly, "when Carrie put on the blonde wig, she looked exactly like Lydia."

When his friends didn't react, he looked injured and said, "Ouch! Tough crowd again."

"Well," said Nora matter-of-factly, "Lydia was a proud Clairol blonde. And Carrie is her identical twin."

Fred cleared his throat and said, "Not sure where this is going, Jack, or what it's got to do with the Balabans."

"I'm getting there," said Jack, lowering his voice, speaking deliberatively. "Want to guess *why* Luis chose a blonde wig for Carrie in the first place?"

"No," said Fred, "I don't. I'd rather you just tell us."

"C'mon," said Jack. "This should be easy. Blonde wig? *Lotsa* makeup?" Still, they both appeared disinterested. "All right," he continued, "you obviously require additional clues. So, then, Luis adds big sunglasses . . . and a faux blue scarf?"

Nora plunked her glass on the table. "To look like Ellie Balaban."

"Bingo!" said Jack, holding out his glass for a celebratory pour. "She's the first 'star' Luis ever met. He's been so enamored."

"What in god's name does that have to do with *anything*?" said Fred.

"Well," Jack answered, smiling sidelong at Nora. "Glad you asked. Because earlier in the day, Carrie had been to a mailbox-rental facility. And, she ran into Ellie there."

"Who's surprised by that?" Fred complained. "Because Ellie sure as hell wasn't home, when I visited Bill tonight. Their parlor was a complete wreck when I got there, like a tornado had passed through it. And when Ellie finally came home, she said she'd been out doing *errands*. Can you imagine that? She had left Bill home alone! We've just got to intervene, and I'm desperate to talk about a strategy."

"Wait!" said Jack. "I haven't told the punch line yet."

Nora shot him a cautionary look, and Fred crossed his arms. Then Jack drumrolled the table with his fingers and said, "Carrie was at the mailbox-rental facility, because she was hoping to track down Bill's neurologist. She used the address we had documented in our system for his office—but clearly, it was wrong."

Nora and Fred exclaimed in unison, "What?"

Finally satisfied with their responses, Jack took a slight bow.

Fred slapped his palms on the table. "Why on earth would Ellie have us believe that Bill's neurologist had an office there? She gave us that address herself! Nora and I were with her in the ER on Friday, when she filled out the paperwork."

"Oh?" said Jack. "That *is* strange. Carrie just assumed it was a clerical error on the hospital's part—mistaking the Balabans' postal address for the neurologist's. But, watch out now—because she's going to be even more upset when she hears that wasn't the case."

"All right now," said Fred. "Ellie intentionally gave us a bogus fax number and address for the neurologist. And a nonfunctioning phone number, as well. My god . . ." He looked wide-eyed at his friends and declared, "There is no neurologist!"

"Well," said Nora, with a meaningful look, "not only is there no neurologist, but—"

The front door opened and Vickie entered, looking haggard. "Thank goodness," she said, noting the brandy. "I could use one of those. Got room for one more at the table, or is this more shop talk about the Balabans? Because, honestly, I'm happy to take mine upstairs."

Pouring a snifter for his wife, Fred said, "Yeah, we're talking about Bill and Ellie."

"It must be getting boring for you," Nora said.

Vickie took her brandy and replied, "I'm actually concerned about them, and all of you as well. It's just that I've had a day-and-some at the gallery."

"And just getting home now?" said Jack, checking his watch. "Hopefully, that means lots of business today."

"Lots of business, for sure—unfortunately, not in sales," she replied. She debated whether to say more about her day, hesitant to make anyone uncomfortable with a reference to Dario Parker. But, since ads promoting the holiday art show would be made public soon, she added: "Lori Greene and Donald Parker dropped off nearly two dozen paintings from their personal collection this morning. So, I spent my day trying to figure out how to show them properly, without compromising the work of the community artists we're featuring in our holiday gala."

Fred said, "But didn't you tell me you were planning a solo exhibit of Lori Greene's work for January? That's two shows, back-to-back, isn't it?"

"It is," she said, shrugging. "And we're still doing the solo. But suddenly, Lori was desperate to be included in the gala. And, under the circumstances, I didn't have the heart to refuse her." Then she raised her glass to the trio and said good night.

After she left, Fred said, "Two shows, back-to-back? Doesn't seem like good business strategy. But what do I know about art sales?"

Jack sighed and said, "It has to be grief at work. Lori is probably desperate for distraction. Though I'm not Luis' father, I can't imagine what I'd be doing if . . ."

Nora heard nothing more of her friends' conversation about imagined loss. She knew firsthand how it felt to lose a child. And in the throes of Dario's parents blaming her for their son's death, she realized now how their accusation had been retraumatizing her the last few days. The guilt she carried over losing her daughter had expanded with the guilt she'd been assigned over Dario's death. She told herself that it was good to recognize this layered complexity of her trauma. And, as painful as that was, it also allowed her to see Lori Greene through a shared lens of loss. *I wonder how successfully she's processing her grief through her prodigious art output. Does she, too, feel guilty about losing a child? Does she also believe she somehow failed to protect them? Is she constantly replaying in her head—?*

"Hey, Nora?" said Fred.

"Still with us?" asked Jack.

Nora looked up and saw her friends as though emerging from a fog bank.

Jack took her hand and said, "I'm sorry. Talking like that in front of you was thickheaded and tone deaf."

"And unforgivable," said Fred. "Still, we hope you'll forgive us."

But Nora's attention had already shifted elsewhere—to remarks they made earlier that were incubating in her subconscious. She recalled Fred questioning the business rationale behind back-to-back art shows. And Jack speculating about Lori needing to distract herself with work.

"You look sidetracked," Jack told her. "You sure we're okay? I'm so sorry."

"We're good," she said. "Honestly. My retreat from our conversation was more than defensive. I was thinking about . . . just, other things." She rolled up her sleeves and said, "Let's get back to the Balabans?"

"All right then," said Fred. "Let's go back to where you left us hanging. Before Vickie came home, you said, 'Not only is there no neurologist . . .'"

"And," Jack added, "I'm dying to hear what happened at Owen Landry's tonight. I must say, it was brave of you to go to his apartment alone, after what he put you through."

Nora rested her elbows on the table. "Well, it's all pretty complicated. So, let's start with the easier question, about the neurologist." She asked Jack, "First, do you know whether Ellie ever used a different stage name?"

"As a matter of fact, yes. Tonight, after Carrie left, Luis and I googled Ellie's storied career. We learned she used her maiden name early on—but, obviously, that's been quite a while. She and Bill have been married forever."

Nora paused for dramatic effect, then asked, "Was that stage name Lopato?"

Jack held up his arms like goalposts and said, "Nora, you've been watching too much *Jeopardy!*"

But Fred responded to the revelation with a dramatic groan. Nora faced him with a wry grin and said, "Yeah—it's pretty audacious."

Jack looked curiously at his chagrined friends and asked, "Will someone clue me in?"

"The punch line *here*?" said Nora. "The name of Bill's so-called neurologist who we faxed at Ellie's direction? It was Dr. E. Lopato."

Jack silently mouthed, "What the fuck?!" Then he said, "Why would Ellie pull such a hoax?"

"Wait," said Fred, getting the gist. "Nora, what's your follow-up to 'not only is there no neurologist'?"

She grabbed the table edge and said, "It's going to be a bumpy ride, friends. Not only are we dealing with a nonexistent neurologist. Bill has been faking dementia and—"

"No effing way!" Jack said.

"*And*," she continued, "Bill has been administering rogue stem-cell injections. *And* I think he's culpable for malicious negligence in Dario

Parker's death. *And*—last big takeaway—he and Ellie have been trying to malign and blackmail Owen Landry."

Weighty silence ensued, during which the three stunned friends glanced at one another. Then Fred picked up the brandy and refilled everyone's snifter.

Jack said, "Wow. Where to even pick up our discussion? So many options. But how about on faking dementia? Nora, you can't be inferring that Bill—"

"No 'inferring' was inferred," she said. "Bill isn't demented—period. Hard stop."

"No, no, no," said Fred, shaking his head.

"Yes, yes, yes," she said, nodding.

"And you know that because . . . ?" asked Jack.

"Because, when I was at Owen Landry's tonight, I learned—" But already her mind was racing ahead of their conversation. So far ahead, gathering speed, moving confidently. Finally, it arrived at the next step they needed to take, and her eyes lit up.

"All right now," said Fred, recognizing that look in her eyes. "You're way ahead of us again, and—"

"Fred," she said, "you still work your Thursday afternoon clinic, right?" He nodded, and she continued, "Perfect. Because you need to book Bill and Ellie for an appointment this week."

"In two days?" said Fred. "I doubt they'll agree to it. Look how resistant they've been to our efforts to help."

"Then you'll have to threaten them," she said. "Say you'll call out APS, or the police for an urgent welfare check. You have to be firm."

"Okay," he said, his forehead furrowing. "I assume you'll explain?"

"I will," she said, turning to Jack with: "And we'll need that blonde wig from Luis, and a favor from Carrie."

Jack shrugged and said, "Sure. It sounds wickedly intriguing."

Nora sank back in her chair with a self-satisfied smile. "And," she said, "I'm going to call on Owen Landry. He owes me big-time." Then she held out a hand to each of her friends, and they readily offered theirs.

Fred's eyes sparkled when he asked, "What's spinning in that wild mind of yours, Nora?"

With calm authority, she answered, "It's our Plan C."

Guest Suite, Carl's Home

Winston headed to the bedroom, excited about his tryst with Fergie, and with three minutes still left on the timer, when her cell rang. Noting the caller, he felt obligated to answer. "Hi, Nora," he said.

"Winston?" she returned.

"Yeah, I'm holding Ferg's phone," he explained. "I only picked up because it was you, calling so late. Is everything okay?"

"Fine enough," she said. "And I'm sorry about the late hour. But, as Fergie would say, I had a 'crazy-times-ten' day. Anyhow, I had to rearrange my schedule, so I wanted her to know I can't meet for coffee in the morning." She withheld her reason for having invited Fergie to coffee in the first place.

"I'll tell her," he said, anxious about the two minutes remaining before he risked forfeiture of Fergie's seductive offer.

"Thanks," she said. "Oh, and I'm glad the Dario Parker case isn't an elephant standing between us now."

"Agreed," he said, kicking off his shoes. "It's nice to feel we can talk again."

"So, what are you working on this late?"

Winston grimaced, fretting over the elapsing time. But because things had been so awkward and strained between them since he began reporting on Dario's case, he chose to engage her in brief conversation. "Oh," he said, "just looking into college scholarships."

"Huh," she said. "Are you going back to school?"

"No," he replied, removing his shirt, preparing to pounce on Fergie. "I'm just investigating how universities recruit athletes on sports scholarships."

"I see," she said, reminded that Dario had a tennis scholarship. "So . . . did I just hear that elephant step back in between us? Because it can't be a coincidence—"

With a concessionary sigh, he said, "Okay, yeah. It involves Dario. I should've known you'd put that together."

"Well, Dario did tell us about his scholarship," she said. "You even reported that in your human-interest piece about him."

"That piece was hollow. But I didn't have much to go on." He pulled off his socks and stood ready at the bedroom door.

"But why *now* such interest in his scholarship?" she asked.

Typical Nora, he thought; so hard to get anything by her, especially when she became curious. He whispered, "Because there's nothing to indicate that Dario had any tennis talent." Hoping that would satisfy her, and trying to end the call with only seconds remaining on the timer, he said, "I should get going. I'll let Fergs know about tomorrow."

"Hmmmm," is all she said.

It was that signature way she said "hmmmm"—slowly, deliberately, a musical hum, the sound of silk-clad genies squeezing out of their lamps. So, Winston picked up his clothes, stepped away from the bedroom door, and asked, "What is it, Nora?"

The Parker-Greene Estate

Donald poured some Gautier 1762 into his wife's glass and soberly toasted, "To Dario. To us."

"And to this being our last night in hiding," Lori added. After savoring the cognac's sweet aroma, she said, "Though it's scary to imagine what tomorrow will bring."

They leaned into one another as they sat on the deck sofa, looking out to their delicately lit yard, to their manicured Japanese gardens and glistening koi ponds. Everything appeared so ordered and tranquil— and, as the minutes wore on, so illusory.

"Yeah," he finally said. "It's going to be rough sailing ahead."

"Squalls," she replied, nodding.

He put an arm around her and sipped his drink, appreciating the peaceful serenity that would be hard to come by after tonight. "Did you know," he said, "that 1762 marked Britain's entry into the Seven Years' War against Spain?"

She finished her drink and said, "I hope our battles won't take that long. Are you having second thoughts about us going public?"

"No," he said. "It's the right decision. I can't live with all the secrets and deceit. And I don't want to fear day-to-day that they're going to ambush us. Besides, the worst that could happen has already happened. Dario is dead."

"I just wish," she said, flicking a tear off her cheek. "I wish we had understood him better . . . loved him for who he was. He'd still be with us if we had."

"Lori," is all he said, firming his embrace.

After steadying her voice, she said, "Yeah, we're making the right decision. And I just can't imagine ever creating art again if I can't face my truth. Art is all I have . . . other than you . . . to help me survive Dario's death."

He offered his glass for her to finish, and she readily accepted it. Then he said, "I'm glad you have art to help you get through. You're going to need it. There's going to be a lot of collateral damage after we tell our stories."

"True," she said. "Lots of cleaning up . . . apologies to make . . . restitution, even."

He kissed her forehead and said, "We'll go through it together."

She asked, "Do you think John Norris will agree with our decision?"

Donald huffed and said, "He's got to. The decision is ours, and he works for us. Though it's probably just going to upset him more. He's already unhappy with us—sorry, with *me*—for vetoing an independent investigation of Dario's death."

"But, after we talked with our doctor about the coroner's report, I see no reason for another investigation. And it would only delay us putting Dario to rest."

"John might understand that, after we explain. But, honestly, we have enough to worry about, without taking on concerns for his feelings. If he can't work with us, he can quit. But we're handing him a golden opportunity, so I doubt he'll pull out. In fact, ten bucks says he'll be negotiating in no time, over who plays him in the film."

"I hope it's Michael B. Jordan," she said.

"Of course, you do. You want him in every lead."

"True," she said, "except the role of my husband."

"A good save," he said, smiling warmly.

She rested her head on his shoulder. "I'm trying not to think too much about tomorrow. Our lives are going to be even more hellish than they have been."

"No way around that," he said. "The notoriety. The legal morass. The financial and social repercussions. And, god, having to relive Dario's death, over and over, through all of it."

"I can't imagine," she shakily began, "any day passing that I'm not consciously living with his death. Maybe that gets better over time. I don't know. And what we're planning to do won't change that. But maybe it'll clear enough air to give us room to breathe."

They sat in stillness. A barn owl hooted, and an airplane rumbled softly above the cloud bank. When a night chill made her shiver, he covered her with his blanket and said, "Speaking of covers, I've got the office covered for the next three weeks, so we can be together through everything. Then we can reassess, and decide if we need more time."

She pulled the blanket up to her chin and reflected on her behavior the past several days. Finally, she said, "I lost my mind for a spell, didn't I?"

"I think we both did," he said.

She closed her eyes, remembering how that had felt—as though the very life of her mind had been threatened, and forced to escape in search of safety outside of her. She remembered existing independent of its jurisdiction—unruly, primitive, and furious.

"What are you thinking?" he asked.

"I'm just thinking back," she said. "About me destroying our home . . . the paint and chaos everywhere . . . I felt possessed by an angry, destructive demon."

His eyes softened as they took hers in. Finally, he said, "I think Nadja would agree with you."

Just then, the house phone rang, flashing a familiar number from "Unknown Caller." Lori muted the deck extension, and, this time, allowed the call to go to voicemail. "It's that reporter from the *Oakland Register*," she said with slight apprehension. "The one we had planned to contact tomorrow."

"Well, he's calling awfully late," Donald said. "Not sure I like that. But let's hear what he's got to say at this hour."

She nodded and said, "Here goes." Then she turned on the speakerphone and pressed the replay button. They held hands while they listened to the voicemail: "Hello, it's Winston Wang again from the *Oakland Register*. I'm sorry about calling so late. And I don't mean to intrude on your grief. But I'd like to talk with you about your son's scholarship. I'd like to give you the chance to comment. Please call me as soon as possible. And, thank you in advance."

Donald and Lori held each other's gaze. Finally, she said, "Sounds like he's ahead of us, already figuring things out. Maybe we should just talk to him now? I mean, we've already agreed to. And John would only interfere with what you and I want to say."

"Still," he said, "I'd like to have this last quiet night, alone with you."

"Good idea," she said. "I'll call him back and offer to meet in the morning. It's late now, anyway."

"Good," he said. "Rough sailing tomorrow."

"Squalls," she said, nodding.

"Together," he said tenderly as she hit the redial button.

Law Office of John D. Norris

John Norris looked out through his office window, relieved to see no police-car lights aggregated near the estuary or flashing in Jack London Square tonight. After closing the blinds, he sat atop his desk and grabbed his maroon-colored stress ball, squeezing it while contemplating about Dario Parker and his parents. Something so dreadful, to lose a child. The raw grief, the unfathomable heartbreak. And the risk of experiencing that, sufficient justification for never having children of his own.

He could understand—though not agree with—Donald Parker's decision to drop the case. But, my god, the coroner's report! If he possessed even a fraction of Parker's wealth, he would pursue an investigation of Dario's death on his own. There were too many compelling and mysterious undercurrents to ignore—even if they were pulling the case in unpredictable directions.

By informing the hospital's lawyers that the case was "suspended," he had hoped to buy time for Donald to reconsider. But having seen him and his unhinged wife in their wrecked home yesterday, he had to concede that the chances were slim to none. And perhaps, given the couple's state, they might be making the right call.

Still, he would appreciate another opportunity to persuade them. But they were making that difficult, continuing to refuse his calls. He dreaded the prospect of driving to their home again, but that was looking like the only alternative.

Now hearing his assistant's ringtone, he answered his cellphone with, "Why are you calling this late? Don't you have a life outside this office?"

Chris O'Dell answered, "Yes, you'd think that someone with my dazzling smile and winning charm would have something better to do than phoning her grumpy boss near midnight. But I just received great news."

"Did you finally win the lottery?" he asked.

"Oh, better than that," she said. "And it's going to make you very happy. You had me calling and texting and emailing and sending smoke signals to Donald Parker all day, until I was blue in the face. And, well ..."

His jaw dropped, he slid off the desk, planted his feet on the floor, and exclaimed, "You got him?"

She spoke in her high-tea voice: "Mr. Donald Parker and his wife, Ms. Lori Greene, request the pleasure of your company tomorrow, eight a.m. sharp, at their estate."

He tossed his stress ball into the wastebasket. "You're the best!" he shouted.

"Tell me something new," she said. "Hey—how about, like, you're giving me a raise?"

"Chris," he said, "all joking aside, I'm so grateful! Dario's case is bursting with questions that are begging for answers. And yes, you made me happy. I'll call Don now so we can start preparing—"

"Hang on," she interrupted. "No! Mr. Parker explicitly stated he didn't want to hear from you before the meeting tomorrow. I'm also supposed to tell you that he sent you an email a few minutes ago. He said it explains the basics of a proposal going forward for him and his wife. And he said he needed you to begin working on immunity for her ASAP."

"What the f—?" he said, hurriedly signing onto his email.

"Oh, and I almost forgot," she said. "He told me that a reporter from the *Oakland Register* would be joining us tomorrow."

Part Seven

Wednesday, December 4

Guest Suite, Carl's Home

FERGIE AWOKE ALONE in bed, and then headed to the dining room. She startled to see Winston slumped over his laptop at the table. After getting no response when calling out his name, she walked up to him and shook his shoulder. When he easily roused and only blithely replied, "Hey," she lightly jabbed his arm.

"What? What did I do?" he asked.

How can he be so obtuse? she wondered. Why hadn't he come to her last night to take advantage of her sexy proposition? Was he losing interest in her? Was he more enamored with his work?

Noting the tears brimming in her eyes, he stood up and embraced her. "What happened?" he said.

"Nothing," she said.

"It was clearly *something*, Fergs."

"It was 'nothing' as in 'nothing happened' because *you* didn't come to bed last night."

"Oh, god," he said, holding her tighter. "I'm sorry."

"You promised me 'ten minutes.' What warped time zone are you living in these days?"

He gently rocked her side-to-side. "I hate that I hurt you. I'm a monster."

"Is something wrong between us?"

Winston flinched. Was there, he wondered? He'd been so preoccupied with work that he hadn't paid much attention to her or their relationship. And, she was right—it was weird to not avail himself last night of her tantalizing sex offer.

"You have to think about your answer?" she shakily managed.

"Honey, no! Your question made me stop because it was *unthinkable* to me. But, unless you tell me otherwise, if there's a problem, I'm guessing it's me working all the time."

"You've been working crazy-times-ten. You've been ignoring me, forgetting dinners and sex—" She stopped, suddenly recalling that she had fallen asleep last night the moment her head hit the pillow. Even if he had shown up in time for their tryst, it wouldn't have been easy to rouse her.

Winston hung his head. "It's my fault, but it's not my intention. And last night . . . god . . . I was standing in the bedroom doorway, ready to pounce on you when . . ." He flipped a hand and said, "It's the same old excuse: My work called me."

Fergie looked gobsmacked at him. "What the hell could've stopped you, when you were that close?"

He withdrew her cell from his jeans pocket and returned it to her. "You set the timer on this—for ten minutes, remember? But when I got to the bedroom—*on time*—Nora called on it. I only answered because it was late, and I thought something might be wrong."

"Well, was it?" she asked, scrolling through her phone log.

"No," he said.

But when she located the log of last night's call, her jaw dropped. "And yet your call with Nora lasted nearly *fifteen* minutes? So, what was that about, if nothing was wrong? You just decided to have a late-night chat instead of having sex with me?"

He held his tongue, concerned about another work-based excuse exacerbating the tension. "Sorry," is all he said.

"No, Win. I want to understand what was so important."

"Okay," he said, sitting atop the table and gesturing for her to take his vacated chair. "Nora wanted you to know that she couldn't meet for coffee this morning. A bunch of stuff had come up."

She refused to sit and remained standing at eye level. "It shouldn't have taken more than a minute, max, to convey that. What about the other fourteen min—?" She stopped herself again and blinked hard, as if trying to clear her vision. What the fuck was going on? She felt as though her speech had been commandeered by a shrill ventriloquist.

He stared anxiously back. "Fergs, you're right. I'm just afraid to tell you that I ended up talking work with Nora."

Struggling to adopt a conversational tone, she said, "So, what did you talk about?"

"You sure?" he asked.

She took the chair and nodded.

"All right," he said. "Nora asked what I was working on so late. I thought I should talk with her a sec, because things had been so strained between us. Anyhow, I said I was pursuing a story on college admissions by way of athletic scholarships. I thought that would be a conversation stopper. But it wasn't. And then she said 'hmm' in that way she does, when her mind wraps around something. You know—that 'hmmmm' that means 'aha!' So, I was curious about what she was thinking."

"And?"

"And, she immediately figured I was investigating Dario's scholarship. Then she said 'hmmmm' again."

"Okay, *and*?"

"She said she'd been bothered by something Fred said earlier in the evening. He had questioned the business rationale behind Lori Greene suddenly scheduling two big art shows at Vickie's gallery, just a month apart."

"Well, maybe Lori needs to immerse herself in work. People cope with grief in different ways."

"But here's the rub. Nora said that's what everyone had assumed, including herself. But while we talked, it dawned on her that Lori didn't add another show to immerse herself in art. Because, according to Vickie, the added show was a showing of Lori's personal collection. In other words, it didn't require immersion in new or creative work! It was a fire sale of pieces she had created in the *past*. And that's when Nora suggested that Lori must have needed . . ." He stopped, looked apologetically at Fergie, and said, "There I go again, getting carried away with work. Anyhow, that's why I went back to my laptop. I knew she was onto something."

"For godsakes, Win! Just tell me what she said."

"Even though it's about my work?"

"You've made your point," she said, gesturing for him to continue.

He rubbed his hands together. "So, Nora figured that Lori must have needed *money*. But then she questioned why Lori, with all her wealth, would sweat over money in the first place, and have to relinquish her private art collection to boot."

Fergie tilted her head. "Maybe Lori had a good reason to sweat? Like, maybe she was involved in something illegal or unethical? And maybe that's why she didn't want to use family money—afraid that someone like her husband might find out."

"Precisely," he said, crossing his arms. "That's what we figured, too. Then Nora did her 'hmmmm' thing *again*, so I waited *again*. Then she questioned the curious timing—asking why Lori was desperate for money *now*, so close in time to her son's death. Then she lined up all the ducks: a dubious athletic scholarship . . . its recipient dies . . . his mother urgently needing to raise money without tapping the family's fortune. And, boom! Nora said flat out: That Lori Greene was doing privately whatever she could to raise money, to cover up evidence of an illicit payment for Dario's unearned scholarship."

Fergie inhaled sharply and said, "A *bribe?*"

"It adds up," he said, shrugging. "I mean, we know Dario wasn't athletically accomplished. And, academically? I didn't find his name on his school's honor rolls. He wasn't mentioned, not once over the years, in the school's online paper—no honorifics, no committee work, no nothing. So, his academic profile also looks weak—not one that a place like UCSM would normally find compelling for admission."

"Oh, man," she said, her brow furrowed. "This is hard to take in. But how are you going to prove the bribe?"

When she saw him hesitate to answer, she said, "Look. I don't know what's wrong with me lately. I haven't been feeling well, physically or emotionally. I even took a pregnancy test at work yesterday. It was negative, so I'm still not sure what's going on. Maybe too much stress at work? Still, there's no way I want to kill your buzz on this story. I think I just need some more 'us' time."

He took her hand and said, "Message received."

Fending off a good cry for now, she asked, "So, what's on your agenda today?"

He scooted off the table, and stood tall like a superhero, with his hands on his hips and chest out. "Amazing things await on the agenda today. After my talk with Nora last night, I left a voicemail with Lori Greene and told her I wanted to discuss Dario's scholarship. I was shocked—she returned my call minutes later. So, I told her everything Nora had speculated about, and I invited her to comment. Then I overheard her consult with her husband, and they invited me to their mansion this morning, eight o'clock sharp. She said she and her husband were ready to talk."

Owen's Apartment

"Son, why are you calling so early?" Mrs. Landry asked, her voice brimming with concern. "I hope you're not worried about forgetting our anniversary? We understand. We know how busy you are."

"No, Mom, please," said Owen. "I mean, yes—you're right. I'm sorry. I intended to call you and Dad for your anniversary. But things got complicated . . ."

"Son," she said, "you sound so serious. Is everything okay?"

He steadied his voice and said, "Can you put Dad on the phone, too? I need to talk with both of you."

For a second, Owen wondered whether he had erred by not jumping off the roof yesterday. He realized he was about to inflict the suffering on his parents that he had hoped not to witness. "Please, Mom," he continued, "I don't have a lot of time. Can you get Dad?"

He heard his mother put down the phone and shuffle away. His hand shook, and he almost terminated the call. But then he remembered the young boy staring up at him with such questioning eyes, and he asked himself: *What are you going to do? Are you going to take responsibility for yourself? What are you choosing for your parents to see about you?* He took in a deep breath. And, with his experience on the roof still so raw and immediate, he chose his life again, in all its disrepair. He was not going to run from it, or take it away from the people who selflessly gave it to him.

"We're both here now," said his mother after picking up the phone. "Hi, son," said his father.

Owen braced himself and said, "First, I apologize in advance to both of you. I'm sorry for what I'm about to tell you. But I got myself into serious trouble."

"Are you okay?" asked his father.

Surprised to hear his father respond with tender concern, Owen stammered, "Uh, no. Not really."

"Do you need money?" asked his mother.

"I wish it was that simple," he answered. Then, cringing, he hastily added, "I didn't mean that. I know money has never been simple for you. And you've given me so much."

"Owen?" said his father. "You sound funny. Not like yourself."

"We are very proud of you," said his mother. "And we are doing fine with what we have. Your father and I are happy. But it doesn't sound like you are."

Owen capped his hand over the phone so they couldn't hear him struggling to stabilize his voice.

His father said, "Son? Tell us why you are calling."

"Because," Owen managed, "I'm probably going to be kicked out of my residency program and lose my research projects. I made some very stupid mistakes at work. And some of them are going to be made public, real soon. I wanted to warn you about that. And I wanted you to hear about my mistakes from me."

A brittle silence ensued. Finally, his father asked, "What do you plan to do about these mistakes?"

"To take responsibility for them," Owen answered. "To apologize to everyone affected by my poor judgment. And I intend to fix what I can."

He heard rustling while his father pressed the receiver to his chest to mute the conversation at their end. When his father returned to the call, he said, "All right, son. That is a good plan. Tell us how we can help."

The Parker-Greene Estate

Nadja escorted Winston to the living room and, after introducing him to Dario's parents, returned to the kitchen. Winston told the couple, "Thank you for agreeing to speak with me. I know this is a difficult time."

Lori Greene replied, "We've appreciated your evenhandedness in covering our son's death. And that you didn't hound us, like other reporters."

Donald Parker put an arm around her and added, "So, we decided to trust you with our story."

"And," said Lori, "you bringing up Dr. Nora Kelly during our call last night? We feel terrible about what we put her through. After looking over the coroner's preliminary report with our doctor yesterday, we know she did nothing to cause our son's death. We want to clear the air about that and make things right. Telling you our story is a start."

Winston only nodded, holding back the urge to inquire about the report, which had not yet been released publicly. But, because his invitation here was predicated upon the couple's willingness to speak about their son's scholarship, he decided to restrict his focus on that.

Donald chimed in, "I saw social media posts of me tearing Dr. Kelly apart in the ER. I'm ashamed. It was reflex, me blaming her—well, that and being told by another physician that she hadn't been qualified to perform Dario's surgery. I also needed to blame somebody other than myself, because the moment I heard that our son died after a surgery on his arm—"

"Not now," Lori said. "Remember our agreement? *My* story first? And then yours?"

Winston's curiosity ramped up a notch. Did they just suggest there was more than one story between them? Again, he counseled himself to stay the course of their invitation, though now champing at several bits. Flipping open his reporter's notebook, he said, "It might be nice to tell all that to Dr. Kelly in person someday."

"We hope to," Lori said. "And, speaking of apologies—please forgive the state of this room. We're having some work done on the house."

The doorbell rang, and the front door's security sensor chimed. Nadja could be heard welcoming visitors and escorting them to the living room. In the doorway, she announced, "Your attorney, John Norris, and his assistant, Chris O'Dell, are here."

Donald thanked Nadja, and waved John and Chris inside. After introductions all around, John faced his clients and said, "I'm here for you two, and you know I have your back. But, as your attorney, I'll repeat what I emailed to you last night: I think we should wait to talk to any reporter until we—"

"No," said Lori, gesturing for everyone to sit down. "What I did was wrong, on every level. And I do not intend to spend the rest of my life fearing that my day of reckoning is just around the corner. I need to meet that day now, head-on."

"*We* need to meet it," said Donald, squeezing her hand. Then he asked John, "You *will* be getting her immunity, right?"

"I'll certainly try," John answered, glancing sidelong at Winston. "But you haven't given me any notice. This is happening too fast. And I'm not comfortable with this arrangement. I'm not even sure what you're going to say in front of Mr. Wang."

"We're going to tell the truth," said Lori.

"Well," said John, "I can't promise immunity if I don't know what we're immunizing you against! All you sent me in your email last night was the suggestion that—" He turned to Winston and said, "Give me a moment with my clients, please? They deserve to at least understand the potential legal consequences of what they're bringing on themselves."

"Sure," said Winston. "I can wait in the entryway."

"Chris will come get you when we're through," said John.

After Winston left, John told his clients, "You might believe that you're going to enjoy a come-to-Jesus moment of redemption after you confess to this 'bribe' you mentioned in your email. But there's going to be hell to pay! Especially if it's a federal case. Prison time, financial penalties, reputational damage—"

"We understand that," said Donald. "And we know the bribe was a federal crime."

John looked thunderstruck. "What the hell did you two do?"

Lori sighed and said, "You'll hear about it in real time, with the reporter present."

Donald said, "Clearly, our situation is stressing you out, John. But we have to do this, we're going to do this, and we don't want you interfering. We want your counsel, but with our truth on the table first. Besides, you'll have your hands full with a headline-generating case. So, no complaining, please."

"Look," said John, frowning, "I'm afraid you're under a misconception about immunity. Only if you've committed a federal crime, and you have helpful information the government can use—"

"I do," said Lori.

"Let me finish," said John. "Especially if it includes information about other criminal activity that you're willing to testify about—"

"It does," she said, "and I am willing."

Donald explained, "What she's about to confess involves a system. So, obviously—other people will be named."

John pressed his hands against the sides of his head. "But if you give away all your information to this reporter, I'm left with nothing to bargain with the government prosecutors to secure your immunity!"

"I want to get this over with," said Lori. "Today. Now."

"Hang on a minute," said Donald, locking eyes with her. "I know we talked about full disclosure. But John may have a point."

"No," said John. "I *do* have a point. If you give everything away now, you're risking your chance to obtain the immunity you want." He internally debated whether to withdraw from the case. "How do you expect me to protect you, when you confine me to the back of a rudderless boat that you insist on steering?"

Lori searched her husband's pained expression. He told her, "The thought of you going away, to prison . . . I can't bear it. Not after losing Dario, too. Maybe you can hold back a few details or names, and still get your story out?"

She had done it before: insulated herself from him while he was suffering and spiraling down. Vowing not to abandon him again, she whispered, "Okay."

Donald's face relaxed. He told John, "I think it's time to call Mr. Wang back."

John D. Norris stared fixedly at his clients, willing them to change their minds about talking to the reporter. But they only looked calmly back. Finally, Chris got up to retrieve Winston.

When Winston returned, he placed his recorder on the coffee table and said, "Are we ready?"

Hospital Cafeteria

Nora walked up to the cafeteria's counter, where Marla poured her a coffee and asked, "Anything else for breakfast?"

Engaging their usual schtick, Nora answered, "I already ate."

"Waffles?" said Marla. If she guessed wrong, the coffee was free.

Smiling triumphantly, Nora grabbed the coffee and said, "A fruit pocket." After Marla waved her away, she headed for a back table, where she put on her readers and began scrolling through her emails. *Yet another internet coupon for Merino-wool socks—how many feet do they think I have? And why must I always "hurry" to buy more Omaha steaks?*

Owen showed up a few minutes later and sat at her table. "Sorry," he said. "I was on a long call with my parents. And I told them everything. Not my proudest moment."

"Everything?" she said, putting down her coffee.

"Yeah," he said, removing his Saints cap. "I didn't want them blindsided by all the shit that's about to come down the pike. And I needed to apologize to them."

Nora again wondered how to read this young doctor. Such a perplexing mix of off-putting and admirable traits. She leaned forward and asked, "How did they react?"

"They were sympathetic. And supportive. I wasn't expecting that. My dad's strict military, and my mom lives by the rules."

She surprised herself by responding, "You're lucky to be loved." *My god*, she thought, *did I just drop into a Hallmark moment with Owen Landry?*

He looked inquiringly at her. "Think so?"

"I do," she said, refraining from appending: *despite yourself.*

"Well, 'lucky' isn't something I've been feeling for a long time. But now, after talking with my folks, at least I know my head is screwed back on." He rested his elbows on the table and said, "So, what's the favor you wanted to ask?"

Suddenly, she felt shy about explaining Plan C for the Balabans. Because now, facing someone with his head screwed on, she questioned whether the plan would stand the light of day. Last night, after snifters of brandy with friends in Fred's cozy dining room, the plan had sounded brilliant. But now? After only a few hours' sleep, and buzzed by her breakfast's sugar rush and a third cup of coffee, she harbored fuzzy-headed doubts. Was the plan too outrageous? Would she be asking too much of Owen?

"Dr. Kelly?" he said. "Last night over the phone, you sounded eager to talk. Did you change your mind?"

She gave him a calculating look over her readers and decided that, at a minimum, having to explain the plan would provide a test run of its reasonableness. "No," she answered. "I'm still eager. And I hope you'll decide to help me."

"Well, I owe you big. And I want to make things right by you."

After pulling her chair up to the table, she said, "Well, here goes. After I left your apartment last night, I visited two old friends to discuss Bill and Ellie Balaban. We had been worried about Bill's dementia and an unsafe home environment, so we wanted to devise a plan to help them."

"I'm not surprised—the Balabans deceived and manipulated you all, too."

"They did," she said. "But the point is, I shared what you told me with my friends. Bill's faked dementia. His stem-cell dealings. How the Balabans were trying to frame you for Dario's teratoma and death."

"Your friends must've been blown away."

She nodded forcefully. "And they had stories of their own that cast the Balabans in a bad light. One had just visited their home, where he was subjected to a disturbance that had been put on for show—an entire room had been destroyed, purportedly by Bill."

"That's sick," Owen said, shaking his head.

"And another," she added, "had just met with a mutual friend, who had been tearing her hair out, trying to locate the nonexistent neurologist managing Bill's nonexistent dementia. So, yes, everyone's shocked by their deceit. Shocked, and angry."

"And to think we were all trying to help them."

"Yeah," said Nora. "So, needless to say, at the proverbial end of the day, my friends and I came up with a very different plan for the Balabans."

He angled his chair to face her.

"Our new plan," she said, "aims to bring them to justice—with a dash of karmic retribution."

Looking searchingly at her, intrigued by her call for justice, he asked, "And this new plan involves a favor from me?"

She nodded.

"Does it require my direct involvement with the Balabans?"

She nodded again.

"I don't know," he said. "I want to help you. But I don't think I could tolerate any more time in their dark universe. They are way too toxic."

"And yet, *they* are continuing to involve *you*, regardless. They're actively trying to pin things on you."

He shook his head. "I've learned the hard way, through failure: I can't control them. And whenever I tried, I just dug a deeper hole for myself. A grave, actually. I've been on the defensive with them the entire time."

"But that dynamic can change, Owen. For your sake, it has to. But you've got to be willing to push back. And besides, your situation is different now. Now you have me and my friends on your side. And justice, too."

Looking down, fiddling with his cap in one hand, he thought about his conversation with his parents. How healing and re-centering it had felt to be reminded of values like truth and justice. And now, glancing at Nora, he considered how forthright and forgiving she'd been—despite himself. "Okay," he said, "how about this? You ask me the favor, and I get to say 'no' if it's something I don't feel I can or should do. And, if I decline, I'll still owe you a favor for another day."

"Fair enough," she said. "My ask is for you to meet alone with Bill tonight and—"

"You're kidding," he said, tossing his cap onto the table.

"Hear me out," she said. "You yourself called the Balabans toxic. And they are! But that's our tactical advantage—because they're also toxic to each other. Nuclear-level toxic."

He flipped his wounded hand. "Their estrangement is old news. Bill has tried every which way to escape his wife and home. Retreating to his lab, hanging out with me, flying to Costa Rica. I don't see how that could possibly be a game changer."

She looked pointedly at him and said, "Exploiting their toxicity and using it against them provides a foundation for us to obtain justice—for Dario, you, me, and my friends. And, for purely selfish reasons, if the plan succeeds, it also gives us front-row seats to watch the Balabans get their comeuppance."

"A comeuppance, too?" he said, tilting his head. "I'm listening."

"Good," she said with evident relief. "Now, the favor I'm asking is a two-parter: First, you meet with Bill tonight and fan the flames of his hostility toward Ellie. And second, I need you to be in the outpatient clinic tomorrow, when the Balabans attend an appointment with Fred Williams."

He put on his Saints cap and squared its visor. His gut was telling him to agree. And, truth be told, he would enjoy a front-row seat at the couple's comeuppance. The Balabans had pushed him to the edge of a roof, and now, as Nora told him, he needed to push back against them. "I'm in," he said. "Tell me what you need from me."

The Parker-Greene Estate

Winston asked, "Is everyone okay with me recording our conversation?"

Everyone in the room agreed: John said "Ready" after pulling out his cell to record simultaneously, while Chris opened her laptop. Donald pulled his chair close to Lori's, and they each answered, "Yes."

After Winston dictated the time and place of their meeting and the names of each participant, he said, "Ms. Greene, let's begin with Dr. Kelly's supposition that prompted me to call you last night. As I conveyed during our conversation, she had wondered about the legitimacy of your son's tennis scholarship. Also, whether you were desperately selling art to replenish, or perhaps cover up, money you had used to purchase a backdoor admission to UCSM for your son, Dario."

After taking a shaky breath, Lori said, "Yes. That is what happened."

"Hold on!" John said. "Self-incrimination is not a legal strategy that I'm willing to—"

Lori persisted undeterred: "I felt in desperate need of money." She pointed to the bare living room walls, and said, "I even put our personal collection up for sale."

Winston had noticed the stripped walls when he first entered their living room. But he obligingly looked now, again noting the shadowy spots, where paintings once hung. He asked, "Can you explain why you felt so desperate?"

She nodded. "Your Nora Kelly was right about that, too. I certainly could have asked Don for the money I spent on that backdoor admission.

But I didn't want him to know about it. It must be understood—he had no part in this."

"You're saying that on the record," said John, anxiously awaiting her fuller description of "this."

Now she pointed to the sole painting in the room, which rested on the mantel. "I kept that one," she said. "It was our son's favorite."

Silence ensued while everyone waited for her to continue. Meanwhile, privately, she recalled the day she painted that simple composition and, hours later, discovered Dario sitting on the floor, transfixed by it, clutching his toy truck and construction crane.

"Lori?" Donald said, concerned about her faraway look. "Maybe we should postpone this?"

"No," she said, leaning back in her chair. "It's just . . . I'm just realizing that painting is where my story actually begins." Looking tenderly at Donald, she continued: "Our Dario loved 'simple.' He never did fancy or complicated. He saw beauty in order and simplicity. But I didn't, or wouldn't, see those things about him. I didn't see him, really."

Donald took her hand, and she turned back to Winston and continued: "So, I kept pushing Dario to be somebody else. At a bare minimum, someone with a college degree. Though his grades were average at best, and he had no interest in school."

"He just always wanted to build things," Donald added. "When he was a kid, he'd beg us to take him to demolition sites. Or hardware stores. He even dressed up as a construction worker for Halloween."

Glancing back at their son's favorite painting, Lori said, "If you can believe it—I hardly can—I even tried to disabuse him of liking that painting. I wanted him to have more sophisticated taste." She steadied her voice and continued, "Anyhow, I knew Dario was never getting into a decent college on his grades. And my husband—making his own way in the world, starting with nothing—I knew how he felt about rich parents 'donating' their kids' way into college. So, when an 'opportunity' to buy a tennis scholarship materialized like an answer to my prayers, I forced Dario to begin tennis lessons—which he also hated. But I wanted him to at least know how to hold a racket for the photographs we included with his college application."

"Dear Jesus," John said under his breath.

"So," said Winston, "that explains Dario not being listed on the high school tennis roster before his senior year."

"That's right," she said. "I was told to start the tennis lessons immediately—an expensive photo op, essentially. And then to apply for admission and the scholarship before October, during the school's early-decision period."

Winston scratched his head and asked, "But didn't Dario or your husband question what was happening? Because it seems—"

"Neither of them knew what I'd done under the table," she insisted. "But, yes, they were both surprised when Dario was accepted to UCSM. Still, we had received his ACT test scores—and they were respectable and convincing."

"But false, too?" said Winston.

"False, too," echoed Lori.

Winston took a beat to remind himself to detach from his emotions and put judgment aside during the interview. He asked, "But the tennis scholarship? How could they not have been skeptical about that?"

Lori buried her face in her hands before answering: "Because Dario and Don believed the coach's letter. That all the photographs and videos I'd sent showed our son's 'great potential.' Some had been doctored, of course. I also submitted a falsified tennis profile."

John's foot started tapping, and Chris sent him a furtive look to make him aware of that. Later, she would inform him that she had fished his maroon stress ball out of the wastebasket this morning—and maybe ask for that raise again.

Staring down at the colorful paint-stained rug that centered the room, Lori continued, "So, with the increasing legal and media scrutiny over Dario's death, I knew it was just a matter of time. Someone was going to discover that Dario didn't earn his college admission or a place on the tennis team. And that 'someone' appears to be you, Mr. Wang. You and your friend, Dr. Kelly."

Donald quickly added, "But Lori had decided to admit everything *before* your call last night. Earlier yesterday, each of us decided to confess the mistakes we—"

"Don—please, again, not now," Lori said. "Like we agreed? Let me get through my confession first."

John shot out of his chair, about to demand another private consultation with the couple. But Donald intuited that and told him, "Please sit down, so we can continue."

Winston's curiosity burned hot; there *were* two separate confessions the couple was eager to make. Although Donald Parker may not have been involved in his wife's college-admissions scheme, he appeared keen to off-load an equally compelling admission of his own.

"The bottom line," Lori said, "is that I bribed someone to get Dario into UCSM next fall. For $800,000, a so-called 'college-admissions counselor' said he could inflate Dario's admission test scores with the help of a test proctor he had in his 'back pocket.' He also worked with a tennis coach at UCSM who could guarantee Dario's placement on the tennis team."

Trying to maintain his journalistic objectivity, Winston steeled himself against the shocking claims. Then, calmly, he inquired, "And the name of the man you bribed?"

"Martin Stanger," she answered.

John whistled softly, and Chris began scouring the internet for information about him.

Winston asked, "How about the names of the test proctor and tennis coach working with Mr. Stanger?"

She shrugged. "I never met them or heard their names mentioned. I think the proctor might've been a friend or a relative of his? I'm not sure. But I do know the head coach's name, only because it was on Dario's welcoming letter."

"Was that name 'Steven McArdle'?"

Lori nodded, her brow slightly raised.

Winston's heart galloped in his chest. "Did Stanger ever explicitly name McArdle as his contact?"

"No. But I've assumed that, only because I thought that any lesser-ranked coach wouldn't have been able to sneak in an undeserving player unnoticed."

Winston nodded; that made sense, though it hardly constituted proof. "Let's go back to you and Martin Stanger. How did you two meet?"

"At a fundraiser for the Oakland Fine Arts Museum."

"Oh? Is Stanger a benefactor? Or an artist?"

"I don't think so. Like I said, he's a self-identified 'college-admissions counselor.' I met him through a mutual contact—an arts patron; she brought him to the fundraiser at my request."

"And, you requested she bring him because . . . ?"

"Because I had talked with her before, about how worried I was over Dario not getting into a good college. And that's when she told me about 'a guy' who had worked magic to get her son into UCSM—for a hefty fee. So, she brought Stanger to the fundraiser and left us alone to talk privately. And when he was through with his spiel, I didn't even have to think about it. I automatically said 'yes' to his proposal."

Flipping his notebook open to his chart of parental connections, Winston asked, "And the name of the arts patron, who introduced you to Stanger?"

"Sonya Wisekof," she answered.

A hush fell over the room. Winston circled that name on his chart, suppressing a grin. John exchanged a knowing look with Donald and Lori but still asked, "*The* Sonya Wisekof?"

Donald nodded and said, "Please. This is extremely hard for my wife. Sonya is a close professional associate. And all she wanted to do was to help Lori with our son."

Winston held his tongue. But it was difficult not to criticize their jaded worldview, using their privilege to excuse the unfairness.

John whistled again, then said, "This is one huge and thorny situation, people. Bribes to cheat the college-admissions system? We're talking serious potential charges. Conspiring to commit fraud and bribery, for sure. And, depending how the money flowed, possibly wire fraud."

With John's escalating alarm, Winston feared that Dario's parents might terminate the interview. So, he quickly pulled them back into conversation with another question to Lori: "Can you tell me how you got the money to Martin Stanger?"

She shifted uncomfortably in her chair. "Stanger ran a charity—well, a sham charity, obviously. I don't recall its name. But it was supposed to help educate the poor. Anyway, I 'donated' to his charity. In exchange, he performed his magic."

"Lori," said John, wringing his hands. "Please don't say you also wrote off that money as a tax deduction for a charitable contribution? Because then we're also talking tax fraud and—"

"I didn't do that," Lori said. "In fact, I'd been trying to cover up evidence of my payment so our tax guy *wouldn't* notice it. But . . ." She cringed, aware she was about to detonate more dynamite within her social circle. "But," she continued, "I knew that was possible to do. Because Sonya told me she and others had successfully claimed sizable tax deductions for contributions to Stanger's charity."

"I'm reeling here," said John, making a spinning motion with his finger. "This Martin Stanger is going to be hit with racketeering and money-laundering charges. Obstruction of justice, too. He'll likely face prison time. And Ms. Wisekof? She's going to need a very good attorney."

"Focus, John," Donald said. "Because we need to finish this story, okay?"

Winston nodded his appreciation for the remark and quickly asked Lori, "What was the 'magic' Stanger performed, Ms. Greene? I mean, how did his operation work?"

"Well," she said, "I don't know all the details, and I never really cared to. But Stanger told me Dario needed two things to happen to get admitted to UCSM—both of which he could provide. One was getting Dario . . . what was the word? . . . yes, 'tagged' by the tennis coach as a recruit. Stanger said the coach's 'tagging' for the team would essentially guarantee Dario's college admission—but *only if* he also met basic academic requirements. And that was the second thing Stanger said he could finesse."

"All right," said Winston, "you've described Stanger's back-channel arrangement with the tennis coach. But, Dario's academic credentials, and his ACT test scores? How did Stanger manipulate those?"

Lori glanced again at her son's favored painting, seeing new beauty in it now. Its basic geometrical forms—so elemental and vital. The purity of the colors—so true to the eye.

"Ms. Greene?" Winston said. "Are we okay to continue?"

"Yes, sorry," she said. "The academics piece. Well, Stanger said he would get someone to compose a hyped resume for Dario. Possibly the same someone to write his 'personal essay.' And he'd also procure a 'score 'enhancement' on Dario's ACT with the help of the test proctor who worked for him."

Winston scratched his head again. "But how can a test proctor do that? The college-admissions exams are usually given publicly, and under close observation."

Chris looked up from her laptop and stared at Lori, eager to hear the answer. Had it not been for her own colossal test-taking anxiety, she would have been able to advance in a legal career. Exactly how, she wondered, did rich people rig the exams that she could never pass? And how outrageous that they could rig a system *already* favoring them.

"I'm not proud of what Stanger and I did," Lori said. "But he advised me how to get Dario certified with a learning disadvantage. Because, once we did that, Dario would be allowed extra time to take the exam at a special designated test site—a site where Stanger's test proctor happened to work. And that proctor would either answer sections of Dario's exam, or correct errors so Dario would score high enough to meet the academic requirements."

The room fell silent again. Winston regarded her with a cautious expression, and Donald looked away. John, aware of his assistant's debilitating exam phobia, glanced at Chris and caught her judgmental eyeroll.

"Okay," Winston finally said. "Let's backtrack a little. Do you know how Sonya Wisekof knew of Martin Stanger?"

Lori thought for a second. "Word of mouth, I think. Because when she was trying to sell me on his services, she said Stanger had worked his magic for people besides herself. She named someone she knew on the state's humanities council—"

"Was that a Mr. Kirk Pendleton?" asked Winston. "The restaurateur?"

"Why, yes, that's right," Lori answered. "And in turn, he'd been referred by . . ." She stopped herself, and looked at her husband, realizing the need to hold back "a few details" for him, for them. He silently mouthed "Thank you."

"That's good," John told her. "We need to hold onto a few bargaining chips. Besides, it sounds like Mr. Wang already knows the score."

Winston's voice softened when he asked Lori, "Were you about to name Ed Cuchelli—the real estate mogul, who donates heavily to the regional theater?"

Lori stared back with a tight expression.

"And," Winston continued, glancing at the remaining name on his chart. "That regional theater is where Kirk Pendleton serves on the advisory committee, alongside Mr. Ryan Newsome. So, I'm wondering if you heard his name mentioned as well?"

John leaned forward, anxious about Lori giving up the name of a beloved movie star. But, after a slow exhalation, she maintained silence.

Winston leaned back into his chair and exhaled, too. He knew he had correctly identified all the parents. And now, armed with Lori's information, he could connect them as a group, with Martin Stanger as the common denominator. Still, how to prove the link to Steven McArdle, who surely was involved? And where was this Martin Stanger? Who was the corrupt test proctor in his back pocket?

"Ryan Newsome," John whispered to Chris, shaking his head. "Incredible. Such a white-hat do-gooder in the movies."

"Winston?" said Lori. "Do you have more questions? I'm exhausted."

He snapped to attention and said, "Just one more, please. I'm wondering if you have any hard evidence of your payment to Stanger? A check you wrote? An invoice from him? Maybe an email or text referring to your arrangement?"

She shook her head. "Ours was a cash transaction, under the table—literally, at the little café down the street." She retrieved her cellphone from the sofa table and said, "But I believe I have Mr. Stanger's cell number. There must be a log of calls between us." After scrolling briefly, she said, "Yes, this number, see? It says 'Unknown,' but it's his. We spoke as recently as Saturday, when I called him to arrange a meeting at the café."

Soon after that, the interview concluded. Donald escorted Winston, John, and Chris to the door, then followed them out to the porch. "As you can see," he said, "this is taking a heavy toll on my wife."

"She's going through a lot," Winston said. "You both are."

John patted Donald's back and said, "And we know there's going to be a helluva lot more to go through, once this admissions scandal goes public. Lori is brave to do what she's doing. But, my god, the firestorm she's igniting, and all the bridges she's about to burn."

"But for now," said Donald, "it's a day at a time. And I need to get back to my wife."

Chris asked, "We're still on for tomorrow at noon?" After everyone nodded their agreement, she left to rush back to the office and begin clearing John's calendar.

"I've got to go, too," Winston told Donald. "You and your wife have provided more than enough information for me to start on tonight's story. And I still need to confirm a few things before we publish."

After Winston left, John stood with Donald and said, "Lori did well. And now we have a few bargaining chips for an immunity plea."

"Thanks," said Donald. "And thanks for not giving up on us."

"I won't lie," said John. "At first, that interview felt like a cardiac stress test. But then . . . Well, you both surprised me. Still, tell me something before I go. What was Lori implying about finishing *her* confession first? Because that made it sound like you had a separate one to make. Do you? Should I ask Chris to clear the whole week for me?"

In a subdued voice, Donald answered, "Yes, I have my own confession. But that's going to have to wait for tomorrow. Besides, like I said, I should be with Lori right now."

"Fair," said John. "But to the question about my schedule?"

Tugging on his mustache, Donald said, "A few weeks, minimum. And months, if you don't hire an associate."

John stepped back. "That big? As big as Lori's story?"

Donald held up a hand. "You're nearing the twenty-question limit. But, yes. It's about vanity financing of trendy research and . . ." He deliberated a moment and continued, "No. It's about me putting my son in harm's way." Then he abruptly turned away and closed the door behind him.

Fred's Home

Vickie straightened Fred's blue-and-white striped necktie and kissed his cheek.

Fred kissed her back—on the lips—and said, "You look happy."

She gazed into his coppery brown eyes and said, "I am happy. Because you *finally* let me in, and felt comfortable talking last night. So, this is me, *finally* understanding what you're going through."

"You know, everything I said was confidential."

"Fred, I understand that. But it's like I've been telling you: Normal married couples talk to each other. Even the courts recognize spousal testimonial privilege. At least they do on *Law & Order*."

He frowned. "Well, I wish what was happening was on the TV. I'd change the channel in a heartbeat."

Accompanying him out to the driveway, she said, "I know this is hard on you. Bill was an important figure in your career. But he and Ellie have veered *way* out-of-bounds. It's unconscionable how Bill treated Dario! It's unconscionable what the Balabans put you and Nora and Jack through—to say nothing of that poor Ortho resident. I think you and your friends are doing the right thing by calling them out and taking them down."

"I wish feeling 'right' also meant feeling 'good.' And, god, the whole thing is still so mindboggling. Bill used to be such an upstanding guy."

She debated whether to remind him that he had neither seen nor spoken with Bill for ages. He, sensing her holding back on that, said, "You're thinking: People can and do change over time, and I should understand that."

She touched his cheek and said, "And haven't we learned that about ourselves, too? The hard way?"

He smiled affectionately.

"Besides," she continued, "I think you always put on rose-colored glasses, when you look back to the old days with the Balabans. But, Fred, I remember you and your gang complaining about having to babysit Bill because he never wanted to go home. All those *long* hours of him insistently teaching you, at night and on weekends? And those monthly cocktail dinners at their house?"

"What about those dinners?"

"Well, they weren't much fun for me or Nora's husband—and not only because we had to listen to you all talk shop. But the banter between Bill and Ellie often made us uncomfortable. It could be cutting and cold, and sometimes outright hostile."

"That so?" he said.

"And, you know, it sometimes stressed me to sit at that table with you and Lydia."

"I know, I know," he said, anxious they were about to revisit that troubling history.

"And Jack—not once do I recall him bringing a date."

"You saying the Balabans were homophobic?"

"Honestly, Fred. Well, they didn't hang 'gays unwelcome' banners in the dining room. They didn't need to."

The corners of Fred's mouth turned down as he began recalling memories on which Vickie was casting a different light now. She and Michael, bored at the dinners? Okay, he could see that now. Jack marginalized because of his sexuality? Yeah, probably. The gang complaining about Bill's obsessive teaching? Definitely, yes.

Still, he thought, everyone had acted with best intentions and good-natured attitudes. So, was Vickie right about the grim interactions between Bill and Ellie? Had he simply turned a blind eye to them? Had he been too focused on accommodating and pleasing his mentor? Too distracted by his own relationship with Lydia, who sat at the same table with Vickie?

"Don't frown like that," Vickie said. "That's all in the past. And you're going to be late for work." After waiting for him to get behind the wheel of his silver Lexus, she said, "Call me later to let me know if you're coming home for dinner. But don't worry—I understand that you and Nora have plenty of planning to do before you meet with the Balabans tomorrow."

"I'll call you one way or the other," he said. "You'll be at the gallery all day?"

"With Lori Greene's work stacked all over the place? Hell, yes!"

Fred pulled out of the driveway and turned on the CD player. He cranked up Carrie Underwood at full volume and headed to the hospital.

Outside the Parker-Greene Estate

Winston sat in his red Subaru in front of the Parker-Greene estate, trying to decide who to call first. He wanted to tell Fergie how right she'd been to suggest a scholarship connection involving the recruits.

But he should also call Nora to thank her for her insights about Lori, which built the case for the bribery scheme. And, of course, his editor—he needed to give her the heads-up about the bombshell story he'd be laying out over the coming days. He also hoped to contact the other recruits' parents for comment, track down Martin Stanger, and—

Someone knocked on the car window. He looked out to see John Norris standing curbside, his blue suitcoat unbuttoned and his red silk tie dangling over his athletic torso.

Winston got out of the car and asked, "What's up?"

John placed his hands on his hips and said, "I just wanted to say: I was impressed. You certainly came prepared. Your investigative work is class-A. And, while I'm not happy about the urgency of my clients' need to confess . . . Well, clearly, that's how they need to deal with their situation. Everyone handles tragedy in their own way."

"Thank you," said Winston. "And, yeah—they seemed more than willing to talk. Aiming for catharsis, maybe."

John nodded. "I also want to apologize for refusing to talk with you before."

"Apology accepted," said Winston, extending his hand. "Still, you know, my reporting is going to cause a lot of grief for you and your clients."

John shook his hand and said, "I'm aware of that. But, as it should, to be frank. And they're expecting consequences, too."

"They're unusual," said Winston. "But it's refreshing to see people accepting responsibility for their actions. Not a common occurrence these days."

A black limousine drove by and bounced a shaft of sunlight onto them. John shielded his eyes from the glare and said, "Still, I feel for them. They're about to become social pariahs after naming names. And them being rich, privileged people acting unfairly to sneak their kid into college? Well, that's just going to play poorly in the media."

Winston was surprised to be feeling sympathy for Lori and her husband, independent of their son's death. He said, "I can only imagine what they'll be going through. They've already been through so much."

"Definitely hard to fathom," said John, arching a brow. "You got kids?"

Winston shook his head, but was suddenly aware of regretting Fergie's negative pregnancy test.

"Me neither," said John. "No time with my career, and, frankly, no desire."

"Well," said Winston, "I should go. I've got calls to make." He reached for the car door handle. "See you tomorrow at noon."

"Hang on a minute," said John, flashing a wry smile. "One of those calls is to the number Lori gave you, right?"

Winston said nothing.

"C'mon," said John, his palms turning up. "You don't trust me?"

Bill and Ellie's Home

Their suitcases were packed—five for Ellie, two for Bill—and they had secured their tickets to the Cayman Islands for tomorrow evening. So, now, they ought to be able to relax. To kick back with a cocktail in their living room. To leisurely contemplate their imminent escape from all the barking hounds at their heels.

But—as Ellie *again* pointed out to Bill—none of that was possible, because of the irksome matter of them having to attend a clinic appointment with Fred *tomorrow*. How disruptive, how inconvenient, how risky. "It was foolish to alarm Fred like that!" she railed at Bill. "And suppose there's a delay on the Bay Bridge, when we get out of that horrid appointment? Or another incident at the airport? You didn't have to be so overly dramatic and destroy our entire parlor!"

"Ellie," he said with a shrug, "what difference does it make? We knew we'd be leaving the house behind."

"But the things you destroyed were important to *me*. And, even my Emmy?"

"You could look at this differently. You could consider it me doing you a favor, by minimizing your packing decisions. Besides, I think my strategy worked brilliantly. I think I fully convinced Fred about the severity of my dementia."

She plonked her cocktail glass down on the coffee table with more force than necessary. "And it's about your *timing*! Pulling your over-the-top stunt while I was away from the house was a mistake. If you hadn't acted so recklessly, we could have appeased Fred by agreeing to a future appointment on a date *after* our flight! But this urgent appointment *tomorrow?*"

"Well, someday, should you ever calm down, you'll understand the wisdom of my strategy."

"No," she said, her face reddening. "You just tossed an enormous monkey wrench into our plans. And if we don't show up, Fred will call out the police and APS."

"You worry too much. You'll see. We're going to sail through the appointment by simply agreeing to whatever Fred recommends. Then he and the others will be satisfied and leave us alone, certainly long enough for us to get to the airport afterwards. The islands await us, Ellie."

His phone chimed a text. He read it and shook his head.

"What now?" she asked.

He stood up, grabbed his coat and hat, and headed out the door.

"Where are you going?" she called out after him.

ER Hallway

Fred pulled Nora aside in the ER hallway and said, "Got a minute?"

"Of course," she said. "'Cuz there's never any work to do around here."

"Okay, no time for sarcasm. Just checking in with you."

She smiled and said, "I was just about to call you and do the same."

He lowered his voice. "So, I had my assistant confirm with Bill and Ellie about the appointment tomorrow."

"Great," she said. "Lola from social services has agreed to sit in. And Owen is meeting with Bill tonight."

"How about Carrie?"

Nora laughed. "She's a little *too* enthused about participating. I made her promise to stay quiet during the appointment. But she's seriously pissed at Bill and Ellie—all their bad behavior and lies, and the maddening 'consult' their dishonesty generated for her."

"Anything I can do to shore up our Plan C?"

She shook her head. "But I am a little concerned about a couple of potential obstacles that popped up."

"You look more than a 'little' concerned, Nora. Tell me."

"Well, for one—I just got off a call with Winston. He wanted to thank me for helping with a story he's writing. But he also mentioned that Donald Parker is planning to 'confess' something big tomorrow."

"Oh? And you think it's about his son's stem-cell injections?"

"I'll bet on it," she said, her brow knitting. "And my other concern? Annie Klumtree texted an hour ago to let me know, that they're planning to release her preliminary report sometime tomorrow."

"Oh, hell," he said. "And you're worried the Balabans might get wind of either before their appointment tomorrow."

"Exactly," she said. "Because, if they do, they're going to clam up, or lawyer up, or flee." She held her hands up toward the ceiling, as if invoking the gods, and implored, "But I *have* to see them held accountable, with my own eyes. And—I don't care if it speaks poorly of me—I *want* to watch them get their comeuppance."

Fred laughed and said, "Well, you've got company there. We've got to nail them tomorrow."

"Got to nail them," she echoed. Then, pointing up the hallway, she said, "That's the room where Dario died. And, after days of news about him, he still seems like such a cipher. A pawn, too. His parents manipulated him to satisfy their goals—even coaxing him into taking useless stem-cell injections. Bill used him, to secure funding for his lab."

"That's so sad," he replied, shaking his head. "Still, I hope you feel some consolation, knowing you're about to give some voice to Dario's life."

Outside the Parker-Greene Estate

After completing his calls to Fergie, Nora, and his editor, Winston opened the car window and told John, "Ready." John entered the car, took the passenger seat, and said, "You won't regret this."

Winston placed his cellphone on the dashboard and turned on its speakerphone. Then he keyed in the number for Martin Stanger.

Martin was home alone, sitting in his favorite armchair—a monstrously large relic from his grandparents, but cozy all the same. Its many poorly matched fabric bandages that had been applied over the decades lent it a colorful resiliency. Drinking a cold beer while halfheartedly listening to the news, he wondered how, and where, his stepson Jason was. "Please, just call me," he said aloud.

Then—perhaps in answer to his prayer?—his charity's dedicated cellphone rang. The possibilities were few—limited to Jason, Steven McArdle, and the parents he had helped. Expecting it was Jason wanting to reconnect, he picked up. But when he answered "Hello?" and the caller replied "Martin Stanger?" he knew he was wrong.

When silence ensued, Winston and John nodded knowingly at one another. Then Winston said, "Mr. Stanger, my name is Winston Wang. I'm a reporter with the *Oakland Register*."

Gathering that he had to be the same reporter who had contacted Steven McArdle, Martin froze.

"We know about your fake charity," Winston continued. "And the college 'scholarships' you sold through it."

After another tense pause, Winston said, "We also know about you greasing college test scores, and bribing the tennis coach at UCSM."

Martin sank back in his armchair and guzzled the remainder of his beer. "Fuck," he muttered under his breath. Then he heard a second voice over the phone: "Mr. Stanger? I'm John Norris, an attorney representing one of your 'clients' who has chosen to go public about enlisting your services. It's to your benefit to speak with us."

Dread flooded Martin's brain. He'd seen the press-conference photograph of John Norris standing by Lori Greene.

Winston waited a beat and said, "I've identified five students you've 'helped' over the years. Do you care to comment about that?"

Martin crushed his beer can and hurled it against the wall. Comment about what? His overwhelming stupidity? How miserably he had failed his stepson? How he broke his vow to Jason's mother to always protect him?

"Mr. Stanger?" said Winston. "I've also identified the parents of those students."

The parents, Martin thought. The parents of the clueless, undeserving students he snuck into UCSM. Did they or their kids have any self-awareness of the unfairness? He, depressed and without the financial resources to support Jason after his mother's death, had been forced to get creative. And his lucrative admissions scheme had worked well—until now—to earn him and Jason a share in the spoils of that unfairness.

"You still there?" asked John.

Throwing his head back and staring up at the ceiling, Martin murmured, "Fuck." But, really, what was so wrong about helping ultra-wealthy parents secure their kids' undeserved college admissions? And how was that different from all the other acceptable forms of stacked privileges that were always available to them? What he did may have been sneaky, but it was also very *normal*.

"Even if you choose not to talk," said Winston, "I can run my story with what I already have. But either way, it's not looking good for you. And soon, circumstances are going to force you—"

"All right," said Martin, privately reaffirming his vow to Jason's mother. "All right. I'll talk with you. Whatever you want to know. But I have one completely nonnegotiable condition."

Lake Temescal Beach House

"What's this about?" Bill asked, emerging into view behind the Beach House.

Owen reminded himself to stay calm. He invoked Nora's advice to keep his fists open, and to remain laser-focused on the meeting's objective. He also remembered his promise to his parents to make things right. He could do this; he *would* do this.

"I suppose I should be grateful," Bill continued, "that you didn't barge into our home this time."

Deflecting the provocation, Owen coolly replied, "I visited the lab Monday night."

"That's your news?" Bill said, casually brushing something off his coat sleeve. Privately, however, he rued the fact that he hadn't changed the lab's security codes, as Ellie had advised. But, god, she always made it so easy to be contrary! Still, this current twist could have been avoided. And, on further thought, it would have been, had Ellie truly gotten Owen on board—as she so boastfully claimed she had. Instead, she made Owen so mistrustful, that he had to check the lab to see whether she had lied about it being cleared.

Taken aback by his mentor's seeming nonchalance, Owen let slip, "Really?" But he quickly recovered his resolve and said, "The news is, I discovered you didn't destroy the evidence of your stem-cell business. In fact, you manipulated it and tried to plant it on me."

Bill looked sternly at him and asked, "Are you recording us, Owen? Show me your cellphone."

After Owen held out his phone for inspection, Bill said, "Okay. So, you're dragging me out here at dinnertime to tell me about that. You couldn't wait until tomorrow?"

"No. I couldn't stand one minute longer of being used—by you or your wife. And I needed to see your face, when I told you I wouldn't be taking the blame for what you did."

Buttoning up his coat, Bill said, "It's getting nippy."

"That's all you've got to say?"

"Well, yes. Because there's no use for further conversation." He laughed sharply, pointed to himself, and said, "Do you actually think anyone is going to believe that this poor demented old man was capable of the sophisticated scheming you just described? Go ahead and share your wild theories with the world. No one will believe you."

"We both know you're not demented!"

Bill shrugged. "And yet, my wife will movingly attest to my cognitive impairment and downhill course over two suffering years. Colleagues— all doctors, mind you—who have visited our house will offer distressed eyewitness accounts of my decline and the attendant behavioral prob- lems that my saintly wife endures. My medical record—the one you illegally read in the ER—documents my failed mental status exams.

And, let's face it—who better than me to know how to pull the whole dementia thing off?"

Stunned by his mentor's emotionless rendering of his deceit, Owen was speechless.

Bill continued, "It's also interesting that, other than my wife, *you* are the only person who has seen me regularly over the past two years. And you happen to be the *only* person with a motive to challenge my dementia diagnosis: You want to pass all blame for Dario's tumor onto me, and then take over my lab."

"So, you admit—you knew about his teratoma."

"Well, you just told me you found the evidence in the lab. I should hope you were able to interpret the ultrasound."

Owen stuffed his fists in his pockets, questioning his ability to contain his rage. Bill was testing his limits and pushing him toward yet another proverbial edge. And, though it deviated from Nora's objective, he asked, "But why did you have to set me up?"

"Well, you don't know my Ellie. But, when she's unhappy? Look out, everyone! The payback was her idea. She deserves the credit. Though, to be frank, I've discovered justifications of my own: your overly charmed existence, your disrespect and ingratitude—to name a few."

Owen pushed up his cap visor, baring his livid eyes. "Why the hell would your wife even care to hurt me? I did nothing to her."

"She would beg to differ. Ellie thinks you've been disloyal, hot-headed, impertinent . . . 'rogue' is the term she uses for you. And she was already unhappy, before you entered the picture. She was afraid I'd lose my lucrative stem-cell practice, after it became known that Donald Parker's son suffered a life-threatening infection from my treatment—"

"You know damn well 'infection' wasn't the complication! You lied to her and Dario about that."

"So literal," Bill said with a tsk. "I thought your question concerned why she hates you."

Owen stood rigid, his jaw tight.

"See," Bill continued, "Ellie and I had figured how to handle that 'infection.' We had planned for me to take responsibility—or, actually, 'irresponsibility,' by virtue of my terrible dementia. But then, it occurred to her—suppose *you*, my mentee, performed the surgery and explored for evidence that we could simply get rid of? That would eliminate worries for her—for all of us. So, imagine how she felt when I informed her you hadn't kept your promise to perform Dario's surgery? Well, now, that pissed her off. She was very unhappy with you."

"But you know why I didn't get to the surgery! It was because you freaked out and phoned me—"

"And later, when she found out the boy had *died*, and the coroner had the body? My god. She became *profoundly* unhappy with you."

Owen stammered, "You set her up against me, with your lies."

With a half-smile, Bill said, "But you put the final nail in your own coffin, when you tried to blackmail me and steal my lab. Because Ellie expected me to return to my stem-cell practice, after Dario's condition settled peaceably enough. And, of course, after my miraculous and speedy response to my new dementia medications."

"Fuck," Owen murmured.

"Did you say something?" Bill asked. "You need to speak up."

Knowing he needed to push back to throw Bill off balance, Owen said, "But it's irrelevant that I didn't take Dario's surgery. Because you knew from your ultrasound, the day before, that he had a tumor in his arm—something you never mentioned to me, to Dario, or to Ellie. And there was no way I, or anyone else, could have found that tumor by exploring his forearm during a fasciotomy."

"Ah, well, perhaps someday you can sit down with Ellie and explain that anatomical nuance to her. Arm . . . forearm . . . I'm sure she would be enthralled. And besides, we both know that if I had told you about the tumor, you never would've agreed to take the surgery in the first place. You had cold feet from the start."

"'Anatomical nuance'?" said Owen. "Say what you want, but that doesn't make it true. And any day now, the coroner's report is going to be made public. Then everyone will know about Dario's teratoma, and they'll trace it back to your stem-cell injections. Dario's father will be—"

"Excuse me—I'm demented. Who is this 'Dario' and his father?"

Owen's face tightened. He urgently counseled himself to stick to Nora's objective as a means of fulfilling his pledge to make things right. But, needing to buy time for that, he said, "I see what you're doing."

Bill doffed his hat. "I doubt it. But, good for you—then there really is no need for further discussion." He pivoted away.

"But what about your wife?" Owen said.

"My wife?" Bill said, turning back.

Emboldened now, Owen replied, "Even allowing for your so-called dementia, people will still file lawsuits against your estate. Not just Dario's family, but all the other people you've put at risk. The press is going to have a field day with your story, too. And I'm just guessing— that whole costly shitshow will make Ellie . . . well, very 'unhappy' with *you*."

Bill considered puncturing his mentee's haughtiness by revealing that he'd already transferred the bulk of his assets to an offshore account. But, calculating the risk of that tipping Owen off to his plan, he only bristled and said, "Ellie's unhappiness is no longer my concern. Except, perhaps, in a perverse sort of way."

Owen shifted his feet, feeling the power dynamic rebalancing in his favor. The conversation's trajectory was bending in the direction that Nora had predicted. He said, "It doesn't seem smart to dismiss her feelings about you—certainly not as her demented husband. Because your unhappy wife would become your legal guardian, and she'd be unhappy around you *all* the time. She'd control your daily life and your estate. You'd need her permission to take a shit, leave the house, go to a restaurant. You wouldn't be able to escape her, Dr. Balaban. And the two of you would be 'unhappy' forever after."

Bill's expression tightened, while he wrestled with the fantasy of smacking the self-satisfied smile off Owen's face. Instead, he decided to leave the confrontation before losing more control. But Owen boldly stepped up to him and said, "We both know you haven't wanted to be around Ellie, even in the best of times. How would you tolerate her 24/7 presence?"

"No need to worry about me," Bill said, trying to recover his bravado. "Just worry about yourself and—"

"The way I see it?" Owen interrupted. "You have two options. One: You leave the country before your stem-cell scandal becomes public and completely destroys your life. Or, two: You murder Ellie, and also expect to be absolved of that, because of your alleged dementia."

"Murder my wife?" said Bill, musing over the fantasy of it.

"You're right," said Owen. "That's not a good idea. Because, even if you murdered her, they'd put you away under state conservatorship, and you'd still lose control of everything." He locked eyes with his mentor and added, "So, I'm betting on option one: You're planning to skip town, ASAP."

Bill's eyes darkened, and emptied of their confident look. "Whatever scenario ultimately plays out in the real world that exists outside of your fevered brain, you won't come out clean."

"I know that. But the difference is, I intend to take responsibility for my part. I shouldn't have given Dario that stupid injection, and I shouldn't have been afraid to disappoint you by declining the surgery. That's all on me." He stood tall and continued, "But, compared to what's on you? Sending Dario home with a compartment syndrome? Lying to him about having an infection? Practicing Wild West medicine with stem cells? Browbeating me to take the surgery and 'explore' his forearm, when you knew damn well about a teratoma in his arm, and you said nothing about that to anybody?"

Uncertain how to put Owen in his place without exposing his hand, Bill reminded himself that this current vexation was temporary. If he could just adhere to his private plan, all would be well by tomorrow night.

Listening to his gut, Owen confidently persisted, "And it's ironic. Because, as it turned out, it still wouldn't have mattered whether I or Dr. Kelly found evidence of the injections, let alone the tumor."

Bill huffed. "What the hell does that even mean?"

"It means, I know what the coroner found."

"Yeah, and?" Bill said, his voice hardened.

Intending to aggravate his mentor's anxiety, Owen yawned artificially. Then he said, "Dario's lungs were filled with tumor emboli—that's what killed him. His teratoma had been metastasizing for weeks to months before the fasciotomy. So, finding any remnant tumor during surgery—in his arm *or* forearm—would've meant squat. Evidence of it had already spread far and wide."

"I'll be damned," Bill said, shaking his head, looking down. "Tumor emboli? And from a teratoma? Well, that's quite remarkable."

Owen shot back, "You don't seem to care that your hubris and greed killed Dario Parker!"

"You're sounding hysterical now. You might want to tone that down. But of course, I regret what happened to Dario. Must have been bad cells I got from—"

"How many other people have you fucked over with your bogus stem-cell 'treatments'?"

"'Fucked over'? That's harsh. Look, people come to me for them—as far away as Costa Rica. And I have private clients here—as you know. But no one is being strong-armed into taking them."

Owen counted to ten, struggling to maintain focus on the Balabans' relationship. "When Ellie hears the news from the coroner's report, she'll know you lied to her. And she'll learn about the deadly tumor *you* created with *your* stem-cell injections. Her unhappiness with you will blow through the roof, and make your life even more miserable."

Patting a hand over his heart, Bill said, "I didn't realize, until now, how much you cared about me."

"When that autopsy report is made public, red flags will go up. And I'll be holding one of them."

"Really, I'm touched. I will never forget your concern. Oh, wait—I will. I have dementia."

Owen crossed his arms. "You think you're so smart."

Smiling insincerely, Bill said, "Well, me having dementia was another of Ellie's ideas. And I have to hand it to her—she was right about that, too. Just don't ever tell her I said so."

And there it was, finally—the tactical opening that Nora had predicted. Owen stepped brazenly into it and said, "It must be difficult—as a renowned neurosurgeon, and as a man—to have a wife you detest, who is so much smarter than you."

Bill scoffed and said, "That's ridiculous."

"Well, she's figured out how to control you and your life with her moods—especially with her unhappiness. And, c'mon. As you've admitted, she's been the 'idea man' behind your plans."

"We're done here," said Bill.

"You can't even live freely in your own home, for godsakes. You're always hiding from her, in your lab or some other country. So, maybe you're a little unhappy yourself?"

Bill narrowed his eyes, while trying to steel himself against revealing his actual plans, only to prove Owen wrong. All the while, Ellie's infuriating charge to *Grow a spine!* echoed inside his head, challenging his ability to think.

"And the two of you?" Owen said. "You *really* don't like each other. That day in the ER, I heard you both talking while I waited outside your room. The mutual disdain in your voices was disturbing. And I felt uncomfortable in your home, witnessing the hostility between you. Then, later, I heard through the hospital grapevine about Ellie's black eye and—"

"We are normal married people. Spouses argue and fight sometimes."

"No. Your mutual contempt is way outside the lines of normal."

"Let's just attribute any bad behavior or attitude to my dementia. So unfortunate—my violent outbursts can be quite unpredictable."

Owen ignored the implicit threat and said, "And for two full years, every Thursday in the lab, I listened to you rant against Ellie. How you hated her acting and her meddling. You couldn't stand her voice or her—"

"What in god's name is your point?"

"She bullies you big time, because you're too weak to stand up to her."

Bill's face burned crimson, and he shouted, "Why does it even matter to you that I hate her?"

It took every ounce of Owen's willpower to maintain a neutral expression. But bringing Nora's plan close to the finish line now, he wanted to thrust his fists into the air and declare victory. Instead, he fixed Bill with a pointed stare and said, "It matters because I can see a way out of this entire mess for both of *us*."

"You got something to say, just say it."

"Okay. But first, I want three things in return for saving you. And one of them happens to be something you also want."

"Well, you can have the damn lab—if you destroy the evidence you found. I presume you took it with you? I haven't been back since my little ER incident."

"You mean, the evidence you doctored and tried to plant on me? Yeah, I took it home. But why would I destroy it?"

"You've got to. If you take possession of the lab, you don't want evidence around that could trace back to it and connect Dario's—"

"Do you have a more selfish reason? Your name's all over that evidence. And it's easy to prove your transactions here, and Costa Rica—"

"Look, I'm demented. But you have no defense."

"All right," Owen said. "The lab is one thing I want. And the other two things?"

Bill's posture stiffened. How humiliating to be at the mercy of his mentee. But Owen's possession of the evidence and his ability to expose the stem-cell debacle threatened his plan. And the clock was ticking faster, because Owen had uncovered his intention to "skip town." Bill loosened his coat collar and said, "Well, you also want to feel safe. You want me to stop plotting against you. So, then, you can stop worrying about that—*if* you keep your silence about my dementia. Besides, if people think I'm demented, no one would believe a word I said against you."

"Yes," said Owen. "It would be nice to be able to sleep again. So, can you guess the last thing? The one we both want?"

"You better have a good strategy, Owen. I don't like this game."

Owen smiled confidently, held up a finger, and drew a triangle in the air.

With sudden realization, Bill let slip out an unguarded laugh. *Of course! I pitted him and Ellie against each other, and look how brilliantly that worked! Now we both despise her.* He answered with a glint in his eyes: "Retaliation against Ellie."

Although sickened by his makeshift alliance with Bill, Owen nodded.

"That makes sense," Bill said. "Because she certainly intimidated you, and humiliated you, and endangered your career. And, as I told you, she also came up with the idea to punish you—"

"Enough," Owen said, holding his tongue, cautioning himself against ruining this hard-won alliance. "I don't need reminding of what she put me through."

"Okay," said Bill, twisting his wedding band. "I've already planned a few things on my own. Still, I'm interested in what you have in mind. We could probably help each other out."

"I think we can," Owen said. "But before I begin—does Ellie know I took the evidence from the lab?"

Bill scoffed. "No! Even I didn't know until tonight. And she'd kill me if she knew I never changed the lab's security codes."

"Good," said Owen. "Then we can talk."

Nora's Home

The pre-fab chicken piccata dinner had hit the proverbial spot, although without delivering its box-label promise of "fresh flavor." *Still*, Nora wondered, *how could any reasonable person expect the taste of "fresh" from something that's been killed, processed, frozen, and mummified in cellophane? And what does "fresh" even taste like?*

She rinsed the plastic microwave tray and tossed it into the recycling bin, vowing (again) to (someday) become proficient in cooking healthy, homemade meals. But with Alex gone the last few days, she had already backtracked in the kitchen, abandoning recent culinary ventures with three-ingredient recipes.

After fruitlessly calling out for Bix (*Where the hell does he go at night?*), Nora turned off the lights and headed to the bedroom. While setting her cellphone down on the nightstand, she remembered promising (but forgetting) to contact Alex today. *How can I be so inattentive to him? He's taking care of his sick parents. Seems the least I could do is call him.*

But, considering the lateness of the hour in Mexico, she instead slipped into bed and pulled the so-called comforter up to her chin. She closed her eyes and imagined herself in session with her itinerant psychiatrist, Dr. Solène Barteau: *Yeah, I think I love Alex . . . Miss him? Not sure. Maybe because our time apart has been so short? . . . Well, I've felt more independent the last few days. And I've had more time to think over things that matter to me . . . Yes, he sometimes interferes with that . . . Lonely? Not really. I'm spending time with friends, and talking things through with them—*

Nora abruptly terminated her imagined therapy session, turned onto her side, and stared at Alex's vacated half of the bed. And, though not understanding why, she reshaped the hollow he'd left in the pillow, and she smoothed out the wrinkles he'd left in the sheets.

Part Eight

Thursday, December 5

Nora's Home

"GOOD MORNING, and where are you?" Nora spoke into the speakerphone, while plating a toasted fruit pocket.

"I'm calling you from the Richmond Bridge," Jack answered. "Heading to work. Or, I should say, crawling toward it."

"Hands-free, I hope?"

"Driving?"

"Funny-*not*," she said.

"Listen," he said, "I'm just calling—hands-free—to wish you good luck with Plan C today. God, I wish I could be there with you."

"You will be, in a way. You've played a critical role in pulling the plan together."

"Still, to be a fly on the wall!"

"Yuck. Not sure I'd like that. I prefer you as a human."

"Call me after the meeting?" he said.

"Too hot," she said.

"Why, thank you!"

"Sorry, not you. I was talking to my breakfast."

"Well, I hope you two have a fruitful conversation. I'm going to hang up now."

"Wait," she said.

"Me? Or the waffle-fruit-tart-whatever?"

"You," she said. "You're sure Carrie's ready?"

He laughed. "She even stopped by the house last night to practice with Luis. They had so much fun. But she's not just 'ready.' I'd say she's lusting for karmic revenge."

Bill and Ellie's Home

At 7:30 a.m., the alarm chirped, "Good morning!"

Ellie punched the off button to silence its unwarranted cheer. Then she rolled onto her side and told Bill, "Wake up."

Bill roused sluggishly and faced her. She looked appraisingly at him and said, "You look terrible. How late were you out last night? And where did you go?"

"And a 'good morning' to you, too," he said.

"I mean it, Bill. We must be on top of our game today. I need you to be alert."

He swung his skinny legs off the side of the bed and sighed. "The meeting with Fred is at noon. We have plenty of time."

"I still want to know where you were last night."

He considered answering, "With my lover," but he knew that would only provoke her. Instead, he replied, "I drove to the Beach House, to see it one last time."

"You fool!" she said. "Someone could have seen you. How would that look? And what truly demented old man drives a car, let alone, at night?"

"No one saw me," he said, pushing off the mattress. "And I thought we agreed to stay calm today. So, please, Ellie—calm down."

Hospital Cafeteria

After waving to Fred, who was seated at a corner table, Nora walked up to the cafeteria counter. Marla poured her a coffee and asked, "Anything else for breakfast?"

Nora shook her head and said, "I already ate."

"Fruit pocket?" Marla guessed, one hand on her hip.

"I'm impressed," Nora said, handing over two dollars. "But, double or nothing—want to guess the fruit?"

Marla slipped the bills into the register while a smile dawned on her face. "I don't want to take advantage of you. I know it's blueberry, because I see the evidence on your shirt." She dipped a napkin into some water and handed it to Nora.

"You're an honest woman," Nora said, trying to blot out "the evidence." Then she thanked Marla and took her coffee to Fred's table. He greeted her with, "Good morning. I hope we're still on track with Plan C?"

"I think so," she said. "All the ducks are lined up."

"Great. But how about follow-up on Owen Landry? I thought you were going to call me last night, after he met with Bill."

"Sorry," she said. "But I had such a long and complicated evening. And Owen called me quite late. Still, it sounded like he got Bill exactly where we want him." She laughed softly and added, "He even got to throw a few punches of his own."

"Good for Owen," Fred said, buttering his croissant. "Any updates on the potential interferences? I read the morning news online, and Vickie scoured the internet—but we found nothing breaking about the coroner's report or Donald Parker's 'confession.'"

She shook her head. "I'm just keeping my fingers and toes crossed that nothing spooks Bill and Ellie before their appointment with you."

"Still, I have to admit," he said. "I'm a little nervous about all the moving parts in our plan. What about you?"

After tearing off a piece of his croissant, she said, "Well, I'm not expecting everything to run smoothly today. But I feel confident that things will move in the right direction. I trust everyone's motivation and intention to see justice delivered to the Balabans."

He moved his plate beyond her next attempted reach and said, "It's been so mindboggling about them. And now I'm questioning whether I *ever* knew them. Then yesterday, Vickie said things that blew my mind even further—or, at least, knocked the 'rose-colored glasses' off my face. I hope you don't mind me asking—but do you remember if Michael found the Balabans difficult?"

"Oh, yeah," she said, with a wistful smile. "He was never keen on attending their cocktail dinners. He found them boring—too much medical talk. And endless—with too much alcohol in the parlor afterwards. I remember him and Vickie sharing lots of conspiratorial eyerolls."

"Huh," he said. "What about the behavior between Bill and Ellie?"

She reached back in time, trying to recall. "I remember Michael commenting—negatively—about their highly traditional marriage. You know—rigid, old-timey, an homage to the patriarchy. And he thought their banter often had an edge."

Fred sighed, wondering what else he'd not seen through his rose-colored glasses. Still, considering how isolated Bill seemed to have been while spiraling downward lately, he said, "Despite their failings, I still wish I hadn't kept canceling on Bill. Because that just says something about me."

"You've got to give that up," she said. "You know how much I value your friendship. But not even *that* would have had the power to compensate Bill for his misery and bad marriage, or to save him from self-ruin. And it wouldn't have given him the purpose in life that he lost in retirement—" She stopped and stared inquiringly at her old friend.

"What?" he asked. "Why are you looking at me like I'm an injured puppy?"

She placed a hand on his arm. "Because I know what you're thinking. But let's be clear—your situation is completely different than Bill's. You're happy with Vickie. You have two wonderful kids. You have interests in life beyond medicine, and you'd never hole yourself up in some dark research cave. And, most importantly, you have me."

A corner of Fred's mouth rose. "So, what you're saying is, you're promising you won't let me spiral into madness after I retire?"

"Yes. When you decide to retire, it will be from your job—not from me."

He patted her hand and said, "Well, thank you in advance."

After they toasted each other with their coffees, he pulled out his inhaler for a dose.

"Hey," she said, after waiting on his exhale. "If you're worried about being able to pull things off today, or you feel too guilty, or Plan C feels wrong . . . Honestly, it's okay to back out now. I'll just show up without you. I'll tell the Balabans you're out sick, and that I'm stepping in."

"No," he said, planting his hands firmly on the table. "It's the right thing to do. I want to be part of it. And if your Plan C—"

"No, *our* Plan C."

"All right then," he said. "If our plan works, scores will be settled, and truth will out."

"That's the hope," she said, holding Dario in mind. "And maybe we'll also shed some light on these Wild West stem-cell exploitations. Maybe fewer people will be hurt in the future."

They held each other's gaze a while. Then he smiled his crooked smile and said, "See you at curtain call."

"See you at curtain call," she echoed, smiling back.

Bill and Ellie's Home

After appraising his grizzled face in the bathroom mirror, Bill put down his razor. It was obvious now—the unshaven look would prove more convincing.

Ellie knocked on the door and barked "Fifteen minutes!" causing him to flinch. But, determined to preserve their fragile truce, he only replied, "Yes, dear," and waited for her retreating footsteps to silence.

Looking back into the mirror, he conceded that she had a legitimate reason to be cross with him. Indeed, his destruction of their parlor the other night had forced today's urgent appointment with Fred, throwing a "monkey wrench" into everyone's plans. And yet, in all honesty, how glorious it had felt to destroy her *purported* acting awards and mementos, and to relocate them to their rightful places in the wastebasket or fireplace. How blissful to have seen her face when she stepped into the ruined parlor and struggled to convince Fred—perhaps, even, herself—that she was taking the destruction in stride, repeatedly stating that she couldn't "take it personally."

Still, today's forced appointment with Fred was going to cost time. To mitigate that, they had strategized about tactics to limit the visit. He would remain nonverbal whenever questioned, and simply stare back when asked to perform evaluative cognitive tasks. They would automatically accept whatever Fred and the social worker recommended. And, if for some reason the meeting dragged on, he would act distraught and demand to be taken home.

Now, picking up his toothbrush, Bill realized how oddly grateful he felt that Fred, Nora, and Jack believed him to have dementia. For, as estranged as they had become, still, he took some comfort in knowing they wouldn't consider him willful or responsible, when news of the stem-cell debacle broke.

And yet, why should he give a damn about what they thought of him? What little, if any, thought had they given him over the years? Still, he had to admit, they mattered. He'd given so much of himself to them; they had embodied his knowledge and skills, carrying him into their futures, like good sons and daughters. At least for that, he felt grateful to them. But, at the same time, all the more painfully discarded, too.

After brushing his teeth, he tousled his hair to complement his unshaven face. Then he nodded approvingly in the mirror and said, "Yes."

Yes, despite a few bumps along the way, he had planned everything well, and tonight would certify proof of that. The prospect of leaving *everything* behind after the appointment with Fred brought light to his eyes.

"Five minutes!" Ellie warned, rapping on the door.

He gritted his teeth and muttered, "One last day." Then he cheered himself by envisioning his wife's inglorious defeat. Within hours, his beautiful new life would begin.

Nora's Office

Nora sat at her desk, staring at the dartboard on the wall, contemplating a toss of her green darts. But suppose she missed the board entirely, let alone the bull's-eye? Would Plan C fail?

She chided herself for entertaining such superstitions. Of course, the plan would work, regardless of her scoring—or lack thereof. Owen, Carrie, and Fred had assured her they were prepared, and she was about to have lunch with Lola to review the details of her participation today.

A knock on the door sounded, and Fergie leaned in.

"Ah," said Nora, holding out her darts. "Here to lose another game?"

Fergie shook her head. "There's a visitor to see you. Got a minute?"

"A minute," she said. "My break's almost over."

Fergie stepped aside to allow Winston in. He carried two Safeway bags that he placed on her desk. "A small thank-you gift," he explained.

Nora's face brightened while she explored the contents. "Corn curls and cheese crackers? Mixed nut packets? Wow, all my favorites!"

"Well," he said, "Fergs gave me hints. I wanted to thank you for staying the course of our friendship during a rough patch. I know my reporting on Dario's case has been hard on you. But I hope you understand—"

She hugged him before he could finish.

"And," he continued, "not only did you hold onto our friendship, but, during a challenging time for *me*, you also helped me out. As I told you yesterday, you were right about Lori Greene's desperation to raise money, and the reason behind that. But I forgot to mention—when I first spoke with her on the phone and shared your theory with her? She said that made her feel better understood and more willing to tell her story to me."

"That's nice to hear," Nora said. "A good outcome, all around. But she's really going to suffer, when news of the bribery and college-admissions scandal breaks. After our call yesterday, I was expecting to read your story about that in today's news."

"Yeah," he said. "I had planned for that story to break this morning. But then I got waylaid last night, because I had an opportunity to interview the mastermind behind the scandal. And he spilled all the beans—well, except one. But Lori Greene's story is huge, and evolving fast. It's going to run over several days, weeks probably. You'll see my first report tomorrow."

Nora wiped the back of a hand across her forehead and said, "Phew! So, can I assume you haven't had time to look into the 'confession' Donald Parker wanted to make?" If true, she could stop worrying about any news of the stem-cell injections leaking and coming to the Balabans' attention before Plan C's launch at noon.

He laughed and said, "Yeah, you can assume that. I've been too busy with his wife's story! But speaking of—I need to get going. I have another meeting at their estate at noon, when he plans his big reveal. And before that, I've scheduled an interview with the parents of another tennis recruit." He kissed Fergie goodbye, waved to Nora, and headed out the door.

After he left, Fergie eyed Nora and said, "Okay, what's bothering you? I know that look. You're not saying something—so, you're saying something."

"It's just," Nora began, walking to the dartboard to gather the red darts and hand them to Fergie. "I think it's right to expose bribery and fraud. But personally, I take no joy in helping to expose Lori Greene. How hard this must be on her. She made a terrible, stupid mistake that she'll have to deal with in the wake of her son's death."

"The *real* answer, please," said Fergie, tapping a foot.

"Well, I'm feeling tense about my own meeting at noon. It's bound to be messy—a confrontation with Bill and Ellie Balaban."

"That couple from the ER? Your old mentor and his wife?"

"Yeah. I didn't tell you about that because . . . Well, I've been concerned about you. You were already having a hard time, and I knew you were worried about me, too. Besides, there's something more pressing I've been wanting to discuss with you."

"Is that why you invited me to coffee the other day?"

Nora nodded. "And it was late when I realized the night before that I'd have to cancel that. Still, I called anyways, hoping we could at least chat a moment. But Winston answered your phone."

"Well, I'm here now," said Fergie, lobbing her first dart, though missing the entire board.

"Oooo-kay," said Nora, tossing a green, hitting the outside ring. "I wanted to talk with you about—"

Fergie's next dart knocked Nora's off the target, and, with feigned sympathy, she said "Sorry."

"Sure you are," said Nora, before landing a dart in the innermost ring.

Taking her last opportunity to score, Fergie stretched her arms overhead and readjusted her bifocals. Then, as she released her dart, Nora said, "I think you're pregnant."

Hospital Visitors' Parking Lot

Ellie parked their white Audi in the visitors' lot and turned to Bill. She scowled and said, "The messy hair is too much." When she withdrew a comb from her purse, he pushed it away.

"Really?" she said. "Don't you think people would expect me to help you with grooming? That would be normal."

"For godsakes," he said. "I'm a neurosurgeon. I know dementia better than you."

"You *were* a neurosurgeon," she said. "And quite a while ago. We're even using the 'visitors' lot now."

He silently counted to ten.

She continued, "But, that's right—you're the one who knows how to *act*. Why take advice from me? Still, I'm telling you—fixing your hair would be expected of me in my role as your wife and caretaker. And that crooked bow tie looks ridiculous."

Now he counted to twenty and reminded himself that this misery would soon end.

She flipped down the sun visor to check her face in its mirror. Then she tutted and said, "Fine, have it your way. But that look does you no favors."

"Well, I rather like it," he shot back, surprised by how automatic his contrariness with her had become.

Reapplying her ruby-red lipstick and then smudging a dab over each cheek, she said, "Our appointment begins in twenty minutes. This is no time to bicker. Do you think you can manage to be civil?"

"Can you?" he said.

She released a weary sigh, flipped up the visor, and gathered her purse. "Just say nothing—as we have agreed. If we can get out of that dreadful meeting by one o'clock, we should have enough time to get to the airport and even grab dinner before our flight. I'd like to try that fancy Rubinstein's that just opened in the international terminal."

"Whatever you say," he said. "*Whatever.*"

Deciding not to question his disagreeable tone, she instead focused on life after the appointment. She shook her head in wonderment and said, "The Cayman Islands! Pristine beaches, wonderful restaurants, interesting shops. And the residents speak English. They even have a decent theater company."

"It's like going to heaven for you," he said without merriment, exiting the car.

Rigby's Diner

Uptown Oakland

Nora and Lola were finishing lunch at Rigby's—a cheeseburger and diet cola for each—when the restaurant's door opened and admitted a cold gusty wind, that uplifted their table napkins. Lola pinned them down before they flew away.

"Good catch," Nora said. "And I suppose we should get going anyway. It's nearing our noontime curtain call."

"You're right," said Lola. "And thanks for lunch."

"A small price to pay for the huge favor you're doing for us," she replied, grabbing the bill. "Any lingering questions about the plan?"

"No," said Lola, rising from her chair and gathering her coat. "Actually, I'll just be doing the job I was supposed to do last week, when the Balabans were in the ER." She winked and added, "But this time, they won't escape me."

"Still, thanks for your help," said Nora, plopping fifty dollars on the table, securing the bills under a ketchup bottle.

"Happy to be of assistance," said Lola, buttoning her coat. "And you know, I'm grateful to you for convincing me to transfer to the ER. Social work is a lot more exciting than—"

Nora looked curiously at her and asked, "What just happened?"

"One of my idols just came in," Lola whispered, trying to appear nonchalant. "She's one of the few black women to make a big name in the art world. And, I'm sorry, Nora. I know about the trouble between you and her—"

"Oh?" said Nora, pivoting around to find Lori Greene standing within arm's distance.

"Dr. Kelly," said Lori, "we met in the ER. I'm Dario Parker's mother."

"Yes, I remember—Lori Greene," said Nora, fearing another confrontation, that she simply couldn't afford right now. Biding time to decide what to do, she introduced Lola—"one of your biggest fans."

Lori thanked Lola for appreciating her work, and invited her to the solo exhibit in January. Lola left the restaurant with a smile on her face and parting words to Nora: "See you soon."

"I'm sorry," said Lori. "I didn't mean to interrupt your lunch. But I had gone to the ER to speak with you, and Lizbeth told me you'd be here."

"Not a problem," said Nora. "But I've got somewhere to be at noon."

"I do, too," said Lori. "My husband and I are meeting at the house with your reporter friend. I assume you know that we're talking with him."

Nora nodded, and Lori said, "My driver has the engine running. We could sit in a warm car and talk? Then I can drop you where you need to be, and I'll be on my way."

As soon as the car doors closed, Lori said, "I wanted to see you in person to apologize for my behavior in the ER. Don wishes to convey the same. I'm mortified whenever I think about the way we treated you."

Nora was blown away, like the flying napkins at her lunch table, and she reflexively planted her hands on the car seat. Yes, it felt good to hear this apology in person—direct and absolute, spoken with sincerity. "Thank you for saying that," she replied.

"And I hope you'll forgive us," Lori said.

"Yes," Nora said in a distracted sort of way, feeling that an entirely different conversation was begging to be had.

Fidgeting with her leather gloves, Lori said, "We also know you did nothing to cause Dario's death."

"I appreciate that, too," said Nora. "But . . ."

Lori looked down and haltingly said, "Of course. It's too early to ask for your forgiveness. But I'll wait on it, however long it takes."

"No, it's not that," Nora said. "The thing is, I do forgive you. I *have* forgiven you." Then she took a deep breath, which instantly lent air and voice to the insistent conversation; she said, "I lost my own daughter in 2015."

Lori felt as though she'd been yanked out of thick fog. Now, looking up at Nora, she could see the nuanced shading in her face, the variant hues in her hazel eyes, the strands of gray in her chestnut-colored hair. She noticed Nora's turquoise-colored earrings that were rimmed with silver, and the blueberry stain on her aquamarine shirt.

"And," Nora continued, "I know it's different for everyone who loses a child. Still, some things are also the same enough."

Slowly nodding agreement, Lori could feel herself emerging within Nora's gaze. All her labeled externalities—of being a wife, an artist, a socialite and public figure, even someone who committed bribery—fell away. Meeting Nora's searching look, and seeing all that it confirmed about her, she felt found.

Waiting Room

Outpatient Medical Clinic

"You must be the Blabbins!" said the cheery desk clerk.

Ellie shot the clerk a censuring glare and said, "No, we are the 'Balabans.' And my husband practiced neurosurgery here for years—" She felt the tap of Bill's shoe cueing her to settle down.

The clerk smiled mechanically while processing their clinic registration. When she finished, she said, "Will you please take a seat here in the waiting room? Dr. Williams is running a little late."

"How late?" asked Ellie, raising her chin.

The clerk shrugged. "Fifteen minutes, maybe?"

"Well, please inform him the *Balabans* are here," said Ellie. Then she turned from the desk and whispered to Bill, "The audacity—butchering our name like that. So unprofessional. And you saw that she had turned over her name badge. If I had the time of day, I'd report her."

After seating themselves in the waiting room, Ellie complained to her husband, "And fifteen minutes late?"

"No, it was fifteen minutes 'maybe,'" Bill corrected her.

She scowled at the clerk and said, "Well, they are fifteen precious minutes we can't afford."

"It's not the clerk's fault," he said.

"Just stop," she said. "You needn't contradict everything I say."

But apparently, I do, he thought.

"Besides," she continued, "we shouldn't even be talking to one another right now."

"Because?"

"Honestly, Bill? *People.*"

He surveyed the crowded waiting room. Everyone was focused on their phones, newspapers, books, kids—on anything but them. He cupped a hand over his mouth and whispered, "No one is watching us."

She tutted, flipped up one end of her iconic blue scarf, and said, "I didn't mean watching *you.*"

Fred's Exam Room,

Outpatient Medical Clinic

At 12:25, Lola Montez received a distressed text from the desk clerk, informing her that the Balabans were demanding to be seen *now*. A second text immediately followed, begging Lola to *Please hurry* ☹

Lola scrolled through the messages on her cellphone—but still, no reply from Nora. She told herself not to worry, and conveyed as much to Fred; no doubt, something important was keeping her with Lori Greene. Then another text arrived from the clerk: an emoticon of prayer hands.

Trusting that Nora would arrive when she was able, Lola braced herself and walked to the clinic waiting room. At the reception desk, the visibly frazzled clerk pointed out the Balabans. Lola approached the couple and introduced herself as Fred's social worker. She added, "You know, the three of us were scheduled to meet in the ER last Saturday. But I understand you had to leave."

"Well, we are here now," said Ellie. "And we've been waiting nearly half an hour." She tapped her cane on the floor for emphasis.

"I'm sorry about that," said Lola, adopting a sympathetic look. But truth be told, she mostly felt sorry for herself and the clerk, both being made to bear the fallout from Nora's delay. "Today's been so busy. But please follow me to Dr. Williams' exam room so we can start."

But, moments later, when they stepped into the exam room, Ellie bristled and said, "And where is Dr. Williams?"

Lola frowned and answered, "He just texted to say he's still running late, and to let you know that he's sorry."

Bill and Ellie exchanged apprehensive looks. She glanced at the clock—12:30, already—and inquired, "And just how late *now*?"

"I'm not sure," said Lola. "He only works in clinic on Thursdays. Naturally, all his old patients try to get in to see him. Then he gets very busy and, frankly, tends to fall behind." She gestured for them to take seats.

They sat across from Lola, who tried to break the chilly silence with "Can I get you some water?"

"We don't need water," Ellie replied. She hooked her cane on her chair and loosened the blue-roses scarf around her neck. "What we need is to move this meeting along. Perhaps there's paperwork we could start in the meantime?"

"We should probably wait for Dr. Williams' medical assessment, so I can tailor my interview and recommendations," Lola said. She furtively glanced at her cell—still nothing from Nora. Knowing the plan was not going to proceed without the starting signal from her, Lola tossed a tense smile toward the Balabans.

"Surely, you've been informed about my husband's dementia," Ellie said. "Isn't there—what?—a home-safety evaluation you could start? You must have general information and referrals you could provide for in-home care options."

Lola glanced at her watch—12:37 now—aware that Fred wasn't going to appear until Nora became available. And, though happy to be doing them the favor of sitting with the Balabans to ensure their continued stay and inability to confer privately with each other, she was increasingly discomfited by Ellie's aggressive interrogations.

"Ms. Montez?" said Ellie.

"That's a great idea," Lola tepidly replied. "Let's start with an Activities of Daily Living assessment." She withdrew her cellphone and asked, "Do you mind if I record our meeting?"

"Is that really necessary?"

"No, but it helps *a lot*. A software program can transcribe our conversation for the electronic health record, so I don't have to sit here and type in everything."

"Well, if that would speed things along, go ahead," said Ellie.

"It will," said Lola, glancing again at the time: only 12:38? How can one minute feel so interminable?

Hospital Backlot Garden

Fergie knew where Lizbeth spent her private time during breaks. Indeed, she found her sitting on the stairway leading out from the hospital's back exit to a small landscaped lot. "Hey, Lizbeth," she said. "I hope I'm not bothering you."

Lizbeth patted the stair one-up and said, "Have a seat."

They stared out at the wintry landscape: The hibernating flower-beds and rosebushes, with their colors browning, their scents fading. The droopy vintage perimeter lampposts surrounding the lot, like tired overseers.

"What's up?" asked Lizbeth, though presuming the reason for Fergie's visit.

Fergie looked warmly at her and said, "I spoke with Nora earlier."

"Ah," said Lizbeth, knowingly.

"And I want to thank you for talking with her. You were right—I'm pregnant. I just checked."

Lizbeth stood and hugged Fergie. "I'm happy for you and Winston."

Fergie wiped her eyes, relieved by Lizbeth's response—her miscarriage had occurred so recently. "My test was negative two days ago. Too early, I guess. But what a great head nurse I am! Believing a negative test result while all the symptoms were present."

"I agree about you being a great head nurse," Lizbeth said.

Returning her smile, Fergie said, "And I get why you expressed concern about me with Nora first."

Lizbeth looked away. "My miscarriage . . . It's still so raw, so front and center in my life. I think about her all the time. And Aditya—he's very depressed."

"God, I'm sorry. That's so freakin' hard."

"Yeah, I didn't think I'd be able to talk with you—not without breaking down and putting a damper on your pregnancy. But I figured you had to be pregnant—your physical symptoms, and, sorry, your mood swings."

"Please don't apologize. Thing is, you were the only person who noticed me. More than my husband, more than my best friend."

"Well, it's holiday time, and people are distracted and busy with—"

"No, I want to thank you for that."

Lizbeth blushed and said, "Well, I should get back to the ER. And I bet Winston is happy."

Fergie shrugged and said, "We'll see. You're the first to know."

Vacant Office, Outpatient Medical Clinic

Naturally, Fred expected Nora to be late. But her exceptional tardiness on this exceptional day was exceptionally concerning. You'd think she could call or text—

Nora burst into the room and plopped herself down in the foldout chair Fred had set out for her. After giving her a minute to catch her breath, he said, "I was afraid you weren't coming."

"I'm sorry," she said, casting off her coat. "But I had this amazing and unplanned encounter with Lori Greene."

"Good," he said. "I look forward to hearing about that later. But we're way behind on Plan C, so I'm just going to text the others. But Lola first—it can't have been easy, babysitting the Balabans."

While he sent off the texts, Nora distracted herself by reading the outdated health bulletins on the walls. "Look," she said, pointing to aged yellowed flyers. "This vaccination campaign ended two years ago. And this health fair is ancient history."

"What can you expect?" he said. "This office has been decommissioned since 2017. No one has used it since—at least, not for official business."

"I think I'm just allergic to any kind of medical disinformation," she said. Then she ripped a flyer off the wall, along with a sizable paint peel.

He shook his head and said, "I'm not supporting your disinformation campaign, unless you promise to repaint the walls."

Then a knock on the door sounded. Owen entered and greeted Nora and Fred with "Hello."

Nora replied, "We'll be ready to start as soon as—"

But then, there she was in the doorway: Carrie.

"All right," said Nora, "we're all here now."

"And ready," said Carrie, with a vigorous thumbs-up.

"Ready and willing," added Owen. "I'm setting my timer—five minutes, right?"

Nora nodded and then extended her hands to Fred. "Showtime," she said, with a tender smile.

He took her hands and echoed, "Showtime." Then he straightened his necktie and walked out the door.

Fred's Exam Room

"Forgive me," said Fred, entering his exam room, greeting Lola and the Balabans. "Things have been awfully busy today."

Ellie replied, "An hour late? Yes, I suppose they must be."

Fred cleared his throat and sat beside Lola. "Well, then," he said, "shall we get on with our meeting?" He turned to Bill and asked, "How are we doing today?"

"Um, fine?" Bill answered. "Who . . . I mean, how are *you*?"

"I'm good," Fred answered, patting Bill's knee. "Thanks for asking."

"Please," said Ellie, "can we proceed with business? It's challenging enough for Bill to linger in his confused state. You understand."

Fred nodded amiably and asked Lola, "So, you've had some time to get acquainted with Dr. Balaban and his wife?"

"I sure did," said Lola, with a stiff grin. "And we completed the IADL and ADL assessments. A home safety check, too."

"An excellent start," said Fred, returning to the Balabans. "Because, as we all know, we're here to come to an agreement on a correctional plan for your home safety and welfare that will—"

A knock on the door preceded Nora's swift entrance. She waved briskly to everyone, pulled up a chair next to Fred, and said, "I hope I'm not too late."

Concerned that Nora's involvement would only cause additional delay, Ellie curtly replied, "I wasn't aware you were coming, Nora."

"Oh, please," she replied, "I wouldn't miss this meeting. It's too important. I want to help us all come up with a plan, that makes good sense for everyone."

Bill began picking at his shirt sleeve, and Ellie said, "Well, as I told Fred, it's hard for Bill to linger in his agitated state. We've already waited an hour."

"I understand," said Nora. "But I promise, we'll be efficient."

"All right now," said Fred. "As I mentioned, we're here today to figure out a correctional plan for—"

The door swung open, and Owen Landry walked in. Nora, intentionally keeping her focus on the Balabans, witnessed what she had expected to see: Ellie flinching.

"Now, what is *he* doing here?" asked Ellie, her voice notching higher.

"So, you know each other?" said Nora.

Ellie looked inquiringly at Bill, who merely looked away. She straightened her scarf and answered, "Well, yes—he and Bill work together in the lab on Thursdays. It's Dr. Landry, right?"

Owen nodded and said, "Hello, Mrs. Balaban."

Ellie tapped her cane on the floor and told Fred, "I expected this meeting to be a private consultation with you and the social worker. What's going on?"

With a shrug, he answered, "It's my fault. I had asked Dr. Landry to see me earlier, ahead of your visit. I was hoping to get his input on Bill, seeing that he appears to be the only person, besides you and the neurologist, who has laid eyes on him in a long while."

"And I apologize for being late," said Owen. "I got hung up in the OR."

Ellie rolled her eyes, and when they landed on Bill he was still looking away.

"I thought Dr. Landry's input would help," Fred explained. "The only medical information we have to go on is the record of Bill's brief ER stay. Obviously, we don't diagnose a chronic condition like dementia based on overnight observation."

"And even then," said Nora, "we had to factor in the possible influence of head trauma from Bill's fall on the steps beforehand."

"Let's be sensible," said Ellie. "You *and* Fred *and* Jack—you *all* saw Bill at the house on Sunday. You saw how forgetful and disoriented he was. And violent, even!" She asked Fred, "In fact, isn't his destruction of our parlor, which you witnessed the other night, what forced this appointment?"

"Well, yes," Fred answered. "That, and the troubling fact that you'd left Bill alone at the house."

Inexplicably, Bill shot up from his chair and, as quickly, sat down. Ellie watched him with a pinched expression, wondering why he was doing nothing to help keep this meeting on track.

"Ellie," said Nora, "it's not even been a week since your husband's ER visit. We're just trying to corroborate the dementia diagnosis to expedite getting proper help for you two."

Owen coughed and said, "Excuse me. But it sounds like we're all in a hurry to settle things. Maybe I can offer what I know to help move things along?"

After Fred gestured an invitation for him to speak, Owen said, "It's difficult for me to say this. But sadly, I have to agree with Mrs. Balaban. I've worked alongside her husband most Thursday afternoons and evenings for two years, and I'll attest to his cognitive decline. The week-to-week changes have been dramatic recently. It's been hard watching him struggle with his memory and judgment. And, yes, I've also witnessed his violent outbursts in the lab."

Ellie regarded Owen with a subtle approving nod, while privately regaling in her domination over him. Clearly, he had chosen to get "on board" with her and follow her lead. And, after this dreadful appointment was over, she would demand that Bill apologize for having doubted her prowess. *Her* skills and *her* strategy had ensured their escape to the islands tonight, ahead of any news about *his* stem-cell fiasco.

"Thank you, Dr. Landry," said Fred. "Your observations are helpful."

"I appreciate them, too," said Ellie. Extending a hand to Owen, she felt a fleeting pang of guilt, thinking: *You are so naïve, and so easy to manipulate. How did Bill have such trouble controlling you? And now, sadly, you'll be left alone to take the fall for him.* She could imagine the young doctor's terrible shock later today in the lab, upon discovering the evidence planted against him.

But when taking her hand, Owen said, "No, I should be thanking *you*. You've been enormously helpful the last couple of years, taking over for your husband and managing the lab. It was a lot of work. But because of you, I was able to continue my research uninterrupted."

Ellie tilted her head. "What are you talking about? Don't be silly."

Bill struggled to conceal his glee. Clearly, Owen was honoring last night's agreement at the Beach House, getting on board with him, not her.

"Don't be modest," Owen told her. "You deserve the credit—the way you helped Dr. Balaban with the lab orders and invoices, and all those communications and reports. And, my god, the budget. You were a real trooper and a loyal partner to your husband. I admire that."

"But I can't . . ." said Ellie, her voice breaking. "No, I *won't* take credit."

Nora countered, "I agree with Dr. Landry. That was very supportive of you."

Ellie removed the iconic blue-roses scarf from her neck, but the room still felt airless.

"But, to be clear," Nora continued, "Dr. Landry's observations don't carry the weight of a formal dementia assessment and diagnosis."

Owen nodded. "Dementia eval isn't in my orthopedist's toolbox— that's for sure. And the fact is, Mrs. Balaban compensated so well for Dr. Balaban, that it probably took me longer to appreciate the severity of his cognitive impairment."

Ellie's heart raced. *What is happening? Is Owen still on board with me, but clumsily overshooting his support? Still, he's lying about me helping in the lab—that's more than an overshoot, isn't it?* When she looked to Bill for guidance, he only stared blankly back.

"Would you like some water, Ellie?" Nora asked. "You look faint."

"No," she replied, listlessly waving a hand, trying to gather her wits. There were too many delays, too many surprises, and too many people at this appointment! It was seriously disrupting her time schedule. And "water" *again*? No! What she needed was to escape this hellish appointment and get onto a plane, ASAP. She grabbed her cane and declared, "I am decided. We wish to cancel the dementia assessment and hospice referral." She gathered her purse and coat.

"Now, hold on," said Fred. "You agreed to this intervention. You leave now, and we call the police and APS for an urgent safety and welfare check." When she stared defiantly back, he continued, "And we know what they'd see if they went to your house. That parlor is scary. And we'd have to tell them about the violence we've witnessed between you two—the raised fist, the black eye. We'd have to share information you provided during Bill's ER intake, about his wandering and agitation at home. And they'd need to know about you leaving him at home alone."

Realizing the mounting risk to their plans for tonight, Ellie conveyed an apologetic smile and said, "It's just too much for us right now. Surely, you can understand that? We are very private people, and suddenly all this fuss? And you and Nora, out of the blue, concerned about us, after so many years of absence in our lives?" She turned to Bill and said, "It's all too much for us, isn't it?"

But he remained fixated on attempts to unbutton his shirt cuff.

Nora leaned toward Ellie and said, "We can't—and won't—sit back while you and Bill are living in such unsafe circumstances."

"We abandoned you before," Fred added. "That won't happen again."

Ellie assessed the facial expressions of everyone in the room—each one alert and expectant, trapping her like fly paper with sticky concern. She said, "I appreciate your good intentions. But my decision is firm. Bill and I will return to our lovely home *now*. And, to alleviate your concerns, we'll take Lola's references and hire in-home support immediately. And Bill will continue to receive his medical care from his private neurologist."

Nora touched Bill's arm to get his attention and said, "I don't know how much of this conversation you've been able to understand. But is there anything you wish to say or ask?"

He looked her in the eyes and asked, "Who are you?"

"Well," said Owen, stuffing his hands into his coat pockets. "I should get going. I've got clinic 'til three, and then onto the lab as usual." But then he hesitated, checked his cellphone, and said, "Shoot! They're texting about another power outage in the lab. Well, I guess I'll be going there first."

Ellie gasped. She had convinced Owen the lab had been cleared of all things stem cell, but now he was about to learn otherwise. Not only that, he would see that the evidence had been manipulated and planted on him. Already, it was later than she had planned to leave for the airport, and his discovery of the deceit could threaten their timely escape. *Thank god,* she thought, *at least I checked with Bill about changing the lab's security codes; that will delay Owen's discovery and buy us some time.*

"Are you okay, Mrs. Balaban?" Owen asked.

With her heart jumping beats, she said, "Surely, the research institute has backup generators."

"It does," he replied. "But my bone-cell cultures are my precious babies. It'll only take me a minute to run over there and check."

Ellie's mind spasmed. And before she could marshal words to form a coherent reply, he added: "Would you like me to check the inbox while I'm there, Mrs. Balaban? I could drop off any mail here on my way back to clinic."

"The inbox?" she said, as though speaking a foreign language. "For the life of me, I don't understand . . . what . . . what you . . ." But she stopped when she saw a faint grin slowly break on Owen's face. Shock and confusion crisscrossed her mind at once, and she could find no words at the intersection. But now she understood. She understood that Owen was *not* clumsily overreaching in support of her. No, he had jumped ship. He was not on board.

"Well, maybe this isn't the best time?" said Owen. "But, tell you what—if I do find mail, I'll just leave it for you in the usual place."

Ellie's trembling hand alighted on her husband's shoulder as she implored, "Bill?"

But he only pulled away from her, while privately celebrating his triumph. Last night's agreement with Owen was working brilliantly, even better than he had imagined. And now, within a few short hours, he'd be on a plane to Costa Rica, leaving his insufferable wife behind, in the limelight of ethics inquiries and criminal investigations. Finally, she would have her time in the spotlight, though on a stage of his choosing.

Watching Ellie's jaw drop while she stared pleadingly at her husband, Nora thought: *I should find this spectacle more painful to watch. But the Balabans are imploding because of their own toxic energy.*

"This can't be happening," Ellie muttered, putting a hand to her forehead.

Suppressing a grin, Bill imagined responding: *My dear, self-centered, narcissistic, imperious wife—so, you are finally seeing what's been happening under your very nose?* He glanced at Owen with a small conspiratorial nod; they each appeared to be reaping the intended benefits of their agreement. And what a bonus to witness Ellie unravel.

"This is a bad dream," Ellie said. "A nightmare."

Only for you, Bill privately mused. *And your nightmare will merely get worse. I'll be gone, far away—yes, sadly, with dementia. But you'll be here alone, living in constant fear of Owen using the evidence to incriminate us.*

"Bill, please say something," she implored.

But he only rubbed his stubbled chin, wishing he could respond out-right: *You failed, Ellie. Owen's on board with me. So don't even think about implicating him or me when the proverbial shit hits the fan. Besides, you can't afford having me or the lab connected to Dario's death—the assets I'm leaving you are too small for you to fight the lawsuits that would follow.*

Sensing the heat between the Balabans was cooling, Nora refueled the fire, using their own hostilities as kindling. "Ellie," she said, "you sound upset with Bill. Judgmental, even. Perhaps you could find it in your heart to show him some compassion? He's impaired, and it's not his fault."

Ellie looked fiercely at Owen, her face reddening. *You,* she thought, *know damn well, that Bill isn't demented! You're lying about that, and lying about me managing his lab. Why are you letting Bill off the hook, but putting me on one? What in god's name is happening here?*

Owen crossed his arms and said, "I agree with Dr. Kelly."

"Stop it, Bill!" Ellie shouted. "Stop this nonsense now! Don't you see what you're doing?"

But his attention was elsewhere, focused on his imminent escape. Within minutes, he would be sneaking out of the building and entering the taxi he had prearranged under an alias.

With evident reproach, Nora asked, "Stop what, Ellie? Bill is just sitting here quietly, doing nothing to provoke you."

As gratifying as it felt to watch his wife fall apart, Bill decided he had exacted sufficient revenge. He and Owen could rightfully claim victory over Ellie now. They had succeeded in humiliating her, wresting con-trol of the narrative, and making her out to be the paranoid one. So, in this triumphant pivotal moment, Bill took the next step in his plan: He stood up and said, "Restroom."

Because Owen had informed Nora about his agreement with Bill, she knew Bill had signaled his next move—leaving the exam room, under the guise of going to the restroom. Owen was supposed to offer to escort him, while secretly providing cover for Bill to sneak out of the building.

Then Ellie shouted, "Wait!" She shook her head, as if trying to eject something out of it. But the insistent truth prevailed: Bill was betraying her with his silence and inaction. Yes, in fact, he was throwing her under the bus! She pointed at Owen and said, "You know I did not manage the lab. I've rarely even set foot inside of it. And, as everyone knows, Bill always went there to *escape* me!"

Nora held up a palm toward Ellie and said, "You need to calm down. Do you want that water now?"

"I don't want any damn water," she replied. "I want the truth!" She faced her husband and demanded, "Tell them the truth!"

Bill held out his hands protectively, guarding his face. Ellie slapped them away and said, "Tell them about your epic stem-cell fiasco. Tell them about the faulty cells from Costa Rica, and all the people you gave them to. Tell them about Dario Parker."

Bill's voice quivered. "I forgot what you told me to say."

Ellie stared back in wide-eyed horror and stammered, "It's time to give up our charade."

Amping up her provocation, Nora said, "Bill's words and body language are conveying fear of you, Ellie. And, frankly, it's disturbing to watch."

In stunned silence, Ellie scrutinized her husband, amazed at his ability to remain so obstinate. She leaned toward him, a hand covering her mouth, and whispered, "When Owen goes to the lab, he'll discover our deceit. And the moment he does, *your* cover will be blown. It will risk us getting to the airport—"

Bill said, "Restroom, please."

Dread draped over Ellie and weighed her down. She groaned in resignation, realizing that her husband had no intention to save her. Under the false cloak of dementia that she had woven for him, he was going to escape responsibility for what he had done, and his silence would allow Owen's false narrative about her to prevail.

Nora told Ellie, "Whatever you whispered to Bill only agitated him more. Your behavior is abusive, and it needs to stop. He doesn't understand you."

"Oh, no, no, no," Ellie said, slowly shaking her head. "Bill understands *everything* perfectly well. He's neither confused nor abused." Then, raising her chin to Owen, she continued, "And you understand, too. You know all about Bill and the stem cells. You know he is not demented."

When no one reacted to her extraordinary claims, she tried one last appeal to Bill: "Why are you doing this? Why have you gone completely off script and ruined a plan, that would have saved us both? Why are you allowing Owen Landry to continue his disrespectful and—?" But then a thudding epiphany smacked her on the head: Bill and Owen were working together as a team. And they were playing the same winning hand against her.

Bill stepped toward the door, but she blocked his path and said, "You aren't worried about Owen discovering the evidence, because you know he already found it. And yet, despite that, he hasn't turned on *you*. So, you must've made another bargain with him. What was it this time, Bill? And why must it entail putting me on the hook?"

"You're sounding paranoid," Nora said, stoking the conflict.

"I assure you—this isn't paranoia," Ellie said, suddenly grasping Bill's hateful intention behind his selective destruction of her acting awards and accolades.

When Bill tried to sidestep her, she repositioned herself in his way. And now, weighing-in his long-standing contrariness, she suffered another epiphany and shared it with him: "You never changed the lab's security codes, did you? Even after I told you Owen was running scared, and warned you about him checking the lab."

Owen scoffed and said, "'Evidence'? I have no idea what you're talking about. And, to be frank, it seems cruel to be browbeating your husband into accepting your paranoid narrative." He thought but did not say, *So, who controls the narrative now? Who is the paranoid one?*

Sweet relief washed over Bill, delighting in Owen's robust loyalty to their agreement. Emboldened now and sensing the exquisite ripeness of the moment to make his exit, he said, "Restroom, *now*."

But Nora was also feeling emboldened. The ripe moment she had been planning for, one brimming with primal hostility between Bill and Ellie, had arrived. She grabbed her cellphone to send off a text while pretending to read one, and exclaimed, "Great news! Our hospice director is on her way with your neurologist's records."

Bill and Ellie glanced furtively at one another. Then Ellie huffed and said, "That's impossible!"

"But we sent that fax requesting them," Nora replied. "Don't you remember? You signed the requisition in the ER and gave us contact numbers for the neurologist."

"But it's not possible because . . ." said Ellie, hanging her head. "Because . . . it's just not possible."

Feeling the rug about to be yanked out from under him, Bill headed for the door. But Nora blocked him and said, "It's not safe for you to go alone."

Bill turned expectantly to Owen, but Owen neither budged nor volunteered to escort him. Then a knock on the door sounded, and Nora said, "Must be the hospice director." Watching the Balabans as she opened the door, she saw Bill clutch his chest when Carrie strutted in, wearing the borrowed blonde wig from Luis.

"Lydia?" Bill said with a shiver, recoiling and stepping unsteadily back. "But . . . but you died." His face turned ashen; he looked dumbfounded at Nora and said, "She died . . ."

"So," Nora said, folding her arms, "you remember Lydia, after all. You also remember that she died."

Fred guided Bill back into his chair, all the while Ellie railed at him: "You fool! You stupid fool! Are you happy now?" Then she admonished everyone in the room: "I told you he was not demented! And all of you here, pulling cruel stunts like this? Raising Lydia from the dead? Pretending you obtained medical records from a nonexistent neurologist?"

"*You* want to talk about 'stunts'?" said Nora, her eyes narrowing. "Because the two of you pulled quite a few, and put on a good show. It took me a while to catch on. But you tried to play us all along."

Carrie removed her wig, sat next to Fred, and whispered, "I know I have no speaking role here, but I'm enjoying this comeuppance." Lola, overhearing her remark, smiled.

Nora continued: "Your pretense of domestic abuse was ruthless and manipulative and cynical. You worried all of us. And you abused us emotionally."

Bill sat up straight and said, "My hostility toward my wife was neither pretense nor show." Then he threw his head back and stared up at the ceiling, wondering how it had come down to this resounding defeat. His brilliant strategy—so clever, so elegant, so well orchestrated, and . . . *so close* to succeeding. He glanced wistfully at the door, envisioning his waiting taxi beyond. But then Ellie stepped into his view, and, with a woeful expression full of injury, asked, "Do you really hate me so much?"

When he simply looked away, Nora replied, "Bill's contempt toward you has been simmering for years. He used his career and his work to avoid spending time with you. Even when Fred and I were residents, he kept us nights and weekends, longer than any of us really wanted—teaching us and reviewing cases. We all knew he was avoiding his home life. But . . ." She shook her head. "But Bill *physically* abusing you? No way. And you both made a mistake to pretend otherwise."

Bill sighed and said, "Just how was that a mistake?"

"No, Bill—let's leave *now*," Ellie demanded. "This hellish appointment is over." When he stayed seated, she begged, "Please, this is not the time to be contrary."

But Fred ushered her back to her chair and said, "I'm sorry, Ellie. You're both going to stay for *our* show now."

The Parker-Greene Estate

"'Stem cells'?" Winston stuttered—in a rare deviation from his journalistic detachment and equipoise. He immediately wanted to backtrack and apologize for his injudicious surprise.

But Donald Parker swiftly replied, "Yes." And the others in the room—Lori Greene, John Norris, Chris O'Dell—fell silent.

Winston shifted in his chair and said, "Sorry. I meant to ask, why did you want stem-cell injections for Dario?"

Donald reached for his wife's hand and said, "I'd been trying everything to interest our son in sports, hoping to improve his chances of getting into college. I thought the injections might help him build strength, and confidence and ambition, too. That's what I told myself." He steadied his voice and continued, "And I believed they were safe. Clearly, I was wrong."

"I don't understand," said Winston. "Why were you 'clearly' wrong?"

"Because on Tuesday, Lori and I reviewed the coroner's preliminary report with our own doctor. We learned that Dario died from a teratoma—a tumor that typically arises from stem cells. And his tumor had metastasized to his lungs."

John inhaled sharply. He looked knowingly at Donald and asked, "So, then, you read the report I left here on Monday?"

Donald nodded.

"But I thought neither of you . . . ," John began. "I thought you couldn't tolerate any discussion about Dario's case."

"But then we discovered it was even harder to tolerate our secrets about it," Donald said. "And it became unbearable to obsessively wonder whether the injections played a role in Dario's death."

"I'm sorry," John said. "I didn't intend to leave the report here, not after you told me you couldn't deal with it. But obviously, you changed your minds."

"We have," Donald said, glancing at his wife.

"Mr. Parker?" Winston said. "It sounds like you were suspicious about the stem-cell injections harming your son. Can you say more about that?"

"Yes," Donald answered. "I suspected them from the very moment I heard that Dario died after surgery on his arm. He'd received injections in both arms, and I . . ."

Lori chimed in, hoping to give her husband a moment to recover his stamina: "Don tried to talk with the doctor who gave the injections. But he kept avoiding Don. And now, we know why."

John leaned forward in his chair, shaking his head. "That's just awful. So upsetting, that a doctor would behave like that."

"Maybe it's my lack of medical expertise," said Winston. "But, if Dario died from a tumor that had metastasized to his lungs, wouldn't he have had symptoms of it beforehand? When he came to ER for his compartment syndrome, wouldn't someone have noted—"

"Please," said Don, holding up a hand. "In retrospect, I think he had symptoms. But I think he was hesitant to talk to us about them because . . ." He buried his face in his hands, then continued: "Because he knew how much we wanted him to succeed, and he feared our judgment if he didn't. And, it turns out, he was right."

"What do you mean?" asked John.

Donald took a deep breath. "A couple days before Dario died, his tennis coach told me that Dario had been making excuses to skip practice. Fatigue, shortness of breath, arm pain—but nothing unexpected from a good workout. And I was too quick to side with the coach. Dario could sense that. I think he was shamed into silence and toughing it out."

The painful admission struck Winston's heart. "So," he managed, "that must be the confession you wanted to make."

"It's the confession I had to make," Donald replied.

John somberly said, "Jeez, Don. I'm so sorry. What a heavy cross to bear."

"It is," Donald said. "But it's a cross I made. Well, with help from a few others. And I want my confession to come out, so other parents—other people—won't make the mistakes I made."

"And," said Lori, "like our doctor told us, people need to understand that most products used in regenerative medicine clinics aren't FDA-approved. They need to know about all the unregulated stem-cell markets operating in the shadow of the law."

"I certainly wish I had known," Donald said. "I wish I'd been more circumspect about all that, when it would've mattered . . . to my son, my wife."

"Well, then," said John, opening his briefcase. "Let's get that information out. Should I give my copy of the coroner's prelim to Mr. Wang?"

Lori and Donald exchanged a wordless consultation and then nodded.

"Thank you," said Winston, taking the copy, but again feeling the need to apologize. *"Thank you"? Thanks for your child's death report? Clueless!*

"You look upset," Lori told Winston.

"Do you have children?" Donald asked him.

Winston gulped hard, as though trying to clear an obstruction in his throat. "No," he answered, though feeling he had just lost something precious himself.

Minutes later, after the interview concluded, Winston declined an invitation to join John and Chris for coffee. "Too much work?" asked John.

"Yeah," Winston answered—it was true. But it was also true that he needed to be alone. So, he drove the Subaru to Lake Merritt, parked lakeside, and stared out through the windshield. *Alone*, he thought, idly tracking all the people on the walkways and picnic grounds. *Whose choice is that but mine? I've practically iced-out Fergs. I'm working non-stop, barely socializing anymore. I keep such distance between myself and the people I write about, and then I'm taken by surprise when I feel something for them.*

And, "Do I have children?" No, I do not! They can die on you—like Dario, and Nora's daughter. They can interfere with your career, like John said. They can make you crazy and overprotective, like those parents in the park. They—

His cell rang, with a call from Fergie. He automatically answered with an apology. "Fergs, sweetie, I'm so sorry for the way I've—"

"Wait," she said. "I want to share some news."

Fred's Exam Room

Nora and Owen stood in the center of the exam room, facing the Balabans, who remained seated across from Fred, Carrie, and Lola.

"So," Nora said to Bill, picking up their interrupted conversation. "You want to know why it was a mistake to pretend physical violence between you and Ellie." She walked closer to him and continued, "That day we saw you through the window, holding your fist to Ellie—that is precisely what you were doing: *holding* your fist. You may have fantasized otherwise, but you weren't going to hit her. I didn't appreciate that at first, because I'd seen Ellie with a partly concealed black eye when we met in the ER. At least, that's what I thought I saw."

To Ellie, she said, "That was clever of you. But you weren't trying to conceal a black eye with makeup. Instead, you had used stage makeup to create the appearance of having one, after you left rehearsal that morning. And your ruse began to dawn on me only after I ran into an ER nurse who was wearing one of your signature scarves, that you had discarded in a wastebasket. That scarf was smeared with makeup of the same colors—red, purple, beige."

"Bravo, Ellie," said Bill, clapping. "Another one of your flawless performances."

"I wouldn't talk," she shot back. "It was your gratuitous destruction of our parlor, that forced this hellacious appointment and ruined our chance to escape!"

"And," he returned with a wry smile, "I'd do it all over again, given the chance. Destroying your ridiculous trophies was a major highlight in my life."

Nora briefly closed her eyes, taking in this bittersweet victory. But now she was certain that the unholy alliance between the couple had been thoroughly shattered by the truth.

Owen asked, "Is this a good time for me to have my say, Dr. Kelly?"

When she nodded and stepped back, Owen told Bill, "You tried to pit me and your wife against each other from the beginning. You threw us in the ring with a pile of red meat between us, hoping we'd destroy each other. You were hell-bent on hurting each of us." Facing Ellie, he continued, "So, yes, your husband made a deal with me last night, that put you 'on the hook.' And he'd been planning all along to get free of you." To both, he said, "Neither of you gave a damn about ruining my life or career. You're sad and repulsive human beings, and you deserve each other."

"How dare you speak to me like that?" Ellie charged—to which Bill laughed. But then the stinging truth of Owen's remarks rapidly sank in, and she shouted at Bill, "You traitor!"

"You entitled narcissist," he returned.

Unable to remain silent, Fred stood up and pointed at Bill. "You don't seem the least bit fazed, that your stem-cell recklessness *killed* a young man. And you don't seem to care about all the other people you may have hurt with your injections. It's criminal. It's wrong and despicable. You're neither the man nor the doctor I knew."

Bill looked defiantly back. "Don't you or Nora talk to me as if you know me. You and your 'gang' disappeared as soon as you settled into your successful careers. And after I gave everything of myself to help you achieve that. Where were you the last years of my dwindling professional life and suffocating marriage?"

When Fred turned away, Nora chimed in, "Despair is a bitch, Bill. But it visits all of us, and you're responsible for the choices you make to deal with it. *You* chose to stay with Ellie. *You* chose to ride your stem-cell hobbyhorse off a cliff. *You* chose to experiment with Dario's life."

"I never intended to hurt Dario," Bill said. "What happened to him was a freak occurrence."

"No," said Owen, "what happened to him was *you*."

Nora glanced at Owen's fists, which he then obligingly relaxed. Then she told Bill, "Granted—you couldn't have predicted that Dario's teratoma would metastasize and kill him. But you recklessly created the possibility for that tumor's existence when you gave him those useless stem-cell injections. And you knew . . . you *knew* . . ." She briefly looked to Fred for moral support and continued, "You knew the tumor was present in Dario's arm the day *before* I did the fasciotomy. I saw the ultrasound you took."

"A *tumor*?" said Ellie, her eyes darting around the room, but finding no one else surprised. "Bill?" she said shakily. "You told me it was an infection. You said Donald Parker's son was at risk for losing an arm because of that. But . . . but your cells caused that young man to die from a *tumor*?"

Nora persisted in confronting Bill: "When you obtained that ultrasound, did it even cross your mind to send Dario for the urgent surgery he needed for his compartment syndrome? And did you wonder if maybe the teratoma you found could have been removed and—?"

"That wouldn't have mattered," Bill interrupted. "Because, as you know, his teratoma had already metastasized before the surgery and before my ultrasound."

"But," she sharply countered, "*you* didn't know that at *that* time."

Bill slumped back in his chair, and Ellie turned away from him in horror.

"You're a coward," Nora continued. "You didn't protect Dario because you felt threatened. You not only tried to escape responsibility for what you did to him. You also tried to blame others—Owen, first, and then . . ."

After a long pause, Fred asked, "Nora?"

"Hmmmm," she finally said, wondering how she hadn't seen it before. Then she pivoted to Owen and said, "That call Bill made to you just before Dario's surgery? That was no last-minute 'freaking out' over his plan. He was intentionally delaying you, so that I'd end up doing the surgery."

Owen tilted his head. "Sorry?"

Pacing slowly now, Nora said, "Also, Bill had to have told Dario to come in earlier, while you'd be out supervising that hospital drill."

"Because?" asked Owen.

"Because we were already set up for Dario's surgery, before eleven. I had finished my exam and confirmed Dario's diagnosis. We'd done the X-rays and blood work. We had obtained his informed consent for the fasciotomy. We'd hung antibiotics at least a half-hour before we started the surgery. So, for all that to have happened, Dario had to have been in the ER, well before 10:15ish. He was fully prepped for the fasciotomy by 10:40–10:45, when we started paging you."

"My fault," Owen replied. "My pager was in my coat pocket at the end of the drill. I had taken my coat off for just a few minutes, and I was about to respond when Dr. Balaban called and kept me on the phone—"

"Not the point," Nora interrupted. "The point is, that I pushed the fasciotomy to the last possible moment, and you would've been there for it if Bill hadn't kept you on the phone." Then she stood still while her eyes widened with sudden realization—and, with surprise, too, that she was experiencing gratitude for Paul Ling. Recalling Paul's remarks that day, she faced Bill and said, "*You* were the 'demented old guy in the hallway' talking on a cellphone, outside Dario's room, peeking through the door window! *You* were monitoring us, and you kept Owen on the phone until you saw me begin Dario's surgery."

Bill crossed his arms and looked away.

"But," Owen said, "why would Bill not want me to do the surgery? I mean, he and his wife were in the ER, *waiting* on me to do it and help dispose of any evidence—"

"No," she said, with a half-smile. "They may have been in the ER. But they had another motive for being there. They were desperate to convince everyone that Bill was demented, and under a ridiculously short timeline that they tried to finesse. But they needed him to be diagnosed so they could defend against his careless indulgence with stem cells, and escape accountability for Dario's tumor—which he, and only he, knew about at the time of surgery."

"It was supposed to be an infection," Ellie said with bewilderment. "Not a tumor."

"Bill may have lied to you about that," Nora said. "But, you, Ellie? The fact is, you were in the ER to help him eliminate evidence of his wrongdoing. You didn't want him fingered for a devastating infection, that harmed the son of a very powerful man."

"But I did not participate in that," Ellie said. "I was with you, in the hallway. And when I returned to Bill's room, he told me it had been 'taken care of.'"

Nora shook her head in dismay. "I don't know whether you can hear all the ways that still sounds bad for you. And I won't even get into how gullible you were to believe Bill about the possibility of recovering infected stem cells in the first place."

"I'll have that water now," Ellie weakly said.

After waiting for Ellie to finish the glass he'd given her, Fred asked, "Feeling better now?"

Ellie stared at him, wondering when, and if, she could ever feel "better." What could improve now, with everything ruined? She didn't even have her acting awards to comfort her. Finally, she said, "Bill misled me about the stem cells."

"Still," Nora replied, "you also willfully lied about Bill having dementia. And you wanted him diagnosed for selfish reasons—to mitigate any claims against your estate. You knew there'd be lawsuits over his negligence and malpractice, once the connection was made between his injections and Dario's 'infection.' And then, when Dario died—"

"Pathetic!" Carrie broke in. "I'm sorry, Nora, but it's hard to keep quiet."

"That's all right," Fred replied. "You're saying what the rest of us are probably thinking."

Nora studied the Balabans' faces, her heart filling with great dismay. "It was shrewd of you to make sure I'd be in the ER on Friday, Ellie. I remember you telling me about checking that out with Jack the night before. You were counting on sympathetic buy-in from old friends like me to build a quick case for Bill's dementia."

"And," Fred added, "Bill knew you'd feel confident doing the fasciotomy without Ortho's help. Which isn't true for many ER generalists these days."

Owen's brow knitted. "Okay. Ellie was in the ER, pushing for Dr. Balaban's dementia diagnosis and intending to help destroy evidence. But Dr. Balaban? Why would he be waiting on me to destroy evidence, yet at the same time prevent me from doing the surgery?"

A smile surfaced on Nora's face. She was masterfully teasing apart the warped threads in the Balabans' stories. And—though hesitant to admit it—she was now enjoying the spectacle of the couple's unraveling. She told Owen: "Bill was *never* waiting on you for that."

He turned his palms up. "And how do you know *that?*"

"For two reasons," she replied. "One: As I explained, Bill intentionally prevented you from doing the surgery; so, obviously, he wasn't genuinely waiting on you to deliver evidence from it. And, two: Bill knew there was no surgical evidence to be found during a fasciotomy, because he knew from the ultrasound, that the tumor was located higher up in Dario's arm."

Ellie pressed a hand to her brow, turned to her husband, and stammered, "Your whole story about that surgery was a complete lie? And I was in the ER only to help you get diagnosed?"

After Bill merely rolled his eyes, Nora answered: "He couldn't have been diagnosed without you. You were the only useful source informant he had."

"Dr. Kelly," Owen said. "I still don't get why it was important for me not to do Dario's surgery. He still needed a fasciotomy for the compartment syndrome. Why not me?"

"The hell with this," Bill said with a disdainful huff. "I've had enough." Then he stood and hurried to the door, praying his taxi was still waiting, and now under the wire of making his flight before the avalanche of incriminating information buried him alive.

But Owen forced him back to his chair and said, "We *are* going to finish this story." Then he turned expectantly to Nora, who obligingly continued: "Bill needed to own you before the truth about Dario came out and ruined his chance to escape the consequences. And, unfortunately, he succeeded far too long. He had you literally scared to death about your life and career. He shook you to your core, and made you doubt yourself and your values—with Ellie's help, of course. Then Bill had you believe you missed a surgery, that was supposed to save you all from suspicion over Dario's stem-cell complication—a complete falsehood, and he knew it."

"He wanted me to miss the surgery, knowing I wouldn't find anything suspicious?" Owen said.

"That's right," she said. "Missing it kept you on tenterhooks with him. Because if you'd done the surgery and found nothing—as would have been the case—you would have been reassured and freed from needing his or Ellie's protection. Bill would have lost his power to control you, and to force your silence over his stem-cell activities and faked dementia. In other words, if you'd done the surgery, he would have no longer owned you."

Shaking his head in incredulity, Owen said, "And then, when Dario died . . ." He tried to finish his sentence but couldn't.

Nora, glancing sympathetically at him, picked up his sentence: "And then, when Dario died, you were made to wait in terror on the coroner's findings. And, meanwhile, Bill was planting evidence against you, knowing the report was going to reveal the teratoma. But, because he owned you and bought your silence, he had time to plan an escape before the definitive forensic evidence could—"

"Stop, please," Owen interrupted. "I need to be the one to say it." Then, with his heart hammering in his chest, he said, "I'm ashamed I kept silent about Dario's stem-cell injections because I was scared. Scared that something terrible had happened to Dario because of them. Scared because I'd given him one myself. And I was afraid of losing Dr. Balaban's research support." He stood tall and persisted, "And I kept silent about his faked dementia because I believed he and Ellie were going to protect me from any fallout from those injections. I also believed I was going to manage his lab in exchange for my silence." Now he stepped up close to the Balabans, and said, "I'm not making excuses for myself. But I'm also not afraid to tell the truth now. And, by the way, Dr. Balaban—I didn't destroy the evidence last night."

Bill leaned forward and buried his face in his hands, trying, but failing, to envision any way out now.

"Look at me, Bill," Nora demanded. "You need to face the truth."

After he sat up straight and met her penetrating gaze, she said, "It was you, who didn't send Dario to the ER, when you knew he had a compartment syndrome. You, who knew he had a teratoma before the fasciotomy. You—*only* you—who knew that tumor wasn't going to allow Dario's normal recovery after the fasciotomy, because it would still be present, pressing on the artery to his forearm. You knew Dario was going to be transferred like that to the recovery room, and supervised by Owen and his team."

Owen's jaw dropped. "I don't believe it! He was going to let that happen to Dario? And, on top of that, leave me red-handed to deal with the teratoma?"

"It looks that way," said Nora. "It wouldn't have taken long before you realized that. Because once Dario's failing recovery became obvious, you'd have done a vascular assessment, and that would've shown obstruction. Then imaging studies would reveal the mass in his arm. You'd remove the mass, and pathology would identify it as a teratoma. And that's when the clock would *really* start ticking for Bill."

"So," said Fred, "Bill was buying time by keeping everyone in the dark as long as he could."

Nora nodded. "The window for Bill's escape was tight, and he did his best to keep it from closing. He'd have days before the genetic analyses proved, beyond doubt, that the cells composing the teratoma were not Dario's native cells. At that point, the likelihood of faulty stem-cell injections causing the teratoma would shoot to the top of anyone's list."

"Still," said Fred, "how would anyone have known to finger Bill or his lab? I mean, if Bill had 'dementia,' and both Ellie and Owen maintained their silence about that and the injections . . . Well, I suppose Dario's father could've come forward and admitted to getting the injections for his son?"

"I doubt that would happen," said Owen, plopping himself down in a chair, exhausted and overwhelmed. Still, breaking his silence and taking responsibility was already feeling less burdensome than his complicity with the Balabans. "Because Dario's father insisted on keeping the injections strictly confidential. And I'm guessing, with his son's death, he'd want that even more."

"And yet," Nora said, addressing the Balabans. "I know for a fact, that Donald Parker is 'confessing' to the press today."

Bill threw his head back and murmured, "Hell." Ellie slapped his arm and shouted, "You bastard! You lied about everything! You only wanted my help to convince people you were demented so *you* could escape consequences. You played me and Dr. Landry against each other, and made us complicit with your deceit!"

"Oh, please," said Bill. "Must you always overact?"

Nora stole a private moment to celebrate Plan C's success. Her strategy to pit the Balabans against each other by exploiting their mutual contempt had succeeded. And now, bolstered by victory, she was eager to reveal the last lingering deceit she intended to expose. She looked clear-eyed at the couple and said, "You've lied and schemed to protect yourselves, and at great expense to others—especially Dario and his parents. But also Owen, Fred, Jack, and me. Yet, it all backfired, and you destroyed your own lives."

Ellie's eyes welled up, but Nora continued undeterred: "Bill had planned all along to get away, before evidence of his stem-cell fiasco surfaced, before the coroner's report was released, before genetic testing proved Dario's tumor—"

"For godsakes, Bill," Ellie interrupted. "We may as well just admit it! Yes, we were planning to leave for the Cayman Islands tonight."

Nora regarded her with a pitying look, and slowly shook her head.

"Well, obviously, that's not likely *now*," said Ellie, her voice trembling with fury.

"Not now," said Nora. "And not before, not ever. Bill never intended to include you in his new life."

"What?" said Ellie, turning to her husband. "But the Cayman Islands... tonight . . . Wasn't that real?"

After exhaling wearily, Bill said, "What do you think?"

"But I saw the plane tickets," she said. "You printed them out. We packed our suitcases."

"And I canceled that flight," he said with a weary scoff. Then he withdrew his solo ticket to Costa Rica and tossed it onto her lap.

Ellie's heart sank precipitously while she examined his one-way ticket. When she looked up, dumbfounded and forlorn, she caught sight of Lola and her still-recording cellphone. And, with murderous intent, she grabbed her cane and swung it at Bill. But Fred wrested it away, and Nora held her back. Then Bill sprang up from his chair and locked his icy eyes with Ellie's, seeing his cold dark future now inextricably and forever entangled with hers, consumed with legal turmoil and financial ruin. And though they had each lost the game, he had a final card to play. He smiled stiffly at her and said, "Clearly, I was, by far, the better actor."

EPILOGUE

Ten Days Later

Sunday, December 15

General Auditorium

OAKLAND CITY HOSPITAL

FRED PLACED HIS COAT on the adjacent front-row seat, saving it for Nora. After accounting for her predictable tardiness, he had advised her to meet him here a half hour before the show began. Vickie and the kids would be arriving soon with the holiday pastries Ella had baked, and the beverages they purchased at Safeway.

But as soon as he got situated, Carrie appeared out of nowhere, removed his coat from Nora's seat, and plopped herself down. She said, "I need to talk with you."

"Oh?" said Fred, taken aback by the urgency in her voice. "Look, I promise we're going to get your phone hooked up."

"It's not about that," she said.

"Okay," he said, turning to face her.

"I need . . . I *want* to apologize for my insufferable behavior."

"Hey, you had every right to be upset about us being slow to settle you in."

"It's got nothing to do with work," she said, her blunt tone reminding him of Lydia's. She continued, "I've been thinking a lot about my sister lately, and how wrong I was to judge her over her relationship with you."

Fred cleared his throat. "Maybe we should talk privately, outside?"

"No," she said, "I'll say it now or never. And I'll be brief."

But suddenly, the hospital auditorium exploded with laughter and excited chatter, as children from the long-term care unit—all festively dressed—entered with their parents and the nursing staff.

Carrie leaned close to Fred and said, "Look—I'm sorry I gave Lydia grief about you. For nearly fifteen years, I refused to speak with her. And I only softened around that after my husband died. Now, living in her home and getting to know her through the people in her life . . . Well, I realize you made my sister happy. That you and she and your wife had an understanding, that was none of my business. So, I thank you for making Lydia happy. And I'm sorry that you lost her, too."

Fred's heart clenched, and he closed his eyes momentarily, trying to stem his sorrow and regret. But when he looked back, expecting to see Carrie, she was gone, and Nora now claimed the seat.

"Hey," she said, appraising him, "what's wrong?"

Fred took a breath and said, "Nothing."

When Nora returned a skeptical look, he added, "Honestly, things couldn't be better."

"Okay, have it your way," she said. "I'll wait for you to tell me, when you're ready."

He nodded and said, "Deal. But what are you doing here on time? I even told you to come earlier, expecting you to be late."

"I had already figured that out," she said. "Still, I was *forced* to be early."

"Pirates got to you?"

She shook her head. "I had to pick up some props for Jack and Luis. And I knew how serious they were about setting up in time for the show."

"Mighty considerate of you," he said. "And Ella's pastries should be arriving shortly."

"Good," she said, "because I didn't have time to make breakfast."

"Technically, you shouldn't use 'breakfast' to describe your ritual grazing from your freezer."

She patted his shoulder, sat back, and asked, "But why are you here early?"

"I had business upstairs," he answered. "But it ended quickly. It was a Zoom meeting with John Norris—the lawyer representing Donald Parker and Lori Greene."

She frowned. "You don't need to remind me who John Norris is. But I thought 'the case' was over."

"Actually," he said, "according to Norris, it won't be over for Dario's parents until they formally—and publicly—apologize to you and the hospital. They plan to do that at a press conference tomorrow. Oh, and the coroner's *final* report will be released then, too."

"That's a relief," she said. "I'm still getting hate mail and online threats. Still, I don't need their apology, not after meeting with Lori a couple weeks ago. Besides, I understand. They were completely traumatized by Dario's death. And let's not forget that Owen Landry essentially *told* them I was responsible for it."

"You're being very understanding. Not just about them, but Owen, too. Though I must say, he did come around in the end."

"That, he did. And he's apologized to me so often, I can't take in another one from anybody."

"Well, you'll be getting a break from him, at least. He's agreed to take leave to be with his parents and think things over. Sounds like a smart move."

"And, speaking of moves," she said. "We *really* need to move beyond all the darkness of the last few weeks. Thank god, the winter solstice is around the corner. I'm so ready for a return to light."

"Amen to that. And, speaking of darkness? John Norris also shared some news about the Balabans this morning."

"Yeah? I've been following Winston's reporting on Dario, and his parallel investigation into stem-cell shenanigans. But the Balabans have consistently declined to comment, even after Donald Parker went public about his dealings with Bill."

Fred nodded. "Well, according to Norris, the Balabans are lawyered up now. But not just defensively against the charges they're facing. They are also lawyered up against each other!"

Nora tsked. "No surprise there. Their relationship was so toxic. I can still taste the fumes from being around them."

A loud thud and breaking glass sounded from behind the stage curtain, and the packed room hushed. Then Jack's quasi-reassuring announcement sailed through the PA: "Everything is fine! Everyone relax, please!"

"Didn't sound all that fine to me," said Fergie, approaching with Winston.

Nora stood up, embraced Fergie, and whispered, "So?"

When Fergie smiled and nodded, Nora exclaimed, "I'm so happy for you two!"

Winston hugged Nora and said, "Thanks! Yeah, all the tests look good. We're jazzed."

"What's going on?" asked Fred.

Fergie patted her belly. "I'm pregnant."

Beaming at the young couple, Fred exclaimed, "What terrific news! And are you still planning to take your honeymoon in China?"

Winston shook his head. "Visiting my family in Wuhan is going to have to wait, with Fergs feeling under the weather so much."

"And I can't believe I'm about to say this," said Fergie. "But I'm happy that postponing the trip gives Win the time he needs to work on the college-admissions and stem-cell stories."

"Well," said Fred, "maybe your folks will travel here instead to meet the baby?"

"They're considering it," said Winston. "They're over the moon about their first grandchild. And if we're lucky, we'll be moved out of Carl's house and into our new place by then. It's got a spare room for guests."

Loud cheers erupted from the back of the auditorium. Nora laughed when she turned to see the children welcoming Vickie and Ella as they entered with trays of holiday cupcakes and cookies. Lizbeth and Aditya got up to help. Carrie set out the paper cups and plates, while Charlie arranged beverages on the serving table.

Fred put an arm around Nora and said, "This place is full! And look at all the people standing along the walls." He smiled when he overheard his daughter sweetly admonish someone: "Not now! These are for the intermission."

Then the overhead lights dimmed, and a bell rang three times. Shoes scuffled and chairs scooted across the floor as the audience settled in their seats. Once the auditorium had silenced, Red snuck onto the stage and waited for his cue. When the bell rang again, he slowly drew back the curtain while a young boy's voice grew louder in the darkness, beginning as an ethereal, melodic hum. Then a light switched on and illuminated Luis at center stage. Gradually, the light expanded and revealed DeeDee in the background, strumming her guitar.

Nora grabbed Fred's hand, and all the while the audience clapped for the duo, she remained focused stage-left, where Jack stood in the sidelines, steadily holding the light.

ABOUT THE AUTHOR

KATE SCANNELL is a physician and author who has written extensively in lay and professional media about healthcare and medical practice. Samplings of her journal articles and newspaper columns can be found at her author's website: www.katescannellmd.com.

Her first Doctor Nora Kelly mystery, *Immortal Wounds*, was published in 2018. The second-in-series, *Lethal Control*, followed in 2021.

She is the author of the memoir *Death of the Good Doctor: Lessons from the Heart of the AIDS Epidemic* and the novel *Flood Stage*.

She practiced medicine in the San Francisco Bay Area, where she currently lives and gardens.

www.ingramcontent.com/pod-product-compliance
Lightning Source LLC
Chambersburg PA
CBHW071347300726
48976CB00006B/1797